THE FEMINIST
AND THE GUNSLINGER

"Care to dance, Harry?"

Without waiting for an answer, Jake Carradine pulled Harriett into the crowd of dancers and waltzed her around the bonfire. Harriett was middling tall, but the top of her head came only to Jake's chin, and her eyes, looking straight ahead, were treated to a splendid view of his neck and throat. Who would have guessed that part of a man could be so appealing, a column of masculine muscle and sinew. Harriett knew she should shift her gaze to some more neutral object, but to look up was to meet his eyes—even worse. The view to either side was blocked by massive shoulders—also bad.

A slow flush crawled up her neck and face until she could take the distress no longer. She pulled away from his grasp.

"I . . . excuse me, Mr. Carradine. I'm really quite tired."

"Let me walk you back to your wagon, Harry."

"No. No. Thank you, but I'll do fine alone."

Without daring to look at him, she fled. But in the dark privacy of her tent, Harriett acknowledged that Jake Carradine was far more dangerous than she had suspected—and not because of the gun he wore.

Also by Emily Bradshaw
CACTUS BLOSSOM

EMILY BRADSHAW

HEARTS JOURNEY

A DELL BOOK

Published by
Dell Publishing
a division of
Bantam Doubleday Dell Publishing Group, Inc.
666 Fifth Avenue
New York, New York 10103

ISBN: 0-440-20872-6

Printed in the United States of America

Published simultaneously in Canada

November 1992

10 9 8 7 6 5 4 3 2 1

OPM

For
Husband MICHAEL, whose patience with me
has lasted through seven novels

and

Friend DENISE, whose advice has made those
novels better than they might have been

Prologue

Willamette Valley, Oregon
August 9, 1849

Jake woke suddenly, his heart hammering in his chest. Another dream, conjured out of a past with too many guns and too much blood. Now he was hearing gunfire in his dreams, loud enough and real enough to jerk him awake.

The sleeping loft of the cabin was black as ink, and out the open window Jake could scarcely discern the tall, straight spears of Oregon pine etched against the starlit sky. Dawn was still hours away. In the other cot snored younger brother Elijah, sounding a bass harmony to the higher-pitched rumbling of little Joshua. A five-year-old kid, Jake thought wryly, had no right to snore that loudly. Must be the boy took after his daddy, Eli.

Once more a gun exploded somewhere in the night, so close, the cabin seemed to shake. Jake jumped, held his breath, then realized he wasn't dreaming. He heard another shot, then another. The forest around the cabin was erupting with gunfire.

"Goddammit!" He bolted from the bed. "Eli, we got company! And they aren't friendly!" Taking four steps

at a time, Jake sprinted down the narrow stairway that
led to the kitchen, his boots in one hand and his trousers only halfway up his long legs. "Dammit, Eli!
Where are my guns?"

Elijah was right behind him. "In the pantry," the
younger man answered.

"What the *hell* are they doing in the pantry?"

"I . . . I didn't think you'd ever need them again."

"And I suppose you unloaded them," Jake growled.
Hell! A man spent two years as a peaceable citizen and
he lost the edge. He jerked open the pantry door.

Eli flinched.

"Yes, goddammit! You did." In seconds he pulled
down the sacks of lead shot and black powder and,
with the quickness of long practice, loaded the pistol's
cylinder and tamped down the powder and shot with
the ramrod.

A small voice intruded from above. "Is it Injuns,
Pa?" Little Joshua, his nightshirt dragging the floor
and his eyes crusty with sleep, stood on the top step of
the stairway.

"Come on down here, Josh! Stay with your pa."
Jake lowered his voice. "Eli, fetch the boy and get
down, dammit! These yahoos, whoever they are,
mean—"

A lead ball whined through the unglassed kitchen
window and pinged off the wood stove, finishing Jake's
sentence for him. Eli yanked his son from the stairway
and ran with the boy to crouch below the window.
Jake came up behind him and handed him a pistol.
"These fellows mean business, Eli. They're not just firing into the air, and I'd guess they're not drunken log-
cutters looking for a good time. You offend anyone
lately? Lay somebody's wife maybe?"

Eli frowned at his brother's half smile. "Don't be
ridiculous! How can you joke at a time like—"

A barrage of lead flew into the cabin, seemingly from

every single window. One shattered the looking glass in the downstairs bedroom. Another smashed the oil lamp hanging from the rafters in the parlor.

"That was my Nell's favorite looking glass," Eli huffed.

Jake popped his head above the window and returned the fire.

"Hit anyone?" Eli asked.

"Course not. I can't see anything."

Joshua, who was clinging to his father's leg, started to wail.

"I'm going to the other window," Jake said. "Maybe I can see better there. Stay here and keep the bastards busy."

Eli looked confused.

"That gun in your hand isn't just for admiring, Eli. Get to!"

Another deadly barrage hammered the cabin just as Jake ran. He dove for the floor and crawled to the parlor window.

"Better come out, boys!" a voice invited from the darkness.

"Kane!" Jake groaned. "What the hell . . . ?"

"Carradines ain't welcome in the Willamette no more, boys," Homer Kane shouted. "This here Oregon's a territory now. Ain't no place in this good timber country for a badass gunman like Jake Carradine. 'Specially not one who steals away his neighbor's crew with lies about better wages." He punctuated his accusation with another shower of lead.

"Did you do that?" Eli asked Jake.

Jake shrugged an admission. "I didn't lie. I told them we pay better, and we do. Dammit, Eli! We gotta have men. Every sawyer and cutter working for us has gone off to California to hunt gold!"

"I told you what would happen if we irritated Kane and his sons!"

"Irritated, hell! They've had their eye on our operation since word came up from California about gold. Timber prices are up, and old Homer's gotten greedy!"

"This house's comin' down, boys!" came a shout from Kane. "Better come out."

"Damn!" Eli set down his pistol. "Let's go out."

"We'd last about two seconds, Eli. Use your head for something other than a target." Jake rose up, aimed, and fired into the darkness.

"We can't fight them off!"

"Sure we can," Jake assured him with a grim smile.

The gunfire outside had stopped, but Jake fired two more shots just to vent his frustration. For two years he had worked sunup to sundown to get the Carradine operation going. A dying father, a brother who could handle an ax with the best of them but had no notion how to handle a crew of rowdy lumbermen, and a small boy with no mother to care for him had not made the job any easier. But he had succeeded, by damn! Jake's father, before he'd died, had seen the Carradine mill become one of the most profitable on the Willamette River. Jake had been the one who did it —the only thing in his entire life that had made him proud.

Now Eli was ready to give it all up to the first man who challenged them. But Jake wouldn't budge. The timber, the mill, and the family had become his whole life, and dynamite couldn't blast him loose.

"Are they gone?" Eli ventured.

"Naw. They're out there thinking up more mischief. Why don't you get Josh someplace safer than that window."

Eli peeled the wailing boy off his leg and told him to go to the downstairs bedroom—the room Eli had shared with his young wife until she'd died of pneumonia. "Slide under the bed on your tummy," he instructed the boy. "Just like a snake. Don't cry. You're a big boy. That's right."

The boy wriggled toward the bedroom as his father directed him, his distressed sniffles leaving a damp trail on the rough planks. When he disappeared into the bedroom, Eli ran across the room at a crouch and joined Jake. Both of them peered cautiously out the parlor window.

"What're they up to?" Eli wondered aloud.

"Whatever, I figure it isn't good."

A shot zinged off the frame of the window. The brothers hastily ducked, then Jake fired off a return shot.

A few moments passed. "We're none of us getting anywhere," Eli complained.

"They're getting somewhere," Jake denied grimly. "Take a sniff."

A new odor mingled with the acrid smell of gunsmoke, and it was growing stronger by the moment.

Eli looked up through the log rafters. "Lord Almighty! There's smoke coming down from above! They're burning the house around us!"

"Not if I can help it!" Jake gritted out. "Damn! One of the bastards is setting the mules loose. We can't do without those mules!"

Eli strained to look. "Can you see well enough to get a shot in?"

"Hell no. I might hit a mule. I need to get closer."

"You can't go out there. You just said . . . !"

"You bide here, Eli." Jake grabbed his brother by the arm. "Dodging lead isn't your style, and it's been mine for a long time. You fire out the window to keep the bastards busy till I get to cover. Then once they've got their attention on me, you grab Josh and get the hell outta here. Go get Amos and the crew."

Jake crawled to the door and crouched there, hoping Eli could provide enough of a distraction. He caught sight of his target—a man moving among the mules in the corral, scarcely discernible in the glow from the flames on the cabin's roof. Time was running out. The fire was spreading fast.

"One of these days I'm gonna catch hell playing hero," Jake muttered under his breath. Then he launched himself from the door and ran.

Eli watched from the window as his brother zig-zagged across the yard toward the corral. The dark forest erupted in a fusillade of firing, and lead peppered Jake's path as he dodged, ducked, and kept running. Eli fired once, twice, three times out into the darkness, and could almost hear the Kanes laugh at his feeble attempt. He didn't have his brother's skill with a gun, or his reckless courage, and for once he regretted it.

He saw Jake take cover behind a big oak tree and return the Kanes' fire. Someone by the corral yelped, and Jake ran again, firing as he went. Eli grinned. Then he coughed. The smoke was descending from the roof in a deadly, stinging cloud. Jake had better finish this business fast.

A shadow detached itself from the dark mass of the outhouse. Eli aimed, but before he could pull the trigger the shadow fired. Jake twisted and fell. His body jerked as another slug plowed into muscle and bone.

Eli's breath choked to a halt. For a moment he crouched where he was, stunned, unbelieving. Then his soul filled with a rage so great the night turned a red that had nothing to do with the flames eating away at the roof. The rage erupted from his throat in a roar. He fired wildly, filling the air with lead until his pistol hammer clicked futilely on empty chambers.

The murderer had disappeared back into the night shadows. All caution abandoned, Eli rushed out into the yard and sprinted for his brother's body. Shots plowed the dirt around him. He ignored them.

"Jake!" he gasped, crouching beside the limp form. Blood oozed from a hole in Jake's side and already congealed around a wound in his shoulder.

"Eli. Dammit!" Jake's voice was a hoarse whisper. "What're . . . ? Eli! No!"

The horror in Jake's face reflected more than the pain of his wounds. The cabin had become an inferno.

"Josh! My God!" Eli sprang to his feet and ran back toward the house. He thought he could hear the cries of his son as he charged into the flames. The sound of Joshua's screams blocked out the scorching pain.

Jake woke in Hell, or so he thought. If the pain in his side was infernal torture, the Devil was doing a fair job of punishing him for his sins.

Then his eyes focused. The face above him, ugly as it was, didn't belong to Old Nick. The broken nose and scars were the property of one Amos Walking Horse, half Cowlitz Indian, half rogue, and for the last year the foreman of the Carradine timber crews.

"Awake are ya?" Amos asked.

Jake tried to rise, but abruptly changed his mind. He collapsed back onto the cot, face white with pain.

"You're in the crew shack," Amos told him. "I figger you're gonna live, most likely." His mouth twitched in a macabre grin. "Man like you—they'd have to shoot you at least ten more times to put you down permanent like. They only hit you twice. You've been out about twelve hours."

"Kanes," Jake croaked.

"I know. They burned the cabin. Me and Cal was fighting the Kane crew at the mill. They just walked into it in the middle of the night shift and took over like they owned it. We didn't think about the house." His voice lowered. "I shoulda gone running to the cabin, Jake. I'm sorry as hell."

Something else was coming. Jake could see it in the
breed's face, feel it in the close air of the little shack.

"They're both gone, Jake," Amos finally said. "Me
and Cal got to the house just as Eli ran back in. Those
bastard Kanes lit out like scared rabbits, but we
couldn't get Eli and Josh out in time. The roof collapsed."

Jake felt a great hole open inside him, far bigger
than the holes drilled by Kane lead. "My fault," he
rasped.

"Like hell."

"I shouldn't have left 'em. Shouldn't have . . ."

"Bull! The Kanes did this."

"They'll pay. I'll make sure they pay."

"Not right now they won't," Amos intruded with the
voice of reason. "Right now they got the money and
the men. You got nothing. The mill's damaged, the pay-
roll's stolen, and the men aren't going to stick around
just for the hell of it, not with the Kanes makin' it hot
here and all that gold waitin' for 'em down in California. And if the Kanes find out you're still breathin',
they'll put those other ten slugs through your stubborn
hide. Next time they won't leave before finishing the
job."

Jake uttered an inarticulate sound of rage.

"You listen to me," Amos warned. "When a man's a
breed he learns to take all kinda crap. He also learns
not to play his hand till all the cards are on his side.
Gettin' yourself killed ain't gonna help Eli and Josh
none."

Jake closed his eyes, but the darkness didn't drive
away the guilt. He opened them again. "Bring me my
guns, Amos."

"You ain't in no shape to use 'em."

"Fetch my guns."

When Amos handed him a pistol, Jake closed his
hand lovingly around the familiar grip. "All the years I

defied Pa and made my living with a gun instead of an ax. I came back and tried to do things his way, and what do I have to show for it?'' He tenderly ran his hand along the barrel, as if he caressed a beloved's flesh, not cold steel. "I still have this,'' he concluded. "It's the only damned thing I do have.''

1

April 27, 1850

Independence, Missouri, certainly did not live up to Harriett Foster's vision of the western frontier. A month ago, sitting in her Boston parlor, Harriett had imagined untainted skies, fresh breezes, and wide, windswept prairies so vast, they would swallow the courageous and enterprising souls who dared carry the banner of civilization into the wilderness. The reality of Independence, however, proved her imagination sadly at fault. The "untainted" skies were clogged with smoke from a thousand campfires; the "fresh" breezes mingled odors of spoiled food and raw sewage—the by-products of an army of people and livestock; and the wide, windswept prairies were littered with a crowded disarray of wagons and tents of every description.

Nevertheless, Harriett girded herself, resisted the temptation to hold her nose, and sallied forth with her mission, as every good soldier must do. For was she not a soldier in service to a great cause? she reminded herself. No true soldier would give up the fight just because the battlefield was not quite up to snuff.

"We shall never find the correct camp!" Lucille Foster Stanwick trudged through the mud behind her niece, commenting on conditions with unsoldierly complaints.

"Of course we shall, Aunt Lucille. The good fellow back there said the Packard and Deere wagons are right across from the camp with the yellow canvas sign. Though I think they might have been helpful enough to put up a sign themselves. "There!" she pointed. "That must be them. I'm sure we have found our way at last."

A stout man who hammered on the iron rim of a wagon wheel looked up at their approach.

"Good sir," Harriett greeted him. "Do I have the pleasure of addressing Mr. Charles Deere?"

He frowned at her under beetling brows.

"Sir?"

"Uh . . . Deere's over there." He directed Harriett's gaze to a tall, graying man who stood several wagons away in conversation with two other men.

Harriett thanked him and trod on. "Mr. Deere?" she began politely.

Deere turned as she strode up to the group. He was a fatherly-looking fellow with impressive side-whiskers decorating heavy jowls. The jowls dropped in surprise before he remembered himself and touched the brim of his hat. "Ma'am."

His tone was polite enough, but his eyes swept with studied contempt from the tip of her beribboned bonnet to the toes of her flat-heeled, high-buttoned shoes. Harriett conceded that her choice of costume might not be wise, for the trouser-like pantaloons she wore beneath her midcalf-length skirt seemed to antagonize most men and offend many women. Nevertheless, Harriett thought of the style as the uniform of the women's equality movement, and she wouldn't tiptoe around her beliefs to please anyone—especially a man.

"Mr. Deere, I am Miss Harriett Foster. And this is my aunt, Mrs. Lucille Foster Stanwick, a widow."

Lucille dropped a small curtsy as Mr. Deere looked her up and down, his regard slightly more approving than the scowl he'd given her niece. "What can I do for you ladies?"

"I wanted to let you know we have arrived," Harriett told him, "and to consult with you about any special requirements of your company of travelers before we purchase our wagon and supplies."

Deere's face went blank. "Beg pardon?"

Harriett regarded him patiently. "I am Harriett Foster, sir. We corresponded. Surely you remember."

"Harriett Foster." He cocked one thick gray brow. "H. Foster? You're H. Foster?"

"Yes sir, I am. Now, Mr. Deere. I have purchased a copy of Mr. Ware's *Emigrant's Guide to California*, which I have been assured is a passably reliable source of information. Mr. Ware outlines in great detail the supplies needed for our overland journey, but if you have any special recommendations—"

"Hold it! Just hold it right there, young woman! My only recommendation is that you and your aunt get the . . . the . . . Go back where you came from!"

"But Mr. Deere!" Harriett looked him straight in the eye, a tactic that she had found made most men back down in only moments. "You agreed that we could travel to California with your company."

He leaned forward and thrust out a bewhiskered jaw. The eye contact didn't seem to bother him in the least. "I thought H. Foster was a man, my girl, and—"

"There was no reason . . . !"

"Of course there was reason! No woman signs her name H. Foster. In fact, no woman should be writing about such business at all! Isn't that right?" He turned to his two companions, who nodded their heads emphatically.

"But you agreed, sir!"

"And you wrote under false pretenses!"

Harriett stiffened her spine and prepared to launch a retort, but he raised his hand as if to ward off a physical blow. "Now, now, little lady. You really have no idea what you're about." The condescending tone raised Harriett's temperature yet another notch. "This is an arduous adventure we undertake—no place for fine ladies like yourself and your aunt. There's dangers aplenty along every mile, and it wouldn't be right to let a gently bred woman subject herself to such hardships."

"Mr. Deere!" Harriett huffed. "Many women have made this journey with every bit the stamina of their male companions."

"But not in these days, dear lady, with gamblers, gunmen, and other assorted ne'er-do-wells headed to California to make their fortunes."

She raised her brows in polite surprise. "Is that the sort of people your Indiana Company of Adventurers comprises?"

"Certainly not, ma'am. But to tell the truth"—he tipped back his hat and revealed a balding pate—"if I was to let you come, I wouldn't need to fear any Injuns on the trail ahead. My own company would skin me alive. They're·in a fair hurry to get to that gold, and they won't be slowed down by a pair of women."

"And those persons over there are not women, Mr. Deere?" Harriett inclined her head toward a nearby wagon whose occupants were clearly female.

"No, ma'am. Those are tarts, going to California to make a fortune their own way."

Behind her, Harriett heard Lucille gasp. But Harriett refused to be daunted. "My aunt and I are every bit as able to keep up as those ladies, Mr. Deere."

Deere shook his head. "No! That's my last word, Miss Foster. If you were traveling with a husband, or father, or brother, that would be different. We have a couple of wives coming along, and someone's sister. But I won't take any solitary ladies." He shot a glance toward the traveling whorehouse. "And they don't count."

"Why not?" Harriett demanded.

"Because they aren't ladies. And you are." His gaze swept her pantaloons once again. "At least on that score I'm giving you the benefit of the doubt."

Harriett frowned thoughtfully as Deere and his companions walked away. "One would think," she commented to her aunt, "that in the forefront of the wave that is carrying civilization to an untamed land, a man's thinking would be somewhat less anachronistic than in the East."

Lucille smiled brightly. "What a shame!"

Harriett didn't think her aunt looked at all upset. Quite the contrary.

The two women picked their way around a steaming pile of mule leavings and walked back the way they had come.

"Don't look so put out, my love." Lucille gave her niece's shoulder an affectionate pat. "At least now we can dismiss the idea of trekking overland with these . . . extremely interesting . . . people and go back to Boston to arrange sea passage. In truth, I don't know why we didn't take sea passage to begin with. It's not as though we couldn't afford to book a comfortable suite, dear. With the fortune your father left you, and the trust fund my Peter left me, we almost could've bought a whole ship."

"And endure seasickness for months on end? No thank you, Aunt! We shall travel overland."

"But dear, you heard the man. We are not allowed to travel in company with his wagons."

"No," Harriett corrected with a smile. "Solitary fe-

males are not allowed. All we have to do is find a man
—a hired helper of sorts—to be our guide and escort."

"I think you're being a bit optimistic, dear."

"No, I'm not. After coming this far, I refuse to turn
around and go back."

They reached the edge of town, which to Harriett's
eyes looked little better than the chaotic jumble of
wagons and tents they had just left behind, though it
was better than the place where the steamer had left
them earlier in the day. When their boat had tied up on
the south bank of the Missouri, at Independence Landing, Harriett had believed the miserable hut that
awaited them at the wharf was the town itself, and her
heart sank clear to her toes. She was relieved to learn
that the actual town of Independence was four miles
from the river landing, and that an army of wagons
and other crude conveyances waited to take the
steamer passengers and their belongings into town—
for a price, of course.

They had hired a crude one-horse buggy, with an
even cruder driver, to carry them into town. Independence had been an unpleasant surprise, filled as it was
with mud, unpleasant smells, and throngs of men,
mules, and oxen. The clamor alone was enough to
make a decent person think twice about venturing
forth into the streets. Blacksmiths hammering, animals braying, bawling, neighing, or barking, each ac-
cording to its own species, and men—sometimes
scarcely discernible from the animals—shouting and
cursing. Harriett had never heard such profanity and
ill language come from the mouth of man, seemingly
every other word.

The first task upon arrival in town had been finding
a hotel room, which was more difficult than they'd anticipated.

"There are so many people!" Lucille objected. "In

Boston, such unruly crowds would never be tolerated."

The first three hotels they tried were full, but at the
fourth the proprietress—an elderly lady with an air of
maternal concern—took pity on them. By that time the
ribbons on Harriett's bonnet drooped pathetically and
the ruffles of her pantaloons were spattered with mud.
They took the room she offered without a single complaint about the cracked ewer on the washstand, the
stained linen, and the single narrow bed. Harriett had
scarcely glanced at the sorry accommodations as she'd
straightened her bonnet, brushed the mud from her
skirt, and set out to find their wagon company, with
discouraging results.

Now Harriett and Lucille entered the town for the
second time since they had arrived. Dusk was painting
the slapdash buildings and muddy streets in muted
tones of brown and gray, but the bustle continued un-
abated.

"Do you suppose this goes on all night?" Lucille
asked disapprovingly.

"I'm sure it cannot."

They trudged up to their tiny room, Lucille droop-
ing, Harriett's back straighter than ever.

"Where are you going to find a man willing to shep-
herd us across the continent, my love?" Lucille sat
down upon the bed and sighed. "Really, Harriett,
when you persuaded me to accompany you on this
journey, you made it all sound so easy. I should have
known better than to listen to you." She gave a ladylike moue. "Not that I could have permitted you to
travel unaccompanied, and not that Boston wasn't
boring me to tears."

"Aunt! Boston is one of the most civilized and pleasant cities in the world!"

Lucille raised a brow. "I'm sorry, dear, but the gentlemen of Boston are stiff as a starched collar. And so

are the ladies. When you suggested this journey, I saw
it as the perfect opportunity to broaden my horizons
and draw some fresh air into my lungs." She sniffed.
"If I could find some fresh air. Really, Harriett, I do
think the trip by sea would have been more pleasant,
seasickness and all."

"You only say that because you've never been seasick. I get sick just riding in a rowboat." Harriett rum-
maged through a satchel and took out her hairbrush.
She pulled the pins from the severe bun at the nape of
her neck and brushed her hair forward over her head.
As she bent slightly forward the shimmering fall
touched the floor.

Lucille sighed. "You've inherited your mother's stubbornness along with her red hair, my love. Combine
that with your father's constant curiosity and it spells
trouble. I should have known."

Harriett flung her hair back and smiled. "Everything will work out, Aunt Lucille. You'll see. I'm sure
there are many men in this town who would like to go
to California but haven't the means. We'll find one and
offer him passage, then let Mr. Deere eat his own
words. It's as simple as that."

"Simple!" Lucille snorted. "Simple indeed! After
seeing this town and these people, you should know
that we are venturing beyond our abilities."

Harriett twisted her hair into a bun, pinned it, and
turned to her aunt with a frown. "As long as women
think so little of their abilities we will never end the
injustices that rule our lives. That is why Mrs. Bloomer
was so anxious to publish my journal of this trip in the
Lily. We must teach women that they are as able and
intelligent and courageous as men." She sat on the bed
beside Lucille and took her aunt's hand in hers. "If I
fail in this endeavor, I fail Mrs. Bloomer, and women
everywhere. Don't you see?"

Lucille sighed and raised one elegant brow. "And

here I thought we were traveling to California to see you married to Edwin. Silly me.''

Harriett smiled. ''Well, of course, that's important too.''

''Has it occurred to you, my love, that if we must hire a man to get us across the continent, then you have not proved a thing about women's abilities?''

''Not true!'' Harriett jumped up, grabbed her bonnet, and motioned her aunt to do the same. ''So we can legitimately say we achieved California through our own efforts, we shall hire a man whom no sane person could consider a protector—some wretch who is the poorest possible excuse for a human being.'' As they went out the door she threw her aunt a dimpled smile. ''And from what I've seen of Independence, there are plenty of those specimens available.''

Harriett was right. Independence abounded in pitiful examples of humanity. She considered hiring a sad-looking boy who fetched and carried for the blacksmith, but Mr. Deere would hardly consider a stripling boy as sufficient manpower. The fellow who swept the floors and emptied the chamber pots for the hotel presented another possibility, but the wad in his cheek and the brown spittle staining his beard convinced Harriett to look for another. The waiter who served them dinner at a crowded little restaurant looked unhappy enough to jump at such an opportunity, but Harriett decided that he was far too old.

Then, as they strolled along the street and Lucille started to talk once again about steamers headed east, Harriett found her man—or rather, her man fell practically into her lap.

The street was busy, but the crowd made way when the doors of Sam's Watering Hole burst open and disgorged a pair of flailing bodies onto the road. The brawlers—kicking, jabbing, and bashing at each other —rolled into the street right at Harriett's feet, then rolled away again. Lucille's shriek was lost in the din of an instant crowd of spectators.

"Of course," Harriett breathed, an idea hatching. "What better place to look than in a place that sells spiritous liquors."

The battling pair crashed back through the saloon doors, and the crowd followed. Harriett moved with the crowd.

Lucille clutched at her arm. "Where are you going? Harriett! Really!"

"Just to the door. I'm not going in!"

"I should hope not!"

As soon as the scruffy gladiators were through the door, three other men joined in the fight, all pounding on the same victim. The poor man who was thus set upon, however, held his own admirably well, considering the odds. He was one of the biggest men Harriett had ever seen, and no part of him looked to be fat. His shirt, damp with sweat and blood, clung to his torso and revealed the bunch and heave of heavy muscle as he returned blow for blow. The crowd alternately heckled and cheered him, except for one ugly, dark-faced man who sat at a corner table and seemed totally unconcerned with the chaos around him.

The fight knocked around the tavern, smashing chairs and overturning tables. Harriett dared not go in, for Lucille regarded her from the street with a most distressed expression. But her heart cried for the poor creature who was so unfairly beset. Strong as he was, he seemed doomed. And indeed he was, for only a few moments passed before the big man's assailants managed to knock him to the floor. Each took one limb, swung him to and fro, and sent him flying through the saloon window with great energy.

"Oh dear!" Harriett hastened to where the human projectile—together with the remains of the window—landed. With the linen handkerchief from her reticule she wiped the bloodied dirt and glass shards from his face. "Have they killed you, poor man?"

"I doubt it." The voice from behind made Harriett jump. She turned and looked up at the one man in the saloon who had ignored the fight. "He's been knocked about more than that, miss, and he generally bounces to his feet and charges back for more."

"You're his friend?" Harriett demanded. "And you didn't help him?"

"When he's drunk, Jake Carradine don't need my help to get into trouble. Or out of it, for that matter."

The man named Jake groaned, and Harriett turned back to her gentle ministrations. Certainly one could not find a more miserable example of manhood than this poor sot. Not even his ugly friend cared enough to help him. Hiring him would be a true act of charity. "Mr. Carradine, are you all right?"

"Goddamma t'ell," he slurred. "Whaddaya think?"

Harriett flinched at both the profanity and the alcohol fumes. "I think you're terribly inebriated, Mr. Carradine. Perhaps you would like some tea . . . or coffee?"

"Wh . . . whishkey!" he demanded.

"Harriett!" Lucille cried. "Come away from that rude man. Surely you're not thinking . . . !"

"He's perfect, Aunt Lucille. We could achieve our purpose and save a poor lost soul at the same time."

Jake stared up at her in woozy concentration. "Whas'say?"

"I'm offering you a job, Mr. Carradine. Free passage to the gold fields of California. Food, wages, a chance to escape from the spell of spiritous liquors. All in return for a few simple camp chores."

"Gold?" He belched. He tried to get up, but collapsed back on one elbow. His grinning friend, rather than helping him, merely shook his head.

"You'll take it, then?" Harriett prompted.

"Shhhure!"

"Oh, dear Lord!" Lucille prayed.

Jake closed his eyes and oozed back to the ground while his friend took Harriett's elbow and helped her to her feet. "You've got a right tender heart, ma'am."

Harriett cast him a curious glance. "And you are?"

"I'm called Amos Walking Horse."

"An Indian?" Lucille gasped.

"Yes, ma'am." He smiled, and for all that he had an incredibly ugly face, Harriett noted, his smile was quite pleasant.

"We're pleased to make your acquaintance, Mr. Walking Horse. I am Miss Harriett Foster. And this is my aunt, Mrs. Lucille Foster Stanwick." She dubiously eyed her new employee, who snored while emitting fumes that would intoxicate a horse. "Your friend . . ."

"Will be at whatever place you say, whenever you want him there. I'll see to it."

She raised a questioning brow.

"Whatever job you're gonna give him, ma'am, it's bound to do him good."

"It couldn't do him much harm," Lucille commented dryly.

Next morning, bright and early, Harriett set out to purchase supplies for her journey. As she walked into one of the many stores advertising "every requisite necessary for the comfort and luxury of emigrants on the overland trails," she felt for the first time that perhaps a great adventure was beginning. Before this day the journey had been tedium. The railroads and steamers that had transported them from Boston had been dirty and overcrowded, and always in the back of her mind was the worry that she would meet trouble in Independence when her traveling companions discovered she was a woman, for the restrictions placed on one's life just because one happened to be female were all too familiar to her. Then, too, the shock of her parents' untimely death in a carriage accident was too fresh for her to enjoy the journey to Independence. Harriett and her mother had been closer than most mothers and daughters, their shared enthusiasm for women's rights and social reform having forged a bond between them that went beyond the ties of blood. To have the bond cut so prematurely had been agony to Harriett. And her father—dear, sweet, intellectual Father—a true Renaissance man whose talents dipped into so many areas of endeavor. Her father was one of the few open-minded men Harriett knew. How Harriett missed them both!

But now, for the first time, she felt a stirring of excitement for the future. Her journey to a new land would be a rare adventure, and her journal, when published by dear Mrs. Bloomer, would allow women all over the country to share her experience. In California, Edwin would be waiting. Their marriage would be a partnership of equals, just as her parents' had been. And together they would make the West a better place for both men and women to live.

"May I help you, ma'am?" the storekeeper offered.

"Indeed you may." Harriett took out her list, copied painstakingly from Mr. Ware's *Emigrant's Guide to California*. With such a detailed source of information about the trail ahead, how could the journey be anything but smooth? "I need fifty pounds of coffee, twenty of tea, seventy pounds of sugar, fifty pounds of rice, four barrels of flour, five hundred pounds of bacon. . . . Let me see. Fruit, salt, pepper, lard, saleratus . . ."

"Going out on the trail, are you, ma'am?"

"Yes," Harriett answered happily. "If I just give you my list, would you be so good as to fill it?"

"Be glad to." He regarded her curiously. "Hard time for a lady like yourself to be going, what with all the no-accounts traveling the trail these days, and the cholera and all."

She shrugged. "There are ne'er-do-wells and sickness everywhere, sir."

"That's true enough, I suppose. I just hope your husband knows what he's doing, taking a gentle lady like yourself along."

"I have no need of a husband to help me along the trail, sir. I am quite capable of being on my own."

The storekeeper glanced at her left hand, then harrumphed. "I'll be!"

"Will two hours be enough time?"

"Uh . . . sure."

"Then good day to you. And thank you. I shall come back with a wagon."

Harriett left the store and hastened along the plank walkway toward the hotel. She had arranged to meet Mr. Walking Horse and her "guide and escort" at ten o'clock, and she estimated that the hour was nearly that already.

The two men were waiting for her on the hotel veranda. In contrast to the night before, Jake Carradine was standing on his own two feet. He was taller than Mr. Walking Horse, and Harriett's first impression of his size had been correct. His shoulders seemed immense, his arms thick with muscle, his legs long and straight. Sun-streaked brown hair fell in an unruly mass to his shoulders, a thick mustache cried out for a trimming, and his clothes looked as though they had very little acquaintance with a washtub. But something in his clear gray eyes made her want to smile. He would do, Harriett decided.

Jake Carradine had other ideas. For the past half hour he had been sitting on the veranda with Amos—some friend the half-breed had turned out to be!—bouncing around ideas on how to get out of the stupid commitment he'd made. Or at least Amos had told him, with unsympathetic glee, that he'd made a commitment. Jake himself didn't remember much past sailing out a window.

"A man oughtn't to be held to the stupid things he says when he's drunk!" Jake had complained.

"You don't like what you say when you're drunk," Amos advised, "then don't get drunk."

"Hell, Amos! You don't really think I should work for this . . . this woman!"

Amos merely shrugged. "I've never known Jake Carradine to break his word, though I figger we've broken every other thing possible this last year. You did give this little lady your word, my friend."

"Some friend! Why did you let me do such a stupid-ass thing?"

Then the "little lady" herself had appeared, walking up the street with a saucy stride and a bold, unfeminine tilt to her chin. Jake had almost groaned aloud. Every inch of the female spelled trouble. He knew that from his first look. She was dressed in one of the most ridiculous getups he'd ever seen—some sort of ruffly trousers under a flounced skirt that came only to midcalf. He'd heard something about the outrageous styles that the more fractious women were wearing back east, but most women in the West had better sense.

"Mr. Carradine. I'm glad to see that you're prompt."

Her cheeks dimpled when she smiled, Jake noted. Another bad sign, as was the red hair that peeked from beneath her beribboned bonnet.

"Miss . . . uh . . ."

"Foster. I guess we weren't properly introduced last night."

"Miss Foster. I . . . uh . . . apologize for any offense last night."

"No offense taken, Mr. Carradine."

He breathed a bit easier. Maybe she wasn't as bad as

she seemed, in spite of a certain glitter in those deep green eyes. Under other circumstances those eyes might have held a certain fascination for him. "Then you understand that . . . that I probably said some things I didn't mean."

"We made a deal, Mr. Carradine." She was still smiling, but the dimples faded. "I offered a job, and you accepted."

"I wasn't myself last night."

"That is a bit of good news."

"What I mean is—"

"That you're trying to back out."

"Uh. . . ." He felt rather than saw Amos's amused smile. Never trust an Indian—even half an Indian.

"Mr. Carradine, I have need of your services, and you did agree to escort my aunt and me on our journey west."

"Is that what I agreed to do?" Jake felt the pall of doom descending.

"It most certainly is. Now, I will pay you fair wages, food, and any expenses you incur in our behalf. I assume you have your own weapons and mount."

"I don't have a horse. I lost mine in a card game two days ago."

She sighed, regarding him for all the world as though he were an errant child. He fought against feeling small. The woman was trouble all right. She barely came up to his chin, and a good prairie wind would blow her right off her feet. Yet she was cutting him down to size like a sharp hatchet.

"Then I will give you funds for a horse," she stated, her rounded little chin thrust out at a stubborn angle. "You will need one on the trail."

"Lady," Jake sighed. "I'm not the sort of man a decent woman wants to escort her across a room, much less a continent. I'm a drifter and a gunman. I drink, gamble, fight, and"—he added a final kicker—"I enjoy whorehouses."

Harriett's face grew rigid, but she didn't twitch an eye. "Are you wanted by the law, Mr. Carradine?" Harriett asked coolly.

Jake thought a moment. "Not right now, I guess. But I could arrange to be, if that's what it takes for me to get out of this."

She speared him with eyes that had turned to green ice. "You agreed to come into my employ, sir. And because I trusted your word—and the word of your friend Mr. Walking Horse—I went forward with arrangements that cost a good deal of money. If you don't live up to your obligations, then you are not only everything you say you are, but you are also a man of no honor."

"Now you're beginning to understand! Hell, Miss Foster! I'm a two-bit gunhand. Why would you want . . . ?"

"I didn't hire you for your virtues, Mr. Carradine. And I am not afraid of a two-bit, dirty, drunken gunman. All I require is your presence beside my wagon on the journey to California. That job shouldn't be too difficult for you to handle."

Hell! The damned woman knew how to get under a man's skin! Jake had never done violence to a female, but Lord, he was tempted! "All right, Miss Foster." Jake slipped his pistol from its holster and had the satisfaction of seeing her face grow a shade paler. "But just so we understand each other—the gun's for hire. But that's the only part of me that is." If that slap didn't get to her, nothing would. Harriett's face flushed to a high color, and Jake was suddenly and uncomfortably struck with what a fine-looking woman the little witch was. But the cold green snap of her eyes spoiled the effect.

"I can't imagine why I would be interested in any other part of you, Mr. Carradine."

Jake grinned, and Harriett's color deepened. Hastily she opened her reticule and fished out a wad of bills. "Go buy yourself a horse. And purchase a pistol for my aunt and myself, and a rifle. I may have hired your gun, sir, but I think I'll trust our defense to myself." With a final look of distaste, she turned and walked into the hotel.

"Well, if that don't beat all!" Jake grabbed his hat off the bench and slapped it onto his head, ignoring the dust that flew. "Amos, you son of a bitch, why did you let me get mixed up with that loco female?"

Amos chuckled. "You did that on your own, Jake boy. I ain't your nursemaid. Least I'm glad to see you've got enough of the old Jake left to live up to your word."

Jake shot him a frown that would have sent many men running for cover. "What's that supposed to mean?"

"Means you've got a devil ridin' you, and it's time you let it go. Ever since we left the Willamette, you've been doing your best to dig your own grave." Amos leaned back against a veranda post, folded his arms across his barrel chest, and regarded Jake with melancholy black eyes. "Eli and little Josh are dead, Jake, and there was nothing you could do to help them. And there wasn't no way we coulda stayed to make Kane pay—with no money and no men. When are you going to let it rest, my friend?"

Jake's face grew rigid, his gray eyes dark and shuttered. He gave no answer.

Amos sighed. "That little lady and her aunt are good people, Jake. Besides, some time away from the booze and the gambling houses will do you good."

"Thought you said you weren't a nursemaid."

"Well, hell! Sometimes you need one. But I think I'll

turn over my nursemaid duties to Miss Foster for the summer."

"You aren't coming?" Jake asked darkly.

"I've got a hankerin' to go back to my own stompin' grounds. Go back to that meadow on the Cowlitz River and talk to the spirits."

Jake snorted.

"You're on your own, my friend." Amos grinned wickedly.

"On my own. Thanks. With two greenhorn females, a wagon train of gold-hungry adventurers, gamblers, and harlots, and close on two thousand miles of river crossings, deserts, and cholera. Not to mention a hostile Indian or two."

"That's a fact," the half-breed admitted. "Now, don't you think it's time you got cleaned up and bought yourself a horse?"

"The hell you say," Jake growled. "I figure it's time for a drink."

He headed across the street, where the tinkling of a piano signaled festivities in progress. A fine mess he was in now. A preacher or two had warned him he'd end up in Hell eventually. But Jake had always figured he had to die first.

Fine time to learn he was wrong!

2

Journal entry—April 30—camped outside Independence, Missouri: Tomorrow it begins—our journey across this vast continent. I sit here in my cozy tent, looking out upon my wagon and many other similar tents and wagons. We are almost a city here on the south bank of the great Missouri, though the strangest city one could imagine, a city of canvas and wheels.

The greatest obstacle to my endeavor—that of convincing our wagon captain to allow me passage—is over. Captain Deere is a gentleman of firm opinions, and he does not approve at all of women making their own way along this trail. Only because I hired a man as guide and helper was he convinced (with some difficulty, I might add) to allow Lucille and me to travel in the Packard and Deere company. And even as he gave consent the captain disclaimed responsibility for the consequences. As are most men, Captain Deere is quite set in his opinion that a woman belongs under the direct care of a man, and any other situation spells disaster. I shall prove him wrong, however, for the guide I hired, male though he is, is certainly not of a type to ease our burden, but rather add to it. When this journey is finished, the credit for our success will remain with Lucille and myself.

Our traveling companions on this odyssey are a diverse lot who have joined themselves together in the Packard and Deere Indiana Company of Adventurers. Many are from Indiana, from whence comes the name, but some are not. Mr. Deere is all too apparent, and Mr. Packard, the other organizer, is nowhere to be seen. I believe he financed several of the travelers in return for a part of their findings in the gold fields.

Gold is a word one hears much too often—not only in our company's campsite, but as one wanders abroad in this strange wagon city. Our Adventurers can think of nothing but reaching the gold fields of California and making their fortune. We have in our company a minister of God—seduced by Mammon, it seems—and a physician who is giving up healing the sick to increase the depths of his pockets (though many argue gold has always been the aim of that profession). Also among us are blacksmiths, farmers, gamblers, clerks, storekeepers, and even (if I may risk censure by daring to notice) a wagon of our fallen sisters who plan to make their fortune from the miners, not the mines.

I think that the argonauts (as they call themselves) gathered here to begin this journey have no notion of the significance of their odyssey, and certainly no care for bringing civilization to a savage land. But I believe that must be the end result of our endeavor.

Harriett closed the book upon her first journal entry and tucked the little volume back into her satchel just as her aunt stepped into the tent.

"You look very satisfied with yourself," Lucille noted.

Harriett hugged herself. "I must confess that I am.

We are provisioned and prepared for any eventuality this land might throw our way. And just think how exciting this journey will be—the new sights and wondrous adventures coming our way!"

Lucille smiled with somewhat less enthusiasm. "I'll admit I'm somewhat more optimistic about this endeavor than I was. The gentlemen of this company seem most gallant, with the exception of that horrid Mr. Deere, of course. And the fellow Mr. Carter whom he's employed as scout is a scurrilous sort. Why, not an hour ago Mr. Carter passed this way—so drunk he swayed upon his feet—and made several remarks to me that I dare not repeat for fear of offending your sensibilities. Why do you suppose Mr. Deere would hire such a man for a responsible post?"

Harriett smiled. "We can't blame Mr. Deere much for hiring Mr. Carter. The man we've employed is not someone I'd call a respectable fellow. Speaking of Mr. Carradine, Aunt—have you seen him about?"

"No, my love. I haven't seen him since this morning." Lucille laughed softly. "When he's not drunk and covered with dust and blood, your Mr. Carradine is a most interesting specimen, dear. You may have chosen better than I thought."

"He's not *my* Mr. Carradine," Harriett replied emphatically. "Aunt, dear, you find every man an interesting specimen in one way or another."

Lucille raised a delicate brow. "Most men are interesting, my love. And the longer one is deprived of their company, the more interesting they become. I've been a widow five years, and that is much too long for a woman to have only herself for company."

"A man's enlightened companionship does make a woman's life richer," Harriett admitted. "I'm certainly looking forward to becoming reacquainted with Edwin after all these years." She frowned. "I do wish I knew where Mr. Carradine has taken himself off to."

"Do you need him for something?"

"Not a thing. I simply don't want him to run out on us at the last moment. Mr. Deere would be ever so happy to put us from the company."

Jake Carradine had reluctantly helped them purchase a wagon and four yoke of sturdy oxen, had obediently allowed Harriett to display him to the wagon captain, and then disappeared. He could very easily back out of his commitment before they left, Harriett acknowledged. She didn't think he would. The man did seem to have at least a rudimentary notion of honor. Then again, she might be giving him too much credit.

"Have you made acquaintance with the others in our company, Harriett, dear? They seem to me not nearly as rough a group as we were led to believe."

"I've met some," Harriett said. "Not many. I've been occupied with rechecking our supplies against Mr. Ware's recommendations, and I wrote in my journal."

Lucille shook her head in admonition. "Always so serious. You should allow yourself more time to make friends and be sociable. After all is said and done, my dear, people are the ones who give us happiness. Not causes and great endeavors."

"I'll try to remember that," Harriett said with a tolerant smile.

"There are several ladies in our company, you know."

"I've noticed," Harriett answered dryly.

"Oh, I don't mean the tarts, dear. I've done my very best not to see them! But two ladies of good character are traveling with us as well. A Mrs. MacKenzie—a newlywed, I believe. And Mrs. MacBride is traveling with her brother and a young son."

"I shall make it a point to meet them. Have you studied Mr. Ware's guidebook, Aunt? Tomorrow we shall be called upon to be competent in the procedures he describes.''

"I've read it," Lucille assured her. "But you shouldn't expect me to excel as a pioneer, my love. His explanation of forming the wagons into a camp goes beyond my understanding entirely, and his description of the devious nature of the savages makes me wish I were in Boston again, safe in my bed." She opened the volume in question and pointed to a paragraph. "And see here—he instructs us to take great trouble forming this enclosure of wagons, and then states that cooking operations should be carried on outside the enclosure. What use is the enclosure, my dear, if we are not protected by it? And I shudder to think of cooking over an open fire, within such a short distance of oxen, and mules, and—heaven forbid!—passing savages."

Harriett laughed. "I think we shall survive in spite of it, Aunt."

"And he doesn't explain how to build a fire, does he?"

"I suppose one simply piles up logs and lights a match."

"I can't picture it, my dear. I hope Mr. Carradine is more competent at these practical things than we are."

"Whatever we need to know we shall learn, Aunt." Harriett's tone permitted no doubt. "We have intelligent minds, and we can educate ourselves, contrary to what most men believe."

Lucille sighed. "Whatever you say, dear."

"Now, Aunt! You must get into the spirit of this adventure. Come walking with me and we'll take a look around the camp."

"No, thank you. I shall save my energy for tomorrow. But you go on, my love."

"I think I will. There's nothing to revive the spirit like an invigorating walk."

As Harriett tucked her shawl around her shoulders and marched away, Lucille raised a brow. "If that is true," she said to herself, "then we will soon be the most revived people on the face of this good earth."

The flickering campfire painted five men in dancing patterns of black shadow and orange light. They lounged around a flat slab of rock that served as a table, regarding the dirty pasteboard cards in their hands with the seriousness of men who knew poker was more than a mere game.

"Jacks or better to open," Jake Carradine said. "Anyone got openers?"

"Not me," Tom Jenkins said.

"I'll open. Fifty dollars." Abel Hawkins tossed two poker chips onto the slab of rock.

Lawrence Steede grimaced. "Fold. Hell, my luck tonight has been crap."

"Hope your luck in Californy is better." Tom grinned.

"Don't worry about me in California," Steede replied. "You fellows can grub for the gold if you want. Wherever there's gold, there's bad poker players stupid enough to take it from their pockets and put it in mine."

"You'll have to get better hands than you've had tonight," Abel Hawkins told him. "How about it, Carradine. You wanna bet some of that money you won tonight?"

Firelight winked off the bottle Jake raised to his lips. He took a swig, wiped his mouth on his sleeve, and glanced at his cards. "Raise you fifty. You in, Carter?"

The scout hawked and spat. "Fold."

"Tom?"

Tom Jenkins shook his head. "Unless you gents will take a pledge on a share of the gold I'm gonna pull outta those hills."

Hawkins snorted. "You might not find no gold."

"I'll find it," Jenkins assured them. "Ain't nothing gonna stand in my way. Injuns, rivers, nothing. I sold all I had to get here, and once we start up these wagons tomorrow, ain't nothing gonna slow me down till I got gold dust comin' out every pore."

"Well, I ain't takin' no gold that's still in the ground," Hawkins declared.

"Your loss." Tom shrugged and tossed in his cards.

Hawkins grinned. "Just you and me, Carradine. How many cards you want?"

"Two." Jake took another swallow from the bottle as Hawkins dealt out two cards to Jake and gave one to himself.

"Bet," Hawkins said.

Jake looked at his cards and hiccuped.

"If'n I was you, Hawkins," Phineas Carter suggested with a leer, "I'd ask Carradine to bet a share of that pretty little piece he works for."

"That would be no bargain," Jake replied with a grimace. "She shoulda put her hooks into one of you fellows instead of me."

"Always was partial to red hair," Carter said. "Li'l gal like her—she looks like she could keep a man nice and warm at night."

Jake snorted. "Wouldn't try to find out if I were you, Carter. Ladies like Miss Foster get right prickly where their precious dignity is concerned. Besides, the woman's made of ice."

"Hell!" Carter sniggered. "I've melted more'n one icicle in my time."

"You'll keep away from this one, if you're smart." Jake gave Carter a meaningful look, then returned his attention to Hawkins. "Another fifty."

"Call."

"What'cha got?"

"Three of a kind," Hawkins gloated.

Jake smiled. "Full house."

"Crap!" Hawkins spat contemptuously. "I ain't never seen a man hold so much liquor and still be able to play his cards. Your luck always this good, Carradine?"

Jake raised the bottle to his lips, and the image of a cabin in Oregon flashed painfully through his mind. "My luck stinks," he said to Hawkins. "I just know how to play the game."

Harriett avoided further complaint from Lucille by taking a walk to admire the stars, only to find that there were scarcely any stars visible. Smoke from hundreds of campfires filled the air with an eye-stinging, acrid haze. But the air at least was cool, and the sounds that underlay the night—the restless commotion of livestock, the soft hum of distant conversation, the rhythmic hammering of someone making late preparation for the journey—were somehow soothing. For a moment she stood and drank it all in, glad to be a part of it, glad to be on a muddy riverbank in Missouri rather than in her safe parlor in Boston, growing old while history passed her by.

She strolled along the perimeter of the wagons. Campfires sent showers of sparks whirling toward the sky, as if to substitute for the invisible stars. Orange light flickered on white canvas wagon covers. In the camps among the wagons men packed, tended livestock, mended harnesses, cleaned weapons. Everyone was busy about his work, a commendable way to begin a journey, Harriett thought approvingly—until she heard raucous laughter coming from a group of men lounging in a rough circle beside a campsite just ahead of her. Harriett recognized one of the men as Phineas Carter, the scout who had so offended her aunt's ears.

"Hot damn! Let's see you beat this!" Carter exclaimed as he laid a fan of cards out in front of him. As the other players showed their cards, his gloating became a groan.

The men were gambling, Harriett realized scornfully. What was worse, the heady odor that hung in the air was most certainly liquor! The Indiana Adventurers should hope that their scout was better than the company he kept.

Harriett started to turn back toward her own wagon when a familiar voice made her stop.

"You gents will just have to win your money back some other time," Jake Carradine's deep voice said. "I've had enough for the night."

"What's the matter, Carradine?" another voice asked. "Run out of whiskey?"

Harriett marched forward. No employee of hers was going to indulge in such behavior when he should be . . . should be. . . . Well, surely there was some chore in their camp that he should be attending to! "Mr. Carradine!"

At the sound of her voice, three of the men sprang up and doffed their hats. Jake Carradine rose in a more leisurely manner, while Phineas Carter remained seated, regarding her with small, piggish eyes.

"Miss Foster." Jake swayed, then steadied himself. His mouth twitched upward in an insolent smile.

"May I speak with you a moment?" Her courtesy was laced with scorn, but he didn't seem to notice.

"'Scuse me, gents. My employer"—he gestured grandly to Harriett—"wishes to speak with me."

The men's laughter followed them as Jake walked with Harriett away from the fire. Her face heated. "You might do well to remember that you are employed, sir." She frowned her disapproval. "Gambling is hardly a good way to start off an expedition such as this, Mr. Carradine."

"Not unless you win," he agreed.

She turned her face away as the liquor fumes on his

breath assaulted her nose. "You've been drinking as well, Mr. Carradine."

He gave her a tipsy grin. "So I have, Miss Foster."

They walked on. Jake's unrepentant insolence rattled her. With effort Harriett gathered her wits to deliver the reprimand she knew he deserved. "Spiritous liquors have been the ruin of many a good man, sir. Drinking weakens the character and destroys the body. I'll thank you to stay sober while you are in my employ."

"Well, now, Miss Foster, I warned you that I wasn't a man that a decent woman would approve of. What you hired is the part of me that handles a gun—not the part that drinks."

"You're splitting hairs, Mr. Carradine."

He merely grinned. Dark as the night was, she could see his white teeth flash beneath the thick canopy of his mustache.

"When we made our agreement, I found it difficult to believe you were the dissipated rogue you claimed to be. But you're working hard to prove your words."

"You shouldn't frown like that, Miss Foster. You'll ruin your looks."

Harriett felt her face grow hot. She halted sharply. Jake stopped beside her and grabbed her arm to steady himself. As if burned by his touch, she jerked away.

"Mr. Carradine!"

He smiled and hiccuped.

She regarded him with disgust. "My looks are hardly your concern, sir."

"Every man is concerned with a woman's looks," he said amiably. "Good or bad, it's what they notice."

"Well, perhaps men should start noticing a woman's more lasting qualities, such as intelligence, sensitivity, integrity, and education—the same things a man notices about another man."

Jake chuckled sourly. "Those aren't the things a

man notices about another man, lady. First thing a man notices about another man is if he looks big enough or fast enough to be dangerous—and where he wears his gun. If he wears it low-slung, tied to his leg, then you can figure he's a man to watch out for.''

Harriett couldn't help glancing at Jake's right leg, where a holstered pistol the size of a cannon was tied firmly to his thigh.

"If he wears it high up on his hip, or stuck into his belt, then he's more likely to shoot off his own pecker than shoot you.''

Harriett's eyes grew wide with horror. "You are unbelievably crude.''

"I try to be.''

"That sort of language and thinking degrades a man to little better than an animal.''

"I'm quite content to be an animal.'' His mouth crooked upward in a humorless smile. "Life's less complicated that way.''

Jake's nearness, his size, his very masculinity, suddenly frightened her. "I think I'd best go back to the wagon.'' Harriett started walking. To her dismay, he walked with her. His eyes traveled over her in a manner that she couldn't quite interpret, but didn't like one bit.

"How is it, Miss Foster, that a lady like yourself is traveling to California with this gold-hungry scum? Almost everyone in these wagons is being pushed across the continent by greed. What is it that pushes you?''

"It's really not your affair, sir, but since you are curious, I'm going to San Francisco to be wed.'' Perhaps it was best that Jake Carradine knew she wasn't a woman alone. "My fiancé is a merchant who's been in the city since we liberated it from the Spanish in 1846.''

They stepped into camp. Lucille's candle-lit silhouette flickered on the side of the tent. All the other camps in the Indiana Company had cookfires burning. Harriett's alone was dark. Jake leaned back against their new canvas-covered wagon, where he was shadowed from the firelight. Harriett wondered if seeking shadows was a habit with him, like a night skulker, or a beast of prey.

"You haven't seen this fellow since '46?"

"I haven't seen him for ten years. But we've corresponded, and he's been a friend of my family since before I was born. He's an extremely amiable and educated man."

"I'll bet," Jake agreed, but Harriett didn't like his tone. "And this fellow you're going to marry is letting you travel alone, two thousand miles, through Indian country, surrounded by some of the lowest scum this country has to offer?"

"I think you exaggerate the conditions, Mr. Carradine."

"You'll soon learn that I don't."

"Besides," she told him primly. "Edwin doesn't tell me what I may or may not do. I have a perfectly good mind to make my own decisions. I considered the route by sea, but it takes twice as long and is just as dangerous. And the shorter sea voyage by way of Panama is beset by savages, disease, and delays."

"And the overland trip isn't," he said wryly.

"On the overland trip," she explained with a small smile, "I shall not suffer from seasickness."

"Tell me that after you've ridden in that wagon for a few hours, Miss Foster."

"I'm sure I can endure any hardship that is necessary, Mr. Carradine," she said frostily. "We women are really not the frail and fainting creatures that most men believe us to be."

"So you wear those"—his gaze dropped to her pantaloons and he smiled, looking very much as though he was enjoying himself—"those fluffy trousers and pick up men in saloon fights to prove you're as good as a man?"

"I am as good as a man," Harriett declared. "Being a woman does not make me inferior in any way. Men prattle of protecting woman, of placing her on a pedestal where she needn't soil herself with the mundane cares of property, politics, and the workaday world. And yet they do not hesitate to cast her into poverty and degradation if her husband takes her properties, her inheritance—even her children, as the law allows him—and then decides to abandon her. Where is man's protection when such a woman is denied even the means to make a living for herself? Half the men of the world prattle that woman's duty is as the moral guardian of society and nurturer of the young, and therefore she should not be distracted from this pure and uplifting work to pursue a profession. The other half would tell you that women are intellectually and emotionally incapable of participating in any endeavor that requires intelligence and thoughtfulness, but I tell you—"

"Harriett?" Lucille's voice interrupted. "I thought I heard you lecturing some poor soul out here." Harriett's aunt, a shawl draped over her head to ward off the chill, came around the end of the wagon. "Ah. Mr. Carradine. I see you are being treated to Harriett's opinions on women's rights. I warn you to tread carefully," she advised with a gentle smile, "or you will be the recipient of similar lectures from here to California."

Jake touched his hat politely as Lucille joined them, a compliment he hadn't paid to Harriett. "All due respect, Mrs. Stanwick, but I doubt that you ladies will make it past Fort Kearney. So fortunately, I won't have to listen to your niece for too many days."

Harriett's eyes narrowed.

"I'll take my leave of you now, if you don't mind. Good night, Mrs. Stanwick. Good night . . . Harry."

"What . . . ?" Harriett choked.

"Since you want a man's role in the world, you should have a man's name. Don't you think?"

"How dare—"

"It fits," he said, cutting her short. "Good night, Miss Harry."

He walked away as she sputtered. "The insolent, forward, ignorant ruffian! I can't think of words vile enough to describe him!"

"You weren't having any problem with words a few moments ago, my love. Really, dear, I don't think Mr. Carradine is the sort of man who would be susceptible to your haranguing."

"I do not harangue!" Harriett huffed. "Besides, he provoked me."

"Doubtless, my love. He seems to be a very provoking sort of man. But he was simply teasing, I'm sure. I vow I saw a gleam of humor in his eye when he was taking you to task."

"The gleam you saw was the Devil's light of liquor."

"Really?"

"Aunt, you would swoon if I repeated the language he used to me just moments ago. Do you know where I found him? Gambling! And drinking! Didn't you smell the fumes?"

Lucille sighed. Gentle brown eyes regarded Harriett with an expression that the younger woman thought of as Aunt Lucille's you're-just-like-your-mother stare. "Try not to be so serious, my love. Lighten your load just a bit. There are wonders in this world to be enjoyed as well as evils to be deplored."

They walked toward the tent. "He seems incorrigible, Aunt. Whatever shall I do with him if he gets in our way during the journey?"

"Oh, I'm sure you'll think of something, dear."

Harriett sighed. "You're right, of course. I shall manage. Here we are," she said, lifting the tent flap. "Our first night spent in a tent. With many more to follow."

"May the good Lord help us," Lucille concluded.

The next morning dawned cold and clear, the air pungent with the smoke of a thousand cookfires. May 1 had become the traditional day of "jump-off" for wagons traveling west, the day when the grass was well enough grown on the prairie to support the horde of livestock that would soon pass over it. The Packard and Deere Indiana Company of Adventurers was only one of many emigrant companies that would begin their trek that day. By late afternoon the bank of the Missouri River, which for several weeks had been crowded with wagons, people, and livestock, would be a nearly deserted stretch of mud and trampled, over-grazed prairie.

By the time the sun rose that morning, Harriett had been up an hour. She should have risen even earlier, Harriett decided, looking with disgust at the pitiful cookfire she had struggled to start. Building a fire was not quite as easy as she had assumed. One did not simply pile up logs and light the pile with a match. And when, after several failures, she had used grass and twigs to catch the flames, the wind had blown her small fire out. Fully thirty frustrating minutes passed before a piece of tinder caught and continued to burn, even though the breeze tried to snuff it. But even then Harriett could not nurse the fire into anything other than a piddling poor thing, with enough heat to make her bacon turn limp and greasy, but not enough to cook it crisp.

"Oh, dear," Lucille said, coming up behind her. "Is that breakfast?"

Harriett sighed. "Well, it's not done yet. Would you

care to finish here while I go hitch our oxen to the wagon?''

Lucille raised a gently skeptical brow. "You're going to hitch those beasts, Harriett?"

"Well, of course I am. Who else will do it? The man who sold me the harnesses explained to me how to accomplish the task."

"Very well." Lucille glanced down at the contents of the iron skillet. "My! Look at that. I wouldn't have thought it possible for bacon to burn around the edges and remain raw in the center." -

"Oh . . . spit! Well, let me try to rearrange the fire. When the bacon's done—such as it is—you can put the corn bread to cook. The batter's over there on the tailgate of the wagon."

"Yes, dear." Lucille sighed. "I do hope one of us learns to cook before this journey is over."

Harriett was sure the next chore would prove her competence. But the oxen seemed reluctant to move from the grassy patch of prairie where they were hobbled, and when they did finally move, they chose their path with malice. After one huge beast had stepped on her foot and two others had come very near to knocking her down, Harriett decided that Jake's recommendation to use oxen instead of mules was a piece of premeditated mischief.

As if her thoughts had conjured him from the air, Jake appeared on the other side of a broad ox back. "Need help, Harry?"

"No!" The harnesses were tangled. They hadn't been tangled when she bought them. How had they become such a mess?

"I guess not," Jake agreed with a chuckle. "Look's like you've got everything under control."

One of the oxen decided to lean her way, and Harriett found herself sprawled upon the muddy grass.

"Is this a new method of hitching oxen?"

Stubbornness is the handmaiden of ignorance, Harriett reminded herself. If she was to gain new skills, she had to learn to graciously ask for help. Even men were not born knowing how to handle these misanthropic beasts. "Perhaps I could use a little assistance," she conceded.

Jake came from where he was leaning casually on an ox and offered to help her up. A faint odor of liquor still clung to him, and his eyes were more red than gray. Ignoring his hand, Harriett hoisted herself off the ground.

"The harnesses seem to have gotten tangled," she admitted.

"So they have." A few deft motions and he had the lines hanging straight and free. "Here. Hold these out of the way." He handed her several of the leather lines, then explained in great detail how to position the yokes in front of the beast's withers, how to connect the harness to the yoke, and then how to fasten the whole rigamarole to the tongue of the wagon. In all, he spent less time accomplishing the whole task than Harriett had spent haltering just one animal.

"You'll learn," he assured her. "It's not that hard."

As if she, being a woman, couldn't learn the process if it were difficult.

"Breakfast!" Lucille called.

Harriett hoped her aunt had done better with the meal than Harriett had done with the hitching.

An hour later the Indiana Company took its place in the line of wagons heading west. Men shouted and yipped, each wagon competing with the others for position in line as if being farther forward in the cavalcade would bring the gold fields all that closer.

A jovial young man by the name of Hobby Smith rode alongside Harriett's wagon as they first began to roll. His horse was far too small for him, Harriett thought—until the youngster hopped off his mount and onto the wagon box to show her the correct way of holding the reins. The problem was not so much a small horse, Harriett discovered, as an overly large rider. Young Hobby was a veritable giant. He was bigger even than Jake, and, fortunately, much more amiable.

"Keep the lines high and taut," he told her, lifting her hands to demonstrate, "and your cattle will feel more secure."

"Your horse," Harriett cautioned him. "You're likely to lose it."

The horse trotted easily alongside the wagon, free of any tether.

"Naw," the boy said. "He'll follow. I got a way with animals. I'm a smith, and you gotta have a way with horses in that business."

A moment passed before Harriett realized he was referring to his trade and not his name.

"My brother Horace is a smith too. We had a livery back in Des Moines, but we figgered that a lifetime of smithin' won't get us as rich as the gold fields."

Harriett murmured a neutral comment.

"Then my other brother—he's the eldest—he decided to come too."

"Is he a smith also?"

"Naw. Horatio breaks horses."

If he was half the size of his younger brother, Harriett reflected, Horatio could probably break a horse in two if he wished.

"Well, ma'am. You remember what I told you about those lines. And if you have any need for smithin' out on the trail, my brother and me brought our anvil. Just give a holler."

"Thank you, Mr. Smith. I will."

At least some of the men traveling to California were gentlemen, Harriett mused. Jake Carradine had been very little help in getting the team moving. She hadn't seen him since he'd choked down his breakfast and made some excuse to leave. Of course, that is exactly what Harriett had intended when she hired the man. He was fulfilling her expectations to the letter.

In the late morning Lucille came forward from the wagon bed and joined Harriett on the front box. "I haven't been much company this morning," she apologized. "This morning's bacon made me quite queasy, I vow. Or perhaps it was the corn bread with the doughy center. I'm better now, though. Would you like me to take a turn at driving, my love?"

"Aunt Lucille, that's very generous of you. But what do you know about driving oxen?"

"Every bit as much as you, dear—which is nothing, I daresay."

"Oh, no, Aunt," Harriett said with a smile. "A very nice young man gave me an impromptu lesson this morning. And now that I've incorporated his suggestions, the beasts are going quite well."

In truth, the oxen were going better than they had gone before. But they were unused to working as a team, and too often each of the cattle decided to go its own direction. By the time they stopped for the nooning, Harriett's hands were blistered, burning, and stiff.

Upon seeing her niece's hands, Lucille insisted on preparing a compress, then took upon herself the task of preparing the noon meal. Harriett had to admit that Lucille built a better cookfire than Harriett had that morning, but the meal was no better. The beans that Lucille placed to boil over the fire simply refused to soften enough to eat, and the two women resorted finally to dining on leftover corn bread, doughy though it was.

"I wonder where Mr. Carradine is?" Lucille asked as they prepared to continue the journey.

"I do hope he hasn't deserted us already," Harriett

replied. "We are still close enough to our starting point for Mr. Deere to put us out."

Harriett found her hired man engaged in a noontime poker game with three of the Indiana Adventurers. She dressed him down soundly as they walked back toward the wagon.

"Your friend Mr. Walking Horse would be sorely disappointed to see you retreating so soon into such vices."

"Amos has been disappointed before," he told her.

"I can imagine," she sniped. She was annoyed, and angry at her annoyance.

"Besides, Harry . . ."

"Don't call me by that name!"

He ignored her objection. "You want to prove that you don't need a man to help you ladies along the trail. I'm just obliging you. And after this morning's breakfast, I figured I'd better find other vittles, or soon I won't be good for much of anything."

"You are an ingrate, Mr. Carradine."

He smiled. "At your service."

"Hardly!"

His eyes crinkled pleasantly when he smiled, Harriett couldn't help but notice. And his chin was square and firm under the stubble of his beard. What a shame he was such a cad.

"I'd appreciate it if you would act a bit more like a hired guide, scout, bodyguard—whatever you choose to call yourself—until we are past the point where Mr. Deere can easily put us out of the company."

"Whatever you say, Harry."

Her lips tightened, but she sternly forbade herself to rise to the bait. The blackguard would only enjoy it.

"Wagons!" came the shout down the line. "Move out!"

The afternoon did not go much better than the morning. Harriett was grateful to note that other wag-

ons and teams were having problems similar to hers,
and many men of the company seemed as inept at harnessing and driving as she. The oxen were fractious,
the road was muddy, the Adventurers inexperienced.
Halfway through the afternoon, on a slight downhill
incline, three wagons slid together and ended in a pile
at the bottom of the hill, causing a delay of more than
an hour. Several wagons had to stop alongside the
road to repair loose wheels, and one wagon almost lost
an inadequately fastened canvas cover to a gust of
wind. The wagon scout, Mr. Carter, was no help to the
bumbling drivers, for as soon as the wagons had
started to roll, he had galloped off on an errand of his
own. Mr. Deere's idea of leadership was to ride up and
down the line of wagons, shouting to the drivers to
"shape up!" Unfortunately, the wagon captain provided little advice on just how they should shape up.

Compared to the flounderings of the rest of the Indiana Company, Harriett thought that the Foster–
Stanwick wagon did quite well, even when Lucille
insisted on her turn driving and almost sent them into
a ditch. Harriett also noted with a twinge of pride that
the all-female wagon of tarts—or entertainers, as they
billed themselves—handled the muddy road, their
wagon, and their mules like seasoned mule skinners.
Let the men of the company take that draught and
swallow it!

By the end of the day the Indiana Company of Adventurers had made only three miserable miles. At Mr.
Deere's insistence the company formed their wagons
into a ragged semblance of a circle—not the complicated oval enclosure described in Mr. Ware's guidebook and practiced over and over again in Harriett's
mind. The defensive formation was little needed so
close to civilization, but the wagon captain shouted
that they needed the practice. Looking at the uneven,

gap-riddled circle, Harriett conceded that Mr. Deere was right.

Hobby Smith—bless him!—offered to help unharness the oxen and stake them out. Harriett was so exhausted that she spent more time leaning against the broad, sweaty beasts than she spent unhitching them. In a moment of weakness she wished Jake were more industrious. She had caught a glimpse of him in midafternoon—five wagons up the line talking to Hobby and his brothers. Other than that one time she saw him not at all. Not that she needed him, or wanted him anywhere near, Harriett told herself with renewed resolution. She and Lucille would cope.

They would cope, Harriett told herself again when, in the dark hours of the night, she woke to a crash of thunder. Rain drummed on the sides of their tent, and two leaks were fast forming puddles—one on the tarp that served as a floor, another on Harriett's blankets. A white glare and loud crack exploded around them, as though the night were ripped in two. Thunder shook the ground, almost drowning out Lucille's shriek.

"Oh, spit!" Harriett dove beneath her blankets, wet as they were. The steady drumming of the rain became the pelting of hailstones. Lightning and thunder bombarded them, deafening, blinding. Missouri in the spring can be playful, one of the shopkeepers in Independence had told her. If this storm was what he meant, he could have chosen a word better than *playful*.

The thunder abated somewhat, dwindling from a continuous explosion to celestial convulsions separated by brief seconds of silence. And in those brief seconds, Harriett heard the terrified bawling of the oxen.

The poor beasts! Harriett pictured a fusillade of hard ice pounding upon her cattle. They would be frantic. And in their desperation to escape, might they not injure themselves—break a leg, strain a tendon? Without their precious oxen, she and Lucille couldn't go on. And then what would her great endeavor amount to?

Harriett shot from her bed. Frantic, she ran from the tent in nightgown and bare feet, ignoring Lucille's protests. The oxen were hobbled not far from the wagon. They were lunging and bucking in terrified protest of their fate.

Flashes of lightning illuminated a small copse of trees about two hundred feet from the wagon. It was the only shelter available for the beasts. Harriett reached for the nearest animal's halter—and promptly got knocked on her backside. She tried again, only to have the frightened ox swing around and almost crush her against one of its fellows.

"Get out of there!" Jake's voice was as loud as the thunder. "What the hell . . . are you trying to get yourself killed?"

Almost in tears, both for herself and the oxen, Harriett obeyed. She watched as Jake calmed the beasts with deft hands and gentle words, then she flitted along, trying to help, as he led them to shelter.

"Lord! What a sight you are, lady."

The oxen were safely tethered, the hail was diminishing, and for the first time, Harriett became aware of the picture she presented. Her flannel nightgown clung to her in sodden folds, delineating every contour of her body. Muddy feet peeked out below the hem to complete the disgraceful picture. Horrified, she crossed her arms over her chest and backed away.

"Barefoot?" He chuckled. "You were in a hurry, weren't you? I'd be surprised if those feet of yours aren't cut or bruised to the bone."

She self-consciously curled her toes. In truth, her feet were so cold, they were numb. The rest of her wasn't much better off.

"I . . . I thank you for your help, Mr. Carradine."
Even her voice shivered. "I'll be . . . g-g-going now."

She lurched forward, but he caught her before she
fell. The cold must have numbed her brain, Harriett
thought, for she didn't feel the least embarrassed when
Jake scooped her up in his arms, cradled her against
his broad chest, and carried her to the wagon, which
was the only dry spot left in their camp. She willingly
clung to him and buried her face against his shoulder
to hide from the hail and rain. He was broad and solid,
a rock in the midst of the raging elements. Through
their sodden clothing his flesh was warm against her.
When he lifted her into the bed of the wagon and left
her there, Harriett felt a chill at the sudden absence of
his comforting warmth.

Only later, lying with Lucille beneath dry, warm
blankets, did Harriett remember the impropriety of
her actions, and she choked with shame.

And while Harriett was remembering, hot-faced
with embarrassment, Jake Carradine was trying to forget how his boss lady had looked with her hair streaming down her back, rain beading her eyelashes, and a
wet, muddy nightgown clinging to her body—and how
she had felt in his arms.

He tried to forget, and cursed himself for remembering.

Breakfast the next morning was as bad as it had been the morning before—with one difference: The corn bread and bacon were burned all the way through instead of only on the outside. Jake was nowhere to be seen, but when Harriett had first awakened and peeked out of the wagon, the cattle had already been brought from their refuge beneath the trees and were munching shoots of spring grass not ten feet away. No doubt, Harriett thought, Mr. Carradine had done his bit to help for the day and had taken himself off to some early-morning poker game.

"I can't blame him for avoiding our cooking," Lucille admitted. "We're all going to starve before we're a week along the road."

"We'll learn," Harriett assured her. She gave half of her corn bread to the sheepdog bitch from the neighboring wagon. The dog had paid them regular visits ever since the morning before, when it had learned that their campsite was a source of abundant culinary discards. "If Mr. Carradine doesn't like our cooking, that's his problem. The food is part of his wages."

In truth, Harriett was grateful for Jake's absence. That morning she had awakened with a rare sense of satisfaction warming her insides, and then she had remembered just exactly how she had been carried from the trees to the wagon. The hail, lightning, thunder, and cold—none of those things were sufficient excuse for her behavior, cuddling up to Jake Carradine like a wet kitten snuggling up to a warm fire. Just the thought made her blush. What would she say when she saw him again? She could picture how he would grin, how his eyes would gleam with malicious amusement, how he would tip his battered hat back on his head and chuckle at her expense.

Mr. Carradine could stay away for as long as he liked, Harriett decided. She could do very well without him.

"Hello."

A soft voice brought Harriett's gaze up from the tin pail where she was washing dishes. "Hello," she returned, smiling.

Before her was a small, gentle-faced woman in brown homespun, a shawl pulled tightly around her shoulders, the drape of her skirt not quite concealing her pregnancy. Harriett couldn't begin to guess the woman's age. Her face was lined and careworn, but her hair, pulled back from her face in a sedate bun, was a soft brown untouched by gray.

"My brother Todd told me there were two ladies several wagons back. I hope you don't mind my being so forward in introducing myself. I'm Sadie MacBride."

"I'm Harriett Foster. And the lady in the wagon is my aunt, Lucille Foster Stanwick. We're very happy to make your acquaintance." Harriett glanced at the kettle that was struggling to boil over into their pitiful excuse for a cookfire. "Would you like some tea, Mrs. MacBride?"

"Please call me Sadie," the visitor told her. "Some tea would be very nice. We have only coffee on my brother's wagon. Todd doesn't care for tea, I'm afraid."

As Sadie glanced at the struggling fire and the discarded remnants of burned bacon and bread, a flash of amusement, quickly hidden, crossed her face.

"I'm afraid my aunt and I have lived too long in a city with servants to build fires and cook for us," Harriett admitted. The woman projected such a mild, accepting manner that Harriett almost didn't mind owning up to the deficiency.

"If you like," Sadie offered, "I could give you some hints at making the chores easier."

"We wouldn't want to trouble you or take you away from your own work."

"All my chores are done," Sadie said cheerfully. "And the truth is, I've been aching for a woman's company. My son Chad and brother Todd are good companions, but sometimes a woman needs the company of other women."

Harriett was astounded at Sadie MacBride's proficiency with an outdoor fire, despite the wind—which seemed ubiquitous in this area—and the wet firewood. Her visitor demonstrated how to build up the flames to a crackling bonfire, then let them die until only white-hot coals were left for cooking.

"You'll get more even heat this way," Sadie explained. "And the coals will last a long time."

Sadie also gave Harriett her second lesson in harnessing oxen. The morning before, Jake had made the process seem easy. But on this morning, once again the straps and lines and yokes and wagon tongue seemed to plot together to foil Harriett's attempts. But with Sadie's patient instruction, Harriett managed the task in only triple the time Jake had taken on the same chore.

While Harriett was struggling with the hitching, she failed to notice that their campsite was receiving more than its share of attention from passersby. Not until Lucille brought the fact to her attention did she realize that the last half hour had seen a parade of men through their camp. Some openly stared at her and Lucille. Some blatantly leered, like the man Harriett recognized as Phineas Carter, Mr. Deere's hired scout. Others were more polite, making lame excuses for a visit or casually strolling by while casting surreptitious glances.

"I feel like some poor creature in a zoo," Lucille complained. She swiped a towel at the last of the breakfast plates and set the dish in its box.

"They're just curious," Sadie explained. "I think before yesterday not very many of the men realized you ladies were with the company. There was a bit of gossip between wagons last night. Only the men don't like to call it gossip. They just call it talking."

"Whoever would gossip about us?" Harriett asked.

"I suppose they wonder why two ladies such as yourselves would be bound for California—and with a man like Mr. Carradine. My brother says Jake Carradine has a rather fearsome reputation that stretches from Independence to the Pacific, or so it's said." Sadie shrugged and offered an apologetic little smile. "You must admit that the situation is a curious one."

"Mr. Carradine is merely a hired man." Harriett sniffed indignantly. "And as a matter of fact, he wouldn't have been hired had Mr. Deere not refused us passage as unescorted ladies!"

"Oh, dear!" Sadie looked sheepish. "I truly didn't mean to offend. Who you travel with is really not my concern. I do hope we can all be friends."

Harriett smoothed her scowl into a smile. "Of course we can be friends. Mr. Carradine's reputation is not my worry, as I can assure you that he will behave himself while in my employ." She shrugged in a gesture of unconcern. "And as for the men who choose to gape, I care very little for what they believe. Men have very rigid minds where women are concerned, don't you agree? If one dares to deviate in the slightest, it sets the poor creatures off.''

Lucille sighed and poured dishwater over the fire, stepping back from the explosion of steam. "Don't get my niece started, Mrs. MacBride. We'll be listening to her decry men's backward attitudes for the rest of the day!"

Sadie's eyes grew curiously wide, but whatever reply she might have made was cut off by the shout to move out. Mr. Deere repeated the command as he rode down the line to hurry the wagons along. When he reached Harriett's wagon, he stopped.

"Mrs. MacBride." He tipped his hat to Sadie, but scarcely acknowledged Harriett and Lucille. "You'd better get back to your wagon, ma'am."

Sadie's chin came up a notch. "Please tell my brother I'll be riding with Miss Foster for an hour or so." She looked to Harriett for approval.

"You're welcome for as long as you want," Harriett told her with a smile. She climbed up on the wagon box and assisted Sadie in following her. Lucille declined Harriett's helping hand and went around to the wagon tailgate.

The captain gave the women a frown of rebuke. "Then let's get this wagon in line. Get those cattle moving, Miss Foster."

"Tyrant," Harriett said under her breath as he rode away. She shook out the reins and the oxen lumbered forward. The wagon creaked as it began to move.

"I imagine he's a bit out of sorts because of the storm last night," Sadie speculated. "My brother Todd and some of the others thought he should have found us better shelter to camp. Our canvas was torn by the hail, and other wagons also had damage. But then, Mr. Deere knows little more about this journey than the rest of us. He was our neighbor back in Indiana. He isn't really so bad."

"It's a shame Mr. Carter isn't more help."

"Yes, it is. Todd complained to Mr. Carter this morning about him being gone so much, and Mr. Carter told him that a scout is supposed to survey the trail ahead, not wet-nurse a pack of bumbling greenhorns. I believe those are the very words he used."

"An unpleasant man."

"Indeed. Did Mr. Deere really refuse to let you join the company?" Sadie asked.

"He did," Lucille told her from the back of the wagon. "And we should have listened to him."

"Fiddle!" Harriett replied. "We're doing fine." She slapped the lines along the oxen's backs and whistled for them to pick up their pace. They ignored her.

"I think you're doing just wonderfully," Sadie said. "I certainly would never have the courage to make this trip by myself. Of course, you've got Mr. Carradine. In spite of his reputation, I would imagine that it's a comfort to have him around."

"Mr. Carradine is just for display," Harriett told her. "We hardly see him."

She'd seen quite a bit of him in the hailstorm last night, a mischievous imp of conscience reminded Harriett—and from very close quarters. She fought against blushing.

"My aunt and I are making this trip by our own efforts," Harriett went on hastily. "And I'm keeping a journal which will be published by Mrs. Amelia Bloomer and will encourage women all over the country to explore their own capabilities and talents."

"Here it comes," Lucille said with a sigh. "Excuse me, ladies. I will be in the back, reading. Call me when the lecture is over."

Sadie looked confused.

Harriett laughed. "My aunt thinks I harangue on the cause of women's rights. And she's probably right."

"Oh. I thought, when I first saw you, that you must

be one of Those Ladies." She emphasized the last two words in a way to set them apart. "I do admire your pantaloon dress. Are you actually acquainted with Mrs. Bloomer?"

"I've met her," Harriett said proudly. "And we correspond quite regularly. Did you know there was an actual convention gathering for women's rights in Seneca Falls two years ago?"

"Well, no. . . ."

"And also—" Harriett cut herself short. Lucille was right. She did have a tendency to harangue. "But enough. I simply believe that women are intelligent enough to determine their own destinies and handle their own affairs."

"Oh, I agree!" Sadie assured her. "But of course my husband doesn't. I'm going to California to meet him. Five months ago he took a steamer down to Panama and was going to get to the gold fields by that route."

"He left you alone to have your child?"

Sadie sighed. "He sold my inheritance—a nice little property I had from my father—to pay his passage. I've been living off my brother's charity for the past months, and now Todd has decided to try his luck also. Neither one of them would listen to me."

"That's disgraceful! Men prattle that women should stay in their 'appropriate sphere' and let their husbands or fathers run their lives. But somehow the men usually manage to exploit a woman's assets to their advantage and leave her to face the consequences!"

"Oh, surely the situation isn't so bad!" Sadie said with a gentle smile. "I do love my husband very much. He's always treated me well and been a good father to our son—before the gold fever hit him."

"Hmmph!" was Harriett's only answer.

Journal entry—May 5—Kansas, approaching the Wakarusa River: We have now endured five days of travel, and it staggers my imagination to think that we have months more of the same—though the sturdy Smith brothers, who seem to have appointed themselves guardians to Lucille and me, assure us that once we become accustomed to the routine, the journey will be like a picnic.

I am proud of our successes, for in these five days we have become much wiser to the ways of the trail. Since Mrs. MacBride showed us how to build a proper fire, our meals no longer alternate between burned and raw. That dear lady also pointed out that beans should soak for a period of time before being cooked, and with that bit of help, Aunt Lucille has become a master at the art of cooking beans—beans with bacon, beans with rice, beans with vegetables, beans with ham. To be truthful, after only these few days I never want to taste another bean as long as I should live!

Mrs. MacBride has become a dear friend. She is one of the bravest souls I know. Her pregnancy is six months advanced and must cause her much discomfort and difficulty along this rough road, but this true lady never utters a complaint. Left by her husband to live on the charity of her brother, then dragged by that brother into a journey filled with hardship and risk, she hasn't a single bad word to say about either of these gentlemen. She has raised her son, Chad, now eleven years old, to be a model of helpfulness and consideration (though I have been witness to the boyish and playful side of the child as well). Getting to know Sadie MacBride has given new strength to my convictions. A society which subjugates one half of the population, handing them into the often irresponsible care of the other half, is dreadfully misguided. I begin to believe that it is men, not women, who need custodians.

Which brings to mind my hired guide—Jake Carradine, a fine example of irresponsible manhood. He has been little seen around our wagon, except two nights ago when we encountered another thunderstorm (lightning and rain seem very common in this countryside. Mr. Ware in his guidebook gives little warning of these frightening storms). Mr. Carradine appeared with the thunder and wind to give us aid in holding our tent in place, though in the end Lucille and I gave up and retired to makeshift beds in the wagon. So far on this trip I vow I have appeared before Mr. Carradine more often clad in nightgown and bare feet than in proper dress. I shudder to contemplate what he must think of me. Not that the opinion of such a man is of any significance.

In general, I must say that the men who travel with the Indiana Company are a fair example of American manhood and are not as crude a lot as I was led to believe. Only a small number are among the lower orders of society—several gamblers, drifters, and a few young men who seek to prove their manhood by being as brutal and crude as possible, to both beasts and fellow men. Unfortunately, my hired man, though he appears to have forged a friendship with the amiable Smith brothers, is seen too often with the dregs of our company. And still, in defiance of all logic, he dares to set himself up as moral guardian of my aunt and myself.

Just yesterday Mr. Carradine, after spending the morning gambling with the wages I paid him, took it upon himself to interfere with my efforts to succor the fallen sisters who travel in our company. You can be sure I gave him a severe dressing-down. But I doubt that he listened at all to my admonitions, for his face was set most obdurately in masculine displeasure.

* * *

Harriett closed her journal and set it on the little table she had set up in the wagon. The incident hadn't happened quite as she had described it, but she had no wish to outline the details of her embarrassment for Mrs. Bloomer's readers.

At the nooning stop the day before she had ventured to have a conversation with the denizens of the "honey wagon," as the men had dubbed the wagon of loose women. The busy nooning was not a convenient time for Harriett to attempt her mission, but during the evening hours the wagon and its women were always occupied with men visitors.

Harriett's intention had been to make friends with the women and explain to them how they were being exploited by men. Some of them had been rude, so far into their unfortunate degradation that all self-respect was gone. Harriett still blushed to remember the woman named Isabelle, who even during the daytime wore a dress that was cut so low in the bodice that only good fortune kept her breasts from spilling out. Isabelle, in particular, had scoffed at Harriett's assertion that the "entertainers" were allowing themselves to be victimized by men.

"Oh, yas!" the woman said in a crude imitation of Harriett's Boston accent. "I do believe I'm being ex . . . exploded."

"Exploited," Harriett explained patiently.

"Yassss! I was exploited"—the whore grinned, revealing two missing front teeth—"five times laaast evening. Poor me." She dug a wad of soiled bills from her cleavage, almost spilling her bosom as she did so.

Harriett grimaced as Isabelle waved the bills in front of her face. She almost retched from the heavy scent of musky perfume and sweat that clung to them.

"Poor little me," Isabelle repeated, though no one with eyes would ever have called her little. "Plowed again and again . . . and again," she purred. A fiery blush rose to Harriett's cheeks. "And only this to show for it."

"Lay off, Issy. Miss Foster there's right. We lay ourselves down when a man's got the urge. The pricks get the fun, and we get the blame for being tarts!" This from a mousy-haired, thin girl who Harriett guessed was scarcely more than a child. But something in the girl's eyes looked as old as the world itself.

"You get paid for spreadin' your legs," Isabelle shot back. "Quit your bitchin'!"

"Now, ladies." The middle-aged woman who had introduced herself to Harriett as Mrs. Hornsby spoke up for the first time. She had explained earlier that she was the women's "employer." "You gotta think of our trade as women usin' men, not men ex . . . uh . . . usin' women. Every gal here come of her own free will, including little Sara." She frowned at the thin, mouse-colored girl. "All you prissy ladies blabber about freein' women up to be like men, but we entertainin' ladies freed ourselves." She laughed, her generous bosom dancing in time to her mirth. "An' we did it by bein' women!"

"That's telling her, Myrt!"

Harriett jumped nearly out of her skin, because the intruding voice was not only masculine, it belonged to Jake Carradine.

"Jake, boy. I warned you never ta call me that!" Mrs. Hornsby smiled as she admonished him—a smile that bordered on obscene, Harriett decided.

Jake opened the canvas flap wider, and a shaft of sunlight fell full on Harriett's flaming face.

"Miss Foster, may I have a word with you?" Jake seemed all courtesy, but his voice had an edge of sharp ice.

"Certainly, Mr. Carradine." She would not lose her composure in front of these unfortunate women, Harriett vowed. But from the look in his eyes, Jake might lose it for her if she didn't do as he'd bid. "If you'll excuse me, ladies."

"La tee da!" Isabelle shot after her as she stepped down from the honey wagon.

As soon as Harriett had one foot on the ground, Jake grabbed her arm in a viselike grip. "What the *hell* do you think you're doing!"

"Mr. Carradine! Please curb your language."

"I'm going to curb you, you little fool! Don't you know what those women are?"

"I know perfectly well . . . !"

"Were you thinking of joining them? Or were you just satisfying your virginal curiosity?"

"Mr. Carradine!" Harriett's blush grew even deeper. Every man within earshot was turning to watch Jake literally drag her back to her own wagon. "Keep a civil tongue in your head, or I'll—"

"You'll what? Fire me? God, lady! I wish you would!"

Lucille popped her head out of the wagon as Jake hauled Harriett up to their cookfire, where the never-ending beans were simmering. Harriett detected a hint of a smile on her aunt's face. "I was simply discussing with the ladies—"

"Those aren't ladies!"

"Would you kindly allow me to finish a sentence?" Harriett almost yelled, her eyes narrowed.

"Harriett!" Lucille reproached.

"For your information," Harriett told Jake, "we were having a very enlightened conversation when you so rudely interrupted! I was making progress to-ward—"

"The only progress you were making, you fool, is toward classing yourself as one of them! Now every man in this company is going to be sniffing around you wondering what your price is."

"Oh, fiddle! That's ridiculous! Besides, I didn't hire you as a bodyguard. You, sir, are forgetting your place!"

"I damn well would like to forget it, lady! You need a bodyguard! And he'll have to shoot the goddamn pants off half the men here to keep you whole for your Edgar."

"Edwin! His name is Edwin. I'll thank you to curb your vulgarity, Mr. Carradine. I will not tolerate such disgraceful language."

"Well, maybe if you started listening to what I say instead of stopping up your delicate little ears, you might survive this journey!"

"You are exaggerating beyond all bounds of reason, sir, and being very rude in the process. As for Mrs. Hornsby and her ladies, I have a right to talk to anyone in this company whom I wish. You are not my keeper, Mr. Carradine."

"Why don't you climb down from your pulpit, Miss Foster, and show a little common sense for the rest of the trip? Elsewise this is going to be a hell of a long trip."

Harriett raised a brow. "I am not the one whose sense needs attention, sir. I repeat. Mend your language as long as you are in my employ. Profanity is not an appropriate form of expression."

"Shit!" He turned away, his fists clenched as though they were aching for something to squeeze. "Redhaired women are always trouble. I should have remembered that." He had stalked away, leaving Harriett to cook in her own indignation and Lucille to shake her head in amusement.

The wagon creaked as Harriett got up to fetch another candle. The one on the table was burning low, but she had no wish to retire as yet. Her mind was agitated all over again, and her face heated at her memories. More than one day would have to pass before she forgave Jake Carradine for the rude words he had thrown her way. Neither was she much in charity with Lucille, who had taken her to task after Jake had strutted off.

She lit a fresh candle, then opened the journal again. She wrote,

This afternoon we departed from the Santa Fe Trail, which we have followed for forty miles. From here we will travel the California Trail, which is also followed in part by emigrants journeying to Oregon. Within a day or so we will experience our first river crossing—the Wakarusa River, which Mr. Ware does not describe in detail, saying only that there are several small stream crossings between the Kansas state line and the Platte River. Therefore we do not concern ourselves; the task should be an easy one, I believe. . . .

If the Wakarusa River was a small stream in Mr. Ware's estimation, Harriett did not look forward to the rivers he described in his guidebook as dangerous. The word came down the line of wagons that several parties of emigrants ahead of the Indiana Company had chosen to cross the river on barges. Standing with Sadie and looking at the river's steep, muddy banks and debris-laden current, Harriett couldn't help but think that their predecessors' decision had been a wise one.

"I do hope Mr. Deere knows what he's doing," Sadie said. She cradled her protruding belly in her arms, a gesture Harriett had learned to associate with distress.

"I'm sure he does," Harriett reassured her.

She had no faith in her words, however. Over the past days Mr. Charles Deere had proven himself a pompous fool who strutted in his position of authority but had neither the intelligence nor the charisma to be a leader. Twice he had chosen disastrous locations for their camp, once bogging the wagons in mud and two days later choosing a low area that had turned into a torrent when a thunderstorm dumped buckets of rain in the middle of the night. The scout he'd hired was little help. Greasy, foulmouthed, and rude, Phineas Carter seemed to think Deere's mistakes were amusing. More often than not, Carter rode off on his own. When he did ride with the train, he paid unwarranted attention to the "honey wagon" and also kept a very close eye—a close, leering eye, Harriett thought with a shudder—on the Foster–Stanwick wagon. Neither Lucille nor Harriett appreciated the attention. If the scout's judgment was as bad as his manners and hygiene, then the train was in poor hands indeed.

"I'd best go," Sadie said with a sigh. "Todd will want me in the wagon." She gave Harriett a reassuring smile. "We shall all be fine, you know."

"Of course," Harriett said lamely. Why couldn't she have Sadie's quiet courage? Her insides were turning to jelly at the thought of driving her wagon through that watery chaos.

Jake was waiting for her when she returned to the wagon. "This might turn out to be an all-day job," he told her. "Deere would have done better to make barges. The crossing would be safer that way."

Even Mr. Carradine had better sense than Mr. Deere, Harriett reflected. That wasn't saying much for their wagon captain.

"I don't understand how we're going to do this," Lucille said uncertainly.

"Each team will be unhitched and walked down the bank to the river's edge. Then the wagon will be lowered over the bank with ropes. The team will pull the wagon across, then be detached again on the far side so the wagon can be lifted." He climbed up onto the front box and looked back into the covered area. "Harry, make sure all the flour, salt, and rice—anything you don't want to get wet—is tied securely high off the floor. The water's deep, and it'll probably come into the wagon bed."

Harriett didn't rise to the bait of her nickname. "The liveryman told me this wagon was caulked to be waterproof."

Jake laughed. "Right. Just like your water casks don't leak."

That fact Harriett had discovered to her sorrow when she had stored the casks, full of water, inside the wagon. She and Lucille had both spent a night in wet bedding.

Jake was correct in his estimation. The crossing took all day and was fraught with mishaps. Before the day was out, the Indiana Adventurers once again were grumbling about Mr. Deere. Harriett's wagon was the last in line. She watched as Sadie and Todd crossed safely, as the MacKenzie wagon almost got swamped by the current, as Mrs. Hornsby urged her mules across the flood with a flamboyant bravado that none of the men had managed. When the Cutter wagon almost foundered and had to be helped along with ropes from the bank, Harriett's nerves almost snapped.

Finally it came time for Harriett and Lucille to enter the swirling water. The wagon was safely, if somewhat awkwardly, lowered down the almost vertical banks. Harriett was determined to drive her team across. But at the last moment, Jake climbed onto the box and took the lines from her shamefully shaking hands. Even more shameful—she let him with only a minimum of protest.

"There'll be lots of other crossings where you can prove yourself, Harry." He grinned insolently. "Let's at least make it through the first ten days alive."

Harriett flushed.

"Besides, the team will go better for me."

"Because they recognize a fellow beast?" she snapped.

"Could be," he said evenly. "Or maybe because I know their names."

"Their names?"

"Sure! All of us beasts have names, you know. The left lead's Curly. And then Sharps, Flytail, and Gus—the one with the freckles on his tail." He pointed to each ox in turn, a twinkle in his eye belying the seriousness of his tone.

Harriett didn't have time to think on the ludicrousness of a professed gunman and badman giving silly names to oxen, for at the next moment he shouted at the team and, after an initial balk that Jake discouraged by a snap of the lines, the beasts splashed into the river. She heard her aunt whimpering in the back as the turbid waters swirled around the wagon box and the whole wagon twisted with the current. Harriett knew she should climb into the back and comfort Lucille, but she couldn't move; for the first time in her life she knew the meaning of terror. The sight of the water swirling around them made her ill, so she dragged her eyes away and instead fixed them on Jake Carradine's face, which was set in grim concentration on the task at hand.

It was a most attractive face, she thought suddenly, even with the mustache in such need of trimming and the shadow of a beard darkening his cheeks. His eyes were the clearest gray she had ever seen, his lashes entirely too thick and too long for a man. The nose might be considered a bit big by some, but its boldness suited his manner. His brows, matching his hair in thick and unruly profusion, curved over his eyes in cynical arches. In fact, if Jake Carradine would ever wash and shave, his face might produce a total devastation among the ladies.

"What's the matter. Do I still have breakfast on my face?"

"What? Oh!"

He smiled at her all too knowingly. They were safely across. Harriett had found a most improper, if effective, method of distracting herself from their danger, and Mr. Carradine had caught her out, it seemed.

"I—I—" she stuttered. "That was a most splendid job, Mr. Carradine."

"Glad you liked it." He grinned, and her mortification grew. Still grinning, he jumped down to unhitch the dripping team. Harriett almost wished she had fallen into the river.

By evening all the wagons of the Indiana Company were safely across. The Adventurers felt they had weathered the first serious challenge of their passage, and in celebration, they built a huge communal bonfire in the center of the wagon circle. Horatio Smith, the brother who "broke horses" for a living, brought out a fiddle and played with surprising skill. His thick, blunt fingers danced agilely across the strings as his bow sawed out a lively tune. And even more surprising, Hobby pushed a guitar into Jake Carradine's hands and commanded him to start strumming.

Jake obeyed, and Harriett was not the only one amazed at the deftness of his fingers and the strength of his voice. With Horatio's fiddle and the guitar as accompaniment, Jake sang a lively and rather crude song that gave an entirely erroneous account of how gold was discovered in California. Then he slowed to a melodic ballad about a woman searching for her lost love in the gold fields. Harriett glanced at Sadie, whose eyes were misting with tears, and wondered how such a cynical and insensitive man could put such feeling into a song. She herself, a woman not generally given to emotional excess, felt swept into the sad story by the deep, resonant tones of Jake's voice.

The song ended. The crackling of the bonfire seemed loud in the silence that followed, until Horatio took up his fiddle again and started to saw away at a jig. The spell was broken, and almost everyone found a partner and began to dance. The "entertainers" from Mrs. Hornsby's wagon were very much in demand. On the other side of the bonfire, Sadie danced with her gangly son, Chad, and Lucille waltzed sedately with a handsome silver-haired gentleman whom Harriett didn't know. The men who couldn't find women partners danced with each other. Sadie's brother Todd do-si-doed around the fire with Hobby Smith, and the doctor found a partner in a bandy-legged little farmer. Caroline MacKenzie, a newly married lady whom Harriett had met only once, danced with her young husband while she sent glances toward Horatio, the handsomest of the Smith brothers. When Harriett saw her a few minutes later she was dancing with Jake, clinging to him like a wet shirt, Harriett thought disapprovingly.

Harriett danced with several farmers and a storekeeper, and did several turns with a calf-eyed Hobby Smith. Before long she was heartily tired of her partners' clammy hands, tobacco odors, and gallumphing feet that smashed her toes. She was contemplating escape routes when she saw Phineas Carter heading her way with a gleam in his eye. Trying to duck between two wagons, she stumbled headlong into Jake Carradine, who seemed to appear from nowhere. He threw a glance at the advancing scout.

"Care to dance, Harry?"

"I thought you were otherwise occupied," she said sourly. Out of the corner of her eye she saw Caroline MacKenzie once again in the arms of her gawky husband. Neither of them looked a bit happy.

"You appear to need rescuing," Jake answered.

Without waiting for an answer, he pulled her into

the crowd of dancers. Horatio had slowed to a calmer tune, and Jake waltzed Harriett easily around the bonfire, his arm holding her so close she was uncomfortably conscious of his heart beating against hers. Harriett was middling tall, but the top of her head came only to Jake's chin, and her eyes, looking straight ahead, were treated to a splendid view of his neck and throat. Who would have guessed that part of a man could be so appealing, a column of masculine muscle and sinew. Harriett knew she should shift her gaze to some more neutral object, but to look up was to meet his eyes—even worse. The view to either side was blocked by massive shoulders—also bad. The heat and hardness of his body made her knees wobbly, and her heart beat much faster than mere dancing required.

A slow flush crawled up her neck and face until she could take the distress no longer. She pulled away from his grasp.

"I . . . excuse me, Mr. Carradine. I'm really quite tired."

"Let me walk you back to your wagon, Harry."

His speaking voice was every bit as deep and resonant as his singing voice. Why had she never noticed it before?

"No. No. Thank you, but I'll do fine alone. Thank you."

Without daring to look at him, she fled. But in the dark privacy of her tent she still didn't feel safe. She lit a candle, picked up her journal, sat for a few moments with it open, then closed the volume without writing a word. Her thoughts at the moment had no place in Amelia Bloomer's publication.

Harriett began to understand how easily an unwary and innocent woman might fall under the spell of a virile man, no matter how ill-suited that man might be for her future happiness. Jake Carradine, she acknowl-

edged, was far more dangerous than she had suspected—and not because of the gun he wore.

Jake lay back upon the thin mattress, listening to
Horatio's fiddle and the laughter of those who still
danced by the fire.

"They'll be goin' strong all night," Clarisse said as
she closed the honey wagon's flap and blocked out the
last of the campfire's light. One candle cast a feeble
glow inside the little canvas chamber, flickering across
boxes, strewn cooking utensils, water casks, pillows,
and mattresses.

"They'll get tired," he replied.

"I could go all night," she said in a husky voice.
Turning slowly, she unbuttoned her bodice. The calico
parted to reveal naked skin beneath, lush white
mounds peaked with distended, wine-colored nipples.
"I never met a man who could tire me out. Can you,
Jake?"

Jake folded his arms behind his head, relaxed, and
surveyed Clarisse's ample curves. She was a fine-looking woman for a whore, one who should be able to
take a man's mind off woman troubles, life's troubles,
any troubles at all. "I could try, darlin'."

"I'll just bet you could."

"You got a bottle?"

"Of course."

She opened a crate and took out a bottle of whiskey.
"This do?"

He caught it deftly as she tossed it to him. Cheap
whiskey, he noted, uncorking the bottle. But whiskey
was whiskey.

Jake let the liquor burn away the tension in his body
as Clarisse unbuttoned his shirt. By the time her deft
little hands worked at the buttons of his fly he was
warm all over. He closed his eyes. Unbidden, an image
of red hair, green eyes, and a freckle-decorated nose

waltzed into his mind. He grimaced and opened his eyes to meet Clarisse's gaze. The whore's hair was brown, her eyes blue—no comparison to warm red and bright green.

"Oh, Jake. You are such a *man!*" she exclaimed as she slipped her hand into his fly, wriggled her way through his long underwear, and circled him with moist fingers. She expelled a gust of excited breath as she grasped his size. He'd been hard and hot since he'd danced with Harry. Even with her stiff spine, her disapproving frowns, her long sleeves, high collars, and tidy, spinsterish hair bun, Harriett Foster had a way of getting a man hot. Who would have thought it?

"Magnifique! I do this to you, no?"

"Sure," he lied. The fake French accent was a sure sign that Clarisse was ready to get down to business.

"Oh, Jake!" She bent over him until her heavy breasts brushed his chest. He took the opportunity to peel down her bodice. She wriggled in delight, bouncing her breasts close to his face. Jake wondered what Harry looked like under those prim gowns she wore. She would be smaller, he decided. Harriett Foster wouldn't have anything that wasn't refined.

"You're going to knock me out with one of those if you don't quit jumping around," Jake warned. He took another swig of whiskey.

Clarisse undressed them both in a matter of moments. The night was cool, but the whore's body shone with sweat in the candlelight. "You like?" she crooned seductively, kneeling beside him.

Her hips were as ample as her breasts, her thighs strong and supple-looking. They could no doubt wrap around a man and pump him straight up to heaven. Jake wondered why his interest was withering. He reached out to caress her breast. Her head dropped back and she purred with pleasure. She thrust her pelvis forward in sensual invitation. "More. Give me more."

Jake realized with dismay that he was bored. He had gone limp, and had no real desire to work hard enough to remedy the situation.

"Come on, Jake," Clarisse urged. She lowered herself to the mattress and opened her thighs. "I'm hot. I'm ready for you."

He wasn't ready for her, unfortunately. He leaned back, sighed, and took a drink from the bottle. "Sorry, darlin'." What a hell of a thing that a good, honest whore like Clarisse couldn't get him hot and a starched, priggish, irritating little spinster like Harriett Foster could set him off without even trying.

"What'cha mean, sorry?" The French accent was gone. She noticed his limp member in dismay.

"That's the way it goes."

"The hell it does!" she cried.

"We could play some poker," he offered. "Got a pack of cards?"

"Poker! Crap! Here I am swimmin' in my own juice and you're limp as a noodle! At least give me some satisfaction."

She was swimming in her own juices, from both sweat and excitement. The tangled mat between her open legs exuded an odor of excitement. "Use it on another customer," he advised, and tossed a couple of coins on the mattress. At her squawk of protest he merely smiled. "I'm the one who paid to get laid, honey, not you."

"Bastard!" she called after him as he jumped down from the wagon. "Fuckin' bastard!"

She had him pegged, Jake thought as he walked away. That's exactly what he was: an asshole fool of a bastard.

Little Harriett Foster would be lucky to survive this trip without finding out just how much of a bastard he was.

4

Three days later they reached the Kansas River, where Mr. Deere informed them they had managed to travel one hundred miles in the ten days since they left Independence. One hundred miles, thought Harriett. The distance seemed more like a thousand—and how many hundreds were there yet to go?

At least this time a ferry awaited them. People and wagons rode across the water in dry comfort. Only the livestock had to brave the current.

Harriett and Lucille sat on the box of their wagon, far back in the line of emigrants waiting to cross. Of the twenty-three wagons in the Indiana Company, Mr. Deere had chosen Harriett's to hold the last place in line, where they had to endure the worst dust and the deepest ruts. Since another group of wagons was ahead of the Adventurers, the day promised to be a long one—long and unpleasant. A cold drizzle had begun an hour after breakfast and threatened to continue into the night.

Jake and Hobby took advantage of the delay to examine a cracked wheel rim on Harriett's wagon. Harriett regarded them morosely from the box as the two men conferred and scratched their heads.

"Well," Jake finally said, pulling himself onto the

box as Hobby waved and walked off. "That rim has to be fixed before you go much further. Hobby says he and Horace will do the job as soon as we can stop long enough to build a decent fire."

"Mr. Ware's guidebook says there's a blacksmith shop ten miles upstream," Lucille told them, pointing at the pertinent line in the book, which was open on her lap.

"That rim won't go ten miles," Jake said.

"I'm sure Hobby and Horace are very competent smiths." Harriett adjusted the flap of canvas she'd propped over the box to protect them from the drizzle. "I'm willing to pay them whatever we would've had to pay the smith upstream."

Jake smiled wryly. "I doubt they'll charge you at all. Hobby seems quite taken with you two. He'd probably build you a whole new wagon if you needed one." He winked. "One of the advantages of being a female, Harry."

Harriett frowned; Lucille hastened to change the subject. "Mr. Ware says the two gentlemen who own the ferry are Indians," she commented.

"Half-breeds," Jake corrected.

"They look very different from your Indian friend Mr. Walking Horse. Don't they, my love?" She turned to Harriett, who was still frowning.

"I suppose," Harriett joined in.

"Do they look different because they're half white?" Lucille persisted.

"Amos is a breed, too, Mrs. Stanwick. But he's a Cowlitz Indian from Oregon. These two fellows are Potawatomie. There's a big difference between the tribes."

"You say Mr. Walking Horse is from Oregon?" Harriett finally abandoned her frown. "Have you been in Oregon, Mr. Carradine?"

"Yeah." He hesitated. "My family had a timber operation on the Willamette River."

Jake Carradine's having family somehow had never occurred to Harriett, and she found the idea oddly intriguing. Even gunmen, she supposed, had parents, brothers, sisters. "Is your family still there?" she asked curiously.

"No." The word was like the slam of a door, and his shuttered expression discouraged more questions. Abruptly he jumped down from the wagon box and stalked away.

"My goodness!" What do you suppose brought that on?" Lucille asked softly.

Harriett watched Jake walk up the line of wagons. Even from the back she could tell that his jaw was set and rigid, his fists clenched. "Best not to ask," she concluded. "Sometimes I think Mr. Carradine has more twists and turns to him than this endless trail we're following."

The ferry could transport only two wagons at a time, and the banks of the river were so muddy from the constant drizzle that loading soon became a problem. The line of wagons seemed to crawl, and by noon the Foster–Stanwick wagon had traveled only half the distance to the river. Following the example of the other emigrants, Harriett and Lucille did not attempt to fight the drizzle by building a fire. Instead they ate ham, rice, and biscuits that were left over from the evening before. As the afternoon wore on, Harriett wrote in her journal, Lucille retired to the back of the wagon to read—she was a great fan of the talented new writer Herman Melville—and they both waited impatiently for their turn to cross. Jake did not return. Harriett supposed he had found one of the card games that started up at every delay—or perhaps was sharing a bottle of spirits with one of the Adventurers. To perdi-

tion with the man, she decided. She didn't care where
he was.

Whatever he had found to entertain himself, though,
Jake did return in time for their crossing. For once
Harriett was grateful to see him. They were the last
wagon of the day to load onto the ferry, which was
nothing more sophisticated than planks laid across
several dugout canoes. The ramp that led onto the
ferry tottered, and the riverbank, which had begun the
day muddy, had been worked by the preceding wagons
into a mass of grease-slippery slime. Except for the
two wagons that would cross on this last trip and several men who were still swimming the livestock, the
Indiana Company was across the river and anxious to
depart.

The ferryman helped Jake position the wheels of
Harriett's wagon onto the front of the ramp. "This
mud's gettin' worse with every wagon," the man complained. "This here wagon is gonna go every way but
straight when we start pushin'."

"Just push," Jake directed. "We'll see what she
does."

Determined to do her part, Harriett pitched in with
the men to push. Lucille, also, put her back into getting the wagon through the slippery mud and up the
ramp. The wagon suddenly lurched forward and
slipped to one side, and Lucille landed on her backside.

"Aunt Lucille!"

Harriett slipped and slid toward her fallen aunt, but
before she had gone two steps a silver-haired gentleman was at Lucille's side. Harriett recognized him.
He was the dandyish fellow who had danced with her
aunt the night after the Wakarusa crossing.

"Mrs. Stanwick," the gentleman said. "Dear lady,
are you quite all right?"

Lucille took his proffered hand and struggled upright. "Mr. Steede. How dreadfully awkward of me. Here . . . oh dear! I've gotten mud on your trousers."

"Don't give it a thought. Careful now! Are you sure you're all right?"

"Oh, yes, perfectly. How very kind of you, sir."

Her aunt sounded like a blushing debutante at a Boston soiree, Harriett thought. And that man! With all the drizzle and mud in this place, his fashionable tailcoat and trousers hadn't a single spot on them before Lucille threw mud his way. Not a silver-gray hair was out of place. Even his horse—an elegant dappled gray—was spotlessly clean. The fellow no doubt had a pact with the Devil, Harriett thought irritably. No other way could he have managed such a feat.

Harriett marched over to the couple. Neither one of them noticed her until she cleared her throat. Then the silver-haired Romeo looked up and smiled.

"Ah! Miss . . ."

"Foster," Harriett provided.

"Yes. Of course." He lifted his hat in courteous— excessively courteous, Harriett thought—salute. "Delighted, Miss Foster. Lawrence Steede, at your service. I had the pleasure of meeting your lovely aunt at our social the other evening."

"So I saw," Harriett informed him. Her aunt was almost batting her eyelashes. Heaven help them all! Lucille was on the prowl. "Aunt, are you all right?"

"Oh, yes, my love. As you can see, Mr. Steede—"

"Yes. I can see. Thank you for your help, Mr. Steede. Aunt, we'd best return to the wagon. The men have managed to get it loaded."

She took Lucille's arm and steered her toward the ferry, carefully picking a path through the mud.

"Don't be such an old schoolmarm!" Lucille complained in a whisper. "You were scarcely civil to the man."

"He's not your sort," Harriett warned.

"He's a very courteous, attractive gentleman. How would you know what sort he is?"

"I just know, Aunt."

Lucille harrumphed. "Your mother raised you to be a prig and a busybody, Harriett Foster. Fortunately, I am a widow and old enough to ignore your interfering."

With that, Lucille retrieved her arm and went on alone. Harriett turned to look back at Lawrence Steede. He had a smile on his handsome face that she couldn't quite interpret. But whatever that smile meant, Harriett didn't like it. Lucille, by her own admission, was lonely for the companionship of a man. Sweet lady that she was, she often credited people with more virtue than they possessed. Harriett didn't like the dapper Mr. Steede, she decided abruptly. She didn't like him at all.

By the time the last wagon rolled off the ferry, the Indiana Adventurers were already moving on. Feeling uncharitably disposed toward men in general, Harriett refused Jake's offer to help with the oxen and bade him ride on alone. Then she hitched the team herself— proud of how accomplished she had become at the task—climbed up on the box, and shook out the reins, calling each ox by name. Curly, Flytail, Sharps, and Gus. Harriett didn't care what Jake Carradine said. The oxen didn't move faster to their names than to a simple "Giddiyup" or "Move, you stupid beasts!"

By the time Harriett caught up, the company was already circled into camp. The distance from the ferry was only two miles, but it was a slow, muddy two miles. The wagon that had been with her on the ferry still slogging through the mire behind her, Harriett guided her wagon into the space in the circle that had been left for them.

Sadie greeted Harriett as she unhitched the team. "There's to be a meeting after dinner—did you hear?

Now that we're truly into Indian country we're to elect new officers, or confirm the ones we have."

"Then we'd best hurry with dinner." Harriett glanced around at Lucille, who was building a fire with the dry tinder they carried in the wagon. "I had a mind to try my hand at fried bread, but perhaps I'll leave it till another night."

Together Harriett and Sadie led the oxen to a spot where the beasts could graze inside the circle. With Indians roaming the country, the animals were not safe outside, at least until a rotating shift of guards was organized—another item on tonight's agenda, Sadie told her. "No need to hurry so, Harriett." Sadie patted Flytail's broad flank as Harriett fastened the last set of hobbles. "We ladies really needn't bother to attend, you know."

Harriett's hands froze at their task, then resumed. "Of course," she agreed. "How silly of me to think the situation would be any different out here, where everyone must work equally to survive." She stood up and wiped her hands upon her skirt. "But I will be there, you can be sure—whether or not I am wanted."

Jake sat on the wet ground, back propped against the spokes of a wagon wheel, his rain slicker spread out beneath him to combat the dampness. Almost mindlessly he wielded his belt knife to whittle tent pegs from wet wood he had collected along the river. Todd Bryant and his sister, Sadie, needed a new set since the last storm had ripped their tent from its moorings, and his lady boss could probably use some extras, considering her aunt's talent for misplacing things.

"My, but you look busy, Mr. Carradine."

Jake looked up to see Caroline MacKenzie standing in front of him. Her voice was soft and melodic, and carried more than a hint of sultry enticement.

"Evenin', Mrs. MacKenzie. Would you mind moving aside a tad? You're blocking the light from the fire."

"Certainly." She took his words as an invitation to sit beside him on the slicker, so close that they touched. "It's a lovely evening, isn't it?"

"It'll do, I suppose."

"Poor man," she said teasingly. "So glum. You men don't have any appreciation for the beauties of nature."

Jake had plenty of appreciation for the beauties that were snuggling up close to his ribs, and he wished Caroline would take them back where they belonged—to her husband's wagon. Damn the woman for a menace!

She sighed. "Today was so boring—doing nothing but sitting and waiting to cross the silly river. And now I'm all wound up with restless energy. Do you feel that way, Mr. Carradine?"

"I'm plumb tuckered, Mrs. MacKenzie." As far as Jake could tell, Caroline's energy was centered between her legs. Tonight wasn't the first time she'd approached him, and he'd seen her swing her skirts toward Lawrence Steede, John Cutter, Joe Riley, Todd Bryant, and all three Smith brothers—even young Hobby, who was scarcely old enough to know what to do with the tool between his legs. The only man she didn't flirt with was her husband, a tall beanpole of a young man with hound dog eyes and a perpetually sad expression. But then with Caroline as a wife, the man had reason to be sad.

"You work much too hard, you know," Caroline told him in her soft, bedroom voice. "You should pause now and then—for rest and entertainment."

"You staying for the meeting?" he asked, hoping to change the subject. The company was starting to gather, and Mr. Deere, conversing with several men by the central bonfire, had assumed the officious manner with which he conducted all meetings.

"Me come to the meeting?" Caroline laughed. "Oh, no!" One of her hands fluttered gracefully and somehow came to rest against Jake's thigh. "You men talk about the dullest things. I'm not one of those women who want to act like a man and intrude on men's business. I enjoy acting like a woman."

Jake would bet a month's wages on the truth of that.

"But my husband, Callum, will be here until the very last word is said, you can be sure."

She sighed and slipped her gaze toward his. Her eyes were a soft fawn brown, he noted. A man could drown in eyes like hers, and no doubt Caroline knew every trick to push him under. She was all soft curves, lush flesh, moist lips, and eager eyes. Jake appreciated a good whore as much as any other man—more than most, usually. But he didn't much like to see a man's wife switch her tail like a mare in heat. Poor Callum MacKenzie didn't need another trespasser on his territory. Jake figured that young man had troubles enough.

"If you get bored, Jake, come around to my wagon and I'll make you some coffee." She rose, pausing longer than necessary with her breasts at his eye level. "Bye," she crooned.

Jake watched her go, hips swaying and skirts swinging saucily. His lusts had become all too discriminating, he mused with regret. Two months ago he would have been after that randy female like a shot. His instincts were going all to hell.

Caroline had not yet disappeared when Jake's gaze swung, as though drawn instinctively, and he forgot about Callum MacKenzie's tempting wife. Female troublemakers were certainly at large this evening, he noted, for into the gathering crowd of men walked Harriett Foster and her tiny band of supporters—her aunt Lucille and the burgeoning Sadie MacBride. Behind them followed the black sheepdog bitch from the

Cutter wagon, strutting as though she, too, were part of the determined feminine parade. A smile came unbidden to Jake's face as he went back to his whittling. The evening's meeting might prove to be more entertaining than a good drunken brawl.

"Good evening, Mr. Carradine." Harriett's voice was just as musical as Caroline MacKenzie's, Jake reflected, but it certainly wasn't singing the same song. Too bad. Maybe if he could lay bare her well-wrapped anatomy, demonstrate to her that women had functions other than nagging, and get her out of his system, then he could get back on an even keel.

"We didn't see you at dinner tonight," she said.

"I had a bite with the Smith brothers," Jake told her.

He looked up. Harriett's eyes weren't on him; she stared in the direction that Caroline had walked—or rather sauntered—away. A tiny frown puckered the usually perfect line of her brows. Were her eyes always that green, or was jealousy adding some color?

Jake chuckled at the thought, and found himself speared on her green gaze.

"Did you say something to Mrs. MacKenzie to discourage her from attending the meeting, Mr. Carradine?"

"No, ma'am," he answered blandly. Not jealous. Indignant. He should have known. He rose, tipped his hat toward Sadie, and ignored Harriett's disbelieving frown. "Why don't you let me fetch a stool for you, Mrs. MacBride. You can lean your back up against the wheel here."

"Why, thank you, Mr. Carradine. But I wouldn't want to put you to any trouble."

"No trouble, ma'am."

By the time Sadie and her protruding stomach were comfortably situated, Mr. Deere had called the meeting to order. Lucille accepted Jake's offer of a seat on his rain slicker, and Harriett continued to stand, arms folded across her chest, back straight and uncompromising as an iron ramrod.

Jake found Harriett's profile more interesting than Mr. Deere's long-winded account of the matters about to be voted on. If she would ease the solemn lines of her expression, Harry's looks would be better by far than Caroline MacKenzie's. The clean line of chin, lips, and nose had to earn her the envy of plainer women. And that hair, shimmering pure red and gold in the firelight, put Caroline's paler coloring to shame. If Harry would just smile, the damned little witch might be downright beautiful.

"Now we got to appoint shifts for the guard," Deere was droning. "We been warned about these Injuns— all the way from here to California. They'll take horses, mules, and cattle just for the plain mean orneriness of it, and if you look at 'em cross-eyed, they're likely to slit your throat as well. Every man here . . ."

"Shouldn't we elect the officers and let them handle the guard?" Caleb Taylor asked. He was a farmer from Wisconsin who had joined the company in Independence. He didn't much cotton to Deere's highhanded manner, and he was a frequent complainer about the wagon captain's mistakes.

"Yeah!" came agreement from Horatio Smith. "You're assumin' a lot, Deere!"

"We'll get around to everything, men! Just settle yourselves down. I'm still captain of this here company."

"Maybe not for long," Jake heard Harriett murmur to Sadie.

The lady did know how to smile, he noted. She was smiling now at something her aunt said. Her teeth were white and even, and two identical dimples dented her cheeks. If she wore that smile more often, he thought, she wouldn't have reached the ripe age of twenty-whatever-she-was as a spinsterish busybody. Some man would have seen that smile, fallen into those jewel-green eyes, and wooed her right off her feet.

"I put up Elias Cartwright as captain!" Caleb Taylor shouted.

"Or Horace Smith!" someone else offered. "Lord! Horace's so big the Injun's'll go galloping off the minute they see 'im!"

Laughter rippled through the crowd. Harriett laughed with them. Her eyes sparkled green fire when she laughed, Jake noted. She was, he decided, one of the most fetching females he'd ever seen. A woman who could look so sweet, so downright pleasing, had no call being a bad-tempered, schoolmarmish prig—no call at all. But then, what man understood women? Not Jake.

Jake had to admit his knowledge of women was limited. His mother—a good woman—had died giving birth to Elijah when Jake was eight. Eli's wife had died of pneumonia only six months after Jake had joined the family in Oregon. The only other women of his personal acquaintance were whores—not a fair standard by which to judge, he conceded. And he didn't rightly understand whores either.

Harriett finally sat down on the slicker. The meeting was dragging on, turning into a forum for the Indiana Adventurers' dissatisfaction with their present captain. The evening was going to be a long one—impossibly long if Harriett Foster continued to sit so close he could smell the lilac scent of the soap she used. The damned female—unlike Caroline MacKenzie—had no idea what she could do to a man's nerves. Every fiber in his body had come to attention, including some that were going to become quite noticeable in a few moments.

Jake got up, muttering an excuse about his legs being stiff. His legs weren't the part of him that was stiffening, unfortunately.

"Well, spit!" Harriett's smile was gone, but Jake found her moue of indignation almost as enticing. "Imagine them letting Mr. Deere bully them into confirming him as captain. Fine bunch of sheep, these so-called Adventurers!"

"He did organize the company, just as he said," Sadie reminded her. "I suppose he has the right to lead it. If he took his employee Mr. Carter and struck out with what wagons would follow him—as he threatened—we would be in a bit of a fix."

"We'd be better off without that dreadful Mr. Carter, if you ask me!"

Horatio Smith piped up from the crowd. "I put up Jake Carradine for subcaptain! And Caleb Taylor!"

Jake came to attention. "What the hell?"

His objection was drowned in vociferous approval from the crowd. Harriett turned and gave him a vexed frown—a look every bit as sour as her expressions during her lectures on drinking, gambling, and general hell-raising. For once he agreed with her disapproval, but she should be directing her glare toward the company, not him.

What were the fools thinking? That his reputation as a gun tough would scare away the Indians, or find watering holes in the desert, or keep the cholera from stalking the company? Fools! Jake wanted no part of the leadership of this company. He hadn't even wanted to come on this damned trip.

He was about to voice his objection when Harriett beat him to the punch.

"Mr. Deere!" she called out loud and clear. "I object!"

The newly confirmed captain raised a brow. "Miss Foster? You have something to say?" Several snickers from the crowd accompanied his question.

"Indeed I do, sir! Mr. Carradine is in my employ. I think I should be consulted before he is given other duties."

Jake grinned, forgetting his own objection. His lady boss was certainly provoked. Could it be she was miffed because the rest of the company didn't see him as quite the rogue she did? Or perhaps she resented the idea of sharing his attention with the others. Unlikely. But an interesting thought.

"Mr. Carradine?" Deere said. "Do your responsibilities to Miss Foster keep you too busy to hold the post of subcaptain?"

"Mr. Deere!" Harriett objected. "I think I am the one to decide that, not Mr. Carradine."

"Mr. Carradine?" Deere persisted, ignoring Harriett.

Jake's grin widened. He was going to catch hell from Harry, but he did enjoy getting her riled. She was as easy to light as a match.

"Miss Foster's right independent," he drawled. "I think I can help you out and still see the little ladies don't get into trouble."

One of the "little ladies" in question was about to cut him to ribbons with her eyes. Harriett's glare almost made Jake want to duck.

"Done then!" Horatio yelled.

Harriett turned her back and stalked off, spine straight as a Pawnee spear. Not until she disappeared did Jake remember that he hadn't wanted to be subcaptain at all.

"Imagine!" Harriett said to Lucille, who sat beside her on the wagon box the next morning. "Men such as these—men who would vote a scapegrace like Jake Carradine a position of authority—these are the same who have rule over the world. The thought is a frightening one."

Lucille grasped the side of the box as the wagon lurched over a rut. "I don't think Mr. Carradine is such a scoundrel. I've never known you to have such lack of charity for someone, Harriett—or to be so full of doom and gloom. If you don't mind my saying so, dear, your attitude on this trip has become quite tiring."

"Not a scoundrel? When he spends all his time drinking and gambling with the lowest elements of the company—and pursuing God knows what other questionable entertainments. He's on a first-name basis with Mrs. Hornsby and her fallen ladies, and he's entirely too familiar with Caroline MacKenzie. You saw the way they danced after the Wakarusa crossing, and only last night when we arrived at the meeting, they were cozy as they could possibly be."

"Did you expect a man you picked out of a drunken brawl to be a saint, my love?"

"Hmmph!"

"I fail to see why his behavior bothers you so," Lucille said, a twinkle lighting her eye. "He's here when we need him—like two days ago, when he fixed our broken axle. He helps us stake down our tent in the wind, he shepherds us across rivers . . ."

"Fiddle!" Harriett declared scornfully. "Hobby and his brothers spend more time at our wagon than he does."

Lucille laughed. "Make up your mind, my love. Do you want the man watching over you or not? One minute you declare your independence, and the next you're berating the poor fellow for not hanging on your skirts. I think you're in a stew because the men in this company regard Mr. Carradine with some respect, even though you've labeled him as worthless."

"I never said he was worthless!" Harriett denied. "He's . . . he's . . ."

"Yes, he is, isn't he," Lucille quipped with raised

brow. "He's a very attractive man, in an elemental sort of way—don't you think?"

"No, I do not!" Harriett snapped. After a moment of silence, she gave her aunt a sheepish look. "I protesteth too much?" she asked, paraphrasing their mutually favorite playwright.

"Forsooth," Lucille returned with a smile.

"Well," Harriett conceded. "I suppose he is attractive—in a strictly physical sense." Attractive, indeed! She had felt the most peculiar sensations when sitting beside him the night before. He was a man who grabbed at a woman's primitive feelings. How fortunate that Harriett controlled those unthinking emotions with cool, calm reason. "He does have nice eyes," she conceded, "and in spite of needing a shave and a haircut, he appears to be fairly clean—at least he smells . . ." Her words faded at Lucille's amused regard.

"Clean," Lucille finished for her. "Is that how he smells?"

"Well . . ." Harriett had the grace to blush. "I suppose, when he doesn't reek of liquor."

"But you are not moved by any of that."

"Aunt Lucille! A woman of true discernment isn't swayed by a handsome face and a strong, well-shaped body."

"A very well-shaped body," Lucille elaborated.

Harriett ignored her. "She is moved rather by nobility of character and mind. And that," she concluded with satisfaction, "I have seen very little of in Mr. Carradine."

Lucille sighed and cast her eyes heavenward. "At times I find it difficult to believe, my love, that common blood runs in our veins."

The days stretched into weeks. The company plodded over a trail made muddy by the almost daily rain.

Seldom out of sight of similar wagon companies both ahead of them and behind, they slipped and slid through the ruts of those who had gone before and left still bigger ruts for those who followed.

Harriett almost grew fond of the oxen whose broad backs and swaying rumps filled her vision day after day. The beasts pulled slowly but faithfully through the deepest mud. Mr. Carradine had chosen them well, she admitted, and wondered where a man who lived by his gun had learned about draft animals. Others in the company were not faring so well, and grumbling and discouragement constituted the after-dinner conversation at more than one campfire.

The Adventurers were anxious for California, and gold; they had no patience for the tedium of the trail. By day they struggled to cover as much ground as they could, perhaps fifteen miles on a good day—a good day being one in which no storm turned the already muddy road to a quagmire and no one broke an axle or lost a wheel. By night the men stood guard in shifts. The Potawatomie Indians were not loath to profit from the strange people crossing their land. They not only charged the emigrants for ferry crossings and bridges that eased the rugged way, but they regularly tried to steal stock. The stock was their only prey, however; the emigrants themselves the Indians let be. Harriett had to give the savages credit for tolerance, for if anyone treated her with the disrespect that some of the company showed toward the red men, she herself might have been tempted to lift a scalp or two. On the whole, she decided, the mortal danger from Indians along the trail was much exaggerated.

Other dangers had not been exaggerated, however. The number of graves along the trail seemed to increase every day—grim witness to accidents and sickness that claimed lives without regard to age or gender or determination to make it to the gold fields. Rumors passed down the trail of a company ahead that had been overwhelmed by the cholera. The Indiana Company had been fortunate thus far. Two of their people were sick, but none had died. Yet.

Harriett saw no reason to expect the dread affliction to pass their company by. She'd read about the toll the disease had taken the year before, not only in the crowded cities but on the trail west. Wherever man fled, cholera seemed to follow.

The prospect was a fearful thing, if one dwelt upon it, which Harriett did not choose to do. She reasoned that the sickness struck where it would regardless of precautions or fretting. All the worry in the world would not keep it away.

5

Harriett's pessimism was justified. By the time the Indiana Company reached the Big Blue River in northeastern Kansas, one of their ill had died. Three more people were sick, and Dr. Silas Fellows, who had left his wagon in the charge of Caleb Taylor's son so he could see to the sick, declared that the cholera was among them in force. During the last two weeks he had been called to the aid of wagon companies both ahead and behind. The dread affliction was taking its toll this season, and the Indiana Company had not escaped its malevolent touch.

The banks of the Big Blue were lush with grass and cooled by the shade of large cottonwood and oak trees —a welcome change. For the last two days travel over rolling, gorge-cut grasslands, neither wood nor water had been available on the trail. Harriett's supply of energy and patience had grown as low as their cache of firewood, and the sight of the cool groves along the river was gratifying indeed.

The company was reluctant to stop, despite the need to rest, nurse the sick, and graze the animals; such paltry needs could not stand against the urgency that drove the argonauts. But even the Adventurers' impatience could not enable the company to cross the Big Blue without rafts. And rafts took time to build.

For two days they camped along the grassy banks of the river. While the men labored to cut trees, hollow out several tree trunks, and fasten logs across them to make two sturdy rafts, Harriett, Lucille, and Sadie rested, washed and mended clothes, aided in nursing the sick, and followed Mr. Ware's recommendations for making pickles from the "prairie pea," which grew abundantly on vines in the grove.

By noon of the second day Harriett was bored. If she never soaked another prairie pea in vinegar, it would be too soon. And Dr. Fellows had shooed both her and Sadie away from his patients, telling them that the sights and smells of the sick-wagon were too much for ladies to tolerate. Harriett suspected their dismissal had more to do with Sadie's remarks about his treatment of the sick. Harriett herself knew nothing about illness or nursing, but Sadie seemed more knowledgeable about disease than Dr. Fellows, no matter the pompous Latin he spouted. She said it was criminal to bleed patients who were already shriveled from loss of fluid. Dr. Fellows just tut-tutted and muttered something about God save him from meddling women.

"Why don't you take a walk?" Sadie suggested when Harriett sighed for the hundredth time.

Lucille had left them earlier to stroll with Mr. Steede, who lately had danced attendance on the widow like a fly buzzing around spilled sugar, much to Lucille's delight. The rest of the camp was quiet, and the afternoon was growing long.

"I can watch the pickles," Sadie assured her.

"Perhaps I'll gather some firewood," Harriett said.

"Chad has gathered enough to last both of us a month," Sadie told her. "Go take some exercise, dear. Didn't you say that guidebook of yours tells about a pretty spring somewhere nearby?"

"It's called Cove Spring. Mr. Ware writes that it's lovely. Perhaps I'll try to find it. Would you like to come along?"

Sadie looked down at her ballooning stomach. "I don't think so," she said wryly. "My walks are limited to short excursions around the wagons."

Harriett laughed at Sadie's expression. "I'm sorry, Sadie. I'll stay here and keep you company."

"Go walk," Sadie ordered. "Otherwise you'll be impossible for the rest of the afternoon."

Finding Cove Spring was not difficult. Many other emigrants had been there before Harriett, and the trail that ran beside the Big Blue and then up the banks of a small stream was well worn. The walk was about a mile, which several weeks ago Harriett would have thought a considerable distance. But now, after so many days of traveling, much of the time driving the oxen while walking beside the wagon, a mile was a mere stroll. She enjoyed stretching her legs and leaving behind the smoke and clutter of camp, the pall of sickness, the fretful impatience of her fellow travelers.

When she caught sight of the spring, Harriett was especially glad she had come. Mr. Ware, usually so wordy in his guidebook, had merely written that the spot was very beautiful. Such simple words were not enough. The spring was like a fairy glade, removed from the world of reality, set aside in its own special dimension of peace and loveliness. Set into the foliage like a pure blue sapphire was a quiet pool edged by sandy banks. From a ledge above the pool issued a flow of water that splattered over the rocks and fell nearly ten feet into the basin. At the other end of the pool the water splashed in melodious cascade into the stream that she'd been following. The scene was so perfect that Harriett was loath to spoil it by stepping out of the surrounding greenery.

Then, as if sensing and resenting her presence, the

pool rippled. Straight from a Greek myth a vengeful god emerged, hurling himself up from the depths of his domain, ready to defend the beauty that was forbidden human eyes. Harriett stifled a scream and backed farther into the foliage, then rebuked her overactive imagination. No Greek god had shot up from the depths and was now floating happily on his back. No indeed! The spring's resident god was none other than Jake Carradine, clothed only in the suit nature gave him.

She turned hastily from the sight, praying that he hadn't seen her. His mind being low as it was, he would naturally think she was spying on him. And of course she wasn't—and wouldn't. But she couldn't leave. If she started crashing through the greenery now, he was bound to see her.

What an awkward dilemma! She closed her eyes and hardly dared to breathe, wishing herself as small and quiet as a mouse. A few moments passed, and all she heard was a quiet splashing in the pool—then a snatch of a less than polite song. The beast didn't know she was here.

Harriett opened her eyes. She turned, slowly, enticed by overwhelming temptation. Though screened by her leafy bower, she could see Jake splashing in the cool water, cavorting like an otter, swimming with strong strokes, plunging beneath the surface, disappearing for long stretches, then shooting from the water like a human geyser. He stood, facing away from her, and flexed his back, shoulders, and long, muscular arms to loosen the tension of vigorous exercise. Harriett remembered thinking him big when she'd first seen him those many days ago in Independence. Now she realized that he was not only big, he was magnificent. No other word would describe him. The man had once done something more strenuous than idle drinking, gambling, and occasionally lifting a gun—that much was obvious. His torso and arms rolled with smooth, supple muscle, his neck and buttocks corded with strength. Her imagination still turned up high, Harriett could almost see power radiate from him like heat from a fire. For one brief, abandoned moment she wondered how it would be to feel those steel arms close around her, to have those broad, muscular shoulders loom above her, blocking the sun, the sky, the world. . . .

She shivered and blinked. Shameful, indecent thoughts! What was she doing—spying on a naked man who trusted that he was baring himself in solitude? Wicked, wanton . . . !

He turned toward her and walked toward the bank and shallower water, revealing a thick mat of hair plastered wetly to a broad chest, lean, narrow hips, muscled columns of legs, and . . . ! Harriett shut her eyes, but the red-hot image of Jake Carradine as nature made him was seared into her brain. She had had no more knowledge of male anatomy than any other decent unmarried woman—until this moment. And she was heartily sorry to lose her ignorance. Sweet heaven! Did all men look like that? Did Edwin? She would likely never know, Harriett comforted herself. Decent husbands and wives didn't offend each other's modesty by exposing themselves. Even Mr. Carradine, she reminded herself, would cover himself if he knew someone was watching. Wouldn't he?

Heart pounding, Harriett opened her eyes. Jake was gone. The pool was quiet, the only sound a trill of birdsong and the splashing of the spring itself. Had the whole thing been a dream? Cautiously she slipped from the trees and eased up to the bank with watchful eyes. No dream after all, for large footprints were deeply engraved in the sand at the pool's edge. Harriett curiously placed her foot in one of the prints. Her foot spanned just over half the distance from heel to toe.

Exhaling a sigh of relief, Harriett sat down on the sandy bank. No harm had been done, she reasoned, except to her own modesty and self-respect. How could she have spied in that manner? Such behavior was completely alien to her nature. But then, since this journey had begun she had behaved remarkably unlike her usual self. Her thoughts had been undisciplined to the point of lingering on the masculine appeal of a man like Jake Carradine. She'd been snappish to Lucille, rude to Mr. Steede, and uncharitable toward Jake. Poor Mr. Carradine. She really should be kinder to the man. He did have some good qualities—other than the ones she had just seen exhibited. The other men on the train seemed to respect him. Many of the argonauts came to Jake instead of Mr. Deere when they had a problem. Whenever Harriett really needed him, he was there—sometimes when she didn't want him to be.

Harriett felt her face grow warm again. No doubt he'd seen no shame in exposing himself to the sun and air. Men seemed much more at ease with their natural state than women. Or could it be that society itself—and a set of rules dictated by men!—declared that women should be ashamed of their bodies? Because men did not wish to fall prey to their own lusts, women must cower within their clothing and be ashamed, even when alone or with their own gender.

The spring cascaded into the pool, and the pool rippled into the stream, producing liquid music that lulled Harriett's senses. With a wanton smile she unbuttoned and removed her shoes, wriggled her toes in the warm sand, and then boldly dabbled one toe in the cool water. How she envied Jake Carradine the freedom of his masculinity. The quiet solitude, the cool, clean water, the trickle of sweat between her closely confined breasts—all combined to tempt her into the pool. If Jake Carradine could take such innocent pleasure, was there shame in her doing the same?

Ridiculous thought. Absolutely mad. Ladies did not do such things!

But why not? tempted a rebellious voice in her head. What harm would be done? The camp was a mile away, and no one else was likely to come.

The air was so hot. And her corset itched. She could almost imagine the feel of cool water slipping past her sticky skin.

Harriett retired behind a leafy bush—for what reason she didn't know, but the privacy made her feel more comfortable. Off came her pantaloons, her dress, her petticoat. Her high-button shoes and cotton stockings were already lying on the sandy bank. And last she peeled away the corset and sweat-soaked chemise —sweet relief! She folded the garments neatly and placed them on a clean nest of leaves, loosened the tightly wound bun that confined her hair, then tiptoed down to the pond, glancing cautiously in all directions like a doe searching for predators.

But all caution and doubt went flying out of her mind when she sank into the water. The delicious coolness wrapped around her, tingling through every pore, and she abandoned herself to the pleasure, gliding smoothly through the glassy calm, diving beneath the surface and twisting round and round in the dim green depths, then shooting back to the surface. How grateful she was that she had learned to swim as a child at her cousin's country home. How wondrous the feeling of cool water slipping past bare skin.

"Uh . . . Harry?"

The infamous name, though quietly spoken, sounded like a thunderclap. Harriett almost jumped out of her skin, splashed frantically in the confusion of wondering what to do, then settled for sinking into the pond up to her chin.

"I was here earlier. Forgot my hat."

Jake Carradine. Who else would it be but her own personal trial from Heaven? Or was it Hell? The devil waved his hat as if it were proof of an innocent reason for his standing on the bank gaping at her. Harriett wanted to sink into the pool and quietly drown.

"Get out of here!" she demanded, her voice trembling. "How dare you stand there and . . . and . . . !"

Jake grinned. "Funny I didn't see you coming up the trail, seeing as I left this place just a few minutes ago. How long have you been here, Harry?"

"Mr. Carradine! Will . . . you . . . please . . . leave!"

He threw his hat on the bank and sat down beside it. Regarding her as if his eyes could see through the opaque water, he smiled in a way that called to mind his long-ago warning. He was a dangerous man, he'd told her—not a man that any decent woman could trust. Her stomach sank down to her knees, dragging her heart with it.

"Cold?" he inquired. "Water's chilly, isn't it?"

"Are you going to leave?" she pleaded.

"Nope." He took a bottle from his trousers pocket, uncorked it, and raised it to his lips.

"Don't you go anywhere without a bottle?" she asked scornfully.

"A gun and a bottle are a man's best friends," he philosophized with a smile.

"They're the Devil's best friends, you mean. For a man to let his character dissolve in alcohol—"

"Dissolve in alcohol," Jake interjected with a wry chuckle. "Very good, Harry. You are really some woman to be able to deliver a lecture even when you're caught under the wide-open sky wearing only your skin." He picked up his hat and twirled it deftly on one finger, regarding her with a less than charitable gaze. "You're a fair hand at preaching at a man, Harry. But right now you're the one who needs preaching up. What in goddamned hell do you think you're doing sitting there buck naked when there's a hundred men less than a mile away—every one who'd love to have a go at you, seeing that you've stripped down for them so nice and convenient."

"You can't talk to me that way!"

"Someone has to!" His voice had gone from mocking to angry. "Lady! You need some sense pounded into your head. And it seems like all the pretty courtesies I've been practicing on you aren't going to work."

"You wouldn't know what courtesy is, you . . . you lout!"

"You don't have a brain in that red head of yours, do you Harry? You saw me swimming in the skin and figured if a man could do it you could too—is that it?"

Harriett wished she could expire on the spot. Or maybe she'd already died and gone to Hell.

"Did the thought ever cross your pea brain," he continued relentlessly, "that no one in camp gives a rat's ass about my bare backside hanging out in the air, but if they saw your pretty little fanny taking the sun, they just might consider it an invitation?"

He was right, of course, but she'd die a thousand deaths before admitting it to him.

"That even I might think all that bare skin is an invitation?" he added ominously.

"That's ridiculous! I . . . !" The words choked in her throat, for the look in his eyes proved his claim wasn't ridiculous at all. "Please go away!" she pleaded, no longer as indignant as she was frightened.

"Lucky for you that I know you're a featherbrain, not a trollop. If I were any other man in our company you'd have earned yourself a roll on the sand."

Even the cold water couldn't keep the heat from her face.

"Now get out of there and get dressed. I'll take you back to camp."

She considered her options, and concluded that she had none. "Turn your back, Mr. Carradine. I'm not coming out with you watching. I'll shrivel and freeze first!"

Again he swept her with a glance that made her feel exposed, in spite of her shield of water. "I'll give you five minutes." He turned, arms folded across his broad chest.

"On your honor?"

"Harry," he said with a sigh. "You're going to find out how much honor I don't have unless you hop to getting dressed."

Jake turned around. He heard a cautious splash as Harriett emerged from the pond. In his mind, he imagined her with water cascading from gleaming red hair to run in curved streams around and between her breasts, over her belly, pooling in her navel, caressing the smooth, long columns of her thighs, until it finally slipped over her calves to merge with the water in the pond. Damned lucky water, he thought.

"Are you ready?" he asked impatiently. A man could endure such imaginings for only so long.

"Y-yes. All right."

He turned. Her pantaloons were twisted, her petticoat askew, and her corset she held behind her back, trying to hide it, no doubt.

Jake shook his head. "Put yourself straight, Harry. Walk back into camp that way and no one will doubt what we've been doing up here." And didn't he just wish it were true!

"You can just take yourself off, Mr. Carradine! I don't care to listen to any more of your insinuating words!"

He smiled, folded his long legs beneath him, and sat on the bank. "Got some of your sass back now that you have your clothes on?"

Harriett gritted her teeth.

"I'll just stick around and walk you back, Harry. Emigrants aren't the only ones you might come upon. There's Indians around here, too."

"Fiddle! I haven't seen those poor Indians threaten anyone."

"Don't ever underestimate an Indian, Harry."

"Well, if you won't take yourself off, then at least turn your back again while I straighten my clothes."

He shook his head in exasperation, sighed, and turned around.

"This is entirely unfair, you know. If I were a man, no one would care one jot about my taking an innocent little swim."

"You aren't a man." Jake chuckled. "I can bear witness to that."

Harriett glared at his broad back, but could think of no retort that wouldn't bounce back and shame herself. She'd been every bit as guilty as he in peeping. Perhaps this was fitting punishment, she scolded herself, righting her pantaloons and straightening her petticoat.

"Are you ready?" he asked. "Goddammit! How long can it take to fasten a few buttons?"

"Just a moment!" Buttons weren't the problem. The corset was. She didn't have time to put the thing on, and walking back to camp with her corset in her hand —unthinkable! Stealthily, with an eye on her self-appointed guardian, she stuffed the undergarment into a tangle of vines and covered it with leaves. She would just have to do without one until she got to California. "All right, Mr. Carradine. I am presentable."

He stood up and turned around, grinning, and gave her a once-over that made her flush. "You were very presentable before," he drawled, one unruly brow lifting in mockery. "A bit too presentable."

Covering embarrassment with indignation, she put hands to her hips. "I'll thank you to keep a decent tongue in your head!"

"Fire me," he offered hopefully.

He had her there. She couldn't.

"I warned you about my manners," he reminded her with an insolent smile.

"So you did," she conceded. "I believed at the time that you were exaggerating. I see now you were not." She scorched him with a glare, then swept past him toward the path that led to camp. Out of the corner of her eye she could see a speck of white where her discarded corset peeked through its blanket of leaves. How many other pieces of her modesty and innocence would be discarded before this odyssey was over?

Journal Entry, May 20—On the Banks of the Platte River: This afternoon we reached the mighty Platte, which will serve as our guide across the plains to the Rocky Mountains. Few of us are in a mood to celebrate the event, however, for now three members of our company have died and four more are ill. Among those near death is Rachel—one of the female "entertainers" who travel with Mrs. Hornsby. She is the only one we ladies have been allowed to nurse, for Dr. Fellows will not have us near the men. Unbelievably, the minister of God who travels with our company has refused to give poor Rachel comfort, and told an indignant Lucille that Rachel is merely reaping the fruits of her sin. I'm certain God will have more mercy on the frightened girl's soul than His minister did. Another of the ill—I am grieved to report—is Sadie's brother Todd, though he seems not so sick as some of the others.

Mr. Ware's guidebook says that we have now trav-

eled 325 miles. I no longer despair of the hundreds
left to go, for I am coming to enjoy the trail, despite
the hardships and sadnesses. This wilderness has so
many new things to see—both small and large—that
my mind constantly whirls.

The Platte River is very different from the familiar
Mississippi and Missouri. It is called Nebraska by
the local Indians, but the first civilized explorers
named it Platte. It is a beautiful stream; when the
sun strikes its waters the river glistens like molten
silver. The Platte is very wide here, and the banks
are a rolling, grassy prairie barren of trees.

This is what I imagined the wilderness to be—
wide blue skies and vast prairie, spoiled only by the
long line of wagons that crawls along the riverbank
and sends dust swirling into the clean sky. Difficult
to believe that Fort Kearney is only ten miles east of
the spot where I now sit; we seem so far removed
from civilization.

Mr. Ware writes that wood can be found on a
large island we can see in the middle of the river, but
the water is very high and swift, and none of the
men have shown any eagerness to brave the current
to fetch firewood. Mr. Phineas Carter, our scout,
tells us that for many hundreds of miles ahead we
will see only prairie—prairie and Pawnee, I believe,
were his exact words. The man seems to delight in
creating agitation; he has several of the younger
men of the company quite eager to show off their
prowess in harassing the savages. It seems to me
that Mr. Carter is more a danger to the company
than any Indians who come riding out of the plains.

The much dreaded Pawnee, though very fierce-
looking warriors, seem more interested in stealing
stock than taking lives, just as the Potawatomie
were. The Pawnee, however, are more proficient
than the other tribes we have met. Two nights ago, in

spite of our vigilant guards, a Pawnee raiding party stole a number of horses, mules, and cattle. One of my oxen—the faithful Gus—was among those taken. Our hotheaded young men, goaded on by Mr. Carter and a young Indiana farmer named Ned White, were anxious to ride after the Indians, retrieve our stock, and mete out punishment. They were all quite ridiculously boastful and bloodthirsty. Fortunately, they were calmed by cooler, wiser members of the company, and the next morning, the savages returned our beasts. Poor Gus was unharmed, much to my relief. Mr. Carradine explained that the Pawnee regard stealing as game of skill. They steal to prove their prowess but often return the stolen items. I confess I do not understand the values of these people.

Harriett closed her journal and stared into the dying campfire. She had hoped that a few men in the Indiana Company would have cool heads in a crisis, but Jake Carradine had surprised her by having the coolest. He had been the one to face down Ned White and Phineas Carter when they'd been so anxious for Pawnee blood. She shuddered to think what might have happened had Jake not won that confrontation. She could still see Ned's flushed, angry face and hear the bloodlust in his voice.

He and a dozen others were mounted and ready to ride. They had reined in impatiently when Jake signaled them to wait. Harriett, standing with Lucille, Sadie, and the Smith brothers, watched anxiously as Ned worked up a full head of steam.

"No damned red savage is gonna take somethin' that belongs to me and get away with it!" Ned had declared, and the mounted men behind him had nodded agreement. "We gotta teach those Pawnee a lesson now, or they'll be after us all the way to the Rockies!"

Abel Hawkins shouted agreement. "Once they feel our lead they won't be so anxious to come around!"

"Feel our lead and see a few of their scalps hanging from our wagons," White added.

Jake had lounged calmly against the rear of the Smith brothers' wagon. The look in his eyes, Harriett had thought at the time, would have given even the Pawnee pause. But White wasn't wise enough to read the warning there.

"More likely your scalps will be hanging from Pawnee belts," Jake told the young man. "And then after you've gotten yourself killed and the Pawnee good and riled, they'll ride back here and make every person in this company pay for your foolishness."

"If you're scared, Carradine, why don't you just go hide behind the bluff over there! No one asked you to come with us."

"I wouldn't mind having him with us," one man in the crowd had muttered.

Phineas Carter simply sat on his scruffy bay mare, chawed his tobacco, and watched in amusement as the trouble he'd caused came to a head.

Jake sighed, pushed himself away from the wagon, took off his hat, and ran his fingers through the shaggy locks of his hair. He seemed unperturbed by White's slur. "You're not going anywhere, Ned."

"Says who? You?"

"You people did appoint me subcaptain of this company," Jake reminded him calmly. "And I imagine Mr. Deere there will back me up."

Mr. Deere would back up whoever won, Harriett noted cynically. He'd done nothing since the Indian raid except fret and look indecisive.

"Well, excuse me, Mr. Subcaptain Carradine. I aim to get me some Pawnee scalps today, and Tom, Abel, George, and a dozen others will ride with me. If you want to add your gun to ours, you're welcome to come. Otherwise, step aside."

Harriett tensed as the two men eyed each other. In spite of Ned's being mounted, Jake seemed to look down at the younger man from where he stood blocking his path. Harriett was close enough to see one of Jake's thick brows arch in unspoken challenge to the other man.

If Ned pushed him, Harriett wondered, would Jake use his gun? He was a gunman, after all, proclaimed so by his own words. She gathered from his stance that he wasn't about to give way, and young Ned White, his face flushed with anger and his lips twisted in scorn, didn't appear ready to back down either.

"Get out of our way, you two-bit Indian-loving gunslinger, or we'll ride right over you." Ned looked to Phineas Carter for support. The scout hawked and spat a stream of tobacco-stained spittle. "I will!" Ned assured Jake.

Jake merely smiled. "Then do it, boy."

Harriett almost stepped forward, but Sadie and Lucille each grabbed an arm. "Jake's going to get hurt!" she protested.

"Don't worry, Miss Foster." Horace Smith stood calmly beside her and watched.

"You could at least help," she said sharply.

"Jake don't need no help. That young pup White's the one who needs help."

Ned White squirmed in his saddle, looking uncertain about what to do. Then someone behind him laughed, and that set the spark to his fuse. "God damn you!" he exploded, and kicked his horse forward, straight toward Jake.

With a quickness that amazed Harriett, Jake stepped aside, reached up, and snatched Ned from his saddle. The horse galloped off without a rider, and Ned dangled ignominiously from Jake's strong hands.

"Put me down, you son of a bitch!"

"Gladly!" Jake tossed his flailing burden in a neat arc that landed him, rump first, into a fresh, aromatic pile of mule droppings. "I don't need a gun to handle the likes of you, kid. If you want to chase Indians and get yourself killed—fine! Just wait until other people aren't going to suffer from your stupidity."

With a final warning glare at Phineas Carter, who blandly sat enjoying his chaw, Jake turned his back on Ned White and walked off. Harriett gasped as Ned's hand moved toward his gun, but Jake didn't hesitate. He merely looked her way and lowered one eyelid in a brazen wink. Ned thought better of his action and instead used his hand to wipe away the green-brown goo that had splashed onto his face.

"Jake knew he didn't have the guts to draw," Hobby told her in a confidential voice. "And even if Ned had gone for his gun, Jake would have blown him off the face of the earth. Would've served him right."

Harriett gave the boy a quelling look.

"Well, it would've!" he insisted.

Harriett wondered, not for the first time, what kind of a man she had hired so impulsively to take her across the continent. She had wanted a mere token as passport into the wagon company, but her token was turning out to be man after all—or was he a monster? What normal man would stand up to an infuriated Ned White mounted on a battering ram of horseflesh? Harriett still shuddered when she remembered the incident.

"Are you cold?" Lucille sat beside her by their cookfire, which had now burned down to mere embers. "We could put more wood on the fire."

"No. Our firewood supply is short enough as it is. I was just thinking about the incident two days ago between Mr. White and Mr. Carradine."

Lucille gave her a shrewd look. "Mr. Carradine is not quite the scoundrel you thought he was, is he?"

"No," Harriett admitted. "I may have partially mistaken his character."

Jake Carradine had been entirely too much on Harriett's mind the last few days. Her conscience—and her pride—still stung from his highhanded scolding at Cove Spring, but the sting didn't keep her wandering thoughts from dwelling on how he had looked as he had emerged, in natural animal glory, from the pond. And now this. . . . She supposed human nature was never as simple as one thought. The man certainly was a mess to any civilized way of thinking, but he seemed to have his strengths as well—strengths of character as well as strengths of the more obvious physical sort. And irritating as he could be, she liked him far better than she had ever believed possible.

She liked him far better than she ought, the voice of her conscience whispered.

What a silly thought! She tolerated him, that was all. She pitied him, as any good Christian would pity a man whose good qualities were buried beneath a burden of vice. She had a responsibility to him. After all, she was the one who had dragged him on this journey.

"Mr. Carradine is a bit of an enigma," Harriett admitted to her aunt. "I believe he could be a far better man than he is, with a little help."

"And of course you are just the one to show him the way," Lucille added with a smile.

"We, Aunt. Not me. The man seems to have a wealth of God-given intelligence, leadership, and courage that he is wasting for some reason or another. Perhaps he merely needs a discreet push to get him back on the right road."

"My love, you and your mother—God be kind to her soul—never learned the meaning of the word *discreet*."

"Fiddle!"

"But perhaps discretion is not required with a man like Mr. Carradine." Lucille had an impish sparkle in her eyes that made Harriett wary. "I think perhaps you both may benefit from your efforts on his behalf."

"Aunt Lucille, I hear a bit of doubt in your voice."

Lucille smiled beatifically. "Not at all, Harriett dear. I look forward to seeing, between you and your Mr. Carradine, just who will manage to reform whom."

6

Two days after the Indiana Company reached the Platte, Harriett ran out of firewood. Phineas Carter was right; for miles ahead and miles behind them stretched only prairie—grass and dust and rock beneath a wide, burning blue sky. All the way from Independence, Harriett had longed for a dry road, but now she found that dust had very little to recommend it over mud. Shade was a thing of the past; not even the side streams that flowed into the Platte supported trees. No trees, no shade, no relief from the sun, which, as true summer approached, became oppressively hot. But more important—no trees meant no wood for a cookfire.

Their third morning on the Platte, Jake joined Harriett and Lucille for breakfast, something he did, Harriett suspected, only when he couldn't find a place at another fire. On this morning he smelled faintly of liquor, and his eyes were more red than gray, though his step was firm and his hand seemed steady when he took the coffee Harriett offered. She noted with mixed feelings the way he flinched at the light of the rising sun and took only cautious swallows of his coffee, ham, and fried bread. The wastrel deserved a pounding head and roiling stomach, she decided. But she couldn't help wondering what drove a man like Jake Carradine—a man with qualities of courage, wit, and phenomenal strength—into destroying himself in such a way.

"Any more coffee?" he asked.

"I'm afraid not," Harriett answered. "We had only enough wood for a very small fire this morning. I hope we come across some wood soon so we can replenish our supply."

Jake chuckled, then flinched. "Harry, there's not a stick of wood between here and Fort Laramie. If you don't want to be eating cold beans and raw meat for the next month, you'd better get yourself a sack and collect some—" He stopped when he saw the distress on Harriett's face. "Didn't your precious little guidebook tell you that the only fuel around these parts is buffalo shit?"

"Dung, Mr. Carradine," Lucille corrected. "Buffalo dung."

He grinned. "It smells the same."

Harriett stared at him, unbelieving. "Mr. Ware did write something about using . . . buffalo leavings . . . as fuel. But I thought he was joking. You can't really mean that . . . that we must burn. . . ."

"Dung," Jake confirmed. He rose gingerly from where he squatted before the meager fire. "Fetch a sack, Harry, and I'll show you where the best pickings are."

Harriett reluctantly climbed in the wagon for an empty flour sack, and Jake met Lucille's amused smile. "What a world this is," he said with a wry grin. "A man hires out as a top gunhand, and he ends up collecting shit."

Buffalo dung, Harriett discovered, was more than plentiful a short distance from camp. All one had to do was look down through the tall prairie grasses to spy the platter-sized offerings the shaggy plains beasts had left behind. The trick was working up the courage to pick up the dried brown mess and put it in one's sack.

"It doesn't really stink, Harry." Jake stood and watched her, his eyes glinting despite their redness, his arms folded across his broad chest in a pose of casual amusement. She looked down at a pile that surely must have come from one of the largest beasts on the plains. Her lips compressed in distaste.

"I should have thought to wear gloves," she said with a sigh. "Really, Mr. Carradine"—she cut him a suspicious glance—"are you positive this isn't a joke?"

"Burns better than wood," he assured her. "Hotter, and without as much smoke. By the time we leave the plains you'll wish you could take a ton of the stuff with you."

She seriously doubted that. Gingerly she bent down and reached for the offending brown mass.

"But make sure it's dry," he warned with a chuckle.

Harriett jerked her hand away. She straightened and glared. The man seemed to delight in provoking her. "Since you're so knowledgeable on this subject, Mr. Carradine, I'll let you do the collecting. After all, I did hire you to help with the chores." She thrust the flour sack his way.

"No ma'am!" he denied with a broad grin. "I warned you in Independence that my gun was the only part of me for hire. The part of me that picks up shit" —he waggled his hand—"is still my own."

"Well, I haven't seen you use that gun of yours," she retorted, hands on hips, "but you've used those un-hired hands readily enough to repair axles and harness oxen."

"Out of the generosity of my heart," he told her.

"Fiddle! I don't think you have a heart, Mr. Carradine." She smiled as she delivered the accusation. The man was certainly an irresponsible scoundrel, but becoming really angry with a man who smiled with his eyes as well as his mouth was hard indeed. "Well," she conceded with a sigh, "I did say I'd make it on my own." She bent down, grimaced, gingerly picked up the buffalo chip between thumb and forefinger, and dropped it in the sack.

The task got less distasteful with familiarity. Jake was right, the dried dung was not that offensive. "Just grass that's been put through a mill . . . of sorts," he commented. After scoring his point, he did help her. They didn't have all day, he told her, and with Harriett's cautious prodding of each pile before she picked it up, the wagons were going to be five miles down the trail before they returned to camp.

The large flour sack was almost full when Jake stopped in midreach and straightened abruptly. "Don't move, Harry."

His voice held a strange note. Harriett straightened and looked over to where he stood. His pistol was in his hand, and his eyes had gone cold as steel. Her heart lurched as she stared directly down the muzzle of what looked to her one of the largest pistols ever made. Was he mad? Had the liquor loosed a monster in his brain?

Then she heard it—a buzzing from the grass at her feet. She'd never heard such a sound before, but some instinct told her what it was. A rattlesnake, poised to strike. Her breath caught in her chest. Cautiously, she started to retreat.

"I said don't move!"

Her reply was a frightened squeak, which was drowned out by the report of his gun. She jumped back, tripped, and fell. As her backside connected with the ground she saw the snake, still alive, close—too close. Jake had missed.

The pistol roared again, and still again. The snake flew through the air, minus a head, its body shredded.

As the smoke cleared, Jake shook his head incredulously.

"I missed." He sounded as if he didn't believe it.

Harriett tried to say something, but she choked as she inhaled the acrid gunsmoke.

"I missed," he said again.

The snake was dead—that was all Harriett cared about. "You hit it," she finally managed to say. "I've never seen such shooting."

He offered her a hand up. "I missed the first shot," he said gruffly. "It could have struck you."

"It didn't," she reasoned. Why did his face appear so bleak?

Harriett shook the dust from her skirt. Her heart still pounded, her ears still rang from the assault of raw gunfire. They walked back to camp, the sack of buffalo chips slung over Jake's broad shoulder. His eyes were almost black with anger—with her? with himself? Harriett couldn't guess. On the way back to the wagons he said not a word.

The next morning Jake joined them for breakfast again. He was at the wagon, building a fire and putting the coffee on to boil, before Harriett was dressed and out of the tent.

"Good morning." Harriett measured out flour for biscuits and dumped it into a tin bowl.

"Morning," he answered—the first words he'd spoken to her since the snake incident the morning before.

She handed him a clean mug for coffee, blinked, and took a second look. For the first time since she'd met him Jake's cheeks were scraped clean of ragged whiskers. The thick mustache decorating his upper lip was trimmed and neat, and his sunstreaked brown hair, which the day before had hung raggedly to his shoulders, was shorn to where it just touched the collar of his buckskins. The buckskins themselves looked clean.

Amazing! Harriett hadn't known he even carried a

change of clothes. And did her nose detect a faint whiff of soap instead of the usual hint of liquor? She raised one brow in wonder.

Jake ignored the subtle inquiry, and the closed, black look in his eyes did not invite more direct questioning. He quickly downed a cup of coffee along with a plate of beans and salt pork left over from the previous night's dinner; then he disappeared.

Harriett resisted following until the faint sound of gunfire reached her ears. The sun was not yet risen; most of the company, including Lucille, was still asleep. The biscuits were mixed, and the rest of the chores could wait. Harriett set the coffeepot where it would not boil over, grabbed a shawl against the chill of the morning, and set out to pursue the source of the gunshots.

Ten minutes of walking placed her at the head of a little draw that sloped down to the banks of the Platte. By that time the sun was inching above the horizon, painting crimson streamers on the muddy river. Jake Carradine faced away from the sunrise. Gunsmoke hung around him in a gray-black pall. Some distance up the draw, shards of glass littered the grass, glittering in the ruddy morning light. And lined up in a neat row, six more bottles—whiskey bottles, Harriett noted with wry satisfaction—awaited their destruction.

Jake drew. His movement was relaxed and fluid, but the fastest Harriett had ever seen a man move. Six shots exploded in quick succession, and six bottles burst into splinters. With much-rehearsed deftness, Jake ejected the pistol's empty cylinder and pushed a loaded one into its place.

Harriett released a pent-up breath, scarcely aware that she'd been holding it. Jake whirled, pistol raised, left hand poised above the hammer and ready to send lead flying her way. She squeaked in alarm.

"Goddammit! Harry!" The tautness left his body. "Don't you know not to sneak up on a man with a gun in his hand?" He tossed the pistol from one hand to the other, then back again, spun it once on his finger, and twirled it neatly into the holster tied to his thigh.

"My experience with gunmen is limited, Mr. Carradine."

"Well, don't do it again!" he warned.

Recollection of an earlier conversation flashed briefly across Harriett's mind. Jake had told her that men assessed other men by the set of their pistol holsters. His was tied down firmly to his thigh, the leather oiled and supple so the gun would slip out without catching—the mark of a professional gunman. Jake had claimed the title all along. But until that moment, when she saw his devilish proficiency with the weapon, the meaning hadn't sunk into her brain. The idea angered her—that when he wasn't destroying himself by drinking and gambling, he was practicing to destroy life itself. Today he shattered bottles with his keen eye and quick hand. But Harriett had no illusions about the real purpose behind such skill.

She watched with a jaundiced eye while he set six more bottles in a row. "Now I understand the reason behind your emptying all those bottles," she said in an acid voice.

As usual, the sound of her irritation inspired Jake's grin. "Learned a hard lesson yesterday," he told her. "Thought I was the exception, that liquor and laziness weren't going to dull my edge. That snake taught me I was wrong."

"I'd be the first to applaud your reform, Mr. Carradine. But can't you imagine a better employment of your time and skill than . . . than that?" She gestured toward the pistol tied to his leg.

He drew the gun and ran his hand fondly over the long barrel. For some obscure reason the action made

Harriett blush. "Harry," he said patiently, "for a man like me, there's nothing more important than being good with a gun. This pistol's the only thing that stands between me and starvation, and many a time it's been the only thing between me and death." He snugged the pistol back into its holster and looked down at her, one brow cocked at a devilish slant. "Having a good gun hand is more important than having a good woman."

She refused to be baited. His last line had been meant solely to provoke her, Harriett was sure. He seemed to enjoy making her angry, and she wouldn't give him that satisfaction.

She gave him what she hoped was a tolerant look and took a seat on a flat outcropping of rock. "You talk as if being a drifter and a gunman is the only thing you can do."

"Maybe it is." His voice had a dark edge that she refused to let intimidate her.

"All of us are given certain gifts, Mr. Carradine. Some more than others. It seems a shameful waste for a man like you to spend your talent and strength in such a way."

She saw a muscle twitch in his jaw, then he shook his head and smiled. "Feel another lecture coming on, do you? Harry, if you'd lay off the preaching and stick to what you oughta be doing, you'd be a right attractive female. It seems a shameful waste for a pretty woman like you to waste your gifts in being a pest."

Harriett didn't appreciate having her own words thrown back into her face, especially by a self-confessed scoundrel. "What ought I to be doing, Mr. Carradine? I suppose in all your educated wisdom you believe that woman's appropriate sphere is wherever she serves the pleasure but does not interfere with the absolute power of a man."

"I don't know about that," Jake said amiably. He turned toward his targets, drew—faster than Harriett could follow—but didn't fire. "What I think," he concluded, once more holstering his weapon, "is that you are a damned busybody who's likely to drive your poor husband to an early grave."

"And what I think—"

"Ever handled a pistol?" he asked abruptly.

Cut off in the middle of losing her temper, Harriett sputtered.

"I didn't think so. Might need a gun sometime on this trip. You told me to buy you one in Independence, remember? Come over here and I'll give you your first lesson."

"You . . . you can't change the subject in the middle of an argument, Mr. Carradine."

"I've learned that arguing with a woman is useless, Harry. When I fight, I fight for real—with this." He unholstered his pistol. "Now come here and get acquainted with this thing, and quit being so ornery."

His disrespectful manner put her off, but the idea of knowing how to defend herself without reliance on a man was tempting. "I'm not being ornery, Mr. Carradine. I'm merely . . ."

He raised a brow and cocked his head.

"Oh, all right." She took the offered pistol as warily as if it were a stick of dynamite with a burning fuse. "How do you aim this thing?"

Jake hastened to step aside as she swung the muzzle in his direction. "Hold it!" He clamped her wrist with his hand. "Don't go pointing a pistol at something you don't aim to kill."

She smiled impishly at him.

"A pistol is not something to fool with, Harry."

"Now who's preaching?"

"Thought you claimed you weren't ornery."

"I thought you were going to teach me how to shoot this thing."

He sighed. "All right. First things first. This is a sin-

gle-action Navy model .44. It fires a .44-caliber lead
ball . . ."

"And weighs a ton! How do you hold it steady?"

"My arm is stronger than yours. The pistol I bought
for you is smaller."

He ejected the loaded six-shot cylinder, then showed
her how to pour powder and shot into the chambers of
an empty cylinder and tamp down the loaded chambers with the ramrod. Extra cylinders, loaded and
ready to fire, he carried on a wide belt—a bandolier
slung crosswise over shoulder and chest. She'd never
seen him wear the belt until now. It gave him a raffish
look—like the Mexican *bandidos* she'd seen in draw-
ings.

"All right," she said, having loaded the gun to his
satisfaction. "How do I aim this thing?"

"Don't aim," he told her. "Point. Pretend the barrel
is your finger." He demonstrated. His long forefinger
became a weapon. He pointed, fired; his arm jerked as
if a real pistol were in his hand. Harriett almost expected to see one of the bottles shatter.

"Point," she confirmed with a sigh. She raised the
pistol, using both hands. It wobbled. She pulled the
trigger; the gun belched fire and slammed back into
her hands with the power of a mule kick. Smoke blew
into her face and stung her eyes.

"Did I hit anything?" she asked, coughing.

"You dug a hole in the dirt about ten feet from the
nearest bottle." He didn't bother to suppress the
laughter in his voice.

She harrumphed. "I'd like to see how well you did
on your first try!"

"That was so long ago I don't even remember," he
said.

"Do tell."

On her next try he stood behind her, supporting her
arm and steadying her hand with his own. As he in-

structed her to squeeze the trigger instead of jerk it, his nearness brought most inappropriate images marching out of Harriett's memory—Jake Carradine, bronzed and lithe and built like a Greek god, rising from the pond at Cove Spring, muscles rolling beneath his skin with every move. Her next shot went as wild as the first.

"You're not concentrating," he told her.

How was she supposed to concentrate tucked up against him as she was, with his breath in her ear and the masculine scent of him—leather and soap and gunsmoke—in her nostrils? He had rolled up his sleeves, and his forearm touched hers as he tried to steady her aim, bare skin against bare skin. A shiver tingled down her spine, so shuddery that he must have felt it, close as they were. Perhaps he did, for his voice sounded strained when he told her to try again.

She pointed and squeezed. A bottle exploded, surely by accident. The pistol's recoil hurt her already bruised hand; she jerked back, by reflex, and came even more firmly up against the solid wall of his chest.

Like a cat landing on a hot stove, she jumped—and didn't go anywhere. The arm that had steadied her now held her prisoner.

"I don't think I want to do this anymore," she said in a breathless voice. Her heart pounded furiously, making the thunderous explosion of the pistol seem trivial in comparison. His arm eased its pressure, as if he had never meant to hold her. She turned, knowing she should escape, but some devil inside her was pumping wicked fire into her veins. When she dared to look up, she saw the same devil echoed in Jake's clear gray eyes.

"Hello, Harry," the devil said, speaking with Jake's voice. His hand pressed into the small of her back, pushing her closer. His body molded against hers, warm and disturbingly hard.

A sultry languor prevented her from backing away, took away the desire to try, even. Slowly, deliciously, his mouth descended toward hers. His shoulders blocked out the rising sun. Harriett closed her eyes. She could feel his warm breath tickle her lips.

"Miss Foster! Miss Foster!" The voice was faint and came from behind the concealing bluffs, but it was enough to dash cold water on the devil's fire. She opened her eyes wide, looked at Jake in sudden panic, and jerked back. His arms didn't block her escape, but his eyes, dark now with something that Harriett found suddenly frightening, challenged her to stay.

"Miss Foster!"

"Over here!" she shouted, dragging her eyes away from Jake's. She recognized the voice now—Chad MacBride. "Chad?"

The boy came running over the bluff. Harriett heard Jake release his breath in a long, shuddering sigh. She didn't want to think about what might have come to pass had the youngster not interrupted them. What was happening to her, that she would allow herself to succumb to such inappropriate urges?

"Ma said you'd probably be out takin' a walk," Chad said. He looked at the pistol in Jake's hand, then at the row of bottles. "Gee! Are you target shootin', Mr. Carradine?" His voice was wistful.

"I was teaching Miss Foster how to shoot," he said with equanimity.

And trying to teach her a good deal more, Harriett added silently.

"Could you show me how to shoot? I mean, if it's not too much trouble? Uncle Todd was going to teach me, but he never gets the time. And now he's sick."

"I probably could do that," Jake told the boy. "But only if your ma says it's all right."

"Oh, yeah! She won't mind! Honest!"

"Chad?" Harriett reminded him. "Did your mother send you to find me?"

"Oh!" The boy sobered. "Yes'm. Uncle Todd took a turn for the worse last night. Ma says she could use your help for a bit this morning, if you don't mind."

"Of course I don't mind. You can take my place in the shooting lesson. I'm sure your mother wouldn't disapprove."

"Yes'm!" His face lit up.

She dared to meet Jake's eyes, where there still lurked the shadows that had almost consumed her. "Thank you for the lesson, Mr. Carradine." She lifted her chin and summoned her coolest, most self-possessed tone. "I'm sure I won't need another."

Gray eyes glinted, then crinkled as he grinned. "Never can tell. You may need to defend yourself someday."

She didn't doubt the meaning of his challenge. "I'm sure I'll be up to it." She met his gaze with a steadfastness much bolder than she felt. "Don't tarry long, you two. I'm sure we'll be getting under way soon."

The company did not get under way that day, however, for Todd Bryant, who had indeed taken a turn for the worse, was too sick to continue. Several others were also dangerously ill. The company voted to lay over the day and rest the stock. Lucille remarked cynically that the decision owed more to hunting fever than sympathy for the ill, for Phineas Carter had spotted a herd of buffalo not far from the river. Ned White was quick to organize a hunting party.

"That man is just itching to kill something," Sadie commented. "I suppose we should just be grateful that his target is animal instead of human this time."

"I'm afraid that some in the company don't agree with you," Harriett said. "They don't credit the Pawnee with being quite human."

"Poor Todd." Sadie touched a soothing hand to her

brother's brow. "He would have loved to ride on a buffalo hunt. He's always been a great one for hunting."

Harriett put her arm around her friend's waist. They were both concerned about Sadie's brother, who had seemed on the mend these last few days. The cholera could kill within hours, or a day, and usually did. Those who survived the crisis of the disease were generally spared, but now Todd had started the vomiting and bloody flux again, and both women knew there was little they could do to help.

"Ma?" Chad intruded quietly, but the anxious energy within the boy could hardly be contained. "Can I go on the hunt? Please? I'll stay out of the way and just watch. All right? Mr. Carradine's goin'. And Hobby is too."

"Chad . . ." Sadie raised a hand to her brow.

"I'll stay outta the way. Honest! I won't even get near the buffalo."

Sadie sighed. "All right. You can ride Dusty. He's so slow that you couldn't get into trouble if you wanted to."

"Thanks, Ma!"

Sadie shook her head as Chad fled. "The boy needs his father." She glanced at Harriett. "Would you like to take Todd's mare and ride up to watch the hunt, dear? I've a sidesaddle you could use."

"Oh, no, really. That's very generous of you, but . . ."

"I would feel better if you were there to keep an eye on Chad," Sadie urged.

"Don't you need help with Todd?" Harriett was half ashamed to admit her lack of skill in riding. Only two times in her life had she confronted a horse. Both times the horse had won.

"You've been such a dear to help," Sadie told her with a smile. "But I'd rather be alone with Todd now.

And Chad will be more likely to stay out of trouble if he knows you're there."

Harriett could find no polite way to say no, and Chad, though surprised Harriett was coming, helped her saddle Todd's mare Blaze—a big, rawboned chestnut that stood placidly while she climbed aboard. The hunting party had left a good ten minutes before, but following them was not difficult. A column of dust hung in the still morning air and clearly marked their trail.

"Gee! Would ya look at that!" Chad was awestruck by the sight that greeted them as they reined to a halt on the crest of a grassy swell. Hundreds of shaggy brown bodies were milling in agitation, churning dust from beneath their hooves. Harriett was struck by the awesome size of the beasts—and the awesome smell. Up until then, her only contact with the buffalo had been their dung.

The hunting party conferred among themselves not far away, and a good distance still from the herd. Harriett wondered if Ned White was having second thoughts about his prey. She certainly wouldn't want to ride in among those beasts!

"We should let the others know we're here. Now remember, Chad, you're to stay well away from the buffalo. We're only here to watch."

"Yes'm."

Jake looked displeased to see them when they joined the little group.

"We'll stay out of the way," Harriett assured him.

"See that you do," he ordered. "On that bluff over there."

"Aw! Can't we get closer?"

"Chad!" Harriett admonished. She saw a gleam of sympathy in Jake's eye and hoped he wouldn't give in to the boy's plea.

"You're not missing much, boy. Those yahoos will be

lucky to bring down one buffalo. Next time we come across a herd, we'll go out, just you and me, and I'll show you how to sneak up on the critters without getting 'em riled.''

"Really?"

"And anything that's brought down today, I'll make sure you and Miss Foster get your fair share. After all, you're part of the hunt, aren't you?"

"Gee, thanks, Mr. Carradine!"

"Now get up on that bluff."

"Yessir!"

Harriett gave Jake a bemused look as he rode to join the others, who were moving toward the herd. If she didn't know the man for a scoundrel, sometimes she might be tempted to like him.

The bluff where Jake had ordered them would have provided an excellent view of the hunt had the dust not been so heavy from the stampeding herd.

"Do you think Mr. Carradine can really sneak up on a herd without them knowin' he's there?" Chad asked her.

"I've found that Mr. Carradine can do most anything he says he can do," Harriett admitted. And some things he hadn't warned her about, she added to herself.

"I can't see nothing!"

"Anything," Harriett corrected.

"Yeah. Anything. How 'bout if I just ride across to that bluff over there. I bet I could see then. All the dust's comin' this way."

"Mr. Carradine told us to stay here."

"But he didn't know they were going to run so far away!"

Indeed, the hunters had not been stealthy at all as they approached the herd, and the beasts—wary, perhaps, from other hunters who had stalked them— broke immediately into a frenzied run. A gunshot or two sounded, and Harriett could see the flash of firing through the dust, but no animals fell, as far as she could see. Apparently, killing buffalo was more difficult than Ned White had thought.

Harriett relented. "All right, Chad. You can ride across to the other bluff. But go directly there, and stay there." Surely the hunt was now too far away to be dangerous.

Harriett had not realized how fast a herd of panicked buffalo could turn. A leading animal fell to Ned White's rifle; the herd veered. Funneled up against the rise of a bluff, they reversed their direction. Chad was directly in the path of the maddened mass of animals.

"Chad! Watch out!"

Chad didn't need Harriett's shout to know he was in danger, for old Dusty had panicked the moment the herd turned their way. Harriett watched in helpless despair as the horse, usually so placid, jerked and bucked when Chad tried to urge it back toward safety. Chad went flying; Dusty fled; and the buffalo herd came on.

Harriett was ready to ride to the rescue herself, heedless of her chances, when another rider broke from the herd and galloped full out toward the downed boy. Harriett recognized Jake's sorrel gelding. Chad stood and had the presence of mind to hold out his arm for Jake to grab. Harriett gasped in relief as Jake reached down, caught the boy by the arm, and swung him up behind the saddle. The sorrel stretched his legs in a run that left the charging buffalo well behind.

Five minutes later Jake lowered a dust-covered Chad to the ground beside Harriett's mare. Tears streaked the dust on the boy's face, and Harriett suspected that her own face looked very similar. She clambered awkwardly down from her horse and hugged the boy to her, her heart still pounding.

"Next time, when I tell you to stay put, you stay!"

"It was my fault," Harriett began, but Jake quelled her with a look.

"The boy's old enough to take responsibility for himself."

Responsibility—such words from Jake Carradine, the self-proclaimed scoundrel? A scoundrel willing to risk his life to save a boy's. Every time she turned around, the man surprised her.

Fresh tears spilled over onto Chad's dusty cheeks. He pulled away from her. For the first time Harriett noticed the dark stain on his trousers.

"Chad. . . . Are you hurt?" she asked gently.

He ducked his head, refusing to meet her eyes. "I . . . I. . . ."

"He peed in his pants," Jake supplied. His eyes crinkled in an amusement he was trying hard not to show. "Chad, boy. If a herd like that had been charging down on me, you can be sure my boots would've filled with a sight more than just pee."

The boy choked, a sound somewhere between distress and mirth.

"Now climb up in back of Miss Foster's saddle and we'll head home. Old Thunder here doesn't take much to carrying two riders. We're lucky he didn't dump us both down there."

A faint grin peeked through Chad's tears. Harriett suspected that Jake had won a friend.

The ride back to camp seemed longer than the ride out, with Jake watching Harriett's awkward horsemanship with an amused glint in his eye. Chad recovered his spirit on the way.

"Do the Indians hunt buffalo with bows and arrows?" he asked Jake.

"Arrows, spears—rifles when they can get them. But they're better at it than most white men. And they use every part of the animal. They don't kill it just for sport." He slanted a look at Harriett. "The men of the tribe do the easy part—they bring down enough animals to provide meat and hides for all their village. Then the women come, butcher the carcasses, and carry the meat and hides to the village on their backs."

Harriett sniffed. He was trying to provoke her again. "At least the Indian men don't think their women too delicate to play a practical role in life."

"No, ma'am!" Jake returned with a grin. "That they don't! Maybe you ought to try your women's equality on some of the Pawnee braves around here."

"Thank you, but I'll stick to haranguing civilized men." Her tone implied that he was only marginally included in that category.

Once they were back at the wagons and Chad rushed off to tell of his adventure, all the bantering left Harriett's voice. "That was an extremely brave and unselfish thing you did out there," she told Jake.

Jake stripped the saddle from her horse, then started on his own mount. "Don't give credit where it's not due, Harry. I knew I could get there before the herd did."

She didn't press the point. "You have a rare skill with children, Mr. Carradine." Harriett was determined he should recognize some merit in himself. "Do you have many younger brothers and sisters?"

"Not a one." He slung both saddles over a shoulder. "Not anymore." His eyes had become suddenly shuttered, his mouth a tight line in his face. Without another word he turned and led the horses away.

Harriett watched him go, wondering what she had said wrong.

7

Todd Bryant did not die that day, though two others lost the fight to cholera and gave up the ghost. One of the two was Caleb Taylor, who had seemed hale and hearty when Harriett and Chad had left that morning to follow the hunt. When they returned five hours later poor Caleb was suffering paroxysms of vomiting and diarrhea, and by sundown he was dead. He was buried with the day's other victim—a slender young farm lad whom Harriett had seen only in passing. The two graves were blessed perfunctorily by Mr. Hawkesbury, a minister of the Methodist faith who had been busy performing similar services for other wagon companies traveling in their vicinity. The Indiana Company of Adventurers had so far gotten off lightly, the minister remarked—small comfort to those whose journey ended so prematurely and so miserably. Small comfort to Todd Bryant, who lay with his face pinched and blue, his hands puckered and cold to Harriett's touch.

"They're waiting for Todd to die," Sadie said. She and Harriett were trying to chafe some warmth back into their patient's hands. "All they care about is going on, getting farther up the damned trail, closer to their damned gold."

Sadie's declaration ended in a sob. Harriett moved

to her side and embraced the weeping woman, rocking her back and forth as though she were a frightened child. Such words from gentle Sadie's lips! Harriett guessed her friend was close to despair.

"He's going to die!" Sadie cried, sniffling into Harriett's shoulder. "It's not fair! He's always been good, and kind, and generous. He didn't say a word of reproach when Chad and I showed up at his doorstep with nothing but our hungry bellies and the promise of still another little mouth to feed. It's not fair that he should die this way!"

She pulled away from Harriett's comforting embrace and wiped at her eyes. "I'm sorry, dear. I shouldn't . . . I shouldn't be falling apart this way. Not now." Despair was still in her eyes. "Poor Todd." She picked up her brother's hand and once again tried to rub some life back into the cold, dehydrated flesh. "He'll not live, and even I find myself waiting for it to be over. If he's still alive in the morning the company won't wait any longer. They'll leave us to make our own way. Mr. Deere said as much to me this afternoon. I don't know what I shall do, Harriett."

"Mr. Carradine would never let the company do such a thing, Sadie." Where did she get such faith in Jake Carradine? Harriett wondered. When had she started to regard the man—often a wicked scoundrel himself—as a bulwark against even greater wickedness?

"Jake can't prevail against them all," Sadie said with a hopeless sigh. "They care for nothing but gold, Harriett. So many people die along this trail that loss of life becomes nothing but an inconvenience to those who still live. If I refuse to move Todd and cause him even more discomfort in his last hours, they will leave us here alone to deal with his death. And if Chad and I die with him, they'll think nothing of it."

"You won't be left alone, Sadie," Harriett assured

her. "Lucille and I will stay with you. And Mr. Carradine also."

Sadie shook her head. "Dear, brave friend. I would
never ask it."

Harriett smiled. "You wouldn't have to ask. Now,
suppose you try to sleep. We are neither of us doing
Todd any good by standing here moaning."

"Knock, knock, ladies. Are you there?"

Harriett and Sadie exchanged a grimace. Dr. Fellows.

"Come in," Sadie responded.

Dr. Fellows was a thin, long-faced man with lank
sandy hair that drooped to his shoulders and made his
face seem even longer than it was. As he ducked into
the tent, he brought the odors of whiskey and tobacco
with him. "And how is your brother, Mrs. MacBride?"

"He stays the same," Sadie told him.

"Ah," the physician commented, the sound neutral.
But Harriett sensed disappointment in his face. He,
too, was waiting for Todd to die so the company could
bury him and get an early start on the trail come
morning. "Let us see, here." He felt for Todd's pulse,
then pried open one of the poor man's eyes, nodded,
and muttered a few Latin words. "He still has the
bloody flux?" he asked Sadie.

"Just a bit," she answered. "Mostly now he just has
. . . spasms."

"Ah." He shook his head, and his dour face grew
even more dour. "Perhaps we should bleed the patient."

"Indeed not!" Harriett denied. "The poor man is
shriveled from loss of fluid, and you propose to take
more?"

Dr. Fellows regarded her down the line of his long,
beaklike nose. "Miss Foster. And where, pray tell, did
you receive your medical training?"

"In the school of common sense!" she snapped.

"Something of which you and your colleagues have very little understanding." She took the doctor by the arm and, ignoring his indignant snorts, escorted him from the tent.

"I suggest, young woman, that you confine yourself to areas where you have some knowledge! It is understandable that you have little comprehension of medicine; the female mind is scarcely fit to embrace such learning, but—"

"Dr. Fellows," Harriett interrupted, mustering every bit of patience in her soul. "Something we both understand is that Mr. Bryant is dying. Suppose we let him die in peace, with what comfort he can find in the attendance of his sister."

Dr. Fellows huffed and straightened the lapels of his black jacket. "I doubt he can be helped in any case. Good evening, Miss Foster!"

"Good evening, Doctor."

Sadie peered cautiously out from the tent. "Is that dreadful man gone?"

"He's gone, dear. And not likely to return."

"Oh, I wish I had your daring, Harriett." Sadie came out and stood beside her.

"And I wish I had your courage." Harriett longed for words to comfort her friend. But what comfort existed for a pregnant woman left with only an eleven-year-old boy to help her over two thousand miles of hardship? And who knew if she could find her husband at the end of her trip? If she couldn't, what would become of her—poor, brave lady. The world had no place for a woman apart from her husband.

An hour later, with Sadie and Todd both asleep, Harriett went back to her own wagon. The night was peaceful and warm, the numerous plains thunderstorms having spared them for this day, at least. Crickets sang in the prairie grass, and somewhere out in the darkness wolves serenaded the almost full moon. It was a good night to die, Harriett decided, a night when God seemed at peace with His earth. Then she wondered at her own morbid thoughts.

The cookfire by the wagon was still burning, a reminder that she'd forgotten all about eating dinner. The strain of the morning's adventure and the hours spent sitting with Sadie and Todd had robbed her of appetite.

"You look done in."

She started at Jake's voice. He was sitting in the shadows, Hobby's guitar on his lap. The firelight flickered and played on his face, darkly emphasizing the lines that creased his brow and etched his cheeks. Now that he had trimmed his mustache, Harriett could see that twin grooves ran from deep dimples in his cheeks down to his jaw, especially when he smiled, as he was smiling just then. A very faint smile. He looked fairly "done in" himself.

"Mr. Carradine." She sat, back propped against the wagon wheel, not bothering to pull up a stool. "We hardly ever see you for dinner anymore. I'm sorry I wasn't here to prepare you a meal."

"Mrs. Stanwick fixed me something," he told her.

"Where is my aunt?"

"I believe she and Lawrence Steede are . . . taking the air."

Harriett sighed. Lawrence Steede again, hovering like a vulture to peck at her aunt's loneliness. Why couldn't Lucille see the man for what he was? She was mature and intelligent, and, if Harriett's mother had often accused Lucille Stanwick of being "flighty" and unconventional, Harriett had always preferred to think of her aunt as fun-loving. More than once Lucille had set Boston tongues wagging with her defiance of the idea that a married lady should be sober and restrained. Harriett certainly wished her aunt would be more restrained when it came to Mr. Lawrence

Steede. She was setting herself up to be hurt by a man who, like most other men, regarded women as little more than a pleasant pastime.

Silence settled around the campfire, broken only by faint night sounds and Jake's idle plucking of the guitar. Softly he hummed the tune his fingers picked on the strings. The melody was a sad one, appropriate to Harriett's mood.

"You haven't asked about Mr. Bryant," she commented.

The humming stopped, and the guitar continued alone. "No need to ask," he said.

She sighed. "You don't care either, do you?"

He continued to play, unruffled. "Everybody dies sooner or later, Miss Foster. Some die sooner—young men, young women, children. Who's to say they aren't the lucky ones?"

"You aren't afraid to die, Mr. Carradine?"

"No."

The one terse word conveyed a volume of emotion. What had Amos Walking Horse said about Jake's trying to destroy himself with liquor and dangerous living? Had he meant that statement literally?

Jake started humming again. His voice was deep and resonant, with dark qualities that reached out to a person's very soul. She was fortunate, Harriett reflected, to be a sensible and mature woman—else she might be swept away by that voice, or the man himself, reprobate that he was.

She leaned her head back against the wheel spokes, closed her eyes, and let weariness overtake her. Why did nothing in life ever go right? She thought of her parents—people worthy of long lives and happiness, surely. And yet her father's gentle charm and acute intelligence had been snuffed; her mother's zeal for reform and diligence on behalf of society's victims had been brought to dust—all because of a senseless carriage accident on an icy road. Todd Bryant, a gentle, giving man, teetered on the edge of death, downed by a senseless, ugly disease that had no regard for human virtue or worthiness. Before this fearful odyssey was over, how many in tonight's camp would follow Todd to the other world? Caleb Taylor had been well in the morning and dead by nightfall, and so had Sara, the frail, mousy "entertainer" who had defended Harriett so many days ago in the honey wagon. Sara had died a few days before, almost before anyone realized she was ill.

Sickness was not the only predator. Chad MacBride, just beginning his life, almost had it trampled to dust that morning in the blink of an eye. Could any of them be certain when life would be snatched away by some cruel and senseless twist of fate?

As depression settled more closely around her, Harriett told herself that it was merely weariness painting her mind so black, but another part of her said she'd led a sheltered life and only now was coming to face the realities of existence. Her causes, her indignant challenges to the injustices of society, seemed insignificant now that she had met the injustices of the universe itself. For a moment she felt as though she were hanging on to her own life, her own self, by a mere fragile thread.

Why did others not see the precariousness of existence? What crime, she reflected, to take the precious, fragile gift of life and waste it. Lawrence Steede—a man of charm, intelligence, and sophistication—spent his life gambling and preying on innocent women like poor Lucille. Lucille—youthful and attractive still—risking her happiness on a scoundrel like Steede, a quick cure for the ache of loneliness. And Jake Carradine. Jake—blessed with a quick mind and strong body, a magnetic charm that led others to give him their trust, and a smile that could melt the ice of a

Boston winter, yet he made of himself a gunman, feeding on violence, drinking, gambling, wasting his wit and his smile on ladies of ill repute, and on women like Caroline MacKenzie.

Harriett's eyes flew open. Mercy! How her mind did ramble into nonsense! Anyone reading the path of her thoughts would think her jealous—jealous of Jake Carradine! The strain of the day and the darkness of night had certainly taken a toll on her sanity.

She looked over at the object of her musings. As if feeling the weight of her scrutiny, he raised his gaze from the strings he still plucked. The night shadows made his eyes more black than gray, or were those windows into a soul colored by thoughts that were as dark as hers? Harriett's mother had once told her that the line between saint and sinner, paragon and criminal, was very thin. Though more sinner than saint, Jake Carradine, strangely enough, was a mixture of both. She still believed a little encouragement, a little push in the right direction, might bump him onto the higher road.

"You look a bit tired yourself, Mr. Carradine," she began. "I hear you went back to the hunt and spent the afternoon showing Mr. White how to butcher the buffalo he shot."

"Um," he acknowledged. "A flank of that beast belongs to you and Mrs. MacBride. I showed your aunt how to salt down the meat and dry it in strips so it won't spoil."

"That was very kind of you."

He flashed her a sharp look. He didn't like the word *kind* applied to him, Harriett remembered. He'd told her once that kind was a label that stuck to a man and branded him a sucker for any Tom, Dick, or Harry who wanted to take advantage of him. She had replied that no one would be stupid enough to take advantage of a man like Jake Carradine. He had merely thrown a mocking grin her way. Tom, Dick, or Harry, he had said. A very specific Harry, his look had told her.

Harriett cleared her throat awkwardly. "My father was very interested in the dependence of the Indians on the buffalo. He speculated if enough people move west, they will force the herds of buffalo off the plains, and the Indians will be forced off with them. I can't imagine that many people emigrating, though, can you?"

"I thought your father was a banker," he said with considerable lack of interest.

"He was, but he was an intellectual with far-ranging interests." She proceeded hesitantly. "You've . . . never told me about your family, Mr. Carradine. Surely you have one."

His gaze grew steely. "Had. The word is *had*."

"Oh. I'm so sorry." Poor man. Without a family's support, no wonder that he had wandered into moral squalor. "What were they like—your family?"

His mouth twisted. "They worked hard—for nothing. They were innocents who played fair—and they got robbed. And they had a son who was supposed to be a tough guy, and he let them be murdered."

Jake rose abruptly, and a bit unsteadily. A half-empty bottle was in his hand—an item Harriett hadn't noticed before. The reprimand that automatically sprang to her lips died when he turned his eyes upon her. As he stalked away, he seemed to take the night shadows with him.

Harriett folded her knees to her chest and wrapped her arms around them. The campfire had suddenly lost its warmth. Jake Carradine had a devil riding on his shoulders, Harriett decided, and she would do well to stay away from him.

But her conscience wouldn't let her off so easily. Jake was in pain, it reminded her, and someone should be courageous enough to help him.

The voice of caution swelled in answer, warning her that one who comforts a wounded bear often gets clawed. Foolhardiness was not courage, and good intentions could lead to disaster.

Jake Carradine wasn't a bear, conscience argued, for all that he sometimes acted like one. Harriett bore a responsibility toward the man. She had forced this journey upon him, separated him from his only friend. And therefore she owed him the same support that Amos Walking Horse might give.

Harriett could almost see her conscience dusting off its imaginary hands and smiling smugly at a job well done. Caution withdrew in defeat. Whether or not he wanted it, Jake Carradine was going to get Harriett's help.

She didn't have to go far. The moment she rounded the wagon into the darkness outside the circle Harriett almost stumbled over him. She could scarcely see him —a dark shadow in an already black night. But she could feel the glare he sent her way, and hear the slosh of liquid as he raised the bottle to his lips.

"Mr. Carradine." She gathered her courage. "Can you not give up your bottle for more than a day? Do you really think to improve your lot by succumbing to the demon of spiritous liquor?"

A low growl came from his throat. Caution, peering from behind Harriett's conscience, reminded her about wounded bears.

"I do apologize," she continued, "for touching on subjects that apparently cause you pain. But you can't expect people to tiptoe around your private devils when they don't know what those devils are, can you? And whatever is bothering you, it's not an excuse for burying yourself in the depths of a bottle."

"Harry," he rasped. "Get the hell out of here."

"And leave you to drink yourself into a stupor? No,

Mr. Carradine, I will not. No person of good conscience would."

"Any person of sound mind would," he grumbled.

"I don't understand you, Mr. Carradine. I can understand Phineas Carter swilling spirits. That poor man doesn't have any resources he can call upon to resist temptation. In fact, fully half the men in this company are so lacking in the qualities that men covet for themselves that I can understand their resorting to the comforts of liquor. I can't approve, but I can understand.

"But you! You have wit and intelligence and strength and—in spite of yourself—a good and courageous heart. Yet when I first saw you I thought I was seeing the most useless, degraded man on the face of this earth. So far had you let yourself slip down the road of ruination!"

"Are you through?"

His voice was hard and cold as steel. Caution squeaked a warning, but Harriett ignored it. She was rolling now, her anger at the world finding a target in Jake Carradine.

"No! I am not through! You once told me you were a dangerous man, Mr. Carradine, but you're a danger only to yourself. I can't imagine why anyone would want to hire that gun hand of yours if the eyes behind it can't see straight. You proclaim yourself to be an animal, but I see only a sulking child—someone who's been given all the gifts he needs to make a lasting mark on this world of ours, but who squanders them in self-pity.

"You know what your behavior is, Mr. Carradine? It's the behavior of a coward. You're ready to risk your life to save a small boy, or face down a poisonous scoundrel like Ned White, or a venomous snake, but you can't face your own devils—whatever they are—without turning tail. Why can't you throw away that evil bottle and stand up like the strong man you really are? You owe that to yourself, to the God who made you, and the family that bequeathed to you all those good qualities that I see dissolving in whiskey."

Harriett folded her arms across her chest and nodded with finality. Silence became a palpable thing that swelled in the darkness. Caution quivered and hid in a corner of her mind and conscience gloated at a job well done.

The bottle sloshed again. Then Jake stood and wiped his hand across his mouth. "Lady. You're enough to turn even good whiskey sour." He tossed the bottle out into the night. It landed somewhere with a faint tinkle of shattered glass.

Harriett was about to congratulate him on his laudable decision when he turned toward her and the faint moonlight revealed the expression on his face. A wounded bear might look amiable in comparison.

He nailed her in place with his eyes. "Isn't there any way I can shut you up? You're worse than a damned preacher. At least a preacher only takes after a man on Sunday."

"Now, Mr. Carradine. I'm—"

"You're a busybody and a do-gooder and a goddamned pest! What right do you have to tell me what I am, or what I should be?"

With every word his anger grew, and caution was whimpering "I told you so" in Harriett's mind.

"What do you know of me, lady? Nothing! Hell! What do you know about life? About the world? Nothing! You've got your head so far into the clouds, you can't see the dirt you walk on."

She drew on all her courage. "This discussion isn't about me, Mr. Carradine."

"It's about anything I want it to be about!"

The words came out as a snarl, and Harriett took a step back. "I'm exactly what I want to be. Nothing more, nothing less. What are you, Harry?—besides a goddamned meddler.''

Harriett opened her mouth to defend herself, but no answer would come. His anger seemed to push against her, confuse her, cloud her thinking, and dull her wits.

''I choose to be what I am, dammit! I choose! A scoundrel, a villain, a rogue, a reprobate, an animal. I warned you what I was! You have no right to expect me to be something else!''

He turned and stalked into the night. Harriett stumbled after him, ignoring caution's screeched warnings. She couldn't leave this anger between them.

''Mr. Carradine!'' she called after him. ''Please, Mr. Carradine. Jake.'' He turned and waited for her— something dangerously deliberate in his action. She caught up with him in a shallow wash that ran down to the river. ''You don't mean that, Mr. Carradine. You're a better man than you know!''

''And you're more of a fool than I thought.''

''I simply—''

She was cut off by his snarl of rage. Before she realized what was happening, he had her by the shoulders. His fingers dug into her flesh, and she cried out in pain and indignation.

''Do I have to prove to you what kind of man I really am, you fool? Is this the only way to shut you up?''

He thrust her back against the wall of the gully and attacked her with his mouth. Sharp rocks dug into her back, but she scarcely felt them. His brutal assault on her senses left no room for ordinary pain.

Harriett didn't struggle; she was pinned much too tightly. Jake's lips ground against hers in hurting, primitive conquest. He ripped open the bodice of her dress and ran hard, callused hands over virgin flesh. Mercilessly, his tongue forced entrance to her mouth while his thigh thrust between her legs. Harriett spun down into a vortex of shame and fear.

"This is the kind of man I am, Harry." His voice, delivered on a gust of whiskey-scented breath, grated against her ear. He locked his hands into her hair, tore away the remnants of her sedate bun, and arched her head back so she was forced to look into his face. "Is this saying it in a way you won't forget?"

He kissed her again, this time a gentler attack. His thigh prodded her in rhythm with the thrusting of his tongue. Something dark and consuming clawed its way through her fear, warmed her blood, sped her heart, and speared strange, aching pain into regions of her body she had always strictly ignored. Helplessly, Harriett succumbed to the maelstrom that reached out to claim her. Her mouth opened wider against his; her thighs relaxed, spreading to the wicked, wonderful pressure of his leg.

Abruptly, he pushed her back. His hands grasped her upper arms in a bruising grip. "Little fool," he growled. "Innocent, ignorant, meddling fool." Blazing eyes stared grimly down at her and made Harriett's heart almost stop.

"Let me go!" she demanded in a voice not nearly as commanding as she wished.

He ignored her plea. "You don't know anything, do you? Anything at all!"

Harriett didn't, not really. But she was struck by a sudden, wicked desire to learn. The Devil himself had hold of her, surely, and had put his mark upon her soul.

"You do-gooders are always so damned innocent. Why don't you learn something about the world before you try to change it?"

Harriett's blood pounded. She could hear her own heartbeat in her head. Or was it his? He was going to kiss her again, she thought. His eyes were eating her alive.

But he didn't kiss her. He released her. Before she

could catch her breath, he was gone, the darkness enfolding him as if he were one of its own.

She stared after him, wanting to weep and laugh at the same time. Her body burned, trembled, tingled, and seemed to belong to another person entirely.

8

Harriett stared at the yellowing canvas above her. It moved, back and forth, up and down, shook, rustled, and flapped as the wagon jolted over the rough trail. The strip of sunlight that came through the back flap swayed and danced in time to the creaking of the wheels.

She should be able to sleep after a day like today—or was it yesterday? Yesterday had flowed into today with no break in between, and Harriett felt as though she were squeezed between darkness and dawn, chewed up and spit out by a world that had somehow gone awry. Somewhere in her mind lurked confusion, anger, and despair, but she felt them as from a great distance. Mostly she was numb. She craved sleep—sweet, black oblivion. But sleep wouldn't come. Her eyes stayed open as if propped that way; her mind whirled in ceaseless repetition around events she wanted to forget.

The night before, somehow Harriett had found her way back to the circle of wagons. She had felt as though she moved in some other woman's body; for surely she, Miss Harriett Foster, spinster, enlightened advocate of female intellect and equality, had not succumbed to the base desire that had reached out from

Jake Carradine's dark, vengeful passion and closed her in its grip. Surely not!

Back in camp, Harriett had pulled her clothing together, straightened her hair, gathered her shredded composure as best she could, and spent the rest of the long night sitting by Sadie's side. As the sun rose over the horizon Todd had breathed his last tortured breath. Harriett had murmured words of comfort when Sadie had clung to her in grief, but what words were adequate for a woman who had lost not only a beloved brother but her last protector?

Todd Bryant had been laid to rest with unseemly haste, in a grave dug the day before, by a preacher who was more interested in finding riches in this world than in the next. The dust had scarcely settled from the last shovelful of dirt on the grave before the company was once again on its way, faces turned once more toward California gold. Few gave a thought to comrades left behind in the ground. They were a fine lot, Harriett had thought—a physician who had abandoned his profession, a minister who had abandoned God, and the rest—farmers, clerks, smiths, storekeepers, gamblers, drifters. All seduced by their lust for gold.

And she herself was no better. As she had ushered Sadie from her brother's grave, Harriett tried to pray for Todd. But her mind was still filled with Jake Carradine and her own shame. She despised the Adventurers for being seduced by gold, but the night just past she herself had been seduced by something much more alluring than gold. She didn't attempt to fool herself by thinking her virtue would have won out in the end. Her virtue, Harriett had discovered, was a weak thing indeed.

Again Harriett shut her eyes, wooing sleep that wouldn't come. The wagon lurched, stopped, then lurched again. Lucille was driving. When Harriett had finally stumbled back to her own wagon, her aunt took one look at her haggard face and insisted she sleep. Lucille was an atrocious driver. Even on a straight, level trail she could get into trouble. Harriett hadn't cared. She'd spread her blankets between the boxes in the back of the wagon and had expected to escape into sleep within seconds of closing her eyes.

And here she was, still staring at the yellowing canvas that curved above the wagon bed, eyes open and mind awhirl. Perhaps she would never sleep again. Perhaps she would continue on awake, haunted by her own foolishness, until exhaustion killed her. And when she was laid in her cold grave, Jake Carradine would erect a marker that labeled her fool, busybody, meddler—and slut.

She was approaching delirium, Harriett decided. She closed her eyes and started counting backward from one hundred, a trick her mother had used to summon sleep. At sixty she flopped over and pulled the blankets over her head. By twenty she was finally asleep.

Jake was in her dreams, sitting by their cookfire, idly plucking at the strings of a guitar. He began to sing, and Harriett couldn't understand the words, but she could see his voice float through the air toward her. It wrapped around her, a sinuous snake of sound— wound around her waist and her arms, and curled between her legs, up inside her, and swelled into a symphony.

She was suddenly naked, and her nudity seemed the most natural thing in the world. Jake didn't notice, didn't even look at her. Others sat around the fire. They didn't look at her either. Caroline MacKenzie sat beside Jake, her head on his shoulder and her hand languorously stroking his thigh.

"You don't know anything, do you?" Caroline asked.

Jake got up to leave. He turned his back toward Harriett, and the symphony inside her fell silent.

"Where are you going?" she asked.

"I'm going away to join my family."

"You can't go," she insisted. "I hired you."

"The gun's for hire. Nothing else."

They were alone, and Harriett's back was pressed against the iron rim of the wheel. The sharp edge dug into her back, and she tried to squirm away, but Jake pressed her back.

"You don't know anything, do you?" he asked.

Harriett opened her eyes. She was soaked with sweat. Her heart pounded, and Jake's smiling, contemptuous face remained seared on her brain, even as other images of the dream faded. Where was she? How had the canopy on her bed gotten so dirty?

She struggled to push away the grogginess that clouded her mind. She wasn't in her bed in Boston; she was in a wagon, on her way to San Francisco and Edwin. Dear, sweet Edwin; safe, sane Edwin. Edwin would never accuse her of knowing nothing. He would never set her awash with such wicked feelings that she feared for her very sanity. He would never make her doubt herself, or the ideals that guided her life.

She sat up and started to pull on her high-topped button shoes. Suddenly she stopped, her fingers still hovering above the row of buttons. The person sitting on the wagon box in front was not Lucille. Harriett could see a broad back, wide shoulders, and a trousered backside that certainly did not belong to her aunt.

Harriett's hands shook so badly she could scarcely manage the buttons of her shoes. Jake Carradine was driving the wagon. How could she face him after last night? He'd called her a fool and done to her things that not even a husband would do to his wife. The strange feelings from her dream still enveloped her, even though the images had faded. He would look into her eyes and know what she'd conjured in her sleep. How could she face him?

The man on the box turned around. Harriett's heart lurched. Lawrence Steede was driving, not Jake Carradine. She was spared, temporarily at least.

"Feeling better, Miss Foster?" Steede inquired.

"Much," she lied. "Thank you. My aunt . . . ?"

"Is with Mrs. MacBride. Mrs. Stanwick was having difficulty with the team, so I offered to help out. And your aunt thought that Mrs. MacBride shouldn't be alone this morning."

"No. Of course not." Harriett finished fastening her shoes and climbed onto the box. The morning was a fine one, though the dust from the wagons ahead almost hid the blue sky. Mr. Steede's gray gelding and laden pack mule—his only accoutrements on this journey—were tied to the side of the wagon and followed placidly along.

"I can take the lines now," she offered.

"I don't mind helping out," he said with a winning smile. "You still look as though you need some rest, if you don't mind my saying so."

Steede's smile made him look young, and his silver-gray eyes were kind. Harriett began to understand why her aunt found him appealing. Perhaps Lucille was the wise one, and Harriett had made another misjudgment of character. Had she judged anything correctly? Harriett wondered.

Journal entry—June 1—approaching the forks of the Platte: Five days have passed since Todd Bryant's death, and Sadie MacBride hourly demonstrates her courage by forging ahead. The hardships of the trail and the discomforts of her condition do not deter her. She drives her mules, cares for her son, and masters all difficulties without a whimper. If men would only open their eyes to examples like Sadie, they would quickly discard their misconceptions about the weakness and incapacity of the female gender.

We plod steadily along the Platte, eating dust by day and being drenched by night. One would think the rains would settle the dust, but by the time we start on the trail, the morning sun has already dried the road. I remember the constant mud at the start of our odyssey and cannot decide which gives the most difficulty—mud or dust.

Our company is far from alone in its journey. Ahead of us and behind us is a long parade of other travelers, and sometimes a continuous line of wagons stretches as far as the eye can see. We can also see wagons traveling on the north side of the river, though they aren't so numerous as the travelers on the south.

Ours is a moderate-sized company with twenty-three wagons. Some are much larger—I had conversation two days ago with a lady traveling with a company of fifty wagons. And some parties travel alone, or with only two or three others. All seem to have only one thing in mind: gold.

Several times during the past week Dr. Fellows has been called to other parties to care for their sick. Our company has lost eight people in all, including Mr. Bryant, and two are currently ill. God grant that they recover!

All but two of the deaths were due to the cholera. Mr. Sattler, a gentleman of fairly advanced years, succumbed to an ailment of the lungs, and a young farmer by the name of Adam Bonny died of snakebite. I'm told that most adults survive the venom of a rattlesnake, but Mr. Bonny became dreadfully ill and died the very day he was bitten. The physician was able to do nothing for him. I narrowly missed a similar fate not too many days past, but my hired man shot the reptile before it could strike.

I do not see a great deal of Mr. Carradine these days.

Lawrence Steede spread his cards flat on the dirty square of canvas that served as a poker table. "Three tens," he declared with satisfaction.

Jake grimaced and folded his hand. "Two lousy pairs."

Four players sat cross-legged around the canvas square. Jake and Steede faced each other, as did Hobby and Horatio Smith.

"Your luck ain't on tonight," Hobby told Jake with a grin. "I never seen you lose so many hands."

"That's what you get for not keeping your mind on the game," Steede said. He picked up a bottle, took a drink, and gave it to Hobby. "Pass it around, boys."

Hobby coughed as the fiery liquid burned his gullet. "'Sgood!" he choked out. He handed the bottle to Jake.

"No thanks." Jake handed it to Horatio.

"My liquor not good enough for you?" Steede asked.

Jake grinned. "You're winning enough off me while I'm sober. I don't need to get drunk."

"Never bothered you before."

"Well, maybe it bothers me now," Jake shot back.

Steede looked up at him from beneath raised brows. "Something bothering you, friend?"

"Let it pass."

"Deal," Horatio ordered uneasily.

Steede shrugged. "Ante up. Five-card draw. Jacks wild."

Jake got a better hand this round—the king and queen of hearts, jack of clubs, ten of hearts, and deuce of spades. But as the betting went around, he had trouble concentrating on the game. The queen of hearts

stared at him from the dirty pasteboard. With her red
hair and primly pursed lips, she reminded him of
Harry. He discarded the deuce. Steede dealt him a
card in exchange—the ace of hearts. A royal flush—
almost a sure winner. The prospect of winning didn't
make him that happy.

He'd scarcely seen Harry since he'd attacked her.
Attacked—there really wasn't any other word for it.
Her image, however, had stuck with him like a burr.
He couldn't get rid of her, or the nagging guilt for
what he'd done to her.

The worst part of the whole incident was that Harry
had been right. He'd been dead drunk not a day after
swearing off liquor—dead drunk and feeling goddamned sorry for himself. She had dared to remind
him that once he'd been a better man, and Jake had
punished her for it. He had meant to shock her so that
she would never again goad him with her expectations
and rub his face in what he had become: a drunkard,
bastard, and coward. His vengeance backfired,
though. The kiss that began as an attack ended as passion. The feel of her tender flesh in his hands and her
sweet curves pressed against his body almost sent him
out of control. He wondered if Harriett Foster knew
how close she had come to being ravished by a
drunken bastard. But then, *ravished* might not be the
right word. Jake had felt her reluctant willingness. No
doubt it had surprised her as much as it surprised him.

"Jake." Horatio nudged him. "Bet."

"Uh . . . right. Twenty-five."

"Damn. I'm out," Horatio growled.

"Cheapskate," Steede taunted Jake. "Raise you
fifty."

"Lord!" Hobby commented with a whistle.

He'd had no right to touch her, Jake mused. She
deserved better. For all her meddling and priggish-
ness, Harry had class and courage. She'd make a good

wife for a decent, settled man—a man like her Edgar, or Edwin, or whatever his name was.

"Well, Jake. In or out?" Steede asked.

Jake blinked. "Yeah. I'm in." He tossed another chip onto the canvas. "Call."

The feeling of resentment that flashed through him at the thought of Harry's intended caught Jake by surprise. It felt a lot like jealousy. Not that Ed wasn't welcome to the little busybody.

"What do you have?" Steede asked.

"Royal flush."

"Shit. Aces and nines. Your luck just turned, my friend."

Some luck, Jake thought with disgust as he gathered in the chips. He was stuck on a goddamned wagon train in the middle of country infested with Indians and cholera; he was nursemaid to two greenhorn females—one of whom was a meddling busybody who could try the patience of a saint; he was losing his concentration at poker and his speed with a gun; and worst of all, he was beginning to think of Harry Foster as a woman rather than a nuisance.

The memory of how she had felt in his arms suddenly made the night warmer and brought a smile to Jake's face. Harry had liked his kiss. She had hated liking it, but she'd liked it all the same. He permitted himself a small grain of hope. Maybe his luck had turned after all.

Lucille smiled at Harriett from across the fire. The night was a fine one, but distant rumbles of thunder promised they would spend the night, as usual, listening to the drumming of rain on the tent.

"You certainly are diligent about that journal," Lucille commented. "I hope Mrs. Bloomer's readers appreciate the trouble you're taking."

"I'm sure they will."

But how little of the real picture they would get. Harriett could no longer write of her true feelings or difficulties—Amelia Bloomer as well as her gentle readers would be shocked. She could write of the dust and the rain, the sad deaths, the small adventures. She could tell them that Jake Carradine had saved her from snakebite. But would they understand how, in this raw wilderness, quickness with a gun and knife could be the measure of a man, as she was beginning to understand? Could they comprehend how a woman could be stirred by a man on a primitive level that was far too deep to be reached by the light of reason? How many would swoon if she wrote about Jake's assault, or the raw instincts it had unleashed in her?

Thank goodness she had been spared his company since that incident. Harriett suspected that Jake wished to avoid her with the same intensity that she wished to avoid him, for she saw him only in glimpses—and those glimpses convinced her that he was not in a good humor. As far as Harriett was concerned, the longer he stayed away from her, the safer she would feel.

"Ladies."

Harriett jumped at the sound of Jake's voice behind her.

"Mr. Carradine," Lucille greeted him. "We haven't seen you of late. Did our cooking finally drive you away?"

"Nope. Mr. Deere's been keeping me busy."

More likely Mrs. Hornsby's entertainers had been keeping him busy, Harriett thought waspishly, or Caroline MacKenzie.

"Have you been floundering without me?" He grinned at Lucille. For a man whose face had been set in a scowl for the last few days, he seemed disgustingly cheerful.

"We seem to be doing quite well, actually," Lucille

admitted. "Harriett was right, you know. We are stronger than I thought."

Her aunt was stronger, Harriett acknowledged. Harriett Foster, for all her posturing, was a good deal weaker. Her hands were shaking where they lay in her lap—her knees as well. How could she face him? And in front of her aunt!

She stood so abruptly that she toppled the stool on which she'd been sitting.

"Harriett, dear. You look as though you've been stung!"

"Your pardon, Aunt. I'm really not feeling too well. I think I'll retire."

"I'm sorry you're sick, Harry."

Except for the ever-present nickname, Jake's words were perfectly proper—unusual in itself; but a note in his voice told Harriett that he knew exactly what she was feeling. She had to say something, or her aunt would think her terribly rude. She turned slowly toward him. He was laughing at her, the villain! The crinkling of his eyes revealed his amusement even though his face was carefully bland.

"It's nothing, Mr. Carradine."

"Then perhaps you could spare me the time for . . . a few words?"

Hadn't they had words enough? "Perhaps another time."

"I promise I won't take more than a few minutes."

"I don't think so."

Lucille intervened with her usual energy. "Harriett, don't be rude. What's gotten into you, child?"

Harriett glared at her aunt, but Lucille seemed perversely determined that Jake should accomplish his mission, whatever it was.

"I'll just leave you two alone for a while." The older woman smiled innocently, but Harriett could see the imp of mischief in her eyes. "I hear Horatio Smith playing his fiddle. Mr. Steede said there would be dancing later."

Harriett watched Lucille go, her heart sinking. Jake smiled—his lips as well as his eyes this time. Harriett backed away and stumbled over the upset stool. He reached out toward her, and she skittered away like a rabbit. But he hadn't been reaching for her; he simply righted the stool.

"Sit," he ordered.

"Really, Mr. Carradine—"

"Sit!"

She sat hastily. He loomed over her. Of course, Harriett tried to comfort herself, a man of Jake Carradine's size and breadth would loom threateningly whether or not he intended it. He grabbed her aunt's stool, swung it under his backside, and sat facing her, not two feet away.

"I've come to apologize, Harry."

For once in her life the articulate Harriett Foster was speechless.

"I'm sorry I frightened you," he said. "And I'm sorry I hurt you. I didn't really intend to, but . . . I got carried away. You have no idea what a woman like you can do to a man."

Perhaps not, but thanks to him, she had a pretty good idea of what a man could do to a woman.

"I guess that's no excuse. But you do have a way of slipping under a man's skin and getting him riled."

He looked sincerely contrite as he sat there, with his unruly brows knitted in concern. Was this truly the same man who had assaulted her?

"I don't like you much when you drink, Mr. Carradine." Harriett's spirit was seeping back, ounce by ounce. "You're too powerful a man to lose your temper so easily."

"And you're too good at prodding a man's temper."

She had prodded something else as well, Harriett

remembered, but he was going to be polite enough not to mention that.

Jake sighed. "To tell the truth, Harry, I don't like me when I'm drinking either. And I lose my temper, and some other things, much too easily. I had no right to treat you like that. Off and on in my life I've sunk pretty low, but I've never before taken my temper out on a woman, and I've never forced myself on a female who wasn't willing. Nothing I can do will take back what I did, but at least I can say I'm sorry." He shifted on his stool. Harriett suspected Jake Carradine was not a man who was comfortable with apology. "I did warn you that I wasn't a man that a decent woman would want as a traveling companion."

He had his back to the fire, his face in shadow. The firelight gave him a bright halo he didn't deserve. The man deserved a pitchfork and horns. She shouldn't forgive him—not after what he had done to her. But Harriett somehow couldn't work up a properly indignant speech. The sight of Jake Carradine contrite must have addled her wits.

"I apologize also—for upsetting you so, Mr. Carradine. I'll admit that meddling is one of my faults. Even my mother, who was quite a meddler herself, used to charge me with it."

"I think I can tame my temper if you'll rein in your meddling."

She hesitated. His temper wasn't exactly what concerned her. What concerned her was the man himself. He'd caught the fancy of some foolish part of her, and the uneasy feelings he inspired went beyond physical attraction to an unreasoning and foolish tenderness. In spite of his recent crude brutality, those feelings were still there, sprouting anew every time she looked at him, every time he surprised her with some bit of courage or gentleness. She could fire him. He would leave, and the feelings would go with him. Jake had never wanted to come, and she would find some way to face down Mr. Deere.

"You're going to have to forgive me, Harry. Once we get past Fort Laramie and into the mountains you're going to need help with the wagon and team."

The firelight played over his face and lit a gleam in his eyes. He no longer looked a bit contrite. No. He gazed at her as if he could see right through her soul to the inappropriate passions he had set to seed. So much for contrition.

"Mr. Steede has been helping us," she told him a bit stiffly.

"He won't be around for long," Jake advised. "He never is."

"How do you know?"

"I've known Mr. Steede in the past."

She would just have to ignore the way her heart lurched when he came into sight. "I would like to forget all about what happened, Mr. Carradine. If we can do that. . . ."

His eyes told her he hadn't forgotten a thing—and wouldn't. "You don't have to be afraid of me, Harry. I won't lose my temper again. I won't touch you again." He rose, turned to leave, then looked back over his shoulder. "Unless you want me to, of course."

The smile that he gave her kept her awake half the night.

The next afternoon they camped within sight of the forks of the Platte, where the north and south branches of the river joined and flowed eastward in a single great waterway. The company traveled a mile or so along the south fork before circling the wagons. The Adventurers were in a festive mood, and as soon as the stock was staked out and supper was started, Horatio pulled out his fiddle. Bottles of whiskey passed from hand to hand, and several of the younger men whooped, hollered, and jigged in time to the music.

Few had felt the wagons were making progress during the monotonous days along the Platte—brittle grass, sandy bluffs, and dust from horizon to horizon were endured day after day. The unchanging scenery would continue for many miles to come, but at least seeing the forks slip behind them confirmed to the travelers that they were indeed going forward, not caught in some nightmare trek where they plodded in the same place, never actually moving, as the scenery tried to convince them.

Harriett was curious to notice that a Pawnee band was camped nearby, just across the South Platte River from the Indiana Company. Pawnee braves had dogged their route since before they reached the Platte, necessitating a nightly guard to protect the stock. Several of the younger Adventurers were vociferous in their boasts of what they would do to any Indian who crossed them, but so far little trouble had arisen other than the one incident with Ned White. Mr. White had grumbled continually since then, but not within earshot of Jake Carradine. Ned White, it seemed, might not be afraid of savages; but he was certainly cautious around the subcaptain who wore a pistol strapped so comfortably to his thigh.

The band of Pawnee camped across the South Platte clearly were not hostiles. Tipis were pitched in a circle near the banks of the river, and children played within the circle's protection. Old men sat in the doorways of their lodges, and women chatted as they moved about doing their chores. Harriett wished she could cross the river and visit the village. They looked so content— those old men and chattering women with their infants. And the younger men, arrogant and strong, scarcely gave the whites a glance. How interesting it would be, Harriett mentioned to Lucille, to learn of their thoughts, joys, and concerns. Were they noble savages, as the idealists said, or filthy barbarians—the opinion held by most emigrants.

Jake laughed, eavesdropping on their conversation as he doctored a sore on Flytail's back. The Indians were people like any others, he told her—some noble, some trash. Most were a little of both.

Harriett arched a brow. "And how would you know?"

"I've spent some time with them. Not this tribe, but some farther west."

"That's right. Your friend Mr. Walking Horse is an Indian, isn't he?" Again she wondered about his past. Had the Indians killed his family? Had Jake been the savages' prisoner? Was that why at times he seemed so haunted?

"Amos is a half-breed," he told her. "Most people consider that worse than a full-blooded Indian."

"He seemed very civilized to me," Harriett commented.

"I doubt that many whites seem civilized to him," Jake said cryptically.

Lawrence Steede walked into their little camp. He smelled of spirits, Harriett noted, but, as usual, his grooming and diction were without fault.

He tipped his hat politely. "Good evening, Miss Foster. Jake."

"Good evening, Mr. Steede." Harriett returned his courtesy. She still hadn't made up her mind about the gentleman gambler. "You left this morning before I could thank you for helping with Gus's sore foot."

"It was no trouble, Miss Foster. That pack mule of mine gets the same condition at least once a month. Is Mrs. Stanwick around?"

"My aunt is in the wagon deciding what we shall have for dinner. Would you care to join us?"

"Why, thank you. Don't mind if I do." He turned to Jake, and the smile left his face. "Some of those young yahoos are getting mighty bold in their talk, Jake. The more whiskey they drink, the braver they get. That Pawnee village across the way is riling them up."

Lucille stepped out of the wagon. "Those Indians haven't done a thing to rile anybody, Mr. Steede."

"Just being Indian is enough to rile some," Jake said.

"Especially Ned White," Steede added. "He's drunker than a skunk, and he's waving a rifle around like he's on the warpath—boasting that he's going to kill himself a redskin. Deere is just laughing at him."

"Well, I don't wonder why." Harriett grimaced. "Mr. White doesn't open his mouth but what he's boasting about something. Nobody ever listens to the man."

"True enough," Jake agreed. "But maybe I'll just have a talk with him."

"That'll quiet him down fast enough," Harriett said to Lucille under her breath.

Jake hadn't gotten ten yards from their little camp before a rifle exploded. Everyone froze.

Steede cursed.

"What happened?" Harriett asked, heart pounding.

The entire company was moving toward the opposite side of the circle, where blue smoke from the rifle discharge rose above the canvas tops of the wagons. A dreadful feeling was in the air. Where the crowd had gathered, several men were shouting.

"What happened?" Harriett asked again, trailing at Jake's heels as he strode toward the crowd.

Jake didn't answer her. He was too busy pushing through the mob of Adventurers who had collected around Charles Deere, Ned White, and Abel Hawkins. Horatio Smith, who stood on the fringe of the crowd, took her arm and drew her away.

"It's that bastard White," Horatio told her. "He took

a potshot at the Indian village. Appears he hit some-one."

Harriett sucked in her breath. She looked across the river. A knot of Pawnee had gathered at the entrance to one of the tipis. More were running to join them. An Indian shouted, then a female wail rose from the knot —one of the most haunting sounds Harriett had ever heard. Another woman broke free of the crowd, shrieking, tearing at her hair, and gouging her own face with her fingernails.

"Lordy!" Harriett heard someone exclaim. "He hit the squaw who was sittin' in front of that tipi. The one who was sittin' there nursing her kid."

"Course I did," came White's drunken claim. "I was aimin' at the red bitch."

Ned laughed. Harriett's stomach turned. She feared that she was going to be ill right there on the spot.

A firm hand landed on her shoulder. "Go back to the wagon, Harry. And stay there."

Jake's voice was grim. A group of Pawnee warriors had mounted their ponies and headed toward the river. The Indiana Company was going to have visi-tors.

"How could this happen?" Harriett gasped. "How could anyone do such a thing?"

Ned White was still laughing. From the sound of his voice he was quite drunk. Even his former cronies were regarding him with a look they might give a mad dog.

"I'm afraid we haven't seen the half of it yet. Go back to the wagon, Harry, and get inside."

She ignored his command, trapped in horrible fasci-nation as the band of six Pawnee splashed out of the river and rode toward the wagons. Their leader was almost as big as Jake, and appeared impressively sav-age. His black hair, obviously dressed with some sort of grease, was shaved into a scalp lock and decorated with bright feathers. Feathers also hung from arm-bands circling his biceps. His chest, scarred and powerful, was bare except for a necklace made from some sort of claws. A loincloth and fringed rawhide leggings tucked into soft moccasin-style boots completed the picture.

He was Harriett's first close encounter with a Pawnee warrior, and his appearance, along with the flat black hatred in his eyes, was enough to make her clasp Jake's arm in fright, not even aware that she was doing so.

The Indian grunted something in his own language.

"Carter," Jake commanded. "Get up here. You claim to speak Pawnee."

Phineas scuttled to the front of the crowd.

"Translate," Jake told him.

"He wants to know who's our chief."

Everyone shifted nervously and looked around. Mr. Deere moved slowly forward, looking like a man who had just seen a ghost—his own.

The Pawnee warrior spoke again, a longer speech this time. Carter listened carefully, grimacing.

"He says that one of us has shot 'n' killed the wife of his son. He wants us to give him the man who would kill a woman—so the Indians can punish him. At least that's the gist of it."

Mr. Deere cleared his throat uneasily. "Tell him we will punish the man. It was an accident. We . . . we mean him and his people no harm, and we'll see that the man's sorry."

Carter conveyed Deere's reply. The Indian's curt answer needed no translation. The braves behind the Pawnee leader scowled and shifted on their ponies.

"Tell him . . . tell him we'll pay for the woman!" Deere said, sounding proud of his cleverness. "We'll pay her family for the loss. That should make 'em happy!"

The Pawnee gave the same sharp reply, only increased in volume. Then he launched into a long, guttural speech punctuated by gestures that were distressingly clear in meaning.

"Uh . . . uh. . . ." Carter's face glistened with sweat. "He's claimin' that he'll punish every one of us here if we don't hand Ned over."

A low grumbling rose from the crowd of Adventurers. Harriett could almost smell their fear—and her own.

"Tell him the man will be shot, just as he shot the woman. And they can be witness to his punishment." Jake's voice was calm.

"Wait just a damned minute!" White complained.

Jake's face was like granite, his tone merciless. "You sealed your own fate, you trigger-happy bastard. I'm doing you a favor, whether you know it or not."

"You can't . . . ! Good God! It was just a damned squaw!" The haze of liquor seemed to have deserted Ned. His face was pale as flour.

Carter stuttered out Jake's proposal. The Pawnee frowned, talked among themselves, then barked a refusal. Jake's lips tightened to a grim line.

"Hand 'im over!" came a shout from the crowd. "Hellfire, Deere! I ain't gonna get scalped just 'cause White there's an asshole."

Deere sputtered. A rumble of agreement rose from the crowd.

"Wait!" Deere ordered. "We gotta have a vote here."

Deere asked for a vote only when he didn't want responsibility for a decision, Harriett reflected cynically. But in this case she couldn't blame him. She wouldn't want responsibility for handing a comrade over to these fierce-looking savages, no matter how much the man deserved his fate.

The vote was unanimous. Ned White was abandoned to his fate. The Pawnee took custody of the struggling man with grim dignity. They circled him with several rawhide ropes, fastened his arms to his sides, and towed him away from the wagons. Their leader stayed behind, until White had been dragged about a hundred feet from the circle of wagons. Then he uttered a single sharp word, whirled his pony, and galloped after his comrades.

"Watch," Carter translated, his voice shaking. "He said we should watch."

Jake pried Harriett loose from his arm and took her hand in his. He pulled her toward the wagon, where a nervous Lucille was waiting in Steede's comforting embrace. Jake seemed in a hurry.

"Both you women get in the wagon and stay there. Take my advice and cover your ears."

This time Harriett was anxious to comply, but before she could climb into the wagon she was riveted to the spot by a bloodcurdling scream. Slowly she turned, unable to not look. The Pawnee held Ned erect in the spot where they had stopped, in full view of the wagons. From all appearances, they were skinning him alive.

9

Lucille whimpered and turned her face into Steede's chest. Harriett looked as though she were going to swoon. Her eyes were wide, her face ashy pale. But she stood rooted to the spot, like all the other members of the Indiana Company. No one moved or made a sound. The air shook with the agony of Ned's shrieks.

The nightmare seemed to last an eternity. When the screams finally stopped, Harriett sagged like a puppet whose strings have suddenly been cut. Jake was there to catch her.

"It's over, Harry. It's over."

She opened her mouth to answer, but gagged instead. "Oh, God!" she whimpered, and proceeded to be violently ill. Jake held her as she retched, wept, and retched again. He glanced at Steede, who held Lucille in his arms. The older woman had fainted dead away.

"I'll take care of Mrs. Stanwick," Steede volunteered. "You look like you have your hands full."

When the spasms had passed, Harriett sat silently where Jake placed her. Her eyes were unfocused, lost in horror, their sparkling emerald green dulled almost to gray. Jake wet a rag and wiped the tear-streaked dust from her face, then bathed her wrists.

"Don't go having the vapors on me, Harry. You're much too ornery a female to start that."

He built up the fire, warmed some salt pork and left-over beans, and offered her a plate. Her face turned the same gray-green as her eyes.

"Yeah, I guess not," he agreed. His own stomach wasn't sitting too easy either. The sheepdog bitch from the Cutter wagon came running when he set the plates on the ground for her to clean.

"Is Miss Foster all right?" Chad peered around the corner of the wagon.

"She'll be fine," Jake told him. "Your ma?"

Chad scuffed toward the fire. "Ma's okay. She hid in the wagon and put a pillow over her head. Made me do the same. I coulda watched, though. It wouldn'a bothered me much."

"If you ever get to the point where something like that doesn't bother you, boy, then you'd better just give up and die. 'Cause you won't be worth the air it takes to keep you alive."

Harriett whimpered. Her eyes grew round, and she bolted up from her seat and dashed behind the wagon. They could hear the sounds of retching.

Jake shook his head at Chad, who looked bewildered. "You go on back to your ma, Chad. She may not be as all right as you think." Jake watched the boy go, then rounded the wagon to where Harriett was doubled over, weeping. He took her by the shoulder and wiped away the tears with his scarf.

"Hold on, Harry. It'll fade. You won't ever forget, but it'll get dim enough to bear." Having had more than a passing encounter with violent death, Jake spoke from experience.

She didn't resist as he pulled her against his chest, but instead unleashed a new flood of tears onto his shirtfront.

"I'll never get the sound and the sight out of my

mind," she choked out against his chest. "I hear it still. Oh, God, I do."

He picked her up. Lost in her weeping, she didn't struggle. "You need to get some sleep, Harry. Then in the morning you can start to forget."

"No!" she gasped. "I'll dream! I don't want to dream. Please, Jake!"

He climbed with her into the wagon, kicked open the roll of bedding, and laid her gently down. "Go to sleep, Harry. I won't let them into your dreams."

She shook her head violently, but didn't pull away as he took her into his arms. "You can't gun down dreams, Jake. You can't."

He smoothed her mussed hair back from her face. "You'd be surprised, lady—at how many dreams I've gunned down." A bitter smile twisted his mouth.

He held her against him until her breathing was calm and regular. In the morning she'd wake up hurting. Knowing Harry Foster, she would hurt almost as much from having lost her composure as from the memory of this evening's horror. She was a strong woman, in spite of some fairly bothersome ideas stored in that pretty red head. The world might be too much for her right now, but someday, he mused, Harry Foster just might be too much for the world. And for Jake Carradine's defenses. He'd have to be sure not to be around when that happened. Most dangers a man could keep at bay with a gun, but what did one use against a woman?

Jake spent the night in the wagon, his back propped against a flour sack, listening to Harriett's even breathing. He slept little, almost as if he were, as he'd fancifully promised, standing guard over Harriett's dreams. How aghast Her Most Proper Ladyship would be if she knew that she'd slept all night not a foot away from him, her hand still spasmodically clutching his arm. Jake smiled just imagining her reaction. All the same,

he left before the first hint of dawn, with Harriett still
safely asleep.

The early-morning moon shone down upon the
empty spot where the Pawnee village had stood. The
Indians were gone. Jake saddled his horse and crossed
the river to the village site. With a shovel taken from
Harriett's wagon he buried what was left of Ned
White. The Pawnee hadn't left very much to bury.

By the time Jake finished, the sun cast a faint glow
from below the horizon, outlining the village site in
shades of blue and gray. Jake was about to mount his
horse to go back to the wagons when he heard a faint
whimper. A chill crawled up his spine. He didn't believe in ghosts, but the past day had been enough to
make anyone's nerves jumpy. He drew his gun. A
movement caught his eye. Staring in the direction of
the movement, he thumbed back the pistol's hammer.
And then he saw.

It wasn't a ghost; it was a puppy. The pathetic thing
whimpered again as Jake holstered his pistol and
squatted down beside the little beast. Its red-brown fur
was as dull as dust; little ribs stood out in bold relief. A
runt, Jake decided. Not even in good enough shape to
go into the stewpot, so the Pawnee had left it behind.

When Jake rode back into the circle of wagons, Harriett immediately spotted his pathetic burden. She
took the pup in her arms and crooned as a mother
might to a sick child. Somehow Jake had known she
would. With the helpless little creature to occupy her
energy, perhaps she would leave him alone for a
change. Except Jake wasn't sure he wanted to be left
alone.

Steede came up beside him and watched Harriett
fuss over the pup, who responded to her affection by
kissing her hand with a pale pink tongue.

"Have a soft spot for helpless creatures, do you?"

Steede's glance encompassed both Harriett and her scruffy charge.

"If you think either one of them is helpless, you're not as smart as I thought you were," Jake growled.

Journal entry — June 4 — approaching the California crossing: Lord, how tired I am of this endless prairie! It rolls on and on until one starts to believe the Rocky Mountains are a myth. The whole world seems to be nothing but grass and sand. To the north is a rise of low bluffs that provide some variety for the eye, but to the south is only flat, flat grassland. Edwin's letters tell me that the mountains of the West are like nothing I've ever before seen, and that San Francisco itself sits among beautiful hills and trees. My mind believes such a place exists, but my spirit looks out upon this plain day after day and insists that it never ends.

The last few days have been cool and rainy—so much so that Lucille and I have both unpacked our wool dresses. I've abandoned my pantaloons—for now. The trail has become so muddy that they are impossible to keep clean. When the mud is deep, we are obliged to walk so that the wagon is lighter for our poor oxen. Not that our paltry weight much lightens the load for the beasts.

We pass numerous graves alongside the trail, and have added one more to their number. Another one of Mrs. Hornsby's "entertainers" succumbed yesterday morning—a young woman by the name of Cassie. No one knew her last name, not even Mrs. Hornsby. She is the third of those ladies to die. I have stopped reading the inscriptions on the graves we pass. Knowing the names of those who have passed away somehow makes their tragedy all the sadder. I wonder if my spirit is sufficient to the sorrows of this trail.

I would not imply that all is gloom, however, for there is joy as well. Lucille and I went for a walk this morning at dawn. The rain stopped—temporarily—and the morning sun sliced through the fog in orange splendor. Everything was fresh and clean, just as it must have been at the beginning of the world. We found wildflowers in abundance and picked a bouquet to bring back to Sadie, who has a special fondness for flowers. We also gave some to Mrs. Hornsby, who seemed quite surprised at our attention. She is very upset over Cassie's death.

Our own health is good, I'm happy to report. Though Sadie is pale and sometimes listless, I suppose one expects that in the late stages of a pregnancy. Mr. Steede suggested that we start to cut our water with a little whiskey, as many others of the company do to purify it. At Lucille's urging, I did try, but the taste was so vile that I spit it out. Mr. Carradine laughed and said that the only result of putting whiskey in water was to ruin perfectly good whiskey.

Mr. Carradine has stayed closer to our wagon of late and smells very seldom of liquor. Now that he pays some mind to his grooming, I must concede he is a well-set-up man. I wonder if my awkward efforts at reform are having some effect or if the trail itself is bringing out the good in him. The puppy that he brought back from the Pawnee village adores the man, and I'm told that of all animals, dogs see through to a man's true character. But Dodger—as I named the little creature—adores everyone. His condition improves daily with proper feeding and abundant affection from us all. As one who has never had a pet, I am amazed at how such an insignificant beast can worm its way into a person's heart. Truly the little dog has become a dear companion.

Rumor has it that tomorrow we will cross the

south fork of the Platte, a ford known as the California crossing. Apparently this ford has no set place along the river, but Mr. Ward's guidebook assures us that the crossing should give us very little trouble. Mr. Deere, Mr. Carter, and Mr. Carradine have been debating among themselves for the last day about exactly where the company should make the ford. We must cross soon, for this river takes us southwest, away from our route. Upon leaving the south fork we must travel northwest until we come to the north fork of the Platte, which will eventually lead us to Fort Laramie.

Jake was not happy about the coming crossing. The river was high, swollen by rains that had drenched the distant mountains as well as the plains. Deere and Carter were anxious to cross. They'd chosen the closest ford possible. A safer ford lay another day upstream, but the wagon captain and his scout wouldn't hear of the delay: They would rather risk people and stock than lose time.

The wagons were lined up in good order, waiting to cross. By now the Adventurers were experienced trailhands. Rivers, mud, hailstorms, lightning, wind—they'd seen them all a dozen times and more. But Jake wondered if any of them had noticed that none of the other wagon companies had chosen this ford to cross.

He rode down the line, checking to make sure that everyone had his goods tied down and secure. Harriett's wagon was last in line—the position that Mr. Deere invariably assigned her. She and her aunt were both smiling and confident. He had to give Harry credit. A woman like her shouldn't have lasted as far as Fort Kearney, and here she was halfway to the Rockies. And he certainly hadn't made the trip any easier for her.

"Where's Steede?" Jake asked. "I thought he was going to drive you ladies across."

"Mr. Steede decided to cross at another ford," Harriett told him. "He took his horse and mule upstream."

Lucille looked a bit shamefaced—or was that sigh one of disappointment? Jake felt a twinge of anger with Steede for taking advantage of the lady's unwary affections, then realized he had very little room to criticize. If Harry didn't put up such a prickly defense, wouldn't Jake have done the same? In fact, hadn't he tried his damnedest to do the same?

"I'll come back and drive you across," Jake offered. "Right now I've got to start the company moving."

"There's no need to bother yourself on our account, Mr. Carradine." Harriett smiled one of her crusading smiles. She was out to prove herself again, Jake guessed. "We're perfectly capable of crossing on our own."

"I'll be back," he answered, and before Harry could argue, he spurred his horse up the line.

Several hours went by. The crossing went smoothly, in spite of the high water, swift current, and muddy banks. Jake was ready to admit he'd been wrong, that the Indiana Adventurers were more competent than he'd thought. Then the MacKenzies' team balked in midriver. As had the others before him, Callum MacKenzie inclined his path slightly downstream. His team of mules spooked when the current carried a long piece of rotten deadwood across their path. The beasts bolted in four directions at once, panicked, tangled their harness, and refused to move another step. Meanwhile the current swung the wagon broadside and rushed against it full force. Poor Callum cursed his mules at the top of his voice, but his shouting was scarcely audible above Caroline's screams.

Jake cursed and urged his horse into the river. The beast plunged into the current with no hesitation. But just as Jake grabbed the headstall of the lead mule, the wagon toppled, spilling passengers and cargo into the water. Callum shouted. Caroline's shrieks rose in volume, then burbled into ominous silence.

The mules brayed pathetically as their harness threatened to drag them under. Jake spurred his horse forward, dodged the team's flailing hooves, and cut the traces, freeing both team and wagon. The mules swam for shore. The wagon pirouetted in the turbulent current, then floated majestically away to lodge in a flood-deposited deadfall fifty feet downstream. Callum had grabbed a rope thrown to him by Hobby Smith and was being dragged swiftly ashore, but Caroline was nowhere to be seen.

"There she is!" a voice yelled from the bank. "In that tangle of brush!"

Caroline had been snagged by the same deadfall that stopped the wagon. The wagon was securely wedged, but the dazed Caroline hung on with only one arm. The wagon captain threw a rope in her direction, but it tangled in the debris out of her reach.

"Son of a bitch!" Jake turned his sorrel gelding toward the deadfall. The horse's response was sluggish. Even Jake, with only half of him in the freezing water, was beginning to feel as though he had ice water running through his veins. Playing hero was hell, Jake thought wryly. How did he get dragged into this, anyway?

By the time he reached Caroline, Jake was practically numb. He could imagine how she felt. But when he hefted her onto his horse she still had enough movement in her limbs to wrap him in a stranglehold.

"Oh, God! Thank you! Thank you!" she sobbed.

"I'm not quite God," he replied, turning his weary, frozen mount toward the bank. "And don't thank me yet."

She hid her head against his chest as the sorrel

struggled toward the bank. Finally they stumbled up onto dry land.

"Now you can thank me." Jake told her.

Caroline thanked him all right—with a frantic kiss aimed to suck the marrow right out of his bones. When Jake managed to push her away, she clung to him as though she was still in the river and he was her only anchor. Her husband finally peeled her off, a stern look on his face for both his wife and Jake. Callum also gave a scowl to Charles Deere, who ambled up leading his horse. The wagon captain had obviously not been anxious to join in the rescue.

"That was fine work, boy." Deere puffed up and clapped Jake on the shoulder.

Legs numb, Jake awkwardly dismounted. "Deere, loan me your horse. Mine's tuckered, and two more wagons are waiting to cross."

Without waiting for permission Jake swung aboard the captain's mount. His feet dangled a foot below the stirrups.

"I'm goin' with you, Jake," Horace Smith volunteered. "I'll drive one o' them wagons across while you take the other."

When they reached the other side, Sadie welcomed them with a sigh of relief, but Harriett regarded Jake with an odd look in her eyes—eyes that were even greener than usual, Jake thought. He chuckled to himself. Having eyes that so truly mirrored feelings must be a terrible inconvenience for a lady. Perhaps her crusading little heart had a soft spot for a down-and-out, no-good gunman after all.

"That was an extremely courageous thing you did," she said, her voice gratingly polite. "How fortunate that Mrs. MacKenzie's husband is tolerant of her spontaneous displays of affection."

Jake grinned and curved one brow into a devilish arch. "Jealous, Harry?"

"Jealous?" she sputtered, then turned scarlet when her aunt gave her a knowing smile.

"Move over, Harry. I'll take us across."

"Don't bother." Her chin lifted stubbornly. "I'm quite capable of driving my own team."

Horace Smith had urged Sadie's team into the river. They were going along nicely, already a third of the way across.

"This is not the time to be stubborn, Harry. In case you haven't noticed, this rain has been coming down all day, and the river gets higher with every wagon that crosses. You saw what happened to the MacKenzies."

"Yes indeed," she said in a caustic tone that had nothing to do with the MacKenzie wagon, and everything to do, Jake suspected, with the MacKenzie wife. "I'm a better driver than Callum MacKenzie, and my oxen are much steadier than his mules."

That happened to be true, but the damned woman made the proclamation as though it qualified her to vote, for God's sake.

"Will you move over, dammit!"

"No. And you may watch your temper—and your language, Mr. Carradine. As you say, the river is rising, so stand out of my way and let me cross."

She shook out the reins, and Jake was forced to either get out of her way or leap from the back of his horse onto the wagon box and wrest the lines from her hands. He figured the little witch would rather drown than admit she might need help.

He breathed an exasperated sigh as the wagon trundled down the bank and into the swollen river. Dodger barked a greeting from over the tailgate, his tail waving furiously in the air, his pink tongue lolling. The dog had more sense than some women, Jake mused sourly. Much more sense.

Harriett had damned well better make it across,

Jake thought, because he certainly wasn't going into the river to pull her out. Playing hero twice in one day was too much to expect of any man.

He spurred his horse into the river beside the wagon. "Keep the lines taut," he advised Harriett. "Any uncertainty on your part and those bonehead oxen will stop."

Lucille clung with white knuckles to her seat on the wagon box. Harriett flashed Jake a withering look. "Giddap, Gus! Move, Sharps!"

The oxen plodded steadily across the river while Harriett pointedly ignored Jake. He had to admit that she was doing a fine job. The woman was a fast learner. The current surging against the sides of the wagon didn't shake her; even when Curly twitched his tail in annoyance and tried to stop, she kept her composure and urged him on in a confident voice.

Not until the wagon rumbled up on the bank did disaster strike—in the form of one undergrown, over-playful puppy. Dodger had yapped in excitement all across the river. Harriett credited the dog with more sense than he possessed, for she hadn't tied him in the wagon. So when the pup spotted a stick floating by that was just too interesting to resist, he scrambled over the tailgate, plopped into the water, and gave gleeful chase. But the stick eluded him, the current caught him, and he found out too late that runt puppies are no match for the South Platte in flood. He yelped, paddling frantically and trailing a plea of pitiful yi-yi-yi's as the current swept him into still deeper water.

"Dodger! Oh, God!" Harriett almost threw the reins at Lucille and jumped down from the wagon box into ankle-deep water.

"Harry! What do you think you're doing, you fool woman?"

Before Jake could stop her, Harriett pulled off her

shoes and charged into the water after the pup. Jake spurred his mount in pursuit, but the horse he had borrowed from Charles Deere had endured quite enough of the cold water for one day. It reared and twisted as Jake prodded it back into the flood.

"God damn it to hell! Fool woman! Sonofabitch horse!"

Jake jumped to the ground, yanked a coiled rope from the saddle, and pulled off his boots. He didn't have time to fight the horse. The current had grabbed Harry as well as Dodger, and they were both being swept past the deadfall that had trapped Caroline and the MacKenzie wagon. The puppy's squeals ceased when Harriett swam to within grabbing distance and snatched him into her arms. So they would drown together, the fools. Both of them could claim equal amounts of common sense!

"Take this!" He handed one end of the rope to the closest set of hands, which belonged to Callum MacKenzie. The other end he knotted around his own waist. "And hold on, dammit! If I drown out there, I'm going to kill that woman!"

As he plunged into the icy water, Jake remembered his earlier vow not to play hero twice. So much for that resolve. The current grabbed him; he helped it along by swimming. The rope reached its limit just as Jake reached out and closed his fingers around Harriett's arm. He pulled her to him. Her face was bluish, her lips white, her eyes green pools of terror.

"Hold on!" he commanded. "I'll pull us back."

She wound one arm around his neck, but her strength wouldn't hold against the current. And Jake needed both hands to pull them back to shore.

"Both arms, dammit!"

Harriett refused to let go of the bedraggled puppy. She tried once again to steady herself with one arm.

"Goddamn son of a bitch!" Fool woman! Useless

dog! Was there anything more dangerous than a red-headed female?

Jake managed to wedge the gasping pup between their two bodies with the dog's head still above water. "Now use both arms, dammit!"

Harriett complied, and he twisted so that the current would press her more securely against his body. He could feel her shivering, hear her teeth chattering even above the rush of the current. His own hands were almost too numb to hold the rope. God curse it all if he got himself killed in this stunt—all because of a half-wit, addlepated loon of a woman!

The pull to the bank, even with the help of the Smith brothers, who'd taken over from Callum MacKenzie on the other end of the rope, took a freezing, bruising eternity. By the time he stumbled up on shore Jake wasn't sure if the burdens he dragged with him were alive or dead. But Dodger wobbled to his feet, coughed up river water, shook, and gazed up at his rescuer with a tongue-lolling puppy grin. Harriett was slower to recover. She lay in the mud, a sodden, gasping, miserable heap, until Jake shook her.

"Harry!" He hated the fear that colored his voice. Before Harriett Foster he hadn't been afraid of anything, not even death. But the thought of losing Harry terrified him.

"Harry!" He pounded her back. She coughed, bringing up a rush of water.

"D . . . d . . . don't!"

He stopped pounding. She would live. Jake didn't know whether he was relieved or disappointed.

"You stupid *fool*!" he shouted down at her. "What the *hell* did you think you were doing?"

The tone of his anger made more than one man cringe, but Harriett only blinked up at him.

"You'd risk your life for a damned dog? You'd risk

my life for a dog? What do you use for brains, woman? Mule crap?''

The tirade went on for a full three minutes without Harriett answering. The onlookers to the little drama faded cautiously out of the range of Jake Carradine's displeasure, some taking odds on the silly woman's surviving the big gunman's fury. The only ones not frightened by his shouting, it seemed, were Harriett and the sodden pup.

"I couldn't have let the poor thing drown!" Harriett finally said.

As if in agreement, Dodger sat with one paw on Jake's soggy stockinged foot, gazing up at him in puppy adoration.

"I damned well would have!" he shouted back.

She grimaced at the volume. "You were the one who saved him back at the Pawnee village!"

"I picked him off a trash heap! I didn't dive into a flooded river after the fool dog!"

"Well, you would have!"

"No I wouldn't have!"

"You would too, Jake Carradine! I know you better than that!"

"You don't know me at all!" he bellowed. "Hell, woman. I thought twice before coming after you! What kind of a sonofabitch brainless saint do you think I am?"

"Oh I don't think you're a saint at all, Mr. Carradine. I'll admit you're quite an accomplished sinner." She climbed to her feet and lifted the pup into her arms. "But I thank you for pulling Dodger and me out of the river. I don't think I could have quite managed the task myself. If you continue to be so heroic, I shall have to raise your wages."

"I'm not a damned hero! I keep telling you—!"

"Of course not," she agreed quickly. "Now, if you'll excuse me . . ." She swayed a bit, her face greenish pale. "I do believe I swallowed a bit too much river water."

Jake stepped aside as she set the puppy on the ground and rushed off to find a private place to be sick. One part of him wanted to comfort her; the other part longed to kick the nicely rounded little butt that was so fetchingly molded by her wet skirts. The combined effect held him frozen to the spot, watching her retreat, feeling like a bigger idiot than she was.

Dodger looked up at him, placed a paw once again on his foot, and grinned.

"You're right," he told the dog. "I'm losing my touch. Grown men used to be afraid of me, and now Jake Carradine, gun-toting tough guy, can't scare one little spinster from Boston."

But the little spinster from Boston was doing one hell of a job scaring Jake Carradine. Indians didn't scare him. Death didn't scare him. Gun-toting bullies, snakes, wolves, bears, and storms didn't scare him—not much, at least. But the feeling that had ripped through his soul when he'd seen Harriett Foster dragged away by the current scared the pants off him. Yes indeed it did.

10

"Everything we own is wet," Harriett complained to Lucille. Kneeling on the bed of the wagon, she held up a pair of pantaloons, grimaced, and wrung them out like a dishrag. "I knew we should've caulked the sides of the wagon after crossing the Big Blue."

The company had made an early camp on the bank of the South Platte—not out of any consideration for Harriett's misery, but to drag the MacKenzie wagon out of the river and restore it to traveling condition. The rain had stopped, finally, but now a cold fog was thickening the air.

"I feel like my very bones are soaked with river water," Harriett sighed.

Lucille sniffed. "You're a fine one to complain! You should be dead and drowned now, by rights. If it weren't for Jake, you would be."

"Oh. You're calling Mr. Carradine by his Christian name now, are you, Aunt?"

"The man's a good friend. I wish you two would stop hissing at each other like cranky cats."

"I don't hiss. And neither does he. He shouts."

"He had a right to shout this afternoon," Lucille admonished. "I still don't know what got into you, Harri-

ett. For God's sake! Putting yourself in such jeopardy
for a dumb animal!"

"Don't you start too!" Harriett brushed back an errant lock of red hair and sat down on a flour sack. "It
was foolish, I'll admit. I wasn't thinking straight at all.
But I've grown so attached to the pup that I just lost
my head."

"You nearly lost a good deal more than your head,
Harriett dear."

"But I had no thought of involving anyone else in
danger."

"You had no thought at all. Did you believe that Jake
would sit idly by and watch you drown?"

"If Mr. Carradine were half as villainous as he believes, he would have."

Lucille simply snorted.

Harriett leaned back against the side of the wagon
and sighed. Dodger cavorted nearby, chasing a grass-
hopper. "He really has stolen my heart."

Lucille looked up from stirring the cookfire. "Harriett!"

Harriett frowned, puzzled, then laughed. "Not Mr.
Carradine, Aunt! Dodger."

Lucille shook a finger in her niece's direction.
"You're a fool, Harriett. I blame your mother, God rest
her soul. And your father as well. They were so busy
stuffing your head with Greek classics and Shake-
spearean plays—not to mention all those revolutionary
writings on social reform—that they completely ignored educating you about your own feelings.

"I don't believe you even know what love is. You
certainly never learned about it from your parents. My
brother was too occupied with his money and your
mother too busy with her causes for them to pay much
attention to each other. You wouldn't recognize love if
it stood up and slapped you in the face."

"Aunt Lucille!" Harriett smiled in tolerant amusement. "We're talking about a dog."

"No, we're not."

For a moment Harriett looked confused. Then her eyes widened. "You can't think that I . . . that Mr. Carradine . . . !"

"You should take a closer look at Jake Carradine. If you can't see what's in that man's heart. . . . Well, I certainly can."

"Lucille, you pick the strangest men to admire. You've never met Edwin, and you're not giving him a chance. Besides, I have no intention of letting any man pull the wool over my eyes in the name of love. You know that. Men use love as an excuse to control women. They—"

"Please, Harriett. I'm really not up to a lecture tonight."

Harriett sighed. "Neither am I, Aunt. I'm sorry."

Lucille walked over and patted her niece's hand. "I apologize also, my love. He is a dear thing."

"I would hardly call Mr. Carradine—"

"Not Jake!" Lucille said with a smile. "Little Dodger. I am glad we didn't lose him. He's a very entertaining companion."

Upon hearing his name, the puppy bounded over and jumped up on Lucille, muddy feet and all. She gently shooed him away and brushed off her skirt. "Ah, well. Everything is wet or dirty anyway."

Harriett climbed down from the wagon. "We won't have time to do a laundry until we reach Ash Hollow." She massaged her brow wearily. Suddenly everything had become a bit too much for her. "I don't think I'll have supper tonight, Aunt. I've really no appetite."

"Harriett! You're much too thin as it is."

"Aunt . . ."

"All right, dear. If you don't mind, I'll just take some

of this buffalo stew over to Lawrence. He does prefer my cooking to his own, you know."

Harriett sat down wearily on a stool and poked at the fire. She was cold to the bone, sore, bruised, aching, and probably coming down with the ague. Her aunt thought she was daft, and Jake was furious—with good reason, Harriett admitted.

Dodger trotted up, gave her a soulful look, and laid his chin on her knee. Unable to resist the invitation, she scratched his ear. "Are you worth all this trouble, little one?"

His expression said that he was. Harriett supposed he was right. The pup was something she'd never before had, something she'd never known that she wanted—a creature who loved her, truly loved her, beyond the bounds of reason and restraint. And she reciprocated in turn. Such a relationship with a human being would be disastrous, Harriett reflected. If she had such a senseless need, how fortunate that need was met by a dog.

Harriett sneezed; Dodger jumped back, yipped, and cocked his floppy ears.

"I'm not playing, you silly dog. I'm coming down with a fever."

"Sounds bad."

It was Harriett's turn to jump at the sound of Jake's deep voice. He stepped into the circle of firelight. Every time she saw him the man looked bigger. "I didn't see you standing there," she stammered.

"I guess not. Otherwise you wouldn't be having a conversation with a dog." He looked around at the wet clothing and blankets spread out on an improvised clothesline.

"Everything we have is soaked," she explained morosely. "Even the bedding, but I suppose everyone is in much the same fix. I know Mrs. MacBride is, because I loaned her our only dry blankets."

Jake gave her an amused look.

"In Mrs. MacBride's condition, sir, it's very important that she not take a chill."

"Oh, I realize that," he agreed.

She sneezed again, then again.

"You really are catching a fever." He sat down on the other stool, appearing very much as if he planned to stay awhile.

"I thought you weren't speaking to me, Mr. Carradine."

"Changed my mind." He eyed her from under lowered brows. "Since I've saved your hide twice now—as you said—I figure you can drop the Mr. Carradine. My name is Jake."

Harriett fastened her gaze on the ground. She wasn't at all sure that she wanted to discard the barrier of that formality.

"Does that come from Jacob?" she asked, still looking at the dirt.

"Yeah."

"Jacob is a very fine name."

"Jake fits me better."

She raised her eyes and was immediately caught by his gaze. "Just as Harry fits me?"

"It does." He smiled wryly. "You don't look like a Harriett. A Harriett should be an old lady with a tiny sharp chin and a mouth that looks like someone stitched a seam across her face."

Harriett returned her gaze to the ground. Should she take that statement as a compliment? "You do look like a Jacob," she told him.

He chuckled. "You don't need to get nasty."

"I wasn't." Jacob did fit him—a strong name, solid. In spite of all his faults, he had those qualities.

As if to contradict Harriett's charitable thoughts, Jake reached around into his jacket pocket and pulled out a flask. He offered it to her. "You should take a little of this, Harry. It'll warm your blood."

Harriett looked at the flask in horror. "Don't be ridiculous! I've never in my life touched spirits."

"Not even wine?"

One of his unruly, devilish brows inched up, and Harriett detected a gleam of laughter in his eyes. But this subject was certainly not a matter for amusement.

"Not even wine, Mr. Carradine." She made her tone as stern as possible, a formidable task when her voice was shaking with a chill.

"Then you really can't know it's so evil, can you? You haven't even tried it."

"One does not need to jump off a cliff to know that the fall will be fatal," she said righteously.

He grinned. "I won't let you fall."

"Fiddle! What poppycock!"

"Tsk, tsk." He sounded so much like a stern schoolmarm that Harriett almost smiled. "Your aunt told me you had a mind that was closed and set, but I didn't believe her. Now I see she was right."

"I do not have a closed mind!" Harriett cried. "Back in Boston I belonged to all of the most liberal ladies' discussion groups, and I. . . . Oh, spit! I'll take a sip of your silly spirits. A strong-minded person who is in control of the base instincts need not fear the evils of liquor."

"Is that so?" he asked mildly.

She took the offered flask, tipped it to her mouth, and imbibed liquid fire. "Oooh!" The word came out as a gasp. She choked, coughed, then choked again.

Jake got up and pounded her on the back, none too gently. "Not so fast, Harry. Sip. Don't drink."

"I've had quite enough!" she rasped.

"You'll get used to it. Take a smaller amount this time."

Goaded by the challenge in his eyes, she took a

smaller sip. The liquor still burned, but for the first time in hours she began to feel warm. The fire was torture on the mouth, but once inside the body it was heaven.

"Yes." She hiccuped. "That is a bit better."

Jake sat back down, one corner of his mouth lifted in a peculiar grin. "Not so bad, is it?"

"The taste is vile!"

"But it warms your insides."

She hiccuped again, a bit sheepishly. "Well, yes. It does that." After a few more sips, the warmth of the whiskey spread and her aches began to fade. Time seemed to stretch as Harriett tried to remember how much she had drunk and how long Jake had been sitting across from her. The campsite grew fuzzy around the edges. Her body felt light as a feather—almost as if she could float right off her stool and drift up into the sky.

Dodger whined and put his head in her lap. She reached out to scratch his ear, but missed her target and hit his nose instead. The pup backed off with an injured glare.

Harriett took yet another sip—or was it called a swig when one drank spiritous liquor? She was beginning to see the lure of the evil stuff. After a while it didn't even taste bad.

"Goo'ness," she slurred. "Th'night's warmer than I thought."

"You may have had enough of that stuff," Jake told her. He pried the flask from her fingers. "But at least that should give you a good night's sleep."

"Zleep?" She giggled. "Can't zleep! Th . . . the blankets are all . . . all . . ."

"Wet," he supplied.

Jake had a smile that was sunlight warm, Harriett decided. She tried to measure the breadth of his shoulders as he got up and came to her. They were broad as the plains, she thought, and liked the analogy. Who would've guessed she was so clever?

Why did Jake have to loom so whenever he was around her? She didn't like to be loomed over—especially by a man. A man of Jake's size should be careful not to loom. He made a woman feel as small and insignificant as a bug—a ladybug! She almost giggled at her own clever thought. A ladybug! So easily squashed. Harriett suspected that it might feel good to be squashed, if Jake did the squashing.

"Um . . . tired." She leaned toward Jake as he took her arm and helped her from the stool.

"Time to go to bed, I think." He guided her toward the wagon, grabbing one of the blankets hanging closest to the fire. "This one feels dry. Come on, Harry," he urged as she stumbled against him. "Damn. No one can get drunk on that little whiskey."

"Drunk?" She stiffened, then gave forth a delicate little belch. "Ooz drunk?"

He chuckled. "You are. Drunk as a skunk."

"Poppy . . . fiddle!"

"Poor Harry. You'll be after my hide in the morning. If you can stand by then."

"After yerrrhide. Don' be z . . . z . . . zilly."

Jake shook his head ruefully. She gazed up at him with unfocused eyes.

"Do you think Caro . . . Caroline's pred . . . pretty?"

"What?" he almost laughed.

"Do you . . ." She hiccuped. "You heard whaddeye zaid!"

"Come on, Harry. Concentrate. You need to climb into the wagon."

"Anszer me. Dammit?"

"Dammit?" He did laugh this time. "You are drunk, aren't you?"

"Is she?"

"Is she what?"

"You know."

"All right. Caroline MacKenzie is a very pretty woman. Or perhaps I should say that she's a very pretty girl. Hardly a woman."

"She likes you," Harriett muttered.

"God damn, Harry. Are you going to make me carry you into that wagon?"

"She didn't need to kiss you."

"You do get nosy when you're snockered, don't you?"

He lifted her into his arms, edged himself onto the tailgate, and swung them both into the wagon. The moment he pulled her against him Harriett seemed to melt. Her eyes closed, her head fell back, a tiny smile twitched at her lips. Her dress was still wet and clammy, but Jake could feel the heat of her skin through the flimsy material. His own blood started to warm.

"Harry! Wake up!"

Her eyes blinked open, crossed, then closed again. He shook her gently, then laid her on the wooden slats and turned to retrieve the dry blanket.

"That wasn't ladylike," Harriett complained.

"What wasn't ladylike?" Jake tucked the blanket around her, then decided that wasn't going to work. The blanket would only get wet.

"You rescued me, and I didn't crawl all over you like flies on . . . on a mule pile!"

"Forget Caroline," he advised with a sigh. "Harry, I never would have guessed you were such a lush."

"Spit!" The word was punctuated by a hiccup. "S'all your fault."

"I warned you I was a villain. Can you get out of those wet clothes?"

"Izzhe . . . is she . . . prettier than . . . than . . . ?"

"Is Caroline prettier than you?"

Jake regarded her with a measuring smile. "Well now, let me see. Yellow hair is generally preferred to red. And you've gotten a whole crop of freckles on your nose over the past few weeks. But I'd have to say you've got the nicer figure, and, when you're not wearing some godawful frown, your face is at least as pretty as hers."

Harriett couldn't quite coordinate her muscles into a proper scowl.

"And of course Caroline is sweeter by far," he added with a twisted grin.

"Spit!"

"I really think you should get out of those clothes."

She was beginning to shiver again, and who knew when her aunt would be back to help; the little lush was going to catch pneumonia and die.

"All right. Let's get that dress off."

Harriett flinched as he crawled behind her and worked on the buttons of her bodice. "Don't worry, Harry. I've seen plenty of women in my time. One more isn't anything special."

"Your hands are cold. Cold," she complained, but she didn't move away when he dragged the wet material down over her shoulders. Obediently she lifted her arms so he could peel away the long sleeves.

"God," he said quietly. He tried not to look at her as he pulled off her shoes, skirts, petticoats, and chemise. She wasn't wearing those ridiculous fluffy trousers that she'd worn for the first days of the trip.

Jake couldn't help but drink in the feminine curves that had been hidden under all that clothing. Her legs were slender and straight, the skin silky soft, her belly taut and flat, and her breasts . . . her breasts were beautiful—high, rose-tipped mounds fine as milky porcelain. Her arms were rounded and firm, and looked as though they could wind around a man and make him forget whatever she wanted a man to forget.

"Lord above!" Jake whispered, unable to drag his eyes away. The exclamation was a prayer for protection as well as forgiveness. A woman like Harriett Foster, Jake decided, could turn a man inside out if she wanted to.

Harriett's eyes popped open. She'd appeared almost asleep as she obediently submitted to his ministrations. She sat up, ignoring her state of undress. "Is she really prettier 'n me?"

"Sweetheart," Jake said with a sigh. "Caroline MacKenzie doesn't hold a candle to you. Not that I've seen as much of her . . ." He smiled wickedly. "But I've never seen any woman who could hold a candle to you."

"Oh." She started to lie back, but Jake caught her and wrapped the blanket around her shoulders. He was a goddamned saint, Jake decided, to cover all that bounty from view.

Harriett sighed in contentment as he wrapped her completely and laid her back on the floor of the wagon. His jacket served as her pillow. Reaching blindly for him, she murmured, "Don't leave. Jacob . . ."

The name trailed out into a long, contented sigh. He could have her right then, Jake realized. She would probably welcome him warmly, submit to him pliantly, following a long-buried instinct but not realizing what she was doing. He ought to take advantage of her. God knew she'd been trouble enough, and a man deserved a little pleasure for his pain.

Then, as he considered the temptation of pleasure, a frightening truth flashed across Jake's brain—a horrifying certainty. For weeks it had stalked him, and Jake had studiously ignored it, dismissing his preoccupation as mere lust. Tonight it pounced, crackling through his brain like a thunderstorm. The river—that swirling flood that had almost washed Harriett away—had swept away his last pretense that he didn't love her, that his life wouldn't be empty without her, scoldings and all. He was roped, hogtied, and branded as thoroughly as any man could be—by a little prig of a spinster from Boston, no less. Jake wanted more of Harry Foster than a boozed-up night in the back of a creaking wagon. He wanted her willing, joyful, passionate, giving herself enthusiastically with all senses intact. He wanted to wake up with her every morning, spend his evenings sitting with her on some homey porch, pestered by children bearing her red hair and green eyes—and her freckles.

He scowled; his stomach lurched in alarm. Here was a reason to start living life again if he could win her. Did he really want to try? Or was he too damned scared?

Many months had passed since Jake Carradine had been frightened of anything. His life had held nothing of value, so what use was fear? Now he was damned afraid. He was afraid of Harriett Foster. And all this time he'd told her that she should be afraid of him.

Jake clambered down from the wagon and quietly closed the tailgate. His gaze lingered on Harriett's sleeping form. He had a lot to think about. Or perhaps he had nothing to think about—no choice, when all was said and done. He was already caught, like a wolf in a steel trap. But unlike the wolf, Jake felt the steel jaws of the trap close with an ache of sharp pleasure. Unlike the wolf, Jake didn't really want to escape. Damned if he would let Harry escape, either.

Ash Hollow was crowded to bursting. At least a hundred and fifty wagons camped in the little valley, and the air was fragrant with woodsmoke as well as the fresh scent of the ash and cherry trees that crowded the creek bank, the rose and currant bushes that carpeted the flat floodplain and the bluffs.

"I thought we'd never get here." Harriett brushed stray red locks back from her face and tucked them into the disintegrating bun at her nape. Seen from the hard seat of the wagon box, through the dusty haze of the late-afternoon heat, Ash Hollow looked like Eden. "I'm exhausted," she told her aunt.

"You do look tired, dear. Are you catching a fever from your dunking yesterday?"

"God only knows what I caught yesterday," Harriett remarked cryptically.

The day had been a terrible one. Aside from the company traveling a record distance over a rough, muddy trail and negotiating Windlass Hill—a decline so steep that the wagons had to be lowered by ropes, with brakes set firmly and the teams led instead of driven— Harriett had awakened that morning with a thousand hammers pounding in her head, a stomach ready to rise into her throat, and a mouth that tasted like mule droppings smelled. She'd not been cheered by an inability to recall anything but the most vague memories of the night before. She remembered taking Jake's challenge to warm herself with a sip of whiskey. She remembered a feeling of woozy well-being and giggly silliness. And that was all. Waking without a stitch of clothing and only a blanket for decency started horrible suspicions brewing in Harriett's mind—suspicions that didn't make her stomach feel any better.

She hadn't seen Jake all day long. If she had seen him, she wouldn't have had the courage to ask the questions that plagued her about the night before. What a horrible day. If she survived this odyssey, poor Edwin wouldn't know her. She wasn't sure that she still knew herself.

The Indiana Company joined the crowd in the valley just as evening fell. The hollow was lush and fragrant, with clean, clear creek water and abundant wood—a true oasis on the grueling trail. The emigrants celebrated their respite together, and a huge communal bonfire was lit that set the valley aglow. Even though they were from several different companies, few of the emigrants were strangers. They had played tag with each other along the trail, passing, then falling behind, then passing again. They'd swapped stories, seen each other bury those who dropped along the way, lent each other healers and potions for the sick, and occasionally celebrated together a successful river crossing or similar small victory. Now they were through the worst of the plains, and everyone felt that a massive festivity was in order.

Harriett was too tired to dance, even though as one of the few women present she was much in demand. Mrs. Hornsby's entertainers were doing a fine business, and even Sadie, large and awkward as she was, was plagued by prospective partners.

The men were hard to discourage, but Harriett managed—with a black scowl if polite refusals didn't do the job. She wanted to retire to her own wagon and sleep, but she couldn't quite tear herself away from the sight of Caroline MacKenzie drooling over Jake Carradine. The blond woman ignored the angry glares of her husband and fluttered around Jake like a moth around a flame. The baggage never did anything overtly wrong, but her intentions, Harriett reflected sourly, must be obvious to one and all. And Jake didn't seem in the least perturbed, the villain.

"My goodness, Harriett! If you don't stop scowling you'll begin to look older than I feel." Sadie sank into a heap beside Harriett and breathed a sigh of relief. "I don't believe I actually tried to dance with Horace Smith. I'm afraid my dancing days are over for a while."

"You looked more graceful than Horace," Harriett told her friend.

Sadie smiled. "The man's an ox. But a nice ox." She eyed Harriett with concern. "You look sour as a pickle. Are you not feeling well?"

Harriett didn't answer, and Sadie followed her gaze to where Jake Carradine was deep in conversation with Caroline MacKenzie. Caroline postured, one hand on her hip, the other resting on Jake's muscular arm. Her hip was cocked provocatively, her eyes peeped up at her prey from under thick lashes.

Sadie grimaced at the scene. "So that's what's scrambled your eggs," she said. "That little hussy's going to earn herself a set-down from her husband one of these days."

"What little hussy?" Harriett feigned unconcern.

"You know very well which hussy, dear. The one with her claws in Jake's arm. And I'll just bet she'd like to get them into several other sections of him as well."

"Sadie!"

Sadie shrugged. "I hope you're not going to let Caroline get away with that?"

"What do you mean?"

"It looks to me like Jake needs rescuing." Sadie smiled at her, a smile that was much too knowing for Harriett's peace of mind. "Seems the least you could do after he pulled you out of the river. Why don't you go ask him to dance?"

"Not in a million years!"

"Oh, Harriett! I know you're sweet on the man."

"Poppycock!"

"You don't have to hide it from me. I think Jake Carradine's a wonderful man. A bit rough around the edges, perhaps. He needs to have a bit put in his mouth and yanked down hard a time or two. But I tell you, Harriett, if that man was a horse, I'd buy him."

Harriett squirmed. "I have a sweet, civilized fiancé

waiting for me in San Francisco—someone who doesn't need his bit yanked to turn him into a decent human being. Mr. Carradine is merely a friend. For heaven's sake! He's my hired man!"

"My goodness!" Sadie's voice lowered to a dramatic whisper. "Do you see where she has her hand? And I'll bet Caroline thinks she's being subtle."

Harriett's vision started swimming in red. "I do wish that woman would grow a wart or two and lose some of that shiny yellow hair."

Sadie nodded in agreement. "That would seem only just. I vow even Jake looks embarrassed. I didn't know that anything could embarrass him."

Harriett had seen enough. After all, Jake Carradine was her employee, was he not? She therefore was responsible for his behavior—and his safety. And Caroline MacKenzie appeared to be closing in for the kill.

"Excuse me, Sadie." Harriett got up and brushed the dirt from her skirts, girding herself for the coming battle. "If Callum MacKenzie won't do something about that shameful display, then I certainly will."

"Bravo!" Sadie cheered.

Harriett marched over to Jake and Caroline like an Amazon marching to war. "Good evening, Mrs. MacKenzie." She put an innocent-sounding emphasis on the *Mrs*.

Caroline turned, casually removing her hand from Jake's thigh. She gave Harriett a sugary smile. "Miss Foster. Poor dear. You look ill." The trollop leaned closer to Jake. Her blue eyes gleamed with challenge. "You really should rest, my dear. A good night's sleep might cure that greenish tinge to your complexion."

Harriett didn't have the patience for such games. "Better to be tinged green than scarlet, Mrs. MacKenzie. If I had your fair countenance, I certainly wouldn't flirt so with my husband's displeasure. Mr. MacKenzie looks as though he might like to rearrange your features a bit."

Caroline stiffened, and she sent a quick glance in Callum's direction. Then her narrow-eyed gaze returned to Harriett. "You are insufferably rude and foul-minded, Miss Foster. It seems that the hardships of this trail bring out the true nature in some of us."

"Yes," Harriett returned firmly. "It does seem that way." She turned to Jake, who had assumed a poker face. Sadie was wrong; he didn't appear embarrassed at all, and could the crinkles around his eyes reveal silent amusement? "Mr. Carradine, I need you."

"Don't say!" He inched one brow toward the sky.

Damn the man! An innocent mistake in choice of words and he pounces. "One of the oxen has a painful foot," she stammered on. "I'd like you to look at it. Now, please."

He grinned. "Yes, ma'am."

Harriett couldn't resist a look over her shoulder as she and Jake walked away. Caroline's face, twisted as it was, didn't seem all that pretty after all. Harriett longed to stick out her tongue in a childish show of victory, but she satisfied herself with a smile.

"That was quite a little act," Jake said as they walked toward Harriett's wagon. "We don't really have a lame animal, do we." It was a statement of fact, not a question.

"No!" she snapped.

"Lying, Harry? I'm surprised at you."

Their camp was dark, the cookfire only embers. Harriett unlatched the tailgate of the wagon and slammed it down. "The only thing lame around here is your sense of decency! Mrs. MacBride thought you needed rescuing, but I think you were enjoying that crude little display. The person I'm concerned about is poor Mr. MacKenzie. He'll doubtless lose his head with jeal-

ousy and challenge you—and he wouldn't stand a
chance against a man like—"

"Harry." He put his hand over her mouth. "You're
babbling. No need to explain how jealous you were. I
could see."

"Jealous?" she sputtered, pushing away his hand.
"Of you? Spit! I'd sooner be jealous of a—"

He cut her off again, this time with his mouth. His
lips slanted across hers as he pushed her back against
the wagon wheel. Harriett struggled for only a moment, then realized the fight was hopeless. She vowed
not to enjoy herself, though. She wouldn't thrill to the
feel of his strong arms holding her; she wouldn't melt
as his tongue thrust past her lips and took possession
of her mouth; she wouldn't ache with forbidden longing as his thighs, his belly, his chest crushed her deliciously back into the night shadows.

When he finally released her, she had broken every
vow. Fighting Jake Carradine was hard enough. Fighting herself, it seemed, was impossible. She had no
more discipline than a wanton.

"Why did you do that?" she gasped, breathless,
shaking, dismayed. A horrible suspicion surfaced in
her mind. "Did . . . did something happen last night
to make you think . . . uh . . . ?"

He pulled her up against him, and all her strength
would not dislodge his grasp. "Yes. As a matter of fact,
something did. You were soused, you know."

Her eyes grew wide. He was too close. How could
any woman think when her breasts were crushed
against a man's chest and every inch of him seemed
molded to her, including several inches that Harriett
was sure were terribly indecent. "I was merely tired. I
don't get . . . soused."

He kissed the tip of her nose before she could dodge.
"You were soused, Harry. You're lucky I'm such a gentleman."

"You're a gentleman?"

"I've decided that everything you've nagged me about is right. I'm a far better man than anyone gives me credit for." He grinned down at her, white teeth catching the moonlight.

"I said that?"

He was incredibly handsome, Harriett realized quite against her will. Trimmed and washed, with straight white teeth, dimples, and eyes framed by thick, dark lashes, Jake Carradine would be hard for a saint to resist. For a moment Harriett felt a morsel of sympathy for poor Caroline.

"You did indeed say that," he reminded her.

"I don't think that's what I meant. Mr. Carradine, do you suppose you could let me go?"

"No."

The man was loco.

"As I was saying, I decided you were right." He loosened his grip and backed her up against the wagon again. Penned on both sides by his arms, she was neatly caged. "I also decided that you need someone to take care of you. And since I'm a fellow of such sterling qualities, I'm just the someone you need."

"What?"

"You're going to belong to me, Harry. You've made me feel alive again—alive enough to see something I want—something that makes life worth the trouble. I've always been a man who gets what he wants."

She pushed against him furiously, to no avail. "I belong to no man! Not anyone, and certainly not to you! I'm my own mistress; I make my own decisions. Jacob Carradine—you toad!—I don't even like you!"

"You like me," he said with an infuriating smile. "You love me, in fact."

Her eyes widened. "Arrogant clod! You're mad."

"I'm sane for the first time in months."

"Who do you think you are to be saying such things! You have no power over me!"

"I have all the power I need."

As if to prove his point, he kissed her again, his mouth gently plundering hers, ravaging her resistance, forcing her to respond. Harriett couldn't help herself. Some part of her had sold out to the Devil. She was helpless in the grip of her own unfamiliar, unwanted passion. Her tongue willingly sparred with his, her arms wrapped around him, hands playing in wanton delight over the muscles in his back. When his mouth moved to her throat, she instinctively arched her head back to give him easier access to her flesh. All the while an ache grew within her, coiled restlessly between her legs and speared straight to her heart.

Finally he set her back from him, supporting her as she swayed. "Don't worry, Harry. I'm not a thief. Whatever I take from you you'll be more than willing to give."

She could only look at him helplessly, stunned, robbed of speech.

Once again he kissed her, a mere brush of the lips that was more affection than passion. He turned to leave.

Harriett stood rooted to the spot.

Jake turned back, one brow angled up in pure mischief. "If you're going to fight me, lady, you'll have to do much better than that."

Harriett stared after him as he walked away. She tried to deny that the fire Jake Carradine had lit inside her was anything but wicked, foolish physical desire. Women like Harriett Foster simply did not fall in love with men like Jake Carradine. True, the man had his good qualities: intelligence, courage, even occasional tenderness and sensitivity. He was handsome. Devilishly handsome. But totally unacceptable. Even if she were in love with Jake Carradine—ridiculous thought!

—she was promised to Edwin, who was a much more suitable match.

She would simply have to temper her feelings with good sense, Harriett decided. Discipline and good sense. Yes, that was certainly the cure.

11

Journal entry—June 20—At Robideaux Pass: The monotonous scenery of the trail has finally changed. These last few days since reaching the North Platte River our eyes have been treated to the most spectacular rock formations that one could imagine, named after the architecture they so resemble. Castle Bluffs, Courthouse Rock, Chimney Rock—they are the first evidence we have seen that this prairie can produce anything more substantial than a molehill. Though perhaps I exaggerate. At times the bluffs beside the river seem substantial enough—when the poor oxen and mules must pull our wagons over them. But to our weary eyes the landscape until now has seemed a flat monochrome of green-gold, pretty enough in detail, with its wildflowers and lush grasses, but to see nothing else day after day is tiring for the soul as well as the eyes.

Shortly after noon this day we reached a prominence known as Robideaux Pass, from which we have our first view of the distant Rocky Mountains. Here the grass is lush, timber is abundant, and a spring of pure cold water is a welcome change from the muddy water of the Platte. A trading post of sorts has been built at this spot by Mr. Robideaux, who is a pleasant enough man with an Indian wife and several little brown children. We have camped here, even though the hour is early and some members of our company want to press on to Horse Creek, which Mr. Ware's guidebook warns is in country that is once again sandy and barren. Wiser heads prevailed, however. We will take our rest here and enjoy Mr. Robideaux's trading post. He has some fine cotton material, and I may purchase some lengths to make myself a poke jacket the like of which the Mormon women seem to find so comfortable. (Yes, my readers, we have seen many of that strange sect traveling the same direction as we.) I should also like to purchase a wide-brimmed straw hat, for I've found that my fashionable bonnets do little to keep the sun from my face. The trading post boasts a smith shop, and Mr. Carradine has taken one of our wheels to be repaired. It has a broken rim —again. I would advise anyone intent on making this trip to bring extra axles and wheels, for the rough road makes the sturdiest of wagons seem very fragile.

"I vow this store would have not rated the least notice in Boston, but here it seems the height of refinement. What a few weeks away from civilization will do to one's taste! Really, dear Harriett. Sometimes I wonder why I let you talk me into accompanying you on this journey."

Harriett smiled and held up a bolt of bright calico. "You wanted to come. Remember all your talk of new places and new faces and how starched old Boston was boring you to tears? Besides, you're enjoying yourself, Aunt. You look younger every day."

Lucille blushed. "I suppose in some ways it has been . . . stimulating. Oh, look, Harriett. There's Mr. Carradine fetching our wheel. You know—I had the most peculiar conversation with him this morning. Do you think he's been drinking again?"

Harriett's ears perked with interest. The past few days she had become an expert at avoiding Jake Carradine, but frequently she felt him watching her. The clear-eyed confidence of his expression unnerved her, as if he were only waiting to pounce, as if somehow he thought that when he did pounce, she would simply stand and surrender.

"I don't believe he's touched a drop of liquor in days, Aunt. What is this conversation you thought peculiar?"

"He took me quite by surprise in saying he was going to marry you. As I've told you, dear, I was quite convinced that he had a certain regard for you, but I would think your attitude toward him would be enough to put any man off."

Harriett laid down the cloth she'd been examining and stared at her aunt wide-eyed.

"You haven't made an engagement with him, have you dear? Without telling me?"

"What a ridiculous notion! Of course I haven't! Why would I do such a preposterous thing? Even if I were so foolish as to have formed an attachment for him, I certainly wouldn't marry him. He's crude, he's arrogant, he's immoral . . . !"

Lucille gave her a bemused look, and Harriett cut short her enumeration of Jake Carradine's failings. Not that there weren't a host more that could be listed, but even she recognized the hint of stridency in her voice.

"I don't know where he got the idea!"

"I didn't ask him, dear. But Mr. Carradine seems to be a man who doesn't speak of something unless he knows it for a fact. Perhaps he sees something in you that you don't see yourself."

"Aunt! Really!" Harriett took Lucille by the arm and

pulled her out of the trading post. A glance at Mr. Robideaux, who was busy with another customer, assured her that he hadn't heard this most embarrassing conversation.

"Well, Harriett." Lucille brushed Harriett's hand from her arm. "I know you insist on marrying that pudding-faced Edwin. But if your mother—God be good to her!—had taught you the first thing about life and about men, which she didn't, you'd have the sense to cast your bait out for Jake Carradine. Not often does a woman of your age find a man so anxious to be hooked. And a good man at that—handsome, kind . . ."

"Kind? Whatever makes you think Jake Carradine has a kind bone in his body?"

"Haven't you watched him teach Chad MacBride how to drive a wagon, or seen him help Sadie with their chores? And when he tends the oxen—even when he puts dreadful ointment on their feet—they don't flick an ear. Your little dog adores him. Animals do know a man's character, dear."

"What do oxen and a dog know? They're dumb creatures without a proper brain between them!"

"It seems they know more than you, Harriett. And wasn't it you who constantly lectured the poor man about living up to his good qualities?"

"I didn't mean . . . ! Oh, spit! Aunt Lucille! This is a pointless conversation. I have promised to marry Edwin Garrett. And even if I were free, I certainly wouldn't tie myself to a man like Jake Carradine. He's the kind of man who would charm a woman out of everything she has—even her self-respect."

"But to be loved by such a man, to see that possessive gleam in his eye . . ."

"Aunt! Don't get carried away." Harriett noted with disgust that Lucille was getting a downright dreamy look on her face. "You're a romantic, and I'm not. I don't give a fiddle for all that mush. My parents had the perfect relationship."

Lucille snorted indelicately.

"Well, it's true!" Harriett insisted with a frown. "Affection and respect are what's important, you know. Romantic love is simply a childish passion of immature people."

"That sounds like one of your mother's maxims," Lucille scoffed. "What are you going to do, dear Harriett, if someday you fall prey to one of those childish passions?"

"I would simply ignore it until it faded!" Harriett answered confidently.

"Is that what you're doing with Jake Carradine?"

"Yes! I mean . . . no! Now you've gotten me all confused!"

Lucille's mouth curved up in a satisfied smile.

Harriet brushed an imaginary speck from her skirt, wishing this conversation could be dismissed as easily. "I'm going back into the store to buy that length of cloth," she told her aunt in a hasty change of subject. "It would do very well as material to make a poke jacket, and also a divided skirt."

Lucille shook her head. "A divided skirt, dear? You'll scandalize the entire company."

"I don't let men dictate to me what I can and cannot wear, Aunt Lucille." Harriett pressed her lips into a stubborn line. "This prejudice against women wearing divided garments is senseless. Besides, the skirt will be entirely modest."

"Well, if you don't mind, dear, I think I'll go back to —Oh, goodness!"

The tone of her aunt's voice made Harriett look up. She followed Lucille's gaze to a couple emerging from the trees—none other than silver-haired, silver-eyed Lawrence Steede with a lissome young woman from another company on his arm. They were completely engrossed in each other. Steede bent down to whisper something in the woman's ear, and she tittered.

Lucille quickly turned away, hiding her face. Harriett's temper began a slow burn. How dare that immoral, irresponsible dandy hurt her aunt! He wasn't good enough to touch the hem of Lucille's skirt, and yet she had condescended to walk with him, cook for him, dance with him, and God only knew what else. How dare he break Lucille's poor heart!

"I think I'll go back to the wagon," Lucille said in a quiet voice.

Harriett took her aunt's arm. "I'll go with you."

Lucille was silent on the walk back, and silent when she took refuge in their tent. Harriett's heart ached for her, but she could do nothing other than grant her the solace of privacy. She considered for a moment going back to the trading post and purchasing her material, but decided against it. If she saw Lawrence Steede there, she was likely to throttle the man, or at least deliver a stern lecture—a waste of energy and breath. Better to start up the cookfire and see to dinner.

"That's what comes of romance," she told Dodger in a world-weary voice. "Let that be a lesson to you. Stay away from the fire and you won't get burned." Who was she trying to convince, Harriett asked silently, the dog or herself?

Suddenly she wondered where Jake was. Dodger had become devoted to the man, and wherever he was, the pup wasn't far behind. Harriett suspected Jake was wooing the dog with treats. The pup thought with his stomach, his devotion a "character reference" that could be bought with a few morsels of bacon.

The man had tried to woo Harriett the same way, but instead of bacon he used kisses and tempting glimpses of a passion she didn't understand—didn't want to understand.

Jake Carradine would just have to learn that such treats didn't work on Harriett Foster!

Two days later, at Fort Laramie—or Fort John on the Laramie, as the outpost was more properly called—Harriett was delighted to find that a most warm and encouraging letter from Mrs. Bloomer awaited her. She wrote a long letter in reply and posted it with her partially complete journal to the *Lily.* She also purchased material for some new garments for both her and Lucille. A woman traveling with a Morman group on the north side of the river gave her a pattern for the poke jacket. Harriett was rather surprised that the lady was such an intelligent, pleasant person, in spite of the rather awful rumors that circulated about the strange sect.

Harriett also purchased a saddle horse, with the help and advice of Horatio the "horse breaker." Everyone in this country seemed comfortable atop a horse except Harriett, and she was determined to remedy this lack in her education. Jake came upon them making the purchase.

"A mule might be more suited to your disposition," he commented, gray eyes twinkling.

Harriett jumped at the sound of Jake's voice, causing her prospective purchase to snort in alarm and toss its dapple-gray head. Harriett gave a little squeak of terror and lunged back—to land right in Jake Carradine's arms.

"Then again," Jake said with a chuckle, "maybe you're not as stubborn as I thought." His arms closed about Harriett before she could escape. "Steady there, Harry. That horse isn't going to attack you."

"Of course it isn't!" she snapped. The beast that worried Harriett was not the horse. She unlocked Jake's hands from around her waist while Horatio watched with interest.

"Thank you, Mr. Carradine," she said with strained calm. "I'll admit I'm a bit nervous around horses." Not to mention being more than a bit nervous around Jake. He'd done nothing overt since that devastating kiss at Ash Hollow, when he'd declared that she would belong to him. But the very waiting for the other boot to drop—so to speak—was straining her nerves.

Horatio and Jake ended up conferring on which horse she should purchase. For once Harriett didn't mind letting the men make the decision for her. Horses were animals she knew nothing about. But she had learned about oxen; she was confident she could also learn about horses.

Her first chance to try out her new mount was at Warm Springs campground, one day out of Fort Laramie. The trail that day had been rough. From now on, Mr. Ware's book warned, they would traverse mountainous, rocky terrain. Debris littered the trail—anvils, chests, forges, trunks, clothing, tents, stoves, sacks of beans—a grim reminder that the mountains lay ahead, and every pound of excess weight decreased the chances of a successful crossing. At last they had left the dreary plains behind and felt that the gold fields were almost within reach. The whole Indiana Company was nervous and excited at the same time.

But the thought of crossing the mountains didn't make Harriett half as nervous as the little chestnut mare that stood before her. With Dodger and the Cutters' sheepdog bitch watching skeptically, she bridled and saddled the beast as Horace had instructed her. That was the easy part. Daisy—as the mare had been named by its former owner—was a well-mannered creature and gazed at Harriett with soft brown eyes that bespoke an amiable and steady disposition. But Harriett wasn't fooled. She knew that the minute she put a foot to the stirrup, all hell would break loose.

Harriett was right. But the poor mare had nothing

to do with the disaster. The horse stood patiently while
its new owner made several attempts to mount, finally
succeeding on the third try. Harriett swung her leg,
neatly clad in her new divided skirt, over the saddle
and grabbed at the saddle horn to keep her whole body
from following. For a moment she wobbled while she
swung her foot in search of the stirrup. Her heel made
solid connection with the mare's flank, and the little
chestnut obediently jumped forward into a brisk trot.
Unprepared, Harriett bounced for a few painful strides
and then took to the air. When the mare halted and
looked around, its new mistress was on the ground
muttering some very unladylike words. The sheepdog
ambled off in apparent disgust while Dodger trotted
over and stuck a wet nose in Harriett's face, then sat
and gave Daisy a look of sympathy.

"You're no help!" Harriett mumbled to the dog as
she picked herself up from the ground and dusted off
her smarting backside. She grabbed Daisy's reins and
put her foot once again in the stirrup, telling herself
that Harriett Foster would not—absolutely would not!
—be defeated by a damned horse.

"Need some help?"

Jake's voice so startled Harriett that she caught her
foot in the stirrup and lost her balance. She clung to
the saddle horn to keep from ending up on the ground
again. "Spit!" she cursed.

She almost died of mortification when Jake took her
ankle and eased her foot out of the stirrup. "How
many times have you been on a horse?" he inquired,
exceedingly polite. But his eyes held an irritating twinkle.

"Three times," she answered tartly. "Twice in Boston. And once when I watched your buffalo hunt. I'm
all right once I'm on top of the beast."

"So I saw," he drawled.

"Mr. Carradine . . . !"

"Don't you think it's time you called me Jake?"

She hesitated, then compromised. "Jacob." Harriett didn't want to argue; she simply wanted him to go away. "After a little practice with Daisy I'm sure I'll be quite competent."

He gave Daisy a sympathetic look, apparently agreeing with Dodger. "I'm sure you're right, Harry. But maybe I'll just ride along this time."

"You really don't need to. I'm only going out to Register Rock."

"Well, I was planning to go see that sight myself. Might as well ride out there now." He swept a glance over her attire. "Interesting getup you're wearing."

She sighed in exasperation. Men were so narrowminded! "I made it specifically so that I can ride astride. Have you ever ridden sidesaddle, Mr. . . . uh . . . Jacob?"

"Well, no."

"You wouldn't like it," she assured him.

He smiled tolerantly.

Once Harriett managed to get aboard her mount, she was more competent, just as she claimed. Her seat was a bit wobbly, her knuckles white where they grasped the saddle horn, but she did manage to stay atop the little mare. Having Jake ride escort stung her pride, but she was wise enough to listen to his pointers on steadying her seat and controlling her horse. By the end of their thirty-minute ride she was feeling as though she might survive, but Dodger, who had trotted along with them, still regarded her with doubtful eyes.

Register Rock was a sandstone cliff in which thousands of emigrants along the Oregon and California trails had carved their names, their initials, messages for loved ones who might follow, and words of wisdom they thought the world should know. Harriett followed the tradition by carving both her name and Lucille's in clear, deep letters. Jake and Dodger both watched her with interest—and, it appeared, with equal understanding.

"There!" she said with satisfaction. "Now our names are preserved for all time in Wyoming Territory. And you said we wouldn't get past Fort Kearney."

Jake conceded his mistake graciously. "I was wrong about you, Harry. You've got more guts than most men."

For once his voice didn't mock. Harriett was touched by his sincerity. She tried not to be, but she was. "Thank you, Jacob."

His eyes had gone from gray to black in a way that made her uneasy. "Jacob . . . I did tell you, didn't I, that I'm going to San Francisco to be married."

"Yes." That knowledge didn't seem to deter him, for the look in his eyes was still there. "Your aunt told me about Mr. Garrett. You don't love him, do you." He didn't so much question as state a fact.

"I like him. I respect him. We believe in the same ideals. Those are the things that are important to me, Jacob. Love is . . . love is much more than heart flutterings and girlish dreams and . . . and yearnings."

He was silent, but regarded her with eyes that mirrored both pity and confidence. He didn't believe her for one moment, Harriett concluded uneasily.

"Aren't you going to carve your name, Jacob?" she asked in a swift change of subject. "I understand it's a bit of a tradition."

A slow smile spread across his face, as though she'd said something funny.

She held out her knife. "Use this. The tip is ruined anyway. You might as well finish the job."

He took the knife, deftly twirled it in the air, then flipped the blade so that, dull tip and all, it buried itself in a patch of soil ten feet distant. Jake looked grim and —Harriett could scarcely believe it, but it was there on his face!—embarrassed. Suddenly the light dawned.

"You can't write, can you?"

He shifted his gaze to the ground, his mouth a tightly disciplined line.

"Oh! I'm so sorry. Jacob, I didn't mean to embarrass you!"

Jake's mouth twitched. He kept his eyes lowered in a humility most unusual for the arrogant Jake Carradine.

"You needn't be ashamed," she comforted him. "Many people can neither read nor write."

"My family never had much time for such things." His voice was strained. Harriett's heart went out to him.

"You wanted to learn, didn't you?" she guessed.

He didn't answer, but when he lifted his face, Harriett could see that his expression was still under stern control. Here was her opportunity to make at least a small mark in the world.

"I'll teach you to read!"

"I'm too old for that," he said gruffly.

"Oh, no! You're a very intelligent man, Jacob!" The more she thought about the idea, the more appealing it became. "You'll learn in no time. We'll spend every evening in the tent with the books I brought with me. Oh, Jacob! This will be an adventure for both of us!"

The slow smile that spread across Jake's face brought an instant's suspicion to Harriett's mind, but she quickly dismissed it. How could she deny a human being who was reaching out to improve himself? She should be grateful that through her inspiration Jake had finally lifted himself from his pit of vice and was climbing toward the light.

"I suppose that's only fair," he conceded. The gleam was back in his eyes. "I'll teach you to ride. You'll teach me to read."

"Yes," she agreed. "That is fair, isn't it?" If he wanted to soothe his pride by considering the lessons an equal exchange, then Harriett would let him. She wouldn't remind him that she could very well teach herself to ride if she so desired.

Her faith in herself as her own riding instructor took a tumble before they got back to the wagons, however. She sat atop the chestnut mare with confidence, reflecting on how the astride position gave a rider a much more stable seat than the sidesaddle. She was congratulating herself on looking every bit as easy in the saddle as Jake when the scrub grass rustled and a dust-colored snake slithered across the trail, almost underneath poor Daisy's hooves. The mare snorted and crowhopped. Harriett squealed, lost her stirrups, and grabbed for the saddle horn. When Daisy pitched forward, Harriett toppled sideways—and landed on the ground in an ignominious, dusty heap.

"Spit!" Harriett started to get up, then froze. Not two feet in front of her was the snake, looking as confused as a snake could possibly look.

"Don't move!"

Jake's pistol appeared in his hand with lightning speed. She'd been in this same spot before, Harriett remembered with a sinking stomach. And Jake had missed. She waited, and waited. Nothing happened.

"Shoot!" her voice quavered.

But Jake laughed. He tossed the pistol into the air, caught it vertically by the barrel, and dropped it in his holster.

"Get up, Harry. It's just a bull snake."

She couldn't quite convince her muscles to move— not while that snake flipped at her with his forked tongue. "Shoot it!" she urged. A snake, no matter what its name, was still a snake.

"No need to kill it," Jake explained. "It won't bite. And if it did, the snake would probably be the one poisoned."

He was regarding her with an insolent amusement

that stung more than her bruised backside. For that matter, Dodger and Daisy were giving her the same look. Wonderful! All three of them thought she was an idiot.

Harriett glared at them all, then picked herself up and limped over to her mount. "I'd at least expect you to side with me," she muttered to the horse. "You are a female, after all." She clambered up, mounting with no more grace than she had earlier.

"I hope I learn to read more easily than you learn to ride," Jake commented in a voice that sounded suspiciously like a snicker.

"You will," Harriett assured him acidly. "You'll have a better teacher."

Journal Entry—June 24—Warm Springs campground: Today I carved my name and my aunt's in the sandstone bluff known as Register Rock—as thousands before me have done. I also increased my equestrian experience by several aching limbs and bruises that modesty prevents me from describing. The mount I purchased is not quite as gentle as Mr. Smith told me, or perhaps I am a slower learner than I thought. My little mare Daisy gave me a lasting lesson in humility today, a more effective lesson, I believe, than Mr. Carradine's instruction in the equestrian art. Though Mr. Carradine was very patient with my lack of ability.

I must admit, dear readers, that I have learned another valuable lesson on this odyssey. Perhaps we who live within the confines of polite society are too quick to dismiss those who, for one reason or another, do not fit inside our tightly prescribed circle of ideals. Yet along this trail I have met people whose nobility of spirit shines so brightly that their rude demeanor and lack of education must be forgotten completely. And some gentlemen along this trail—persons of respected position and pleasing manners, persons whom any gentle hostess would gladly welcome into her parlor—reveal a true nature that is all out of keeping with their outward refinement.

We must all learn from our mistakes, so I will confess that I gravely erred on the character of my employee Mr. Carradine, a man I have cited as being the poorest possible specimen of a man. He has proved a valuable friend—a person of many fine qualities. As he does his best at times to hide those qualities, perhaps I can be forgiven the injustice I did him.

Harriett closed her journal and snuffed the candle, too tired to write any more even though the hour was still early. She wearily donned her nightgown and settled herself into bed. The loose flap of the tent provided a view of Lucille still sitting at the fire. Her aunt would sit so for several hours still, Harriett knew, and once in bed, would waste the night in restless tossing.

Another lesson learned—one that Harriett couldn't write about in her journal. Lucille had lost much of her sparkle since she'd seen Lawrence Steede with another woman on his arm. What price women paid to discover the folly of romance! Her mother had the right of it, Harriett thought, when she said that the truest and most fulfilling passion was that expended on good works and noble causes. Harriett was exceedingly grateful that she had inherited her mother's pragmatic nature. How troublesome a romantic heart would be—a heart that might allow her to succumb to the charm and almost overpowering masculinity of a man like Jake Carradine. Harriett almost shuddered at the thought.

Or was the shudder a shiver of something quite different?

Jake Carradine was a man hard to dismiss from one's mind. Harriett had always considered herself a competent judge of character, but Jake defied rational judgment—a gentle man who rescued puppies and refused to kill a snake unless it was a threat; yet the riffraff crossing the prairies with them feared his gun and his temper. He had held her in true compassion that terrible day when Ned White died; he had risked his life to save Chad MacBride from a herd of charging buffalo—the same man who had bashed heads in a saloon in Independence and drunk himself into a useless heap more times than she could count. Still the same man who had attacked her in brutal intimacy to prove to himself and to her that he was no better than an animal.

Had there ever lived a man of more contradictions? Were there more surprises in store?

And this man said he wanted her, declared he would have her, and she would have him.

Harriett closed her eyes on the thought. God preserve her from temptation.

12

Journal entry—June 26—crossing the Black Hills:
Since Fort Laramie our trail has been very rugged,
just as Mr. Ware promised. If our wheels are not
mired in sand, then we are bouncing over rocks and
cobbles; our poor oxen are quite worn out dragging
our wagon up the steep inclines—and our wagon
must be one of the lightest in the company. The
Smith brothers—who have become our very dear
friends—have talked of discarding their anvil and
forge, but the company convinced them not to do it.
We all have made use of their trade; just two days
ago young Hobby replaced the shoes on two of our
oxen. This road is very hard on the poor beasts' feet.

Though we follow the general route of the North
Platte, the river is now quite a distance from the
road. It is visible only occasionally through the haze
of heat that covers this land. Fortunately, fresh, cold
springs are abundant—and firewood also. We no
longer have to burn dried buffalo piles for fuel. In
fact, we have left the buffalo far behind us.

These evenings the Indiana Adventurers are very
quiet. Everyone is much too tired to dance and tell
tales around the central fire, as was done earlier in
our odyssey. My nights of late have been spent giving

Mr. Carradine instruction in reading. He is adept at his letters—amazingly so. We are frequently joined by my aunt and Mrs. MacBride, and twice Mrs. Hornsby has sat with us. Not that these ladies need instruction in reading, but they are interested in the volumes I use to teach Mr. Carradine recognition of letters and words—the Holy Bible, Mary Wollstonecraft's *Vindication of the Rights of Woman*, and Margaret Fuller's essay *Woman in the Nineteenth Century*. Poor Mr. Carradine, surrounded not only by women but by literature that expands or outright defies the concept of women's "appropriate sphere." He does not seem much put out about it, though. In fact, he takes a lively, if sometimes adversarial, part in our discussions.

Harriett eyed Jake as he lounged on the blankets that constituted her bed. She wasn't at all sure she approved of his resting place. But asking him to sit on the floor would be rude, she supposed, and every stool was occupied—by Sadie, Lucille, and Myrtle Hornsby, who had surprisingly become a regular member of what had grown into a discussion group. Harriett herself sat, as gracefully as she could, on a sack of rice that she had brought into the tent for just such a purpose. She had debated whether to have Jake sit on the rice and recline on the bed herself, but that would be even more improper.

Still, tonight the scent of him would linger to disturb her rest. Not that his scent was unpleasant. But the combined odor of leather, fresh air, and clean male sweat was simply not something a decent unmarried female should be smelling in her bed.

"Can you read the third sentence on page twenty?" she asked him.

Squinting at the words of Margaret Fuller's essay,

Jake shook his head. He looked up, a twinkle in his eye, and declared, "They don't make sense."

Harriett raised a reproving brow. "I didn't ask your opinion of the sentiment, Jacob. I asked you to read it."

He read it, sounding out the words with almost theatrical effort, then grimaced.

Harriett repeated the passage, her words flowing more smoothly than Jake's. " 'Woman . . . the other half of the same thought, the other chamber of the heart of life, needs now to take her turn in the full pulsation, and that improvement in the daughters will best aid in the reformation of the sons of this age.' "

"It still doesn't make sense," Jake commented, a spark of mischief lighting his eyes.

"You think women shouldn't be educated, Jacob?"

"Why should they?" He shrugged a broad shoulder. "Suppose a woman should desire a trade or profession?"

"Women have a profession—running a home and being quiet, obedient wives."

Mrs. Hornsby laughed and winked. "Some of us have another trade, Jake. You seemed to like that well enough in St. Louie and elsewhere."

Jake grinned at the madam, who dimpled at his attention. "I don't think Miss Foster was referring to your particular profession, Myrtle."

Harriett and Lucille both stared at the other two in the tent. "I take it you knew each other before you met on this journey." Harriett's softly spoken question stretched like velvet over a razor's edge.

"Oh, Jake here gets around, don'tcha love? When was it—five years ago? What happened to all them big plans o' yours with your family in Oregon, honey?"

Jake's grin faded.

"Don't wanna talk about it, huh?" The madam

glanced at Harriett and Lucille, as if they were the cause of Jake's reticence.

"Mr. Carradine," Harriett interrupted primly, "this conversation is not teaching you to read. I want you to read that whole page silently and take note of the words you don't know. We will go on from there."

Once her pupil applied himself, Harriett turned to Mrs. Hornsby. "I believe you said earlier that you were interested in learning something about the property laws that apply to women?"

Mrs. Hornsby looked from Jake to Harriett with a knowing smile. "Yeah. I got me a nice house in St. Louie. Jake's seen it. He'll tell ya it's a real gem. I got a friend takin' care of it for me. Remember Charlene, Jake?"

Jake's mouth twitched as he grunted noncommittally, but he didn't take his eyes from his lesson. Harriett thought that he looked a bit too studious.

"From what you said t'other night," Mrs. Hornsby continued, "I'm guessin' my rotten slime husband could come back and take that house away from me, just like it was his."

Sadie interjected her own sorry experience. "My husband John took my inheritance. He even sold our house to pay for his passage to the gold fields. He left me with nothing but promises about how someday we would be rich. Not a penny to live on."

Mrs. Hornsby glanced at Sadie's burgeoning figure. "Looks like he left you with something, at least."

Sadie blushed.

"You call me when that kid comes, Mrs. MacBride. I've delivered a few babies in my day. You might say it comes with the entertainin' profession. Now"—she turned back to Harriett—"about my house."

"I don't know the specific laws of Missouri," Harriett said. "But many states allow a husband to dispose of his wife's property as his own, and the wife has no say in the matter—and no legal recourse to recover her property even should her husband abandon her."

"Well, I'll be twiddled! I guess if that piece of dog shit shows his face again, I'll just have to kill 'im before he can sell my place for 'is gamblin' debts. If I know him, he'll have 'em stacked up higher than a bird can spit."

"Are you going to California to find your husband also?" Sadie asked.

"Hell no, sweetie. And I cain't imagine why you are, either. That man of yours sounds like he's worse 'n my Joe."

"John's a good man," Sadie said with a sigh. "Just full of . . . of foolish dreams."

"Fulla crap if you ask me!"

Lucille spoke for the first time. "When you love a man, sometimes his faults don't matter all that much."

Harriett turned a frown on Jake's quiet chuckle. This discussion certainly wasn't going the way of her ladies' discussion groups in Boston. "All the more reason not to become mired in such foolish passions! A woman who lets her heart rule her head is very unwise," she said acidly.

Lucille looked hurt, and Harriett felt instantly contrite. Her aunt was still bruised from her encounter with Lawrence Steede, and rubbing her nose in the mess of her emotions certainly didn't help the wounds to heal. Sadie also seemed surprised at Harriett's vehement outburst, and a little taken aback. Only Mrs. Hornsby nodded in agreement.

"That's the attitude, ya know! No offense, friend Jake, but men and women go together about as well as nitro and glycerin, if ya know what I mean. A man's a good thing on a shivery night when a gal needs a bit o' lovin', but let him into your life more'n that and he'll walk away with it. An' that's a fact!" She turned to Harriett, a gleam of naughtiness in her kohled eyes.

"Ya know, missy? You've got the makin's of a smart whore if ya only knew how to use what the good Lord gave ya."

Harriett was too stunned to reply, and before she could gather her wits Mrs. Hornsby had bid them all good night with a promise to return for the next evening session.

"It's damned good—all this educated talk!" the madam declared as she left.

"What an extraordinary woman!" Sadie breathed.

"Well, I think I shall also say good night," Lucille said. "Harriett, dear, I hope you don't mind too much if I sleep in the wagon tonight. It does look like rain, and this tent leaks so that the last time we had a storm I didn't get a moment's sleep."

"I'll probably join you in a short while, Aunt," Harriett replied.

Sadie left with Lucille, but only after extracting Harriett's promise to take a walk with her early the next morning. She claimed it relieved the discomforts of advanced pregnancy—and a backside sore from sitting all day on a hard wagon box.

"She's looking pale and worn," Harriett worried aloud when Sadie was gone.

"Sadie's a brave woman," Jake replied.

"I wonder if I could be as brave in her position."

"Harry, you would never be in her position. A man who did to you what Sadie's husband did to her would be lucky to get out of your reach with all his parts still attached."

Harriett didn't answer. Once she would have been quick to agree, and glad that Jake recognized she was no weak-willed pushover. But Sadie was neither weak-willed nor a pushover. What was the fatal quality in so many women—in Sadie, in Lucille—that allowed them to love to their own destruction? Were all women cursed with the same failing? Was she?

"Why didn't you tell me that you'd met Mrs. Hornsby before?" Harriett asked a bit sharply.

Jake set aside his book. "Such adventures are not for the ears of a lady."

"Fiddle!" Harriett pulled over a stool and sat. "Mr. Deere says I'm no lady," she recounted with a grimace. "I heard him say so to Mr. Hawkesbury."

Jake regarded her with a warm look. "Charlie doesn't like your fluffy pants—"

"Pantaloons," Harriett corrected.

"Pantaloons," he conceded. "Or your divided skirt. Or your riding astride. Me . . . I think what a woman wears or how she rides doesn't have much to do with her being a lady or not. And I think you're quite a lady."

Harriett studied the dirt of the floor. It wouldn't do to let Jake see her blush, but his praise did bring a certain warmth to her face. For five evenings they'd been in this tent together, two of them alone most of the time. The more she talked to him, the more she saw of him, the more her foolish heart strayed out of line.

"Thank you, Jacob. I appreciate that." What Jake thought of her mattered. His opinion shouldn't matter, but it did.

For the past few weeks Harriett had scarcely been able to get away from Jake. He was in her camp for every meal, spent his nights sleeping beside her fire, his mornings and evenings lightening the work for Harriett and Lucille, Sadie and Chad. Since Sadie's wagon was always next to Harriett's in the line, helping Sadie didn't take him far out of Harriett's sight— and in Sadie he had gained a powerful champion for his cause.

Harriett knew exactly what Jake was up to. After all, he'd made his intentions clear enough that night in Ash Hollow, and several times since. He was pursuing her like a wolf chasing his dinner. Her many reminders that she was already promised didn't discourage him. And Harriett's stern lectures to herself couldn't quiet that undisciplined part of her nature that responded to his attention. In spite of knowing Jake's intent, in spite of fully understanding the impossibility of his suit, Harriett couldn't banish the man from her thoughts, and worse, from her dreams. There was something frightening about the way his smile caught at her, the way his gaze could make her lose the focus of her thoughts. Beneath his tough exterior was a gentleness that was visible only in rare moments, and it fascinated her. She wouldn't have admitted it to anyone else, but she had to be honest with herself: A female given to fanciful notions might think she was falling in love. Harriett was grateful that she had more sense than to think such a thing. She acknowledged only that the weeks away from civilization had robbed her of proper perspective.

Spending every evening in close company with Jake, tucked away in her tent, bending together over a book, did nothing to improve her perspective. Even the frequent presence of Lucille and Sadie didn't much diminish the intimacy of their togetherness—and Harriett suspected that was what Jake had intended for his lessons. She wasn't even sure he didn't already know how to read—the wretch! The thought of such deception ought to make her flamingly angry. But it didn't. The very fact that it didn't was frightening.

Jake sat on her bed looking very comfortable, showing no inclination to leave the tent.

"I was teasing, Harry," he said.

"What?" She realized that his eyes had been on her all this time, taking in all the unguarded expressions that must have crossed her face, ending with her present frown. "You were teasing about me being a lady? That's not very flattering."

His eyes never left her. "No. I was teasing about women not needing an education. I think everyone has the right to learn what they need to survive—and whatever else they please. If a woman wants to be a storekeeper, or a teacher—or hell!—even a banker, it's no skin off my nose."

"That's very generous of you," Harriett commended wryly. "But would you deposit your money with a woman banker?"

He grinned. "Hell, no. If I had money, I wouldn't give it to any kind of a banker."

"I suppose you think it would be safer with you."

"That's a fact."

Maybe it would. Even the worst sort of criminal might hesitate to rob a man so big, with a body thick with muscle and a hand so fast with a gun.

She was too tired to argue. "You might be right. I suppose you're very good at that sort of thing. If I had much money, I might give it to you to keep safe."

"You'll give me more than that to keep safe." The easy confidence in his voice approached arrogance.

"Jacob . . . !"

He held up a hand as if to fend off her rebuke. "Don't jump like a scared rabbit."

"I wasn't . . ."

"You were. But there's no need. I'll behave myself . . . until you tell me not to."

"Where did you learn to handle a gun the way you do, Jacob?"

Jake grinned. "Changing the subject?"

Harriet looked stern.

"All right. All right. I spent eight years making my way by a gun, Harry. From the time I was sixteen. When a man's life depends on a weapon, he gets good with it. Or he doesn't live very long."

"Sixteen? My heavens! Didn't you have parents . . . or . . . at least a guardian to see to your welfare?"

He leaned back on her bed, cradled his head in his hands, and stared up at the tent canvas. "I had a father and a younger brother. Ma died when I was eight. We were whipsawyers in California, going from lumber camp to lumber camp. A hard life, axing trees and sawing timber all day. I got tired of it real fast. And when I could, I skipped out."

"You've lived in California? I had no idea."

"I've been across the country a time or two."

"This journey must be child's play to you, then."

He chuckled, rose up on one elbow, and gave her a warm look. "No, Harry. With you along, I don't think any journey would be child's play."

Harriett flushed and steered him back to a safer topic. "Do you still have relations in California?"

His face tightened, and the gray eyes froze to steel. "My family's all dead. Every one of 'em."

Harriett swallowed hard at the expression on his face. Once again she had blundered into forbidden territory. Jake had told her before that his family was dead, but most everybody had some family, somewhere.

Jake fixed her with a gaze that made her stomach drop. "The only family I had left—my brother and his five-year-old boy—were killed in Oregon by a man named Homer Kane. They burned to death in our cabin."

"Were . . . were you there?" Harriett asked quietly.

"I was. Fat lot of good that did them! I'd gone up to Oregon two years before. Figured it was time to settle and help my family build their own lumber business. Kane wanted our timber stands, and when he and his sons came around throwin' lead, I ran right into one of their slugs like some stupid greenhorn. Just when Elijah and Josh need me I'm laid out like a dead log." His mouth twisted into a bitter smile. "Lot of help my fast gun was right then."

The pain and bitterness in Jake's voice hung in the air, and his eyes gauged Harriett's reaction, as though he expected her to cringe from the evil he had just confessed—or at least cry out his guilt. When she did neither, the tension in his body eased somewhat. But he still looked like a whip about to be cracked.

Harriett wished that she could take Jake into her arms and soothe him as though he were a small, hurt child. Obviously she couldn't. He wasn't a child, he was a man—a strong man whose pride wouldn't allow him to reach out for comfort or help. Or had he reached out just now?

"Jacob . . ." she began hesitantly. "Surely—surely! —you don't hold yourself responsible for what happened."

His face was like granite. "If I hadn't been so hot on pulling some yahoo stunt and going after those boys alone, I could've gotten Elijah and Josh out of that house. Somehow I could've. I'm going to carry that with me for the rest of my life." His mouth flattened into a grim line. "I've been kicking myself around the country for the last year—kicking poor Amos around, too, I guess—trying to run away from that fact." His eyes came up again and fastened on hers with a hold that all her determination couldn't break. "You slowed down my running and made me look at what I was doing, Harry. Guess what I needed was an unstoppable busybody who would nag and nag until I couldn't stand myself any longer."

"I had no business . . ."

"Well, no. You didn't. But has that ever stopped you before?"

Harriett pulled her eyes away from his.

"Harry, I love you just the way you are, nagging and all."

"Jacob . . . !"

"You gave me back my self-respect. I haven't been this sober in a year, or"—he chuckled—"this clean."

"You only think you—"

"Love you?" he finished as her voice stuck on the last two words. "I don't fool myself on something as serious as that, Harry. You're the one who doesn't know how she feels."

"You haven't listened to one thing I've told you over the past few weeks, have you?"

"Maybe you haven't been listening to yourself."

Her eyes narrowed in exasperation.

"I won't press you, Harry. Not yet. I've got some business to take care of before I can settle down. The last year I spent fighting for other men I should have been doing some fighting of my own."

Harriett got up, uneasy with the way his eyes had turned to cold gunmetal gray. Neither did she like the tone of his voice. "What do you mean, Jacob?"

"Just this. Homer Kane needs killing. He and his vicious sons should have been bleeding their lives out before my family's ashes were cold. If I hadn't been shot I would've seen to it. As it was, by the time I could properly lift a gun I'd already drunk myself into oblivion."

"Jake! You can't deliberately set out to kill a man!"

He chuckled and shook his head. "Harry, Harry." Unfolding himself from the bed, he got up, came to her, and gently took her chin in his big hand so she couldn't look away. "How are you going to right all the wrongs in the world when you're so innocent yourself?"

His hand held her still as he lowered his mouth to hers in a gentle kiss. Harry was too stunned to struggle, her whole body rooted to the spot and melting in the tender warmth of his caress.

"But I like you this way," he whispered against her

lips. "And one kind of innocence—well, we'll see to that soon enough."

He released her, but she couldn't move. Not until he ducked out of the tent did some of her composure return, only to be shattered again as he stuck his head back in. "Besides, lady," he taunted with a grin, "where would we live when we get married if I don't get my land back?"

The Indiana Company plodded steadily onward. At the beginning of their journey, the emigrants had considered fifteen miles a good day. Now they often made over twenty, in spite of rough roads and tired animals. Harriett was amazed that she had never felt better in her life. She could walk all day beside the wagon, and frequently did, without a single sore muscle. Though her feet were often blistered, her face and arms stinging from sunburn, her clothes sweaty, her hair bedraggled, her nose clogged with dust, small discomforts didn't cause the misery they once had. She still saw the beauty of the wildflowers and the clean blue sky. She still delighted in the fresh smell of the rain, the musical trickle of a creek, the mournful, wild howling of the wolves, and the quiet crackle of a cookfire. At times she wondered if she could ever again enjoy city life. Boston seemed a dimly remembered dream, San Francisco a goal too distant to even think about.

A little over a hundred miles out of Fort Laramie the company crossed the North Platte River for the last time at Mormon Ferry. Here the river turned south, and the wagons would continue west toward the mountains—and beyond them the gold fields. Not a single Mormon was anywhere within sight of the so-called Mormon Ferry, at least not as far as Harriett could see. Two enterprising Indians operated the raft, and several others conducted a lively trade with the wagons lined up to cross.

Jake bargained with the Indians for soft walking-moccasins for Harriett, Lucille, Sadie, and Chad.

"Now you won't have to take off your shoes every time you sit down," Jake told Harriett. "These won't rub blisters."

Harriett blushed as she thanked him. All this time she'd thought no one had noticed the rude habit she'd allowed herself. She'd always kept her feet well hidden under her skirt. But Jake Carradine didn't miss much, and she warmed toward him in spite of her chagrin. The blisters were such a nuisance.

They left the Platte, that silvery ribbon that had been their guide for so long, and struck out across fifty miles of barren waste and alkali swamps. In this land, Harriett discovered, the birds seldom sang, the sky was white-hot instead of blue, and carcasses alongside the trail bore grim witness to the poison in the water. Phineas and Jake both warned the company to fill their water casks from a pure spring they passed not far from the ferry. Those who were driving cows and drinking the animals' milk were told to abstain until the company reached the Sweetwater River, as the herbage along this part of the road was sufficiently vile to poison the cows' milk.

The road across the wasteland, however, was not quite as rough or steep as it had been through the Black Hills. Lucille volunteered to take a turn driving the wagon while Harriett rode Daisy and practiced her new equestrian skills. Jake was a better teacher than Harriett cared to admit, at least in riding. During one riding lesson he had promised to be a good teacher in more intimate skills as well, but when Harriett had refused to speak to him for a full day, he left off his private teasing and behaved himself. Even when the man behaved with perfect decorum, however, his smile was still warm with a slow heat that told her he was simply waiting for the time to be right, for her to be ready. Harriett despaired of convincing him that she would never be ready for what he wanted. Sometimes she despaired of convincing herself.

Finally the wasteland fell behind them. In one momentous day they caught their first glimpse of the Sweetwater River and camped near the famous Independence Rock. The same day was made even more momentous by Sadie going into labor.

"Oh! Dear Sadie, you should have told me earlier! When I think of you driving that wagon all day . . ."

Sadie laughed quietly, the rich color of her laughter at odds with the ashy paleness of her face as she lay down on the blankets Harriett had prepared. "Don't fret so, Harriett. Babies seldom come in much of a hurry. Besides, did you expect Charlie Deere to halt the whole train because a woman's labor begins at midday?" Her voice trailed off into a groan as another contraction racked her thin body.

Harriett let Sadie squeeze her hand, ignoring the pain of crushed fingers, beside herself with worry. "I should fetch Dr. Fellows."

"Don't you dare!" Sadie groaned. "Harriett! Don't you let that quack near me. These physicians with all their Latin phrases know nothing of women and babies. A birthing room"—she looked around her and smiled wryly—"or tent, is not a place for a man."

"But Sadie . . . !"

"No!" Sadie squeezed her hand again, not from pain but friendship. "Harriett, dear—this is a woman's world. This is the joy and the mystery of being a woman. To give birth. To give life." She smiled. "A man isn't capable of understanding. His presence profanes something that is for women alone."

Sadie's little speech ended in another groan. Her breathing raced, shallow and desperate with pain. Harriett's own stomach cramped and twisted as if in concert with the laboring woman. She took a wet rag and wiped sweat from Sadie's face and neck, then looked to Lucille, who was hovering nearby. Lucille shook her head helplessly. She knew no more about babies than did her niece.

"Sadie, dear," Harriett said, striving for calm. "Tell me what I must do."

Sadie's gasps slowed into normal breathing. "We have clean towels and sheets to wash the baby?"

"Yes."

"A sharp knife to cut the cord?"

"Yes," Harriett gulped. "Just as you instructed."

Sadie looked up into Harriett's white face, took her hand, and patted it comfortingly. Lucille appeared to be in equal need of comfort. "Perhaps we should fetch Mrs. Hornsby after all," Sadie sighed. "And best you hurry, dear."

Mrs. Hornsby needed no explanation when Harriett rushed into her camp. She already had the necessaries gathered and an enormous apron fastened over her gown. They were back in Sadie's tent before the next pain arrived.

"What are the needle and thread for?" Harriett asked as she set out the woman's things.

"Sometimes the mother needs a bit of stitchin' up," the madam answered matter-of-factly. "Some babies just can't squeeze through the space we give 'em."

Harriett thought she was going to faint, and poor Lucille almost did.

Many times that night Harriett again thought she was going to faint. But she didn't. Early in the night Mrs. Hornsby, complaining that she'd never seen a female so prone to the vapors, sent Lucille from the tent. But Harriett stayed. She held Sadie's hand as the laboring woman screamed, wanting to scream herself. She mechanically and competently performed every task Mrs. Hornsby asked of her, trying not to think, or to feel, for fear that she would give in to the vapors just as Lucille had.

All through the night, Harriett saw none of the mystery or joy that Sadie had talked of with such reverence. She saw only blood and pain. And at the end, the product of Sadie's terrible labor was red, ugly, and misshapen—more of a monster than a baby. But Sadie and Myrtle both exclaimed over the lump of flesh as though it were perfectly normal and a joy to behold.

Sadie laughed weakly at Harriett's expression. "Don't frown so, Harriett. All babies look this way just out of their mother's womb." Her hair was tangled and damp with sweat, her face was a grayish shade of pale, but Sadie was lit from within by a rapture that gave radiance to the whole tent. Her new son lay upon her breast, waving his tiny hands and squinting his displeasure with his new home.

Harriett helped Mrs. Hornsby clean Sadie and dispose of the soiled sheets.

"Ya done jest fine, missy," the madam said. "You've got more backbone than I woulda guessed."

"Thank you," Harriett said sincerely. "I'm ever so grateful for your help."

"Ya jest keep an eye on Sadie, there," the madam warned. "That babe's a strapping lad, and Sadie's no bigger than a minute herself. It were a hard birth, and the little lady could use a few days o' rest, I'm guessin'."

"I'll speak to Mr. Deere about camping for a few days."

"Fat lot that prick cares."

Harriett blinked.

"You jest take care of 'er."

"Oh, I will."

Mrs. Hornsby left, and Chad came in to see his new brother. Harriett noted that the youngster wasn't quite the boy who had started out with his mother from Independence. He had grown a bit, true, but the main difference was in his eyes. Chad was no longer a child.

"I'll sit with Ma awhile, Miss Foster," the boy offered. "You look tuckered."

Sadie was fast asleep, and so was the child who snuggled in her arms.

"Call me if you need me, Chad."

What Harriett had seen and felt that night desperately needed sorting out in her mind, but just then exhaustion's demands were too great to be ignored. She stumbled through the pitch-black night back to her own camp, and literally fell into Jake's arms.

With all the things in camp to trip over, she had to stumble into Jake. It was one straw too much. One sob escaped, then two, then a whole flood of tears.

Jake set her back from him, still imprisoning her with a hand clamping each shoulder. "Is Sadie all right?"

Harriett nodded tearfully.

"The baby?"

"Fine," she choked out.

"Then what are you caterwauling about?"

"It . . . it . . . !"

In the dark Harriett could still see him smile, as if he finally understood her tears. If so, he understood a deal more than she did. Unresisting, she allowed herself to be eased against the hard wall of Jake's chest. His arms wrapped securely around her.

"Sadie named him Independence," Harriett sobbed. "For the rock."

Jake chuckled, and Harriett could hear the deep vibrations in his chest. "Better than naming him for Devil's Gate. That's just down the trail a bit."

Her laughter came out as weeping. She couldn't stop herself, and she didn't even know why. She couldn't push Jake away from her, though she knew that she ought.

Her world was shifting—a whirling storm of ideas, emotions, fears, and realities was overwhelming her. The old Harriett was being swept away with the cyclone, a new Harriett kicking and screeching in a painful birth, just as little Independence had fought and screamed when he'd discovered the inhospitable world he'd entered.

Harriett didn't blame the new babe. It hurt. God, how it hurt!

13

Journal entry—July 8—Green River crossing: We have finally conquered the Rocky Mountains, and I must say that I expected more of a barrier so much talked of. Though the scenery was quite beautiful in its way, I had somehow pictured our trail passing through majestic alpine peaks of stupendous heights. But such was not the case.

We followed the Sweetwater River west along its narrow course, crossing it six times in all to stay on a passable trail. Lucille and I—and our faithful oxen —think very little of river crossings after having done so many, but were very interested in this new sort of country; it is so very different from our road along the Platte. The Devil's Gate especially caught Lucille's interest, and young Chad MacBride could scarcely be persuaded to return to camp when we took a walk to see it. Here the Sweetwater River rushes through a narrow gorge of pinkish granite rock, with a great roar and much foam and turmoil. I've never seen the like.

At the headwaters of the Sweetwater we ascended to South Pass, which our scout Phineas Carter tells me is the continental divide. Instead of being the rugged spine of mountains I had expected, the pass was a wide, grassy valley—very high, for we could see snow on either side of us, and this in July. Mr. Carter assures us that we will have our fill of rugged mountains. The Sierras, he claims, are so steep and frightening that he's seen grown men turn around and travel the trail back the way they had come, just to avoid crossing them. Personally, I think Mr. Carter delights in tall tales. I cannot imagine anyone coming as far as we have and not seeing this journey through to its end.

Once through the gentle pass we followed Pacific Creek to the Big Sandy River, which led us down to the Green, where we now make camp with numerous other parties waiting to cross at the ferry. This ferry, like the raft over the Platte, is also called Mormon Ferry, and this time seems to be actually operated by members of that sect. The Great Salt Lake is only two hundred miles west of here, or thereabouts. The closer we come to the stronghold of these people, the more parties of Mormons we see traveling toward their mecca. They keep apart from other companies, but seem friendly enough when we are forced together. A very pleasant Morman lady sold us a goat for a very reasonable cost. Sadie's milk has turned sour, I fear, and little Independence will not take cow's milk, which our party has in plenty. On the goat's milk he is doing very well.

Poor Sadie is not doing well, however. Of course, Mr. Deere refused to rest the company for the time she needed to mend, and Sadie refused to stay behind, though Lucille and I would have stayed with her, and I believe Mrs. Hornsby's wagon and the Smith brothers would have also. But Sadie insisted on moving with the company, and thus has not recovered properly from the birth. When she finally allowed Dr. Fellows to help her, that "learned" man gave her only the most superficial examination, declared she was fading from lack of strength, and prescribed a tonic which I believe is naught but opium.

Why is it that physicians believe women are malingering when they complain of ailments that are exclusively female in nature? I dearly wish that women were allowed to train as physicians so that we might do the same to them. That sentiment sounds like petty spite, to be sure. But I believe that walking a mile in women's shoes might give the male gender a better perspective on masculine attitudes.

We have been camped for a full day at the Green River Ford, and another day may yet pass before our turn to cross. The campsite is lovely, with lush grass and big cottonwood trees growing on the banks of the river. But most of the Indiana Company are restless to move on. Gold is still in their eyes, and they complain of the length and boredom of this trip, though how they can be bored with every day presenting new experiences and new sights, I do not know.

Half of our company was so restless that they have taken a different road. Shortly after passing through the Rockies they veered west on what is known as Sublette's Cutoff—I suppose after the man who opened the trail. In fact, this is the route that Mr. Ware's guidebook recommends, as it supposedly shortens the trip by seventy miles. However, I have heard from others that it shortens the trail not at all.

The Adventurers who wished to continue on the Fort Bridger road elected a new captain—my employee Mr. Carradine, who has proven his leadership many times on this odyssey. The division of the company was no pleasant undertaking, for the group at the beginning of the journey had agreed to remain together until their destination was obtained. Hard words flew when so many of our number—fourteen wagons in all—would not continue on with Mr. Deere.

I believe those of us that took the Fort Bridger road are happy with our new leadership, however. Mr. Deere, however good his intentions, was not a man of sound judgment or decisive temperament. I wish that his scout, Mr. Phineas Carter, had not chosen to continue with our party. We certainly do not need his scouting. Mr. Carradine knows the trail better than he, and when Mr. Carter imbibes spirits he is truly a menace. Mrs. Hornsby has complained several times that her "entertainers" have been subject to his abuse, and he loiters around our wagon much too often for my comfort, especially now that Mr. Carradine, with his new responsibilities, is occasionally not with us in the evenings.

Our little Dodger is growing to be quite protective, and he particularly does not like Mr. Carter. He growls whenever the scout comes near our camp. Mr. Carter finds great amusement in growling back at the dog, but I do not find it amusing at all.

Harriett sat beside Sadie's bed in the back of the MacBride wagon while Chad collected firewood and water for all of them. They had combined their parties into one single camp since the birth. Harriett cared for Sadie and the baby—almost a full-time job since Sadie was not at all well and required at least as much care as her thriving infant son. Lucille cooked and washed, and when Jake was otherwise occupied, Chad saw to the animals, tended the fire, and hauled water.

Harriett missed the peace of their evenings on the North Platte. Seldom now did she and Jake find time for reading instruction, though Harriett had come to admit that on her part as well as his, the lessons were merely an excuse to spend their evenings together. Nor did Harriett have time to ride. Poor Daisy was so lacking in proper exercise that Jake had taken to riding her every third day or so.

For all intents and purposes Harriett had become the mother of two children, a role she had never thought to play. The rewards were almost as great as the trials, she found. In her concentration on the limitations of being female, she may have overlooked a few advantages that were inherent to her sex. Whenever little Indy, as Independence was called, looked up at her with his bright baby-blue eyes—unfocused though they were—Harriett's heart grew warm. And she grew to appreciate Chad more each day. With his new responsibilities, the boy was quickly growing to be a man. He had taken to mimicking Jake's habits and speech, and Jake tolerated—perhaps even enjoyed—the boy's tagging after him. Dodger often joined them to make the group a threesome, and Harriett laughed with Lucille and Sadie at the sight of the big bad gunman with his entourage of a gangly, worshipful puppy and an equally gangly, equally worshipful eleven-year-old boy.

But right at this moment Sadie wasn't laughing. Pale and thin, she looked close to sleep as Harriett read quietly from the Psalms that Sadie had requested. Sadie's skin seemed almost transparent, the blue tracery of veins showing starkly against the white of her eyelids, her arms, even her face. She had the ethereal, insubstantial quality one might expect of a ghost.

Harriett's mind caught on the image, dismayed. For the first time she allowed herself to admit that Sadie might not survive to see California, and the realization filled her with anger. Sadie MacBride should not have to lie in a crude grave beside a wilderness trail while her self-serving husband, who had abandoned her to a merciless world, chased adventure and riches in California.

"Miss Foster?" Chad stuck his head into the wagon and peered at his mother. "Is Ma all right?"

"She's fine, Chad. Just sleeping."

"Oh. Well, Horace Smith and Jake are gonna have a wrestling match. Everyone's betting on Horace, but I know Jake can win. Do you suppose Ma would mind if I watched? I don't wanna wake 'er up to ask."

"Your mother doesn't approve of fighting, Chad."

"Aw. This ain't . . . isn't''—he corrected himself at Harriett's frown—"real fighting. Wrestling's a sport, you know. No hitting or gouging or anything dirty like that."

The hopeful look he gave her was too much for Harriett to resist. He affected the same expression Dodger wore when begging treats.

"All right, Chad. But no betting. You understand?"

"Oh, sure! I don't have anything to bet."

The whole wagon shook as Chad launched himself off the tailgate. Before Harriett could utter a word of reproof, he was gone. Awakened by the commotion, Sadie smiled up at her.

"Make sure he stays out of trouble, will you, Harriett? He's a good boy, but . . ."

Harriett knew exactly what was implied in Sadie's *but*, having been in charge of young Chad long enough to learn his talent for scrapes.

"I'll see him safe in bed whether or not he wants to end up there." Harriett patted Sadie's thin hand. "Will you be all right alone?"

"Oh, of course. Dear Harriett, I don't really need a nurse."

"Then I'll go see how un-nasty this wrestling match really is."

The match was not nasty, perhaps, by the onlookers' standards. Horace and Jake both stripped down to their trousers. Barefoot and bare-chested, they grappled in the orange flickering light of the central fire while the rest of the company cheered, booed, hooted, groaned, and yelled advice. The scene reminded Harriett of a particularly lurid illustration of her father's copy of Dante's *Inferno*. Her mother had spanked her the one time she'd caught Harriett perusing the little volume, but no one was there to spank her now. And her conscience, it seemed, was incapable of halting the most improper feelings that washed through her at the sight of two nearly naked men straining against each other like battling bulls.

Horace was huge. Blacksmithing had given him muscles piled upon muscles. He was built like an ox, square and powerful. But Jake was also huge. Swinging an ax must rival smithing in physical stress, Harriett noted, for Jake's body, gleaming with sweat that emphasized every contour of his physique, was every bit as muscled as Horace's. Horace was broader, thicker. But Jake was faster and had a longer reach. When the two giants grappled, muscles bunched and straining, tendons corded, Harriett could picture the gods of Greek mythology struggling in just such a way —more stories that her mother had forbidden her, though Harriett had regarded the taboo as a challenge rather than a barrier.

Harriett gasped involuntarily as Horace threw Jake over his shoulder. The ground shook when Jake landed. In the blink of an eye Horace squatted beside his victim and locked him in an armhold that looked capable of breaking the neck of an ox, never mind a man.

But Jake broke the hold with a deft twist and slammed Horace to the ground. Horace heaved upward, but Jake's weight pinned him to the dirt. The smith heaved up again, this time with success. Jake toppled, rolled, and came to his feet in a feral crouch. For a split second Jake's eyes met Harriett's. He grinned salaciously. To any other watcher, the expression seemed directed toward Horace, a taunt of challenge. But Harriett knew better. She saw—or rather felt—that grin in her very bones, even after she managed to pull her eyes away and turn from the contest.

Heart pounding, Harriett glanced back toward the crowd. Chad had wriggled in between Horatio and Hobby, both of whom had one hand on the boy's shoulder. He was safe enough, Harriett decided. But she definitely wasn't. This was no place for a maiden spinster with an overactive imagination. With Jake's grin still burning in her mind, she retreated.

Back at camp, she checked on Sadie, who was fast asleep in the wagon. Lucille sat in the tent, reading, her silhouette dancing on the tent canvas to the tune of a flickering candle flame. Harriett needed to unburden herself, but not to her aunt. Lucille had troubles enough, for Lawrence Steede—who had disappeared for the last weeks to ride with another company—had reappeared and was sniffing around their camp once again. Lucille was very painfully trying to ignore him.

Cheers from the wrestling crowd floated through the night air. Mrs. Hornsby's girls were whooping up a storm for their favorite, who, Harriett had noted earlier, was whichever man happened to be winning at the time. And above the general chorus of yelling Harriett could hear Horatio groan. Horace must be losing, then. Caroline MacKenzie would be having a time of it cheering Jake on—if she were here. But Callum had literally dragged her off on the Sublette trail with Mr. Deere's party. That had been quite a scene between husband and wife, Harriett recalled.

Harriett snatched at any stray thought to keep her mind off the match that was taking place just beyond her sight. But images of Jake's knowing, carnal grin kept intruding. She pulled over a stool and sat, leaned her back against the wagon wheel, shut her eyes, blanked her mind. But Jake's face, his broad shoul-

ders, his glistening arms and chest rippling with muscles—and most of all the raw, confident, animal smile
—stayed. Sweat popped out on her skin, in spite of the
cool night air, and a peculiar ache coiled in her belly,
an ache that was becoming distressingly familiar.

The turmoil in her system served her right. Proper
spinster ladies did not subject themselves to such a
scene, and if they did, they certainly didn't let the raw
carnality seep into their veins and set every nerve afire,
as Harriett had done. Heaven above! What was happening to her? And how could she stop it?

Three days later the Indiana Company rolled into
Fort Bridger—a rather grandiose name, Harriett
thought, for such a primitive log structure. But the
land itself was grand. All around were sweeping flat-
topped hills covered with gray-green sage, and to the
south a range of mountains cut jaggedly upward into
the skyline. Harriett was grateful the trail turned
northwest at Fort Bridger instead of continuing south.
The sight of those mountains made her appreciate the
unspectacular ascent at South Pass.

The little settlement that greeted them at Fort
Bridger was a trading center rather than a military
outpost. The traders wore buckskin and beards, which
seemed a uniform of sorts among white men who lived
by dealing with the Indians. They also accumulated
Indian wives—sometimes more than one. Crude wigwams huddled up to the fort like children crowding
around a mother's skirts. These housed the wives and
families of the traders. The women were of the Shoshone and Snake tribes—a beautiful people, Harriett
observed, not unlike the Pawnee. But the sight of Indians had made her flinch ever since Ned White's gruesome death. Not that these women with their shy
smiles brought to mind the vengeful cruelty of the

Pawnee. How could one race combine so much beauty with such barbarity?

When Harriett expressed her confusion to Jake, he merely shrugged. "Indians aren't the only dealers in brutality." His face grew hard, a reminder that he had abundant experience with the white man's version of that vice. "What you think of as cruelty is the Indian's idea of justice. It's simpler and more effective than the white man's so-called justice."

"You sound as though you approve, Jacob."

"It works. You can't argue with that."

The chill in his voice sent a shiver down Harriett's spine. She thought of the man named Homer Kane, who had killed Jake's brother and nephew, and wondered if that villain wouldn't be better off facing the Pawnee than reckoning with Jake Carradine.

A small herd of children gathered around as the company parked the wagons and tended the stock. Young girls held infant brothers and sisters on their hips. Younger children toddled here and there, fearless of oxen, mules, horses, and whatever other dangers the camp presented. The braver ones begged treats. Others played hide and seek among the wagons. Harriett just managed to rescue poor Dodger from the determined tail-pulling of one little boy and pull a toddler away from the bared teeth of the Cutter's sheepdog bitch— all with little Independence tucked under one arm.

Jake lounged against the back of their wagon with a complacent smile. "You're getting quite good at playing the mother. It's nice to know that even females in pantaloon dresses haven't lost the touch."

Harriett sent him a shriveling glance, but its effectiveness was dampened by her kneeling to show Independence to a little brown boy who pulled insistently at her arm. Jake shook his head and chuckled.

The trading post was well supplied with mules and oxen, and Jake suggested that they trade Curly and

Sharps for one fresh ox and buy another fit beast to complete the team. Gus and Flytail had held up very well so far, but their yokemates were sorely in need of a rest. The exhausted oxen would be allowed to graze and recuperate, then later traded for some other weary animals and complete their journey to California.

Harriett was reluctant to see the two beasts go, for she'd grown very fond of her faithful oxen—something she certainly wouldn't have understood that first morning when she'd labored and sweated with frustration trying to harness them to the wagon. But Jake was right, as usual. It was almost frightening how much she was coming to rely on his judgment.

While Jake struck a bargain with a trader who dealt in stock, Harriett petted the two oxen and told them how much they would enjoy the grass meadows of Fort Bridger. A man in greasy buckskins and a battered beaver hat stood nearby listening to her words and smiling.

When Jake led the oxen away, the man approached and doffed his hat respectfully. The sparse hair on his head was white, and his long, full beard was dark gray shot through with silver. Age hadn't affected the whipcord leanness of his frame, however, and he moved with the grace of a much younger man.

"Are you Miss Foster?" he inquired.

"Yes, I am."

"My name's Joe Woodford, ma'am. Most folks around here call me Montana Joe. A Mr. Smith in your wagon company suggested that I talk to you."

"Well . . . I'm happy to make your acquaintance, Mr. Woodford. Can I do something for you?"

Joe put his hat back upon his head and sighed. "I got me a young wife who's sick, ma'am. I heard your company had a doc . . ."

"Dr. Fellows."

"That's the fella. I asked him to look in on my

woman but the bas . . . uh . . . he says no. Guess
he's too blasted busy to bother with an Indian gal. Mr.
Smith told me you was a lady who wasn't likely to turn
down a man in trouble, and you had some skill in
tendin' the sick."

Harriett hesitated. She had very little skill, to tell the
truth, but the man had a desperate look in his eye that
was close to pleading. She supposed taking a look
wouldn't hurt.

"Mr. Smith probably exaggerated my skill, Mr.
Woodford, but I'd be glad to look in on your wife. Do
you have any idea what ails her?"

He grimaced. "I'd say it's the cholera, ma'am."

The cholera. The Indiana Company had left the sickness behind when they left the plains. But it certainly
wasn't impossible that the disease could show up here.
God only knew what caused the sickness or what made
it strike some people and not others.

Mr. Woodford's wife was indeed in the last stages of
the cholera. Her name was the Shoshone word for
Bright Bird, and she was much younger than her husband, perhaps in her mid-twenties. Two somber children squatted beside her bed—a plump brown toddler
and an equally plump, equally brown boy of about
eight years.

"Can you do anything?" Woodford asked, his voice a
plea.

Harriett sighed and took the woman's hand, which
was cold and puckered. Her skin was bluish gray instead of the fine healthy brown of her children. "Will
she take water?"

"I've tried to get some down her. She just spits it
up."

Sleepy-eyed, almost unconscious, Bright Bird didn't
have the strength to swallow. For two hours Harriett
did what she could, which wasn't much. She bathed
the woman's skin, chafed her cold hands, and inter-

mittently helped her husband force water down her throat to combat the dehydrating effect of the sickness. The sun was long down when she finally left.

Word that Harriett was tending Woodford's wife had spread around Fort Bridger, and another trader waited to ask her help for his wife and daughter, who were both suffering the same symptoms as Bright Bird. Harriett went with him, and then with a Snake woman whose husband was sick. In the small hours of the morning, when she left the last of her patients, she was exhausted and depressed, convinced that she'd done none of these people any good except perhaps make them more comfortable in their last hours. It was small comfort that Dr. Fellows would have been able to do little more than she, and infuriating to think that he'd refused even to try—just because they were Indians.

"You are good woman," the Snake wife said at the door of her crude wigwam. "You try to help my man. Other whites who travel this way do not care."

Harriett shook her head. "No one knows how to cure your husband's illness."

"You try. That is good. Maybe he live now."

"Remember to make him drink fluids, if he can. And keep him warm and clean. That's the only thing I can tell you."

The Snake matron nodded gravely. "You are good woman to tell me this." She pressed a package into Harriett's hands. "You take this as gift, and may your God reward you also."

The bundle contained vegetables from the little garden in back of the hut—squash, peas, green beans, and wax beans—treasures indeed. Harriett doubted that the woman could spare the food, but to decline would offer insult.

"I thank you," she said, closing the bundle tightly.

"You are very generous. I hope your husband recovers."

The woman nodded, but her face was already set in mourning. Before the sun rose, Harriett guessed, her husband would be dead.

So much death. And so close. Death was no stranger to Harriett. It had visited her own house and swept her parents away from their comfortable lives. But in Boston society death was euphemized, prettified with words and rituals that hid the grim realities. Harriett wondered if the world she'd known in Boston was not like the smooth facet of a stone that has been polished by a river. On this journey she was seeing the underside of the stone—dirty, rough, elemental. Which was real? Or were both real, in their own ways?

Harriett was too tired to think more on the subject. The wigwam she'd just left sat against the far side of the log fort, and her camp was a good long walk through the darkness. Fortunately, the stars were out in force. The Milky Way girdled the sky in a luminous white band, and a three-quarter moon floated above the hills to the west.

But she was uneasy despite the brightness of the night. A chorus of wolves sang in the distance—a nightly serenade she scarcely noticed when in camp. But without the familiar comfort of the campfire, wagons, and tents, the eerie sound sent a chill up her spine. The moonshadows were black as ink, and some had shapes that would set any imagination to conjuring dangers—bears, wolves, wildcats, wilder Indians. As Harriett walked she could almost see eyes staring out at her from the depths of the darkest, deepest shadows, fangs that caught stray light from the moon and gleamed in obscene malevolence. She scolded herself for such wild fancies. Nevertheless, the urge to run helter-skelter back to camp was almost too great to resist—until another sound joined the night noises. A human voice raised in song.

Well, perhaps *raised in song* was a bit too grand a phrase to describe what the voice was doing, Harriett admitted. Someone was slouched against the log wall of the stockade just ahead, spouting the words of a very improper ditty in a wavering and broken tenor. She recognized the voice too late to take evasive action.

"Why, Miz Foster!" Phineas Carter pushed himself away from the wall and lurched toward her. "Pretty Miz Foster. What you be doin' out here so late, sweet gal?"

Harriett could smell a waft of alcohol on his greeting. But he was solid on his feet—steady enough to be a substantial barrier between her and the camp. A prickle of uneasiness crawled up her spine.

"I was tending some people who were ill, Mr. Carter."

"Those Injuns? They been botherin' you, missy? Someone oughta teach 'em not to bother good white folk. Mebbe I'll do it. Yeah, mebbe I will."

Harriett had seen Carter leering at the Indian women—even the scarcely adolescent girls—but he apparently didn't think them worth treating as human beings. He and those like him were maggots on the underside of her rock, Harriett decided. She was too tired to scold herself for the insult to the maggot.

"They weren't bothering me, Mr. Carter. I was glad to do what I could for them."

"Well, you're just right saintly with them redskins, ain't ya?"

Harriett sighed. The man was drunker than she'd thought. Or was it the distance from safe camp that made him so bold?

"Excuse me, Mr. Carter. I really should get back to my wagon."

She moved to step around him. He moved to block her.

"No hurry, pretty Miz Foster. You got time fer Injuns, then you got time for me." He reached inside his buckskins and pulled out a bottle. "Here. Have a drink. That'll make ya more sociable."

"I don't drink spirits," she said flatly.

"That so? Guess you're too good for plain whiskey. You an' your high-minded ways and fancy talk. You figger you're too good for much of anything, don'tcha missy?"

"Mr. Carter, really . . . ." She tried to dodge around him again, but this time he grabbed her arm. His fingers felt gritty where they closed on the flesh of her wrist.

"'Ceptin' mebbe there's one thing you're not too good for, is there? Makin' eyes at that know-it-all Jake Carradine. Oh, I seen ya, gal. Yer eyes go all soft and gooey ever' time you look at the man. An' I saw ya watchin' the wrestlin' match, too. If'n ya was any hotter, you'd a caught fire. Now, don't open that sassy mouth o' yours to tell me t'ain't so. I know a hot, wet woman when I see one. An' you was heated an' slicked up like a mare ready ta get humped. Oh yes you was."

Harriett was too stunned to answer. Half the things Carter said she scarcely understood. But she got the evil gist of it.

"No answer for ol' Phineas?"

"Mr. Carter! Let me go at once! I tell you, sir, your imagination has gotten the best of you. I am engaged to be married to a fine man in San Francisco, and I assure you . . . ."

"There go those fancy words again!" Carter was panting now, whether from anger or passion Harriett didn't dare to think. "I don't care how many men you got, gal! That don't keep you from putting out for Carradine. I figger you can put out fer me too."

He jerked her close. Harriett screamed, but her scream was smothered by Carter's grimy hand closing over her mouth.

"I like it noisy, too, sweets. But this ain't the time."

One of his arms pinned her to his body while the hand gagging her mouth pushed her head back. He forced her to look at him, to smell his putrid breath, the sourness of his body.

"Go on and fight, pretty gal. I like it when you move. You rub me just right . . . just, just right." He ground his hips against hers to demonstrate how much he liked it.

"Let me go!" she mumbled into his hand. His grip was like a vise. Harriett saw spots before her eyes as he tightened his hold.

"That's better. Relax and enjoy it."

Carter slid his hand from her mouth, but the moment Harriett tried to scream he clamped his own mouth upon her lips. His sour tongue thrust inside, licked, prodded. Harriett bit down and fought the urge to vomit. Carter screamed, spraying spittle on her face.

"You bitch! You high-talkin', snooty bitch! I done my best to woo ya the nice way, and whaddaya do?"

Blood ran out of his mouth, and Harriett gagged on the taste of blood in her own.

"You do want it the hard way, don'tcha! Friggin' bitch!"

He pushed her to the ground and pinned her with his weight while he worked her skirts up past her hips. She squirmed and screamed, but her screams got only as far as the hand he had clamped once again over her mouth, and her struggles lent fire to his cravings.

"I'll have me some of this, bitch!" His hand, gritty and rough, slid up her thigh. He cursed anew. "Damned female. Only female I ever did see wears trousers under her skirts!"

He ripped away her last remaining protection and squeezed the bare flesh of her thigh. "I'm doin' you a favor, gal. I'd wager the only thing Carradine's got that's this hard is his pistol! You're gonna have a treat here."

His "treat" poked and prodded at her hip and thigh, a hungry snake looking for prey. "Quit buckin', gal! If'n ya wanna act like a horse I'll turn ya over an' stick it in yer backside. Hold still!"

Harriett managed to free one hand from his grip. She slapped and hit at him, to no avail. Her stomach was rising into her throat and a red haze of rage and desperation blocked out the sky.

Suddenly Carter was gone. Off. Pulled away, his weight no longer grinding her into the dirt.

"You want to see something hard, Carter? I'll show you something hard!" Jake's voice roared like thunder in Harriett's ears, followed by the crack of bone hitting bone and a gargled scream from Phineas.

Harriett scrambled away from the melee, jerking her skirts down to cover exposed hips and thighs. Blood pounded through her veins, her whole body aflame with both fear and humiliation.

Carter picked himself off the ground and wiped at the blood that streamed from his nose. "You're a real big man with that gun on your hip, Carradine. I ain't got my gun."

"I don't need a gun to deal with you." Jake unfastened his gun belt and tossed it on the ground near Harriett. She gingerly pulled the belt toward her.

Carter chuckled. "You got balls, Carradine. But yer stupid." The scout launched himself forward. Seemingly from nowhere, a wicked-looking knife appeared in his hand, the blade glinting coldly in the moonlight.

Harriett cried a warning, but Jake was prepared. He merely stepped aside and let Carter's momentum carry him past. At the last moment he grabbed the scout's knife arm by the wrist and gave it a vicious twist. The snap of bone was sickeningly audible, and Carter's scream made Harriett's stomach rise into her throat.

The scout doubled over in agony and cradled his wrist, but Jake mercilessly jerked him up straight again. Carter swung a punch with his one good arm; his fist landed with a meaty thunk on Jake's jaw. Jake staggered, blocked the scout's next swing, and delivered a solid blow to Carter's middle. The scout folded with a groan, but Jake once again brought him upright, this time by a grip on his throat.

"You leave Miss Foster alone, Carter," he commanded quietly. "She belongs to me. And if you touch her, or her aunt, or anyone else who's under my protection, I'll make you wish you were dead. Understand?"

Carter choked out a curse, his face darkening. Jake lifted him so that his feet dangled off the ground.

"Understand?" he growled.

"Yes!" the scout rasped. "Yes!"

With an effortless heave, Jake tossed Carter into a groaning heap. He watched as the scout got up and staggered away. In the pale moonlight, Jake's face seemed chipped from cold marble. A muscle twitching in his jaw seemed the only part of him that was alive.

Harriett tried to hold back her tears, but despite her determination they welled out of her eyes and streamed down her cheeks. Jake's pistol wavered in her trembling hands, but she couldn't seem to put the weapon down. When Jake finally turned to look at her, his eyes black as the moonshadows, she wanted to run, to cry, and to throw up, all at the same time. Immediately his features softened. He knelt beside her and touched her wet cheek with his finger.

"You can put the gun down, Harry." His voice was quiet, no longer like splintered shards of ice.

"I c-c-can't," she stuttered.

He gently pried the cold metal from her fingers and then gathered her into his arms. "You're all right, Harry. You're all right."

He was trembling too, Harriett noticed, his pulse pounding just as loudly as hers, his heart beating almost as fast. Lifting her to her feet, Jake pulled her back into his embrace. She melted against him, buried her face in his shirtfront, and let the tears flow. Propriety be damned. She needed his arms around her, his broad chest as shield against terror.

"Did he injure you, Harry?" His voice was soft with a core of steel.

Harriett nodded against his chest. What a question! Of course Carter had injured her. She was bruised, slobbered upon, humiliated . . .

"Harry." He took her chin in his hand and turned her face up. His eyes, oddly grave, caught at hers. "I know he . . . hurt you. But did he"—Jake's mouth tightened. He actually looked embarrassed, Harriett thought—"did he come inside you?"

Harriett's eyes widened.

"If he did, there's an Indian woman here at the fort who can mix you a potion to make sure you're not pregnant."

She choked. "P-p-p-pregnant?"

Jake couldn't mistake the confusion on her face. "Harry, you don't have to worry about it if Carter didn't . . . if he didn't . . ." He scowled. "God save the world from innocent women! Harry, don't you know anything?"

"No," she sobbed.

"Goddammit! Did Carter shove himself up inside you, between your legs?"

"No!" she shouted, her face flaming. She twisted to get out of his grasp, but he wouldn't let her go.

"You're not running away from me, Harry."

Jake's face was bloody, his mouth set in a harsh line. He, also, was part of the underside of the rock, Harriett realized—powerful, raw masculinity with a talent for violence that was frightening. That he used his strength to protect her was of no matter. She wasn't born to this world, and she couldn't protect herself against the creatures it spawned—not the Carters nor the Carradines.

Harriett pulled back, a desperate plea in her eyes. "Stay away from me, Jake. Please. Just leave me be."

"Not a chance, Harry." He pulled her toward him, back into his arms.

Harriett struggled frantically, then suddenly drooped against him as if all the fight had drained from her. Her tears soaked Jake's shirtfront.

Jake smiled grimly. He had recognized the plea in Harriett's eyes. Slowly but surely he was winning. Harriett knew he was winning, and the prospect frightened her almost as much as Carter's attack.

14

Journal entry—July 20—Fort Hall: I am ever amazed at the variety of topography on this continent of ours, and the vast potential for our nation's expansion. Until I came upon this journey, distance was a small word—encompassing a ride of a few minutes between my home and the city shops and theatres, or at most the piddling little trek to the seaside or to New York, which was the furthest distance I had known. Now I have traveled for months without seeing another civilized being other than my fellow travelers. The vastness of this land is unimaginable to one who hasn't seen it with his or her own eyes. Our great cities which pride themselves on being the center of America merely perch upon a narrow border, and their influence here is felt not at all. This is a different world, peopled by characters and animals that the most fanciful storytellers would shun as being outlandish. But here, where distances go on forever, where civilization is a word from another world—here they are real.

In the two weeks since we left Fort Bridger we have traveled northwest up the valley of the Bear River—a valley as lush and green as any I have known. Curiously enough, among all the greenery of that beautiful valley issue a host of poisonous springs. A case of nature imitating life, I believe. How many things in this world seem beautiful, only to hide evil beneath their beauty!

We left the Bear at Soda Springs (a most remarkable boiling spring that had Chad MacBride awestruck, and myself not much less amazed). From there we crossed over dry hills to the Port Neuf River and followed that stream to the Snake. We are camped now at the confluence of the Port Neuf and the Snake, at Fort Hall, a post of the Hudson's Bay trading company. The valley around us is wide and rich, with good water and abundant grass for our oxen and mules. We will stay here for several days to rest, do our wash, and tend to our faithful animals. Other companies are doing the same, and the valley is crowded with wagons.

I am told that at Fort Hall we are directly north of the Great Salt Lake which the Mormons have made their home. The majority of our journey is behind us, but perhaps the hardest is yet to come. The company can talk of nothing now but the trek over the high Sierra range.

Harriett massaged her brow. The writing on the page before her blurred. She hadn't been this tired since the first few days of their journey. Of course, she had more work to do now than ever before—and more on her mind. Sadie was still ailing, and very seldom could she rise from the pallet they'd made for her in the back of her wagon. Harriett willingly stepped in to care for infant Indy and keep an eye on Chad. Children, she discovered, had a way of running a mother ragged—even a substitute mother. Lucille did as much work as she, though, and Jake was a help. He was quite accomplished at dealing with Chad and most endearingly gentle with the baby. Harriett really didn't have that much excuse for her lethargy—except for one horrible possibility.

Could she be pregnant?

Harriett had tried her best to forget that horrible night at Fort Bridger, telling herself that dwelling on things she couldn't change was a useless and painful mistake. But the ugly incident came back to haunt her in a variety of ways, catching her off guard at odd moments, changing a smile to a grimace, stilling a bubble of laughter, making nights blacker and lonelier than they had been before. For a week after they left Fort Bridger, Harriett had feared sleep, for sleep brought nightmares of Phineas Carter and the horror of his assault. The dreams were less frequent now, but disgust and rage still lurked in a dark corner of her mind—and unreasoning fear, wearing the faces of both Phineas Carter and Jake Carradine.

Every time she looked at Jake, she had to remember how comfortable he was with violence, as if anger and bloodlust were old friends. How casually he had wiped his hands on his trousers, as if they were soiled with mere dirt instead of Phineas Carter's blood. When Jake had turned to look at her, she'd seen the wolf in his eyes—for an instant before the predator was gone. That instant had been enough to convince her that Jake Carradine could be a far more dangerous man than Phineas Carter would ever be.

But conversely, Jake had such patience in teaching Chad how to drive a wagon, had become an expert at dandling little Indy on his knee, and only laughed when his efforts got him a warm and spreading wet spot on his trousers. That same man, the man with the wolf in his eyes, had only to smile and Harriett Foster, a sensible, civilized, educated, liberal-thinking woman, lost all claim to reason and crumbled before the assault of his magnetism.

Of course, Harriett was in good company there.

Chad worshiped Jake, Lucille found him "charming," and Sadie treated him like the brother she'd lost. But Chad was just a child; Lucille thought most men were charming; and Sadie was ill. Harriett had no such excuse. She was merely a fool.

Now, as if she didn't have enough on her mind, came the possibility of being pregnant. Could such a disaster be possible? Harriett had only marginally understood the questions Jake had put to her on that horrible night, and she certainly had been too embarrassed to clarify her doubts. Had Carter done what a man does to get a woman with child? He had certainly touched her with a very unspeakable part of his anatomy.

The thought of having part of Phineas Carter growing inside her body made Harriett feel even more ill. For once she was sorry that young ladies in Boston were not exposed to the mysterious secrets of marriage until they had husbands to demonstrate those secrets. What she would give to know positively that she was free of Carter's taint.

She could ask Lucille. But the thought of telling her aunt what had happened with Phineas Carter made Harriett blanche.

She could ask Sadie. But Sadie was so ill, so uncomfortable, so worried about her children. How could Harriett add to her woes?

Or she could ask Jake. He seemed to know plenty about such things—certainly more than any decent unmarried man should know. He would no doubt be delighted to explain everything in great detail. From the gleam in his eye when he looked at her, he'd probably be even more delighted to demonstrate. No. She couldn't ask Jake.

For the first time in her life Harriett began to understand hatred. If she ever saw Phineas Carter again—which wasn't likely since he'd slunk off and not re-

turned to the company—she would gladly give him to
the Pawnee as another subject for their harsh justice.

The Indiana Company left Fort Hall two days after
they arrived, turning southwest to follow the Snake
down to the Raft River, a difficult trip of three days.
Grass was scarce, and water could be reached only by
a hazardous descent from the black-soiled, rocky up-
lands to the river below. The ascents and descents of
the trail oftentimes forced the wagons to be lowered or
hoisted by ropes.

For the first time on the journey, Harriett could not
force herself to be cheerful. She was snappish to Lucille and impatient with the MacBride children, and
wouldn't speak to Jake. Only with Sadie did she have
patience. The increasing discomfort in her stomach
and bowels convinced Harriett she was pregnant with
Phineas Carter's babe. She was tempted to cry on
Sadie's shoulder. But what could Sadie do for her?
Nothing. What could anyone do for her?

Two days out of Fort Hall, Harriett collapsed. Doubled over on the ground, a spasm of pain knifing
through her abdomen, she turned her face away as
Jake bent over her. Others gathered curiously around,
but a sharp look from their wagon captain sent them
quickly about their own business.

Jake picked Harriett up, climbed with her into the
back of her wagon, and kicked open a roll of blankets.
"Go get her some water," he commanded a distraught
Lucille. "And send Chad to sit with his mother."

Harriett kept her face turned away as Jake laid her
gently down. She couldn't meet his eyes and let him
read her shame.

"Harry." He forced her head around to look at him.
"How long have you been sick?"

She shook her head. She wasn't sick. She was
tainted, disgraced, soiled, filthy.

"Have you been vomiting?" he asked relentlessly. "Stomach cramps, bloody flux?"

She nodded weakly. Why couldn't he spare her the interrogation? Most women got sick with pregnancy. Did the whole world need to know the ugly details?

Tenderly he brushed her damp hair back from her brow. His expression was heavy, his mouth set in a grim line. "Harry. Lady mine, you've got the damned cholera."

Cholera?

Of course! Cholera! "Thank God," she mumbled. The puzzled frown that darkened Jake's face seemed to grow farther and farther away as she drifted off into comforting blackness.

Mrs. Hornsby picked up Harriett's pale, bluish wrist and felt for a pulse. Then she peered under the patient's eyelid and clucked dolefully.

"Too bad. She were one o' the few decent women I ever met who weren't a bitch. An' you too, o' course, Widow Stanwick."

Lucille sniffed and wiped at her streaming eyes. "Oh, my poor Harriett! Poor sweet baby!"

"She's not going to die!" Jake cursed, and both Lucille and the madam backed away at his vehemence.

"I suppose you could send round for that Dr. Fellows," Mrs. Hornsby conceded. "But if I was you, Jake Carradine, and I was fond o' this gal, I'd let her slip away peaceful like without that quack pokin' and proddin' her to death."

Dr. Silas Fellows, when he came, said much the same thing but in much more learned and pompous language.

"Most strange," the physician reflected. "We have had several instances of bilious complaints among our company these last few weeks, but no true case of the cholera since we left the Platte. But of course there were those sick savages that the lady did insist on visiting. God only knows what filth she encountered in those huts."

"She brought back some vegetables from one of the wigwams," Jake remembered.

"Did she eat them?"

"She ate a few of the peas," Lucille said, sniffling mournfully into a handkerchief. "About a week ago."

"Anyone else eat them?" Fellows asked.

"No. I took some, but I didn't eat them. I don't care much for peas. Jake and Chad were off somewhere with the Smiths."

The doctor sighed. "I doubt very much that the disease can be passed in such a way, but I would discard those vegetables if I were you, Widow Stanwick. As for Miss Foster, there are a number of remedies currently in favor. It's a shame we haven't the equipment for electric shock. Many of my colleagues have found that most efficacious. But I do have supplies of strychnine and morphine, which may also prove effective."

"Have they cured your other patients?" Jake asked suspiciously.

"Well . . . ah . . . no. But there are other remedies—cayenne pepper and jalap, calomel mixed with laudanum. A dose of sulfur is very well thought of, and when all else fails, a tobacco-smoke enema may bring the patient around. And, of course, she must be bled. That is a certainty!"

Jake began to feel that the physician had certainty of nothing whatsoever. The quack seemed delighted to have another cholera patient. To him, Harriett was not so much a suffering human being as another experiment for his remedies.

"The lady really should have followed my example and stayed away from those filthy savages. These modern women who feel they must dabble where they have neither the necessary wisdom nor capabilities—well, we see before us the sad result. This one should have been married years ago to a man who would have taught her a woman's place."

Jake clenched his fists, scarcely able to keep himself from taking a swing at the man's arrogant face. Harriett Foster had more wisdom and capability in one little finger than Dr. Fellows had in his whole stringy body. And the man dared to pontificate about Harry being taught her proper place!

The physician pulled a small blade from his bag.

"What is that for?" Jake asked darkly.

"For the bleeding. A small incision in the vein is all that's required."

"I don't think so."

Dr. Fellows looked at Jake in surprise. "But my good man, she must be bled!"

"Get near her with that knife and you're the one who'll be bleeding, Fellows. I don't think your services are going to be needed here."

The quack drew himself up in righteous indignation. "Then her death will be on your head, sir. And on her own, the foolish woman!"

"Get out, Fellows."

The good doctor made haste to obey, for the black glint in Jake's eye didn't match the mildness of his voice.

"I will have some of our comrades prepare a grave."

"Don't bother," Jake sent after the physician. "She's not going to die."

Jake turned back to Harriett, not at all as confident as he sounded. She was so still, so pale, with an ugly tinge of blue replacing her usual rosy glow. Perhaps he should have let the quack treat her. But how many times had he heard Harry decry the physician plying his powders and potions while ignoring the sufferer's most acute needs—fluids, warmth, comfort. Those things he could give her. Those and all the strength of spirit that was his to lend.

"Oh, Jake!" Lucille looked up from her weeping, her eyes red, her hands fluttering in worry. "Should you have told Dr. Fellows to leave? He might have . . . might have . . ."

". . . done her more harm than good," Jake supplied. "We can deal with this ourselves."

Lucille released a new flood of tears. "Oh, my poor Harriett. Poor baby. I just . . . just don't believe this is happening."

Harriett moaned and stirred. Her eyes flew open, and she groaned again. Jake brought a bucket to the edge of her pallet, a chore he'd done with frightening regularity over the past two hours. Patiently he supported Harriett's cold and clammy body as she retched bile and blood into the pail. Lucille turned away, weeping.

When the spasm was over, Jake wiped Harriett's face with a cool, wet cloth and brushed damp tendrils of hair from her face.

"Lucille, I can take care of this."

Lucille wept even harder. "It's not at all proper!"

Jake clenched his jaw. As if he didn't have enough on his hands!

"Proper be hanged! Lucille, you're only upsetting Harry. Why don't you go sit with Sadie and make sure that Indy is looked after." Gently but firmly he moved the widow toward the canvas opening. "I'll let you know if . . . if anything changes."

"You won't let her die without me being here?" Lucille sobbed.

"I won't let her die at all. If she tries to die on us, I'll make her wish she'd done it before she met me!"

Lucille didn't stop to question his logic, and as her sobs trailed off into the night, Jake turned back to Harriett.

"Just you and me now, Harry. Don't you even think of caving in on me."

Harriett turned her face away, tears streaming down her ashy face. She cried as a new spasm racked her, but this time her body was rebelling from the other end. Her tears were from shame as well as pain and weakness.

Jake took her hand. "Lady mine, you're just going to have to put up with me doing for you. You did the same cleaning up after Todd. And you didn't think a thing of it."

Jake wished he hadn't thought of Todd. Young and fit as he'd been, Todd Bryant hadn't survived his ordeal, despite Harriett's and Sadie's constant care. What chance did Harriett have when a man like Todd couldn't win through?

"You're not going to die, dammit! You hear me, Harry?"

For most of the night, Harriett was beyond hearing. Time and time again she convulsed, seemingly intent on discharging every drop of fluid in her body. If it were possible, Jake thought grimly, she would bring up her very guts. The water he forced down her throat always reappeared within minutes, bloody and sour. The blankets he wrapped around her shivering form did nothing to warm the cold, puckered clamminess of her skin. His words of comfort, of encouragement, met with protests that she wanted to die.

In Harriett's few lucid moments she wept with embarrassment at the intimate nature of Jake's care—until the night wore on and she no longer had the strength for shame. She clung to Jake's hand as if he alone could anchor her to this world. The wagon rattled with the sound of her harsh breathing and stunk with vile sickness. She didn't declare her resignation to death, as in her earlier moans, but Jake saw it in her eyes.

"You would've gotten me, you know," she rasped in the small hours of morning. "You were . . . quite irresistible. Frightening, but irresistible."

With difficulty Jake summoned a cocky grin. "I still am, Harry. You're not getting away from me so easily."

She grimaced in an attempt to smile. "Not . . . really easy."

"Easy compared to what I'll do to you if you try to die on me, lady."

"Oh, Jake!" she whispered. Tears of weakness welled in her eyes and dribbled down into her hair. "I wish . . . I wish . . ."

He saw the longing in her face and wished for a wild moment that just once he had forgotten his good intentions and seduced her. How many times had he felt the need so hot that it scorched from the inside out. He could have made her love it—love him. And they at least would have had that little time together.

But Harriett wasn't going to die! He wouldn't let her, dammit. He wasn't nearly finished with her yet, and still had his victory to savor.

"You'll get whatever you wish for," Jake promised her gently, then smiled. "As long as it's the same thing I wish for."

"I do love you," she said weakly. "I don't care how foolish it is."

"You're going to live up to those words, Harry, if I have to drag you back from Heaven to make you."

She closed her eyes, and for a desperate moment Jake thought he'd lost her. But when he looked carefully, he could see the barely perceptible rise and fall of her chest, and a thready pulse still moved through her veins.

When Harriett opened her eyes again, the lids drooped lethargically.

"Will you sing to me, Jake?"

"Sing?"

"I . . . I do like to hear you sing."

He sang. Gathering her cold body in his arms, he sang every song and ballad he knew, and made up some he didn't. Softly, almost in a whisper he sang, rocking her as she so often rocked little Indy when the baby was fretful. Jake sang until his voice was hoarse, until no more words or melodies would come to mind, until Harriett was fast asleep in his arms. Then he wrapped her in clean blankets and laid her gently on her pallet.

Tears flowed freely down Jake's stubbled cheeks as he sat and looked at the blanket-swaddled form. He never would have let Harry see them had she been awake. For a man to cry was a hard thing, and Jake remembered crying only once before in his life—when his mother had died. He was eight years old and had never wept since, not even when Elijah and Joshua burned to death in a house he should have been protecting. But Jake wept now.

He would lose her before the sun rose, despite his threats, despite his demands to the contrary. Even now Harriett was closer to Heaven than to earth. Jake could see it in her face. Nothing he could do would keep her with him. Nothing he could do . . .

Abruptly he rose and climbed down from the wagon. The night was still dark; the stars glittered icily in a black velvet sky. Jake tilted an agonized face toward the dark vault of the heavens. Was there anything in that great vastness that cared what happened to Harry, what happened to him? For all the many prayers that people launched toward the sky, were any ever answered?

"Are you listening?" he cried out to the sky.

Nothing answered him, not even in his mind. Wearily he hunkered down on the ground, head in his hands, and listened to the silence.

"It's damn well not fair!" he protested. If God existed, He could stand to listen to a complaint or two. And if He was annoyed—well, what could He do to Jake that He hadn't already done?

"Everyone I've loved has died. You've got every single damned one of them. And now Harry. It's not fair, dammit!"

Silence. Stone-cold silence.

"Listen!" Jake stood and started to pace, each step an angry demand for attention. "Maybe I'm not one of your favorites. All right. I can understand that. I don't go to church and I haven't read the Bible since Pa made me read it for punishment when I was a kid. I drink and gamble; I can be a mean son of a bitch when I'm riled. Worse yet, I've helped a few souls on their way to Hell and made a few others wish they were already there."

Jake stopped and stared at the sky. "But I've never shot a man who wasn't trying to shoot me. And I've given up drinking and cards in favor of chasing Harry Foster. As for being a son of a bitch when I'm riled"— Jake sighed in resignation—"you've got me on that one."

He felt none of the comfort that preachers promised with prayer. The night, the world itself, seemed utterly desolate. Nothing and no one was listening.

"I'd be good to Harry if You let her live," he promised lamely. "I'd make something of myself, build her a nice house up in Oregon, give up my gun, cut trees, raise kids. Hell, I'd even let that toad-sucker Kane keep on living, if he stays out of my way. Good enough?"

Jake wasn't accustomed to negotiating deals when he didn't hold all the cards. For once he couldn't obtain what he wanted with his fast gun or his equally fast charm. God, if He existed, had the deck stacked in His favor, and He probably had a hundred reasons to enjoy watching Jake squirm.

"She's not going to die, dammit!"

Silence seemed to be the Deity's last word. No trumpets thundered or angels sang—not even a miserable falling star appeared to offer comfort. The night was bleak, with cold, distant stars spangling an empty sky.

Jake dropped his head to his hands. He would gladly face man or beast, with or without a gun, and give himself better than even odds of coming out on top. But death had always managed to whip him.

Harriett didn't die that night. Jake held and comforted her all through the hours of darkness, listening to her shallow breathing, forcing water down her throat, and holding her through the frequent episodes of bloody vomiting and flux. As the stars faded and the eastern sky paled, she grew quieter, her breathing steadier. Jake didn't allow himself to hope. Her poor body had nothing more to yield, he figured.

"Jake!" came a hail from outside the wagon.

Jake pulled the blankets up to Harriett's chin and stepped out of the wagon. Joe Riley and Abel Hawkins stood outside. Lucille sat by the morning cookfire, looking almost as gray as Harriett. Jake knew Harriett's aunt had been up all night, for every hour or so she'd stuck her head into the wagon with questioning eyes, and when Jake shook his head, she'd left, looking even more bleak than before.

"We gonna move soon, Jake?" Joe asked. "We'd like to make twenty miles today, and I feel a storm blowin' in from the west."

Jake could see the morbid curiosity in the men's eyes, the concern on Lucille's haggard face. He himself probably hadn't looked this bad since his last all-night drunk.

"We don't move today," Jake said. "Miss Foster's too sick."

"Well, hell, Jake!" Joe said. "We're awful sorry for the little lady. But if we'd stopped for every person in this company who took sick, we'd still be on the Platte. She'll likely be the same whether we move or no."

"We don't move," Jake repeated, his voice steel hard.

"Well, I'm gonna move!" Abel Hawkins declared. "An' I figger just about ever'one else'll move with me. You can just stay here if ya like, Carradine. We can get another wagon boss."

"Now, wait a minute, Abel," Joe said. "Ain't no one knows this country like Jake here. Maybe . . ."

"No maybe! Hell! We've diddled and dawdled all summer while others is diggin' gold in Californy. I'm goin'!"

The wagons moved out with the rising sun. Only the Smith brothers hung back, offering to stay, until Jake urged them to go.

"You can't do any good here," Jake told them. "It's not like we're alone. Hell! There's a line of wagons stretching from here back to the Platte. When Harry's well enough to travel, we'll move out."

Horace looked at the ground. Horatio shuffled and harrumphed, and Hobby turned his hat through his fingers in a nervous circle.

"Sure, Jake." Horace shifted his weight uneasily. "We'll see you all up ahead."

No one mentioned the freshly dug grave that lay waiting on the edge of the encampment.

But Harriett fooled them all. As the sun rose higher in the sky, she struggled to gain ground. By noon she could hold down small amounts of water. The bluish tinge of her skin began to fade. Jake began to hope.

In the afternoon Lucille helped Jake clean and scrub the inside of the wagon, visibly trying not to gag as they washed linen and applied lye soap to every exposed surface. By evening Harriett was able to swallow a few spoonfuls of broth made from boiled strips of dried buffalo meat. The patient managed a smile for

Jake and, better still, laughed weakly when Dodger jumped into the wagon and touched his nose to hers in canine concern.

Once Harriett was safely tucked away in the clean wagon and peacefully asleep, Lucille grabbed an embarrassed Chad and waltzed around the fire in giddy relief. Even little Indy seemed to croon in delight.

Jake didn't dance, or celebrate. He scarcely had the strength to smile. But he did look at the sky, where stars were popping out one by one. Somehow tonight those pinpricks of light didn't seem quite so cold.

"You took long enough to let on," he accused.

15

Journal entry—August 1—City of Rocks: How sad I am as I write tonight, for all the time I was growing stronger from my bout with the cholera, my dear friend Sadie MacBride was losing her strength. Two nights ago she died, and only now do I have the composure to write of it.

In a strange way I find myself angry with Sadie. I myself have lately visited the door between life and death. I know how tempting that passageway can be —not an entryway to darkness and grief, as so many believe, but a promise of freedom from pain, of peaceful rest. I turned my back on that doorway and struggled back. But Sadie stepped across, leaving all of us who love her behind. My heart aches from the betrayal, though my mind tells me such feelings are pure foolishness.

How I miss her! How it hurts to see poor Chad's confusion and grief. And little Indy will never know the brave woman who bore him. That women must so often destroy their own lives to bear new life seems injustice, but this is one injustice that cannot be eradicated by petitions to the legislature or fine speeches at a convention.

Perhaps I am angry because I feel so helpless. The

only thing I can do now for my dear friend is care for her children. How ironic that I, who never had ambitions of motherhood, at the age of twenty-three have instantly acquired two sons, an eleven-year-old and an infant, temporarily, at least.

The rest of the Indiana Company was also camped at City of Rocks, Mr. Deere's group as well as the other wagons that had traveled on the Fort Bridger route. Jake's little caravan was invited to join the reunited company, but after discussing the matter with Harriett and Lucille, Jake politely declined. Harriett was in full agreement. She had a lingering resentment, Harriett confided to Lucille as they set up camp, that the people who had shared so many weeks of hardship and peril could have left them behind so callously. She was raised to believe that companions should support each other in adversity, but on the California Trail, every person's mind was turned only to his own profit.

"We will do very well on our own," Harriett concluded.

"On our own?" Lucille snorted. "This place is more crowded than Boston Harbor, and I've heard that there's almost a solid line of wagons from here to the Sierras. California's going to be a very crowded place, I think."

"I don't believe so, Aunt. The trail may be crowded, but this country is so vast I don't think it will ever fill up with people."

"Well, from what I've seen of this bunch, I hope there's enough gold in California for everyone, because if there's not I wouldn't put it past these fellows to start slitting each other's throats."

"Not everyone is after gold," Harriett reminded her. "We aren't."

"No. But I wouldn't object to finding a man who's

got some to spare. I think after surviving this trip I at least deserve that much."

Harriett laughed, but she knew her aunt was only half teasing. "You may be sorry if you give up your independence, Aunt Lucille."

"Bah. Independence is a poor companion on a lonely night."

"One should not grant a man control over one's affairs—as the law does in marriage—without being sure he has wisdom and intelligence."

"Wisdom can be boring as well. You may discover that someday, my love, when it's too late."

Harriett snorted and changed the subject.

"I think I'll stew some of the dried buffalo meat for dinner. Jake's gone hunting, but with the traffic in this area I doubt he'll bring anything back."

Lucille sighed. "Oh for one of those glorious beef pasties that Clarissa used to cook. The partridges, the fish stuffed with sausage dressing, the fine apple pies. To think we used to eat that way every night." She sighed again. "You'll never find another cook like Clarissa."

"No," Harriett agreed. "I suppose not." For a moment she wondered if Edwin had a cook or servants. How would it feel to be waited on again after having learned so painfully how to do for herself?

Two hours later, dinner was cooked and eaten and Indy settled for the night. Chad was off with Horace Smith—learning how to whittle, he had informed Harriett proudly. Harriett was tired. Her strength was still not up to snuff. But she was too restless to go to bed.

"I think I'll take a walk, Aunt. Will you join me?"

"In the dark?"

"The moon is bright. It's almost as light as day."

"You go on, dear. My feet have done enough walking for today. Or for all this year, in truth."

Before she left, Harriett found the small pistol Jake

had bought her in Independence and slipped it into
her pocket. She'd learned the hard way that a woman
didn't walk alone and unarmed at night, and the
crowd that made camp at the City of Rocks was a
rowdy one. Always before some of the companies in
the mass campgrounds had been northwest bound—
taking families and farmers and honest merchants to
Oregon Territory. But the Oregon and California trails
diverged where the Raft River meets the Snake,
and now the moderating influence of the northwest
emigrants was gone. Camped at the City of Rocks were
only the argonauts—rowdy, fractious, impatient, with
gold in their eyes and, frequently, whiskey in their bellies. Few of them would hesitate to grab at a solitary
female.

Harriett strolled away from the wagons and toward
the edge of the bowl-shaped valley that comprised the
campground. A path led her through the grassy meadows, up the flanks of the valley, and into a little alcove
guarded by pillars of granite. There she sat, grateful to
be alone. Back in Boston, Harriett had anticipated the
trail west as a lonely trek, but in truth she hadn't been
alone once since leaving Independence. Solitude had
become a precious thing.

Stretched out before her, the valley called City of
Rocks seemed to glow in the pale moonlight. Carved
by nature into fantastic spires and improbable towers,
the granite monuments that rimmed the meadows
looked like shadowy giants who watched the wagons
below with haughty, frozen disdain.

The analogy was uncomfortably close to her own
life, Harriett concluded. She had mapped out a path
that kept her on the boundaries of living, a frozen
statue observing life from a cold, lofty perch. An amiable, intellectual marriage steered her clear of messy
passion or demanding children; a dabbling in reform
and women's rights allowed her to salve her con-

science and pat herself on the back, deploring the state of society's filth without getting close enough to gag from the smell.

How close she had come to having that carefully laid path jerked out from beneath her feet! Harriett was still somewhat surprised that she was alive. When the cholera had twisted her bowels and reduced her to the level of a heaving, filthy animal, death had seemed so certain. The depths of her innards hadn't been the only thing pulled to the surface; the depths of her soul had also been laid out for examination. Truths that she'd shoved into the dark corners of oblivion burst out and paraded before her mind's eye—the awful realization that she was a coward, that she had lived her life on the safe paths and never had the courage to look beyond, that she had reduced the wonderful complexities of the world to simplistic rules, safe haven for a small mind.

And that she loved Jake Carradine.

She'd picked a piece of human offal from the street and convinced him to become the man he really was. And in so doing she had created a monster who would devour her, who would trample her carefully laid plans to dust and thrust his own chaotic passion in their place. And she loved him with a swelling madness that Harriett's gentle mother had never warned about. This passion was no childish game, no coy and silly emotion, as her mother had labeled it. It was a consuming desire, a dictatorial fascination, an irresistible excitement that had come to rule her heart. For weeks she had ignored it and denied it, all the while it rooted itself so deeply in her soul that it had become a vital part of her. A brush with death had forced her to look into her own soul and see what grew there, and who—Jake Carradine.

The thought was frightening. Right and wrong had become fuzzy; Harriett was losing the very sense of

who she was and where she belonged in the world.
One part of her wanted to jump back to safe ground,
another part longed to dive off the cliff and wallow in
the new world she had discovered—safety be damned.
Suddenly Harriett felt very alone, with a loneliness
that had nothing to do with the solitude of her grassy
hillside perch.

"You should be in bed."

Harriett jerked upright at the sound of Jake's deep
voice. He stepped into view, coming out of the inky
darkness that clung to a granite pillar—almost as
though he had materialized at the juncture of moonlight and shadow.

"Lucille told me you walked this way," he explained.
"I found the path."

"Keeping track of me?" she asked, half flattered,
half annoyed.

"Like a mother hen," he admitted. He came to sit
beside her. "You should be resting, Harry. You're not
that strong yet."

"You are like a mother," she accused with a chuckle.

"Of course. I'm the one who sang you to sleep. Remember?"

Harriett did remember, most uncomfortably. She
sat for a moment, feeling silence thicken around her.
Finally she spoke. "I haven't thanked you properly for
. . . for what you did for me, Jacob."

"I wish you'd call me Jake."

"And I wish you'd call me Harriett," she returned.

He smiled, conceding the point.

"Seriously," she continued, "I would have died if it
weren't for you. How does a person thank someone for
that?"

He didn't answer. The silence swelled, and for some
reason Harriett's heart stepped up its pace. She
jumped when Jake touched her hand where it rested
on her knee.

"Part of me was dead until I met you," he said quietly. "Perhaps we should just call ourselves even."

"That's hardly the same thing."

He regarded her seriously for a moment, then grinned. "All right. You owe me."

She gave him a startled look. Slowly, the grin faded. Deep in his gray eyes flickered a light that started warmth coiling through Harriett's loins.

"Harry. Don't you think it's time we stopped playing games?"

Harriett didn't ask what he meant. She knew.

"You said you love me. I'm going to hold you to those words."

"And do you love me?" she asked in a small voice.

"I do."

His words had none of the hesitation or uncertainty she had expected. Probably because she had sucked all the world's uncertainty into her own soul and none was left for anyone else.

"I'm not . . . prepared for a man like you, Jacob."

"My good luck. If you were, I couldn't have ambushed you so easily."

"Is that what you did?"

"It is. Jumped you fair and square, got you at gunpoint, and I'm going to keep you there, slave to my every whim."

"Jacob. Don't be ridiculous."

His presence beside her made the lonely, aching hollow that had opened in her heart fill with warmth. The urge to reach out and touch him was almost irresistible.

"Well, it might be a toss-up as to who's the slave," he admitted.

As if infected with her longing to touch, Jake reached out and brushed a finger along Harriett's cheek. A shiver of longing traveled the length of her spine, and an illogical well of tears burned her eyes.

She could almost see the mighty pillar of her will-power, her resistance, her reason, crumble to dust. The need to come down from her sterile perch, to abandon her cowardice, to live life instead of observe it, was overwhelming.

She caught his hand. "Jacob . . . I . . . I . . ." Harriett didn't know where to start, hardly knew what she was doing. "I do love you."

Jake smiled, folding her hand in his. "Don't make it sound like a death sentence, Harry. It's not."

"No. Of course not. It's just that . . . I thought I would never feel this way about a man. I feel . . . almost like a stranger to myself these days."

"You'll like yourself once you get acquainted."

Her mouth twitched as she tried not to smile. "Do you think so?"

"I know so."

He gently turned her face upward and met her mouth with a kiss, a long, lazy, thorough kiss that seemed to coil every nerve in her body into a spring of tension. Harriett had taken the plunge from her lofty perch. She could feel herself falling, but a strange elation left no room for fear. Tomorrow was forever away. Yesterday was gone. The world was only Harriett and Jake, together.

"Jacob . . ." She reeled from his kiss, gentle though it had been. His arms seemed her only anchor against spinning away into darkness. "I need . . . I want . . . something. I don't know how to get it. Please. Help me."

Jake took a deep breath. He was shaking, Harriett noted in wonder. She could almost smell his desire, musky, warm, reaching out to pull her to him with a strength even more irresistible than his arms. "Don't tempt me, Harry. I'm not a man noted for his restraint."

"I thought you—"

With a finger across her mouth Jake cut off the confused disappointment of her voice. "You're a woman who needs wedding before bedding, Harry. You're a woman . . ."

"I'm not a woman at all." Tentatively she put a hand against his broad chest, then didn't know what to do next. She spread her fingers uncertainly and slid them between the buttons of his shirt.

"God!" Jake closed his eyes as he gusted out the exclamation. "You'd better be certain, lady."

Harriett's breath caught in her throat. She couldn't think about reason or certainty. Decent women remained pure, modest, virtuous—she'd been taught such rules all her life. Were those edicts another attempt by men to control women? Harriett found she didn't care. She simply longed to be closer to the man she loved. That love was such a compelling emotion, yet still somehow distant, incomplete, needing something more. . . .

"You're special, Jake. And this is a special time. Isn't it?"

Jake drew a long, shaky breath. "It is, little Harry. Sweet damn, but you do know how to sabotage a man's gentlemanly intentions."

Slowly, as if afraid of startling her, Jake reached behind her to unfasten the buttons of her bodice. "You're going to like making love," he promised in a husky voice.

"What . . . what are you doing?" She felt suddenly naked as he slipped off her bodice. The cool air caressed her shoulders, and her chemise seemed indecently flimsy.

"This isn't an activity you have to dress for, sweet lady." He slipped the strap of her chemise down her shoulder, gazing at her bare skin like a cat looking at rich cream. She felt paralyzed by his eyes, and even the cool evening air couldn't keep a hot flush from crawling up her neck and cheeks.

Enveloping her face with big hands, Jake leaned down to taste her lips, gently at first, a soft, tantalizing brush of his mouth against hers. His mustache tickled her nose; his tongue touched the corner of her lips, then circled her mouth, sending a thrill of pleasure washing through her body. They sank down into the grass. This had to be very wicked, Harriett thought lethargically. Very, very wicked. And very wonderful.

"Was that so bad?" he teased.

"No." She looked up at him. His darkened gray eyes held more than passion, and Harriett's heart swelled. If Jake truly loved her, could she deny him anything? She was no different, no more sensible than Lucille, than Sadie, than all the world full of women who loved so well and so unwisely. But right now none of that mattered. "No. That wasn't so bad."

He smiled, satisfied, a little arrogant, very male.

"That wasn't bad at all," she breathed. "It was nice."

Once again he bent his head to her, this time parting her lips with his own and thrusting his tongue inside. Harriett closed her eyes and let her world narrow down to just the two of them. She was lost, and she might as well enjoy the losing.

He kissed her nose, her ear, her throat, and then trailed his mouth along her shoulder until he reached the chemise strap that she had instinctively restored to its place. He pushed it aside and brushed his lips across the bare skin where the strap met the chemise itself.

A sudden attack of modesty inspired Harriett to object, but he merely looked up, his eyes smoky with desire.

"We haven't even started yet, sweet lady. We've got a long, long way to go."

"Jacob . . ."

He put a finger to her mouth. "I wouldn't hurt you for the world, Harry. Trust me just this once."

Gently he pushed her back down and resumed his exploration, disposing of the other strap and peeling her chemise down to her waist. The cool air rushed against her bare skin, raising goose bumps and puckering her nipples. Harriett's face and throat grew hot as his eyes drank in the sight of her.

"God but you're beautiful!"

Harriett's face grew hotter. His gaze was like a palpable caress, his eyes hot as flame. Almost worshipfully he touched her, his fingers brushing the sides of her flattened mounds, pushing them up and together, circling, caressing. A moan escaped her mouth as the ache in her loins became a twisting, coiling hunger.

"Feels good, doesn't it, Harry?" His voice was husky, a deep, sensual caress. "You know the very sight of you makes me want to bust right out of my pants."

Harriett's body took over from her mind. She wasn't embarrassed when he took her nipple in his mouth and suckled like a child; she wound her fingers in his hair and pressed his face closer to her flesh. And when he peeled away the rest of her clothing, she frantically helped.

But Jake seemed in no hurry. One by one he revealed her hidden treasures, savoring each one thoroughly before moving on to the next. His hand spread possessively over her flat belly, his tongue teased and tortured her navel until she cried out. Each smooth rounded thigh received ample attention, the backs of her knees tingled with his kisses—even her feet received their share of his ardor. And all the time Harriett burned, not knowing quite what she burned for. If this was passion, this raw ache with no relief in sight, then no wonder that married ladies clacked together with complaints about the marriage bed.

"Harry," Jake whispered, his warm breath torturing her ear. "You're everything a man could want—a treasure, pure gold with red hair and green eyes."

"What are you doing to me? Oh, please . . ."

A wry smile twisted his mouth. "You don't even know what it is you need, do you, Harry?" He trailed one hand up the inside of her thigh and brushed the soft down between her legs.

"Jake . . . !"

"It's all right, sweetheart." He stroked gently between her legs. Out of control, Harriett gasped and arched her hips desperately against his hand. He shouldn't be touching that most private area of her body, Harriett was quite sure. But his caress felt so good, she could hardly breathe.

"Harry, if I could spend the whole night touching you, I would." His voice had a strained quality that made Harriett open her eyes in alarm. "But truth is I can't wait much longer."

He'd peeled off his shirt a few moments before, and now he unbuckled his gun belt and stripped down his trousers and johns, freeing a manly appendage that was more than ready to join in the game. Harriett shut her eyes tightly. She'd seen horses and bulls. How amazing—and horrifying—that men were so similarly built.

His hand slid up her thigh again and he bent down to taste her lips. Uncertain now, she tried to wriggle away, but his weight held her prisoner. For one desperate, frightening moment her mind flashed back to the horror of Phineas Carter. She stiffened.

"Harry," he whispered against her lips. "Don't be afraid of me."

Long, supple fingers slipped inside her. Wet and aching, her body responded, relaxing as he stroked her with a slow rhythm that set her nerves to throbbing. This was Jake. This was love. Her nightmares had no place here. Desire was eating her alive; uncertainty couldn't survive.

Shyly she touched Jake's bare chest, ran her hands down his ribs to his lean hips.

He took her hand. "You're going to touch me."

"Oh, no!"

"Yes."

He molded her fingers around the turgid rod that hung threateningly between them. It warmed in her hand, soft velvet over hot steel.

"A very friendly weapon," he told her with a smile.

Still stroking her, feeding her desire, he nudged her legs apart with his knee. "Innocent little Harry. God how I love you!"

His hungry, friendly weapon pushed into her, only a little way, enough to make her moan with delight. Back and forth he rocked, each time pressing on a little farther.

"I'm going to cause you pain, love. Just this once." He kissed her hard, then eased fully into her, conquering as gently as possible the barrier that stood against his possession. Harriett clutched at his shoulders, moaning now in distress, not desire.

Tears rolled down her cheeks, the salty drops caught by Jake's lips as he kissed them away. "Never, never again will I hurt you, Harry. I promise."

He moved inside her. She gasped.

"Relax, love. Relax. Let me love you."

Grasping her knees, he pulled them up and around his waist, then cupped her buttocks in his hands and rocked her with him as he gently, carefully thrust again. As she relaxed and began instinctively to move with his rhythm, he thrust harder, deeper. Harriett felt the ache build again, stronger than ever. The pain was gone, only dimly remembered as his possession became an urgent command that her body strained to obey. The sight of him arched above her set her afire— his face tense with his arousal, the muscles of his splendid body rippling with his effort. She wanted to melt into him, to have him melt into her, to have him push up inside her until they could no longer be separated, ever.

She ached, burned, strained, and thought she was going to swoon. But she didn't swoon. Jake arched back his head, his body suddenly taut and still, his throat rumbling in a growl of victory just as every muscle in Harriett's body convulsed in ecstasy. Harriett sobbed out her relief. Jake captured her sobs as he kissed her, openmouthed, sensual, possessive—a seal of their irrevocable union.

For a long while they lay unmoving, looking at each other, feeling the heat and sweat of each other's bodies, smelling the musk of their lovemaking, enjoying the intimate, unbroken union of their flesh. When Jake reluctantly rolled to one side, Harriett clung to him. He cradled her against him, her head pillowed on his broad chest, where in a few short moments she fell peacefully and soundly asleep.

Jake closed his eyes. He'd never been where they'd gone tonight, never been quite so desperate with desire or quite so choked with love. The feeling was almost scary, and he wasn't a man who scared easily. Scary, but worth whatever it cost.

For Jake Carradine had finally won. Harriett had surrendered, had almost forced him to conquer. She would never escape him now.

Harriett woke in the tent to the sound of Lucille's soft snores. Pale dawn peeped around the edges of the door flap. Dimly she remembered Jake carrying her back to camp, setting her down in front of the tent, and kissing her good-bye—a tender, possessive, very thorough kiss. He'd teased her about the little pistol in her pocket, asking if she was going to shoot him for taking advantage of her. Who had taken advantage of whom? Harriett had answered. She'd laughed with him, wantonly unashamed, totally under his spell. Tomorrow had seemed so far away. But now it had come.

She turned her face into the blankets. Surely last night had been a dream, a wicked, erotic dream. But the burning soreness between her legs testified to the reality of what had happened.

When she stripped off her dress, which she'd been too tired to remove the night before, Harriett found further witness to Jake's explorations—an irritation on her belly where the stubble on his jaw had scraped her skin, a red mark on the side of her breast where his teeth had left a brand. She remembered too well how he'd nipped her there—a bite of pleasure, not pain. The pain was in the remembering.

What had she let herself become? The Harriett Foster who sat in her tent at City of Rocks certainly wasn't the same woman who had left Boston in the spring.

Her hand mirror—for weeks unused—confirmed Harriett's fears. She scarcely recognized herself. Her face was browned, with freckles showing through the tan; her hair tumbled about her shoulders in a chaotic fall of red. Her eyes, green as ever, held a shadow of sadness—and knowledge that no spinster lady should have.

What kind of wicked, wanton creature had she become, that she no longer even knew herself?

"Harriett, dear. Are you all right?"

Harriett turned. Lucille was awake, gazing at her in concern—and past her, to where Harriett's discarded cotton drawers lay in a heap upon her trunk. For the first time Harriett noticed that the drawers were splotched with crimson. The sight brought home what she had done, and she felt herself go cold.

Lucille noted her distress and smiled. "My love, don't look as if the world had ended. Very few women remain virgin forever. Although I was beginning to think that you might."

"Oh, Aunt Lucille!" Harriett covered her face with her hands. She felt like snatching up the blankets she was sitting on and draping them over her head. "I don't know what to think!"

"You must love Jake very much to have yielded yourself to him. I know he would never have forced himself upon you."

"No. Of course he didn't." Almost the opposite, Harriett admitted to herself. She'd been shameless. Absolutely shameless. But she didn't feel as contrite as she ought. Peeping through her fingers, Harriett slowly lowered her hands. "Oh, Lucille, he did the . . . the most . . ."

Lucille chuckled. "No need to elaborate, dear. I do have some idea of what he did to you."

Harriett turned crimson as the virgin blood that stained her drawers. "I . . . I don't know what's come over me, how I let this happen! I'm not acting like myself at all."

"Not necessarily a bad thing," Lucille commented with a lift of one brow.

"He's a hired gun, for heaven's sake! He has violence in his blood. I've seen him do the most . . . frightening things. He can be brutal, arrogant, debauched . . ."

"Patient, kind, tolerant, loving," Lucille added. "Harriett, this is not a civilized land. The men who live here survive by cunning and strength. Do you suppose your father would be the same gentle person if he had been raised out here, or Edwin? . . ."

"Oh, Edwin!" Harriett groaned. "I've betrayed him, and wretch that I am, I didn't even think of him until you said his name!"

"Which shows just how much you loved him."

"I never said I loved him!" Harriett denied hotly. "I hold him in respect, affection . . ."

"In boredom," Lucille suggested.

Harriett got up, pulled a dress from her trunk, and yanked it down over her head. "Edwin is not boring!"

"But you love Jake Carradine," Lucille reminded her.

For the first time in several weeks, Harriett pulled on pantaloons under her skirt, then proceeded to brush out her tangled locks and confine them in a tightly wound bun at her nape.

"Harriett, all the noble ideas in the world—all the respect and affection and mutual causes—aren't worth one night of genuine love in a man's arms. And a lifetime of that love is worth gambling all one holds dear."

The note of wistfulness in Lucille's voice caught Harriett's attention. She dropped down beside her aunt on the blankets and took the older woman's hand. "And what of the pain when you lose, Aunt Lucille? Isn't it better to found a life on reason rather than emotion?" Daylight had come, and with it the return of rationality.

Lucille shook her head. "I loved my husband Peter with everything that is in me, my dear, and when he died, I wanted to die also. But I wouldn't give up one minute we had together just because I suffered his loss."

"And Mr. Steede?" Harriett asked, remembering her aunt's pain when they had spotted the charming gambler with another woman on his arm.

Lucille laughed. "Lawrence Steede was a diversion, sweet. He's amusing, attractive balm for a widow's loneliness. But no woman in her right mind would count on him for a future. I was hurt at his desertion, but most of the hurt was to my pride."

"And you think Jake Carradine isn't cut from the same cloth as Steede?"

"Harriett, dear. You know Jake much more intimately than I. You must answer that question for yourself."

16

They left the City of Rocks in company with a solid line of other wagons. Splitting off from the Indiana Company had not condemned them to brave the trail alone. In fact, Harriett had heard that head-to-tail traffic was common all the way to California.

Lucille minded little Indy, Jake had taken Daisy for a much-needed run, Chad drove the Foster wagon, and Harriett drove the MacBride wagon, which was the larger of the two vehicles. She had learned to drive the MacBride mule team almost as well as her own oxen. Dodger sat beside her on the wagon box, tongue lolling, eyes sparkling, apparently delighted with the cool morning and the prospect of a beautiful day. Harriett wished she could say the same for herself.

Breakfast had been a disaster, at least for her. Jake's manner had been outwardly unchanged, but a knowing twinkle in his eye whenever he looked her way made Harriett want to run—from him, from herself, from the stomach twistings and heart somersaults that were inspired by his proximity. She was numb and breathless at the same time, and when he'd handed her a cup of tea, his knuckles brushing her hand, she'd jumped like a frightened rabbit and dropped the cup. He'd only smiled, an infuriating, heart-stopping smile that fastened her unwilling gaze upon his mouth and made her remember the miracles that mouth had worked the night before.

What kind of casual breakfast conversation could she have with a man who had only hours before done such unspeakably intimate things to her body? How could she calmly knead the biscuit dough while Jake watched—when he'd kneaded her breasts, her belly, her buttocks, in much the same way while she'd shamelessly moaned her pleasure? How could she move and act and talk as if this were a normal morning, that last night had been an ordinary night, when her wicked mind was recalling the feel of his weight pressing her down, the heave of her body arching toward his, the plunging of his hard, hot flesh into hers—knowing that he was remembering the same things?

Harriett had eaten her breakfast off the wagon's tailgate rather than sit on the one unoccupied stool, which was too near Jake. He'd watched her closely, amusement making his eyes crinkle and the grooves in his cheeks deepen. Lucille had attempted to draw them both into polite conversation, but Harriett's only comments had been stilted and stammered, and Jake had seemed content merely to watch her with glinting eyes.

Harriett stared morosely at the broad rumps of Sadie's mules. Every time she saw Jake Carradine, her composure fled, her brain froze, and coherent speech deserted her. No doubt everyone on the trail knew exactly why she was acting such a fool. She might as well have a broad scarlet *A* embroidered across her chest, and *N* as well—for ninnywit. She ought to be ashamed as well as embarrassed. But she wasn't. That was the most upsetting realization of all.

At the end of the day they reached Goose Creek Hill, a steep descent where some of the more cautious emigrants lowered their wagons down the hill by means of ropes. At the top of the hill Jake told Chad to wait with the Foster wagon by the side of the road, tethered Daisy to the back of the MacBride wagon, shooed Dodger off the box, and climbed up beside Harriett. He urged the mules forward, crooning and soothing as they slid down the hill. One of his booted feet constantly pressed the brake.

Harriett longed to jump down from the wagon box, but she couldn't without being obviously rude. Her thigh and shoulder brushed against Jake's on the narrow confines of the seat. Her blood pumped furiously, her lungs couldn't get enough air. He squeezed her hand when they stopped at the bottom of the hill, and she thought her heart would jump into her throat.

"That wasn't so bad," he said.

The words echoed from the night before. She jerked her hand away before she could control herself.

He frowned. "You're pale as a ghost, Harry. Are you all right?"

She wasn't all right! Her emotions were swinging wildly up and down, totally out of control. Harriett hated to be out of control.

"I'm perfectly all right," she lied crisply.

"Is that so?"

"I . . . yes! That's so!"

Jake lifted a brow. His knowing eyes made Harriett's heart thump alarmingly.

"I'm a bit under the weather. That's all."

"I expect you're sore," he said in a shockingly matter-of-fact manner. "I'm not surprised, sweet lady. It'll go away"—he grinned wickedly—"along with the blushes."

Harriett's face promptly betrayed her by growing hot with color. She turned away. "I suppose you . . . you've had so much experience in such things that you know."

"Harry"—he took her stubbornly set chin and

turned her back to face him—"let's get something straight. I've laid a pantload of whores and a few good women who were lonesome for a man, but you're the first woman I've ever loved. And you'll be the last. You'll do me for the rest of my life. I'll take care of you, I'll make you happy, and I'll try my damnedest to be the best thing that ever happened to your life."

Her eyes grew wide. "You want to marry me?"

Jake gave a short bark of laughter. "What did you think I wanted? You're not a woman to tumble in the grass for a quick thrill. You think last night would've happened if I wasn't set to make things right?"

"Last night . . ." She colored an even deeper red. "Last night was my decision. I tempted you into something that . . . that . . ."

"Don't take all the credit, Harry. You gave me a beautiful gift, but I never would've taken what you offered if I hadn't known that soon we'd be wed. It wouldn't have been fair to you."

"Jacob," she said quietly, "I never said that I'd marry you."

"You'll marry me," he assured her.

Tyrannical, arrogant male. They were all alike! "Marriage," she began hotly, "is more than just . . . just a night of foolish . . . foolish . . ."

"Love," he suggested. "You love me, Harry. You were a virgin—scared as hell. Last night would never have happened if you didn't love me."

Harriett's lips tightened into a line. She stared at the ground, at the rumps of the mules—anywhere but into Jake's knowing eyes. She was caught, and there was no sense in denying it. "All right, Jacob. I love you. You're right. I never would have . . . would have . . ." Words failed her, and her face grew hotter. "But marriage is more than love."

"Like hell."

"You're a man!" she accused. "That's why you can

be so cavalier about doing such a thing! When a woman marries she gives not only her love, but her whole life to her husband. By law she is no longer a person, no longer exists. Her husband controls her property, her income, her person—even her children belong to him!"

"I don't give a damn about your property or income. Your person"—he grinned—"that I want."

"Be serious!"

"I am serious! I want to marry you, Harry. Forget your damned stupid laws. Forget everything except that I love you and you love me. We'll tell Edwin to jump into San Francisco Bay, and then we'll go to Oregon, get into the timber business, cut trees, and raise babies. Lucille can go with us. And so can Chad and Indy. And dammit, you can control me and everything I have if you want!"

"I don't want to control you, Jacob. I only want control over my own life. Edwin understands that. It's the only reason I said that I'd marry him."

"But you don't love Edwin," Jake growled. "You love me."

Harriett stared at the mules, her face set.

"You don't trust me, do you, Harry?"

Unwillingly she dragged her gaze around to meet his, shamed by the tears that trickled down her face. "I do love you. And I don't trust anyone anymore, not you, not Edwin, not even myself."

He sighed, then brushed his hand across her wet cheek. "Don't think I'm going to give up this easily. You're going to marry me if I get my way. And I generally get my way."

The tenderness in his eyes was too much to bear. "Please understand, Jacob. Part of me wants to say yes. And another part of me knows I'd lose myself in you. Lord but I hate indecision!"

Harriett forced herself to uncurl her hands, which

had been wadding and clenching the material of her skirt. She'd made a mess of her clothing, just as she was making a mess of everything else.

Jake was silent, giving her no comfort. She sighed and turned her face away. "I'm not always this dim-witted. Really. I'm usually quite firm about what I should do. But I've taken myself quite by surprise, you see, and I don't know if I should scold myself or give myself a pat on the back. It's all very confusing, and I'm being a complete ninny."

"That's nothing new, lady." His smile took the sting from the words.

"Give me some time, Jake."

"You can have your time." He leaned forward and brushed his lips across hers, tantalizing her mouth with light touches of his tongue. "I won't promise not to fight dirty, though," he warned. "And I'm the dirti-est fighter I know."

Harriett closed her eyes and felt herself melt inside. Her lips burned where he had touched them.

"I'd better get up the hill before Chad decides to drive that wagon down on his own. That boy thinks he can do anything." Jake grinned. "Can't imagine where he learned to think that way."

Journal entry—August 19—Sink of the Humboldt River: How can I begin to describe the marvelous variety of the lands through which we have passed these last several weeks? Just southwest of the City of Rocks we traversed the Valley of Thousand Springs—cool and green with good water abundant from springs after which the valley is named. Water was hardly our concern, however, for rain followed us from one end of the valley to the other.

How glad we would be to have that cooling rain right now. For the past days we have plodded beside the infamous Humboldt River. I must take Mr. Ware to task for his erroneous description of this part of our road. It is the most desolate part of the earth that I have yet seen, with danger abundant for unwary travelers—alkali springs; deep, burning sands; treacherous bogs; and scorching heat. Quite a contrast to the lush valley with grass and timber "requisite for the emigrants' comfort" that our guidebook describes. The only accurate part of Mr. Ware's description concerns the Digger Indians, who, though not as fierce as our longtime acquaintances the Pawnee, are so accomplished at thievery that our possessions and stock must be guarded at all times.

Because of the rains, the river is overflowing its banks, and grass is abundant. However, our animals could not get to the fodder because of the bogs and quicksand. Our wagons had to take to the sandy hills that border the valley, and the going was very difficult. Fortunately, Mr. Carradine is well acquainted with this river course and, being forewarned, we filled our water casks and stored up sweet grass to provide fodder for our animals. Our little party has more animals than people now, with Dodger, our goat Jasmine, who provides milk for little Indy, my little mare Daisy, Mr. Carradine's Thunder, the four faithful oxen, the MacBride's four mules, and a pinto pony that we purchased from another party for Chad, who is very keen on horses.

Young Chad has become quite accomplished at driving the smaller wagon, thanks to Mr. Carradine's patient tutoring. Even through the difficult deep sands he has little trouble coaxing the oxen through. His help has freed Mr. Carradine to ride ahead on Daisy or Thunder to scout out the difficulties of the road and the best campsites.

Harriett felt like a liar every time she wrote Jake's name in her journal, for she continued to write of him as though he were just a hired man. She didn't say—she couldn't say—that she ached every night to feel his arms embrace her one more time, to feel his mouth move on hers, his breath warm her hair, his body possess hers with such vigor and passion that she almost died of ecstasy. Of course she couldn't write that. She didn't even want to think that.

But she couldn't control her thoughts. Always, every night, and all day—as she drove the wagon, or walked alongside the mules, or rode atop Daisy—her mind wandered to Jake. Frequently he rode ahead of them, and she missed him terribly. She missed the way he looked at her, smiled at her, even the black scowls he gave her on occasion.

Jake almost seemed to be avoiding her, riding out so much of the time. But that was exactly what she had wanted, wasn't it? Time to think. Time apart from him so that the giddy feelings he inspired couldn't influence her reason. So why did she feel so empty when Jake was nowhere in sight?

He had threatened to "fight dirty." Had she been looking forward to that dirty fighting, to whatever devious methods he might use to make her need him? He was a master of low-down sneakiness. That Harriett had discovered one day in pulling dirty laundry from his saddlebags. Along with soiled shirts she had inadvertently pulled out a book by James Fenimore Cooper, *The Pathfinder*, published ten years earlier and still a popular novel. Jake's copy was dog-eared and soil-stained—it had been around a long time. The hours Harriett had spent trying to teach that rogue his letters, when all he had wanted was to spend time alone with her in the evenings! His duplicity had made her fume, then laugh.

"Never trust a man in love," Lucille had commented when Harriett told her. "They're the sneakiest creatures on this earth."

Harriett set aside her journal—and her thoughts of Jake—and filled a large kettle to heat water over the fire. A mountainous pile of laundry awaited her, as well as a number of other chores. They planned to stay in this grassy meadow at the Sink of the Humboldt River for at least two days to rest the animals and themselves. Just ahead lay forty-five miles of desert with no water and no vegetation. The last twenty miles of the desert was dubbed Destruction Valley, and Harriett had heard dreadful stories of the deep sand and scorching sun that gave the valley its name. The trailside was said to be littered with the bleached bones of both men and beasts who had not survived the crossing. Lucille had been in a dither of worry since a woman from another company camped at the Sink had told them the story of her son, who had traveled to California two years ago and had almost not made it across Destruction Valley.

The Sink was crowded with parties resting themselves for the ordeal. Here where the Humboldt River sank into the ground, losing itself in bogs and desert sand, grass grew abundantly and numerous ponds and springs provided ample water to fill the wagons' casks. Almost everyone camped at the Sink seemed nervous about the road ahead, and at the same time heartened that Destruction Valley was the last difficult barrier east of the Sierras. Once the Sierras were conquered, California was theirs. An undercurrent of excitement enlivened everyone's preparations. The long journey was almost over.

Lucille stepped out of the tent, Indy cradled in one arm.

"Did he eat?" Harriett asked.

"Goodness, did he eat!" Lucille smiled. "His tummy's round and fit to burst. You're going to grow up to be a big boy, aren't you, Independence?"

The baby grimaced, milk dribbling from one corner of his mouth.

"And a smelly boy, too," Lucille continued. "He needs a bath."

"The water won't be hot for some time yet," Harriett said. "I found a nice secluded little spring yesterday. Why don't we take him down there and give him his bath?"

"In cold water?"

"The day is hot. He'll be fine." Harriett sighed. "I could use a bath myself. After these last days along this awful river I feel like every pore is clogged with dust."

Harriett's discovery lay at the edge of the big meadow. A few scrubby pines and high reeds sheltered a shallow, sandy-bottomed, spring-fed pond. The water was clear and cool, but not so cool that Indy didn't thoroughly enjoy his bath. He splashed and gurgled in a fashion that Harriett thought quite precocious, drenching both his foster mothers in the process.

"Well, I suppose we might as well bathe also." Lucille laughed. "I'm already soaked to the skin. Who would think that such a little thing could have so much energy?"

Lucille shed her wet clothes and washed while Harriett wrapped Independence in a clean blanket and sang him softly to sleep.

"You've got quite a talent for motherhood," Lucille said with a smile, climbing from the pool and donning her damp clothes. "Does Jake like babies, too, or is he just faking with Indy to get in your good graces?"

"Lucille!"

"My dear, haven't you noticed that our trip is coming to an end?" She turned her back so Harriett could fasten the row of buttons that closed her bodice. "If you don't make up your mind soon, you're going to lose that man. I can't imagine Jake Carradine pining after a woman who doesn't want him, or being without a woman for very long after one has refused him."

Harriett sighed. "I don't know what to do. Edwin is waiting for me with the future I always thought I wanted for myself."

"Boring," Lucille commented, turning back around.

"All right. Boring. And I suppose marrying Edwin is out of the question anyway, after . . . after . . ."

"You discovered the delights of love in another man's arms?" Lucille suggested.

Harriett colored. "But Jake makes me feel so out of control. And what do I know about him? Nothing. At least nothing that would recommend him as a husband."

"Except that you love him."

"A wise person is not carried away by emotion."

"A wise person forgets wisdom once in a while," Lucille countered. "Love doesn't follow any rules. It creates chaos out of order."

"And sometimes brings disaster in its wake."

Lucille shook her head in disgust. "Jake Carradine is a good man, a strong man, a man who could give you more in one loving night than that pudding-face Edwin Garrett could give you in a lifetime. You don't need to know his family tree or his personal history. You've seen what he is. He's got courage, wit, and compassion—and a strength to shield you from the worst this uncivilized land can offer. What more do you want?"

"I want to be my own master! And something inside me, every time I see him, wants to bow down and yield everything I am to him."

"Well, at least that part of you has some sense! Harriett Foster, if you don't run into Jake Carradine's arms and thank your guardian angel for giving you such a man, then you're a fool and a coward. Your parents—God rest their souls—did you a great disser-

vice in raising you with no understanding or appreciation for love.'' She huffed indignantly. ''Give me the
baby. I'll take him back and settle him for a nap. You
go ahead and take your bath—and while you're at it
clean some of that useless garbage out of your mind!''

Harriett took her bath, but the garbage in her mind
didn't wash away as easily as the dirt on her skin and
in her hair—perhaps because she wasn't quite convinced it was garbage. She'd lived for twenty-three
years under her parents' tutelage. Their relationship
had seemed perfect—affectionate, respectful, harmo-
nious, quiet. A chaste peck or two on the cheek was all
the physical contact Harriett had ever seen between
them, and if there was anything more in the privacy of
their bedroom, it was a well-kept secret. Harriett's
mother had once told her that physical passions were
the childish fancy of men's minds, and women's passions were reserved for higher causes. What was
wrong with Harriett that she was prey to the baser
passions? Or had something been wrong with her
mother?

Harriett climbed from the pond and pulled on her
chemise. The cool water had cleared her mind, making
her wonder if she'd been moonstruck when she'd surrendered to Jake that night—moonstruck, tired, prey
to foolish night vapors and fantasies. The decision of
what to do with her life should be made in the light of
day, illumined by reason and sensibility.

But being in love was harder to ignore than she'd
thought.

''My, don't you look clean!''

Harriett nearly jumped out of her skin as she jerked
around and saw Jake lazing against a scraggly pine.
His arms were folded across his broad chest, and the
sun struck gold sparks off his hair.

''Where did you come from?''

''Lucille told me I'd find you here.''

"She would! Must you always sneak up like an Indian?" Harriett grabbed her dress and held it up to her chest. "Turn around right now, Jacob Carradine! I'm not dressed!"

"Don't you think it's a little late for modesty between us?"

"Easy for you to say! You've got all your clothes on!"

"I could remedy that."

"Don't you dare!"

He laughed, pushed himself away from his piney perch, and knelt down to scoop up a handful of water. "Pretty spot. Nice and private. Why didn't you tell me about it? I could use a bath myself."

"Because I wanted to use it to bathe. That's why."

"Tch! A bit testy today, aren't we? In fact, I've never seen a woman in such a foul mood as yours the last couple of weeks."

"Me? In a temper? How would you know? We've scarcely seen you these last days."

He sent a knowing look in her direction. "Miss me?"

"Of course not! Why would I miss you?"

Backing away as Jake rose and came toward her, Harriett shook her head in denial. He took her all-but-bare shoulders in his big hands and repeated. "Harry. Did you miss me?"

She melted at his touch, just as she had feared she would. "All right!" she snapped. "I missed you. Satisfied?"

"No. Not nearly."

His mouth descended, and Harriett didn't have the will to turn her face away. Warm lips covered hers, teased her mouth to open, to receive his playful tongue, which quickly became more demanding than playful.

When he pulled back from her, Harriett swayed toward him. She almost couldn't keep her feet. The victorious smile on his face didn't make her mad enough to drive away the longing that blossomed in the very core of her.

"Well, I think I'll take a bath." He released her shoulders. Her skin burned where he'd touched her. "Care to join me?"

"Don't be ridiculous,"

"I'm only being sensible." He managed to look hurt. "You can't put those clothes on. They're still wet. Might as well entertain yourself while they dry."

She hugged her dress closer to her breasts. "You have a scandalous lack of morals, Jacob."

"Now, that's not true," he denied, stripping off his shirt. "I'm a reformed man. From now on I don't shoot people on Sundays and I only gamble when I know I can win. I don't cheat at cards on Sundays either." His gun belt joined the shirt on the ground, and his trousers were about to follow.

A smile tugged at Harriett's mouth. How could any woman stay mad at Jake for long? "You are a hopeless rogue!"

"You need a rogue in your life, Harriett. I figure I fit the bill."

Harriett knew she should turn around, because every glorious inch of him was now revealed. But she couldn't resist looking at him, fascinated beyond her ability to control herself. His shoulders were broad as twin ax handles; his chest and arms rippled with supple muscle—a bronzed statue of male strength, marred only by scars that spattered his left shoulder and curved around his side. The sculptured columns of his legs rose to meet lean hips, and at their juncture rose that which Harriett knew entirely too much about.

"Like what you see?"

She turned crimson. "You have absolutely no modesty at all, have you?"

"A man isn't supposed to be modest in front of the woman he loves. Same goes for the woman."

"That's not what I was taught."

"Well, then," he said, advancing toward her. "I guess I'll just have to teach you differently."

Harriett stood rooted to the spot as he pried her dress from her hands and carefully laid the garment out to dry. Next he attacked the buttons on her chemise.

"Why is it I let you do this to me?" she whispered wonderingly.

The chemise fell in a heap around her ankles. The slight breeze caressed her breasts, curled around her naked thighs and made her want to squirm.

Jake swung her up into his arms and started toward the pool. "You let me do it because you love me, Harry. And you know that you're going to marry me and have my babies . . ."

"And be your devoted slave in an Oregon timber camp?" she guessed, one brow slanted skeptically.

He grinned. "I think we can do better than a grubby timber camp, and I can't imagine you being anyone's devoted slave."

Before she could answer, he tossed her unceremoniously into the water. She came up sputtering, hair plastered to her head and shoulders like a bright red hood.

"You can swim, can't you?" he asked.

"Fine time to ask!"

He dove in and surfaced beside her, grinning wickedly. She paddled away, a smug look on her face.

"Going to make me chase you?"

"What makes you think you can catch me?"

Harriett discovered the part of her that was still a child as she dodged and feinted around the pool, laughing, splashing water into the face of her pursuer, and delighting in taunts and near misses. But when he finally caught her, the woman in her came back in force.

She gave up squirming and stood still under his hot scrutiny.

"You are a beautiful woman, Harriett Foster. And I'm beginning to think that under that prim exterior lies the heart of a tease."

The dark glow in his eyes warmed her to the very marrow.

"Is that bad?" Her voice quavered. She couldn't catch her breath—and not because of the exercise.

"Not as long as the tease knows when the game is over and it's time to yield up the prize."

He lifted her effortlessly, the muscles in his arms rippling with strength. When her breasts were level with his face, he brought her forward so that he could caress her nipples with his mouth and tongue. Harriett gasped and dropped her head back, arching toward him. Every nerve in her body caught fire.

After giving each breast its due, Jake brought her slowly down against him, her body sliding wetly along his. He'd moved into water that was chest-high on him, chin-high on Harriett. But he didn't allow her feet to touch the sandy bottom. Instead he wrapped her legs around his waist and settled her on his hips.

"Give up, Harry," he advised. "Some people were meant to be together. You and me. We fit one against the other like a glove on a hand."

She dropped her head upon his broad shoulder, savoring the feel of his arms around her and at the same time flinching from a spark of insistent reason that swam up through the turmoil of her desire.

"We have nothing in common," that reason insisted, using Harriett's voice almost against her will.

He kissed the nape of her neck. "Yes, we do. We both like dogs. We both despise changing Indy's nappies. And we both"—he nipped at her ear—"like to make love in the water."

"Oh, Jake!" Her cry was half sob, half laughter, but

it changed to a gasp of pleasure as the hands that supported her bare buttocks moved and Jake's fingers brushed the delicate, desire-swollen region between her legs.

"And there's this," he rasped in her ear. Very carefully he lifted her and settled her onto his swollen shaft. "Funny that this water hasn't cooled me off one bit."

Harriett buried her face in the muscled column of Jake's neck, inhaling the wet, masculine scent of him. She clung to him with her legs as he slowly filled her with himself. The feel of his skin against her mouth, the chafing of coarse chest hair on her naked breasts, the helpless, vulnerable, utterly delicious glory of him filling her, impaling her, thrusting again, again, again, and still again—her world narrowed down to these sensations. Reason spun off into oblivion, passion chasing it into nothingness.

"We have more than this," he whispered, withdrawing slowly, deliberately, then driving into her again— so deep, so hard, that she thought she would explode with aching desire. "Much, much more, Harry."

Harriett's body contracted around Jake's, trying to draw him inside farther, faster. "Jake . . . Please."

"Patience, lady mine."

Three long strides brought them to the edge of the pond, where Jake knelt with her on the grass. He laid her back, still locked inside her warm flesh. With his hands beneath her bottom, he lifted her to meet each powerful thrust. Harriett felt herself dissolve, felt her very being melt into the man who crouched above her. She grasped his taut buttocks and urged him to plunge deeper, faster. Strung tighter than a bowstring, every fiber of her body seemed to hum with tension. The whole world narrowed down to Harriett and Jake, Jake and Harriett, merged, united, together climbing a mountain of aching, soaring need.

Until her body imploded, all the tension bursting inside her with twisting, spiraling ecstasy. She cried out in joy, clinging to Jake as he convulsed in climax and emptied himself deep within her flesh.

Panting, sweating, twisted around each other like two clinging vines that were never meant to be separated, they waited to settle back to earth.

"I love you, Harry."

Words Harriett wanted to hear, and yet didn't. He kissed the tip of her nose, the lid of each eye, the corner of her mouth. She smiled.

"I love you too, Jacob." There was no denying it, and refusal to say the words wouldn't make it any less real.

"Marry me."

"Jake. Don't push."

"You need to be pushed, Harry. Come with me to Oregon."

"Where Mr. Kane lives. You're still determined to get your land back?"

For just a moment his eyes clouded. "Don't change the subject. First I'm going to marry you. Then I'll see about Mr. Kane."

Harriett closed her eyes against the promise of violence in his voice—a reminder that he was from a far different world than hers. If she let love rule her reason and gave her life over to Jake Carradine, how could she survive? He loved her; she loved him. But by the standards of her world Jake was a savage. He was set on conquering a wilderness—probably the only place big enough to hold him. He would use guns, fists, muscle, and the sweat of his brow to get what he wanted and defend what he loved. While before the last weeks, Harriett was accustomed to sedate parlors where the hardest work had been stitching a sampler and the bloodiest violence came from sticking oneself with an embroidery needle.

She rolled away from him. With Jake looming above
her she couldn't think.

"This isn't me, Jacob."

Jake smiled. "Well, whoever you are, you look a lot
like Harry Foster." He twirled a lock of her hair between his fingers. "Green eyes, hair so red it should set
your head on fire, a body so beautiful that—"

"Be serious!" She slapped his hand away. "I mean
it. I don't know who I am anymore. The Harriett Foster I knew didn't do things like this—with men like
you."

"She didn't drive a team, ride a horse, cook over an
open fire, care for two children, or play nurse to sick
Indians either. You're growing up, Harry. That's nothing to be afraid of."

She dodged another caress, got up, and grabbed her
clothes.

"I need time, Jacob."

"You've had time! For God's sake, Harry, after
you've given yourself to me, how can you still think of
marrying Edwin?"

Harriett fumbled with the buttons of her chemise,
her hands shaking. "I didn't give myself to anyone! I
made love with you. I still belong very much to myself,
thank you! And of course I'm not going to marry Edwin. What makes you think I have to marry at all?
Maybe I don't need a man! Maybe I can run my own
life!"

"I don't want to run your life! I just want you, goddammit!" He yanked up his trousers so hard that a
seam ripped. "Shit 'n' damn!" he cursed.

Fully dressed now, Harriett clutched her arms
around her chest. Jake's anger frightened her. Somehow she'd thought herself immune from the darker
side of his passions.

"I need to know what person I've become before I

make such a serious decision, Jacob. Please understand. I do love you."

Jake snorted contemptuously. "You don't know how to love, and you're afraid to learn! You want to live your life in a safe little shell where nothing can get in that would make you feel, or laugh, or cry."

"That's not true!"

"Isn't it? I thought you'd grown up on this trip, but I was wrong. I'll take you to San Francisco and deliver you into the safe hands of your genteel Edwin. I hope he doesn't want much more than a parlor decoration in a wife, because that's what he's getting!"

"Jacob!" Each biting word gnawed into her heart.

"And you can quit worrying about me, Miss Foster. I won't bother you anymore. You're safe from me—a hell of a lot safer than you are from yourself!"

Stunned, Harriett couldn't get her mouth to close. Neither could she utter a word. Jake's pursuit had become one of the constants of her life. She couldn't believe that he would give her up, after all they'd been through together.

"Come on!" Jake swung his gun belt around his hips and buckled it with jerky motions. "We've got work to do before we can get going, and I want to end this trip as soon as I can."

17

Journal entry—September 4—Hangtown, California: At last we have reached the end of our long trail, an accomplishment that brings joy and sorrow in equal measure. The tasks of our journey have become almost second nature to me, the oxen, mules, and horses valued companions. The daily discovery of new wonders of this land—be they as insignificant as a new bird or a flower not before seen—are pleasures I have taken for granted all our months on the trail. Here in a Hangtown hotel, sleeping in a real feather bed for the first time in months, eating food not cooked (or burned) by my own hands, luxuriating in hot-water baths, I find myself longing for my tent, my little kettle that sat for so many mornings over our cookfire, our sturdy wagons that saw us through so much sand, mud, rain, hail, wind, and dust.

The last part of our trip was rigorous in the extreme—first the trek through the desert, and then, only a few days later, the trail that took us over the rugged Sierras. The desert was as fearful as we had been led to believe. Though we crossed at night, the heat was intense. Deep sand caused our poor oxen and mules to falter time and time again—and our-

selves as well, for we could not add to the animals'
burden by riding in the wagons. The last ten miles,
an area of very deep sand known as Destruction Valley, was particularly difficult. Along the trail was
strewn the most amazing collection of discarded
property: bedsteads, stoves, boxes of china, pots, ket-
tles, sacks of flour, and even wagons. Travelers
across this earthly Hell discard anything they can
spare, and some things they cannot, to lighten their
loads. Still, some do not make it across. The dried
carcasses of mules, horses, and cattle that could not
endure the crossing also litter the desert. I was
grateful indeed that our wagons were light and our
animals, though they struggled, were strong and
willing.

Thanks to Mr. Carradine's foresight in storing up
animal fodder, taking on extra water, and distribut-
ing the weight in the wagons, we made the crossing
in good form. Five miles before we reached the Carson River we met men on the trail who were selling
water—for ten cents a pint! It is a sad commentary
on human nature that men will leap in to profit from
others' difficulties.

We camped for two days in the lush valley of the
Carson River while our beasts recovered and we
ourselves garnered our strength. The campground
provided a lovely view of Mt. Davidson, which is
beautiful to the eye but remains in my memory as a
harbinger of the terrible climb we were about to begin. The Sierras are certainly one of God's most
spectacular creations, but surely one He never
meant man to cross with wagons. Most of our fellow
travelers by this time had sold or discarded their
wagons, packing their belongings on mules instead.
The descents were so treacherous that our wagons
frequently had to be lowered by ropes, and our poor
oxen and mules were hard-pressed to pull to the top

of the ascents. But with perseverance we succeeded. The descent from that tortuous climb saw a number of raucous celebrations, for the last barrier to the gold fields was finally conquered. Talk of the latest and best strikes was all the conversation one could hear, and parties started departing the trail, singly and in small groups, each man heading for the area he hoped would be a rich strike. Most of the gold seekers stayed on the trail for Hangtown, however, which is a bustling village not far from where gold was first discovered at a sawmill on the American River.

Evidence of gold is everywhere I look. Even the stream that runs through the center of town is littered with workings where prospectors have staked claims. The merchants here do a fine business in selling equipment needed for wresting gold from the ground or from the streams where it has been deposited. Prices are unbelievably high, and I have observed that many people pay for goods and services with gold dust. Common money seems to be in great shortage here, though the proprietor of our hotel was happy enough to take mine.

Our hotel room here in Hangtown is much finer than the one we endured in Independence, and even with a cradle moved in for Indy we are not crowded. Chad disdained staying with us, however, and declared that he was much too grown up to room with women. Fortunately, Mr. Carradine did not mind sharing his room down the hall. Dodger also deserted us and elected to stay with the "men."

My aunt Lucille has caught the excitement of the town, and we have entertained ourselves by going from store to store, looking at the strange merchandise—and the even stranger people. Everyone in California seems to be afflicted with gold fever, merchants and prospectors alike. The prospectors all have a similar stamp upon them—bearded, often ragged, dressed in flannel shirts, heavy denims, and sturdy boots. Aunt Lucille says they're colorful. I might use a less complimentary phrase.

My aunt has quite recovered her spirits. In truth, we happened upon the notorious Mr. Steede in the mercantile store this morning and he and Lucille were quite cordial. How fortunate that women recover in such good form from men's abuses. If we were not so resilient, then very few of us would survive this world.

There are not many women here, compared to the herd of men, and Lucille and I do draw some uncomfortable attention as we go about our business. Only this afternoon two prospectors stopped and stared as if they'd never seen a woman in their lives. And they seemed particularly fascinated with little Indy. In a town of single men and men long separated from their wives, an infant must be quite a novelty.

On the whole the men of Hangtown are extremely courteous, even the most rough-looking of them, and we go our way without fear of interference. If anyone offered us insult, I believe we would have at least fifty defenders around us before we could blink an eye.

A knock sounded on the hotel room door.

"Come in," Lucille called, looking up from her mending.

Jake stepped into the room—one step only—and kept a hand on the doorknob. "Afternoon, ladies."

"Hello, Jake." Lucille slid a glance toward Harriett, a plea to behave. "Were you successful?"

"Yeah. Good wagons and healthy teams are in demand. The horses too. I sold them for a good price. Except Thunder. I stabled him. Good mounts are too hard to come by in this country. You can take his price out of my wages."

"That won't be necessary." Harriett felt a foolish surge of regret. Daisy was gone. Of all the things that had been with her over the long trail, Daisy was the hardest to let go. Who would've thought she would ever become fond of a horse?

"Did you buy tickets for the stage to Sacramento?" Lucille asked.

"Tomorrow morning's stage," Jake confirmed. "We'll have to buy the steamer tickets when we get to Sacramento."

Harriett closed her journal and drummed her fingers lightly on its worn cover. "You really needn't escort us, Jacob. Lucille and I and the children will do very well traveling to San Francisco on our own."

Lucille sent her a scorching look, but Harriett ignored it.

"You might not do as well as you think, Harriett. I'll deliver you to San Francisco and make sure you're safe with your Edwin. I'll see you ladies at the stage at nine tomorrow morning." With a tip of his hat to Lucille and a tight smile for Harriett, he left.

Harriett stared at the door that closed behind him, her mouth bowed down in a dispirited curve. "Harriett," Jake had called her for the last few weeks of their journey. The name grated on her ears much more than her despised nickname ever had. When he'd called her Harry, a note of warmth, humor, even affection had gone along with the nickname. But "Harriett" was a sound as cold as a Boston winter—a sound befitting his new manner toward her.

Harriett hadn't really believed Jake that day on the Humboldt River when he'd cried finish to his courtship. But he'd stuck to his word. All through the desert to Ragtown, every day of the long trek up the Carson River and over the Sierras, he'd acted the courteous, businesslike, cold hired man. Lucille had prodded her with meaningful glares during the day and sharp scoldings at night in the privacy of their tent. Harriett was a fool, a ninnybrain, an idiot, passing up a chance that very few women got in their lives—not only passing it up but doing her best to drive it away.

Harriett was inclined to agree with her. She'd been terribly wrong to expect a proud man like Jake Carradine to trail along like a devoted dog while she put her confused mind in order. But pride stuck the words in her throat the many times she vowed to apologize. Not that Jake made himself very accessible to an apology. He was distant, made a show of being constantly occupied, and seem to take great pains at avoiding her. Jake was determined to "deliver" her to Edwin like a sack of flour, and he treated her with almost as much warmth as that sack might deserve.

The situation was for the best, Harriett told herself time and time again. She and Jake were too different, too often at odds. Love was a mere feeling that would soon fade.

If she could only believe her own counsel!

Sacramento was as frantic as Hangtown. Frenzy and excitement hung in the air, shone in every face, buzzed through every conversation. All the talk, the business, even the entertainment seemed to concern gold. Like Hangtown, Sacramento was a town of men. A scattering of strumpets could be seen if one peeked past saloon doors, and even on the streets a few women of ill repute plied their trade. Decent women were rare, and Harriett and Lucille once again drew attention, most of it courteous. Any that wasn't courteous quickly became so when the ever-watchful Jake stepped to their side. He now went armed to the teeth —a gun slung low on his hip, a bandolier of preloaded pistol cylinders stretching across his chest, and a wicked-looking knife scabbarded on his belt. Even without the weapons, his arrogant carriage and cold gunmetal-gray eyes would have given many men pause. Harriett felt quite safe in his company. Too safe. And completely frustrated.

In her Sacramento hotel room, after a polite but chilly conversation with Jake about the next day's steamer schedule, Harriett realized that she would regret her cowardice the rest of her life if she didn't garner some courage and talk to him. She was quite sure the man was beyond her reach, in spite of her aunt's idea that Harriett need only crook her little finger and Jake would come back to her on his knees. Harriett wasn't sure that Jake wouldn't get a similar response from her if he but crooked his finger. But did she want to go running back? Or go with him at all? Harriett wasn't sure, but she knew that she couldn't bear to part with him with ice frosting the air between them.

Not until the following day did she get her chance. Lucille and she were among the fortunate few who had a cabin to themselves aboard the vessel that steamed down the Sacramento River toward San Francisco Bay. The steamship was grossly overcrowded—passengers ranging from nattily attired successful gold seekers to somber merchants to prospectors whose odor testified that they hadn't seen soap and water in at least a year. The crowding was almost shoulder to shoulder, and every inch of deck not taken up by passengers was reserved for cargo. Harriett had feared that poor Dodger would be relegated to the livestock area with Jasmine. But no one said a word when she brought the dog on board. Many of the passengers, after all, were dirtier than Dodger, and their personal habits no more tidy.

Harriett's cabin wasn't much of a refuge from the crowd. Airless and hot, it banged and vibrated with noises from the engine room. With Lucille, Harriett,

Indy, and Dodger all in residence, both women were hard-pressed to find room enough to turn around, much less make themselves comfortable. They were fortunate that Chad had begged to sleep on deck with Jake.

Harriett preferred the deck, if not to sleep, then at least to while away the evening hours. Cool breezes from the river somewhat relieved the closeness of the air. Jake found her sitting in a crude but private little alcove between a bulkhead and a lifeboat, Dodger at her side, both woman and dog looking out upon the moonlight-rippled river.

"You shouldn't be here alone," he snapped.

She looked up. "Dodger's here with me."

The pup, grown into a gawky and angular canine adolescence, whined a glad greeting and thumped his tail.

"Fat lot of good Dodger would do if someone decided you were ripe for the picking."

"No one's going to bother me, Jacob. Everyone on this boat is busy drinking and talking about gold. Besides, every man on board has been looking at that gun of yours and giving you the widest possible berth. Since you've made it very clear that Lucille and I are with you, I doubt that any man will dare so much as to tip a hat in our direction."

He sat down beside her, took off his hat, and ran restless fingers through his hair. "I figured you'd be a bit smarter about human nature by now," he said. "I can see that you aren't. You still think that men as a whole are a bunch of snakes, but for some reason you're immune to getting bit."

"I never said that!"

"Lady, you don't have to say it. You act it out."

Back to their beginning, Harriett thought sadly—a cynical, sniping standoff. They'd come full circle, stiff-mannered, hostile, with hackles raised, as if the intervening months of hardship, companionship, and love had never happened.

But he was right about her in part. If the journey had taught her anything at all, it had pressed home her lack of wisdom about human nature. Before this odyssey, she had believed that she knew it all—the black, white, and gray tones of human foibles and strengths, including her own. The journey had taught her that she didn't know anything. Anything at all.

Dodger whined and licked her hand, as if sensing her dispirited mood. Harriett looked up. Jake was gazing at her, his face darkened by the night shadows, his mouth a tight, unrevealing line, his eyes narrowed in a manner she couldn't interpret. But in spite of his forbidding expression, Harriett remembered her vow to speak.

"Jacob." She diverted her gaze to the river, where the moon laid a silver path from bank to bank. "You've been right about many things, you know. And you've been a good friend. Most men would have said bad riddance and gone their way when I proved to be such a muddlehead. But you stuck with a job you didn't even want in the first place. I . . . I'm very grateful. You really are an extraordinary man."

"A snake. But an extraordinary snake?"

"I never . . . !" She swung her gaze around and saw his mocking smile. "Well, perhaps I did. I am sorry that I treated you so badly." She was sorry now, and would probably be sorry the rest of her life. For weeks she had admitted to her love, but only now did Harriett realize what a vital part of her that love was. Without Jake Carradine her life was going to deflate like a punctured balloon.

"What are you going to do?" he asked blandly. "Are you going to marry Edwin?"

"Oh, I don't expect so." A part of her longed to ask Jake if he still wanted her, throw herself on his mercy and hope that some spark of his passion lived. "But I do owe him an honest explanation of why I've changed my mind."

"Always the honorable Miss Foster, honest with everyone but yourself."

"It's harder to be honest with yourself than with others."

She couldn't quite pose the question, fearing his answer so. Harriett could too well imagine the contemptuous glitter in those steel-gray eyes as Jake explained that her ninnyhammer behavior had killed any feeling he'd had for her. He would be vastly amused that she'd finally been brought to the point of pursuing him, the man who so long and diligently had pursued her.

"What are your plans, Jacob?"

"Back to Oregon, I guess."

"To kill someone," she surmised in a sad voice.

"To get back my land. And pay some debts."

Blood debts, Harriett thought. And the blood might turn out to be Jake's. If she had married him, could she have kept him from such a destructive path?

"I wish . . . I wish . . ." She sighed, pride choking the words in her throat.

He regarded her with a shuttered expression, eyes like chips of steel. "What do you wish, Harriett? What do you want of me?"

The intense tone of his voice frightened her—as did the sense of expectancy that shivered in the air between them. For moments she fought with herself, fear battling hope, pride wrestling with need. Jake gave her no help, not a single sign of softening. The implacable steel that curtained his eyes finally decided her.

"I don't want anything," she said softly, bowing her head. "You've done enough. More than enough. I don't need anything from you or anyone else."

Dodger sent Jake a confused look as Harriett rose and walked calmly toward the refuge of her cabin, then the pup trotted faithfully after her. Jake watched the dog catch up with Harriett, watched her kneel down to give Dodger a quick, almost desperate hug.

"You lie," he said softly to her retreating back. "You lie to both of us."

Journal entry—September 6—Sàn Francisco: This city which has recently garnered so much fame is not precisely what I had expected. I looked forward to a city—small, perhaps, since it was wrested from the Spanish only four years ago, but a city nonetheless. Instead I find a ragged conglomeration of tents, hovels, and buildings piled beside the bay in a half-moon-shaped crescent.

On first arriving in San Francisco one discerns very little order and an equal lack of charm here. But on a closer examination I see a town of raucous energy and explosive growth. The captain of our steamer informed me that two years ago the village boasted only about a thousand people, and now more than twenty that number call San Francisco their home—not to mention the hordes that pass through on their way to the gold fields. It is no wonder that the town's growth has outstripped its abilities to provide the trappings of civilization.

Edwin's letters to me did not begin to describe the conditions here. He wrote only of the great opportunities for commerce—about the lines of trade opening with Hawaii, the Far East, Latin America, and Europe. Being a merchant, he understandably holds these things close to his heart, and I suppose the excitement of such opportunity blinded him to the mud and garbage that clog the unplanked streets and the other conditions that I find incredible. Huts of scrap timber and canvas vie for space with more substantial buildings—also of timber but of better construction. Along the muddy waterfront (such a thing as a clean sand beach does not seem to exist on this bay) saloons and brothels rub shoulders with warehouses and merchants, many of whom construct their buildings on wharves over the water. Getting from place to place by boat is much more practical than any other mode of travel in the town, because of the wretched condition of the streets, though I understand there is some plan to plank the main thoroughfares and provide omnibus service very soon.

The harbor is crowded with ships—quite as many as I was accustomed to seeing in Boston, I think. Our loquacious steamer captain also told me that San Franciso is the unloading point for the ships carrying cargo and passengers for the booming inland towns. Here they must transfer the cargo to smaller steamships that carry the goods up the San Joaquin and Sacramento rivers to Stockton and Sacramento. Apparently the building of wharves has not kept up with the bustling trade, for goods must be lightered in. It is quite a sight, these busy flat-bottomed barges plying the waters from the great oceangoing steamers and the tall, graceful clipper ships—which look every bit as fast as they are reputed to be.

My aunt Lucille is enraptured by it all. Every new sight of the harbor and town seems to lend her new energy, and she takes every unfamiliar experience in her stride.

When our little ship steamed into San Francisco harbor, I was quite astounded by the crowds, and a bit dismayed, I admit. But Mr. Carradine, our faithful friend and guide since Independence—which seems a world away—got us all through the confusion in good order, and even convinced young Chad to contain his many questions until we had more time to answer them. We hired a hackney to take us

to Edwin's residence, and the driver didn't blink an
eye at carrying our motley group, including a muddy
dog and protesting goat, though we did receive a few
stares from passersby.

Lucille and I did a bit of rude staring ourselves, I
fear. The population of this town surely sets it apart
from any other place on earth, for it is a sampling of
almost every culture one can imagine. On just our
short ride to Edwin's residence we saw pigtailed
Chinese, Negro dandies, Japanese, Indians, and one
tattooed gentleman who our driver informed us is a
New Zealander. One can also commonly see Aus-
tralians, Russians, and Turks, the driver told us, and
seemed quite pleased at our astonishment.

Edwin's residence is among several newer houses
on Stockton Street, which lies outside the most chaotic part of the town. There we were greeted by a
most intriguing fellow. . . .

" 'Oo did ye say ye was?" The little man who greeted
Jake at the door of the Garrett residence was grizzle-
haired and bandy-legged. Round black eyes and the
upward slash of heavy brows lent him a remarkable
resemblance to a horned owl.

"Jake Carradine. Tell Mr. Garrett that Miss Harriett
Foster is here."

The gnome gave Harriett and Lucille an appraising
look, then disappeared into the gloom of the hallway.
Moments later Edwin appeared.

"Harriett!" He enfolded her in a warm embrace.
"You're here at last." Edwin stepped back and gave
her a fond once-over. "You look marvelous. Just as I
expected. I told you years ago that you'd grow up to be
a beautiful woman. Remember?"

Harriett colored.

"Amazing!" Edwin exclaimed. "I haven't seen you
since you were thirteen, yet from your letters I knew

exactly how you would look, even though you seldom said a word about yourself. Character is the true determination of one's appearance, as I have always said."

"Edwin . . ." Harriett pleaded.

"Ah, yes! I'm being unforgivably rude. Introduce me to your friends, my dear."

"Edwin, this is my aunt, Mrs. Lucille Foster Stanwick."

"Dear lady." Edwin bowed over her hand. "I am absolutely charmed."

One of Lucille's brows inched upward. "Indeed, Mr. Garrett. The daguerreotype that my niece showed me does not do you justice."

Harriett could almost hear Lucille mentally taking back every time she'd called Edwin pudding-faced. In truth, Edwin was a very handsome man, in a dignified sort of way. He looked no older than when Harriett had last seen him, ten years ago, just before he left to make his way west. Tall, with silver wings of hair framing chiseled features, Edwin carried his fifty years with grace. And if the youthful, adventurous gleam in his eyes had dimmed somewhat, that was to be expected in a man who had spent so many years struggling to open the floodgates of trade into an uncivilized country.

"This is Mr. Carradine," Harriett continued. "He's . . . uh . . ." For a moment she was at a loss for words, not having planned beforehand how she would describe Jake's role in their journey. Apparently she should have given the matter more thought, for when Edwin's eyes turned upon Jake, traveling swiftly up and down the broad-shouldered, formidable frame, his expression stiffened.

"I'm the hired man," Jake smoothly interjected. His wry smile made Harriett's heart skip a beat. "Miss Foster hired me to quiet a wagon captain who didn't think she could take care of herself."

Edwin regarded Jake for a moment more, then visibly relaxed. "Obviously the man wasn't well acquainted with my Harriett!" he said with a chuckle.

"Obviously." Jake's smile only broadened as Edwin put an arm fondly about Harriett's shoulders.

Harriett breathed a quiet sigh of relief. How Edwin had been fooled by Jake's innocent, forthright smile she would never know. Jake Carradine didn't have an innocent bone in his body, and most of his smiles either set women's hearts to fluttering or men to ducking for cover. She wouldn't have thought Edwin so easily fooled. Harriett was surprised that her own transparent face hadn't revealed that Jake was much more than just a hired man.

Not that she wouldn't tell Edwin the truth soon. But she was grateful that she could choose her own time.

Next Harriett introduced Chad and Indy—and Dodger. Chad's eyes stayed fixed on the ground; Indy spit and gurgled; and Dodger plunked his shaggy butt on the ground when Harriett told him to sit, but his eyes spoke plainly that he was only humoring his mistress this one time. Edwin regarded children and dog with somewhat limited enthusiasm, and only nodded when Harriett explained how she had taken responsibility for Chad and his infant brother.

"Well, Harriett—a lovely aunt, a hired man, two children, a pooch, and—Lord!—is that animal a goat? You've gathered quite an entourage." Edwin turned to Jake. "Mr. Carradine. Do you plan to stay in San Francisco?"

Harriett imagined an undertone of strain that shouldn't have existed in a simple, friendly question.

"No." Jake glanced briefly at Harriett. "I'm headed up to Oregon. Got some business up there to take care of."

Edwin looked relieved. "Excellent country that. Spent a couple of years up there myself—dealing with the Hudson's Bay Company. Not British territory any more, though, is it?"

"No, it's not."

"Well, you'll want a hotel for a couple of nights, at least, won't you?" He raised his voice in a sharp summons, and the little owl-eyed gnome appeared from behind the entrance door, where no doubt he'd been eavesdropping. "This is Matt Loggins. He'll help you get situated in a hotel. Rooms are a bit scarce around here, you understand, but my name should get you a place."

"I'd appreciate it."

Jake moved with Matt toward the waiting hackney.

"Wait!" Harriett cried. She handed Indy to Lucille and took a step in Jake's direction. "You . . . you're leaving already?"

Jake's mouth pulled up in a smile—one of those that could set ladies' hearts fluttering. "Journey's over, Harriett."

Harriett felt her throat close, her eyes grow hot. He couldn't just leave her like this, just turn and walk away without so much as a good-bye. Her insides were turning to mush and her knees to water.

Jake ruffled Chad's hair and thumped Dodger's ribs. "You take care of this crew, you scraggly mutt. And you"—he turned to the boy—"behave yourself. You're not a kid anymore."

Lucille gave Jake a peck on his cheek. He squeezed her in an undignified hug. "Take care, Lucille."

Good-byes for everyone but Harriett. She bit her lip as Matt and Jake climbed onto the hackney. Dodger whined and slurped his tongue over her hand, his brown face puckered in concern.

Jake turned as the hackney lurched forward. "I'll send you word where I'm staying." He grinned. "You still have to pay me my last wages."

Harriett's heart leapt as the hackney rattled away.

She would see him again! Of course! At least one more
time! She had to pay him his wages.

When she turned back to the group by the door, Edwin was regarding her with a forced smile. "Good-
byes can be painful after such a long journey, can they
not?" he commented. "Even with just a hired man."

Lucille shook her head at Harriett in disapproval as
they followed Edwin into the house.

A plump, blue-eyed cherub of a woman whom Edwin introduced as Martha Loggins—presumably Matt
Loggins's wife—showed Harriett to an airy second-
story room that, unlike the rest of San Francisco, had
all the trappings of luxury.

"The mister done this room just fer you, miss! A real
labor of love it was! That carpet there's English wool—
the best there is. He had it made up just fer this room.
The dresser cloth's real silk from China, an' the pitcher
an' basin's from Italy. An' look, miss!" She pointed to
a bowl on the dresser that held—of all things!—plump,
juicy-looking oranges. "Them's from a place called
. . . Tahiti. The mister knew you was comin' sometime
this month, an' he had 'em brought in special."

Edwin had done all this to please his bride. Harriett
felt like the lowest form of louse, because with all this
evidence of Edwin's affection in front of her eyes, all
she could think about was Jake.

Dinner was a trial. The dining room was formal, and
after spending so many weeks eating beans, rice, bacon, and buffalo meat around an open campfire, Harriett felt uncomfortable with a tablecloth and candles.
Edwin, Lucille, and Harriett were waited upon with
punctilious efficiency by Matt and Martha Loggins.

"He's Australian," Edwin explained when Lucille
asked about the little man's strange accent. " 'Sydney
ducks' they call them here in San Francisco, and the
common belief in the town is that the lot of them are
convicts. Of course it isn't true, but the prejudice

makes it hard for them to get a job. Matt's a loyal worker, though, and Martha too. She's not Australian, though, as you can tell from her speech.''

Edwin talked about the two as if they weren't in the room, which struck Harriett as strange. She'd forgotten the common practice of treating servants as nonpersons. She herself had probably done much the same in Boston.

The children did not join them. Chad had been fed earlier and, along with little Indy, was asleep in a part of the house that had hastily been transformed into a nursery. Edwin had been persuaded to allow Dodger upstairs with Chad, and when Harriett had tucked the boy into bed the dog had curled happily beside him, all the while keeping a vigilant eye on Indy, who slept peacefully a few feet away. After this invasion, Edwin would no doubt be grateful when he learned that Harriett wasn't staying permanently, but she certainly couldn't discuss the matter with him until they were alone—and until she had made some plans of her own.

That discussion wasn't going to be an easy one. In the heat of Jake's presence, Harriett had forgotten how fond she was of Edwin. He was an exemplary man—attractive, considerate, educated, witty. Their correspondence over the last years had provided her with hours of pleasure. In spite of the difference in their ages, Edwin was the closest thing to a true friend that Harriett had while growing from a girl to a woman.

Of course, he was a bit on the stuffy side, an ornery part of her noticed.

Edwin wasn't stuffy, Harriett chastised herself. He only seemed so because she had grown unbecomingly casual over these last months. Edwin would make a wonderful husband for any woman.

As long as that woman wasn't Harriett Foster, the ornery little voice insisted. Edwin was as starched as his shirt collar, which rose stiffly behind his conservative black cravat and then turned down in precise, pointed perfection. His ostentatious house, his servants, his manners and dress, his very gallantry, was like a breath of musty air in a fresh new land. She might as well be back in Boston.

What was wrong with being back in Boston? Harriett asked her rebellious self. She'd lived in Boston all her life and enjoyed every minute of it.

Harry the Ornery just snickered in silent contempt.

"I say, Harriett. Are you listening?"

"Um?" She looked up from her plate to find Edwin gazing at her with a faint expression of reproof. He had been as engrossed in conversation with Lucille as Harriett had been in conversation with herself, but now he apparently expected her attention. "I'm sorry, Edwin. I was off wool-gathering. What did you say?"

"Your charming aunt and I were discussing the MacBride children. I can understand your sense of responsibility toward them, dear, seeing that you and their mother became so close. But don't you think some attempt should be made to find Mr. MacBride?"

"Who?"

"Their father."

Harriett had long ago dismissed John MacBride from her mind. "Edwin, Mr. MacBride left his wife and children with no means of support so that he could follow a childish dream to search for gold. Do you think such a man is responsible enough to care for children?"

"My dear," Edwin said—a bit condescendingly, Harriett thought. "It matters not what the man is. A father is entitled to his children."

"Fiddle!" was Harriett's reply. "We don't even know if John MacBride is still alive."

"Obviously we must find what the true situation is, Harriett. If Mr. MacBride is no longer living, then certainly we must discharge our duty to his orphans."

Duty? What of love, and caring?

"There's a man in town who's quite competent at investigation. I shall request him to call sometime tomorrow, and we shall set him on Mr. MacBride's trail."

An idea flashed into Harriett's head. "I have a better man!"

Edwin raised a quizzical brow, and Lucille shot her a knowing look that made Harriett's face grow warm. But she pushed on. "I'll hire Jake Carradine to search out Mr. MacBride."

Edwin frowned. "I believe your Mr. Carradine said he had plans to travel to Oregon."

"I can persuade him to do it." Harriett's heart raced at the thought of delaying the final good-bye with Jake. It was wrong, she knew. She should let him get on with his own life and dismiss him from hers. She should try to forget about him. But the unruly, perverse part of her that had been born somewhere between Kansas and California had the bit in its teeth and was running full out. "Jake is dependable, and he's very good at whatever he sets his mind to."

"Oh, yes, he is," Lucille agreed with a subtle smirk that made Harriett blush.

"If John MacBride is alive, I'm sure Jake can find him."

If Jake found him, Harriett would have to think of a way to keep the children. They had become almost like part of her own flesh, and she couldn't bear to let them go now. But even that thought couldn't keep her heart from singing.

Not quite yet would she have to tell Jake good-bye. She had him just a little while longer.

She would live for that little while longer—and then think about the future.

18

Jake's hotel was the St. Francis, one of the fanciest places in town, Matt Loggins claimed. He gave Harriett the address, declaring that her friend Mr. Carradine was a right good sort of a fellow and a mean poker player as well.

"That explains where Matt was all yesterday afternoon," Edwin said with lifted brow.

For propriety's sake, Lucille insisted on accompanying Harriett on her mission. Edwin instructed Matt to drive them in his carriage, even though the hotel was within easy distance for two women who had just walked much of the way across a continent. The ladies would have every gentlemen they saw offering to carry them through the mud-clogged streets if they walked, Edwin declared. Apparently such gallantry was accepted custom in San Francisco, but Harriett agreed with Edwin that she would rather not be carried about the streets in some strange man's arms, custom or not.

"Since when have you been concerned about propriety, Aunt Lucille?" Harriett asked once they were alone in the carriage. "You certainly didn't pay much mind to it on the trip out here."

Lucille shrugged daintily. "Then is then and now is now. Besides, you've made up your mind to give Jake the boot, so you shouldn't be playing patsy with him in a hotel room. Love, my dear, justifies intimacy. Pleasurable diversion does not. At least not"—she added with a twinkle—"until you've achieved the status of being a widow of independent means."

Harriett snorted.

"You have decided to give poor Jake the boot, haven't you?"

"He wasn't the one who got the boot, Aunt Lucille. I still have his footprint on my backside."

"Your what?" Lucille gasped in mock horror. "My dear, you should remember that we're back in civilization again. Or at least what passes for civilization in this part of the world. Edwin surely won't approve of such colorful language."

"I'm not going to marry Edwin. So he has very little say over my language or any other part of me. I intend to talk to him later today."

"He'll be very disappointed, Harriett." Lucille was serious again. "I do hope you'll be careful of his feelings."

"Of course I will. I'm very fond of Edwin. But what's this, Aunt? You seem terribly concerned with the feelings of a boring pudding-face."

Lucille had the grace to blush. "Your daguerreotype didn't do the man justice. And he is very sweet."

"Yes," Harriett agreed. "Edwin is very sweet."

Lucille slanted her a perceptive look. "But he isn't Jake Carradine, is he?"

If the St. Francis was one of San Francisco's best hotels, Harriett pitied the rest. From the outside the building looked like a dozen or so prefabricated cottages thrown together side by side and stacked one upon the other. The inside was little better, with unplastered walls of thin boards and little in the way of decor—at least by Boston standards. The place was so flimsy that Harriett was sure a mere sneeze in one room could be heard in all the others.

The clerk behind the desk of the hotel was a spare, graying man who looked like he disapproved of just about everything and everyone, including Harriett. He took one look at her pantaloons and greeted her with a smirk.

"My, my," he commented loudly to the one guest sitting in the lobby. "Look at this. If women can't have men's jobs, they'll take our pants."

Harriett skewered him with an icy glare. It had no effect.

"You gals go sell your wares elsewhere, sweetie. We don't allow such business in here during the day."

Prostitution was second only to gambling as the local pastime, so Harriett wasn't really surprised at being taken for a streetwalker. She was insulted, however, and did her best to look down her nose at the clerk—a difficult feat since he was taller than she.

"We are not trollops, sir. We're here to talk to one of your guests."

"Come back after sundown, sweets, and you can 'talk' all you want."

This was really too much. "I'll talk to the manager of this establishment if you do not immediately mend your manners, sir!"

A shadow of doubt crossed the man's face. "Mighty fancy talk there."

"I happen to be Edwin Garrett's fiancée," she told him with narrowed eyes.

Lucille nodded in confirmation when the clerk gave Harriett a skeptical look.

"Perhaps you would like to explain to him the insults you have offered?"

The man began to pale as the ring of truth in her voice sank into his brain.

"I am also Mr. Jacob Carradine's employer, and I need to speak with him. His room number, please."

"Room eight," the clerk offered reluctantly. "Uh . . . listen, ma'am. I apologize. It's just that . . . Wait! You can't go up there! This is a respectable hotel!"

"And I'm a respectable woman," she threw over her shoulder as she headed for the staircase. "I wish to have a conversation in private."

The clerk sputtered and glared at Lucille, who made no attempt to follow her niece. Instead she sat primly on a velveteen-upholstered settee and smiled in satisfaction.

Room eight was at the end of a hall that was wallpapered and carpeted in a slapdash floral design. The garish patterns did nothing to cool Harriett's ire. She was still fuming when she reached the correct door. Why did all men assume that the moment a woman was alone with a man she would try to seduce him? Women were evil tempters, men innocent victims. Typical masculine reasoning!

Jake opened the door to her knock, face covered with shaving lather and chest covered with nothing at all. His eyes opened wide in surprise when he saw her. Grabbing her arm, he pulled her into the room and closed the door quickly behind her.

"What in the devil's sweet hell are you doing here? The vultures will be pecking at your reputation!"

"Fiddle!" Harriett scoffed. "Reputation is something invented by men to keep women in line."

Jake cocked a brow. "Edwin throw you out already?"

"Don't be ridiculous." She sniffed the air, getting a faint whiff of musky perfume, and her face soured. "I thought they didn't allow whores in the hotel until after sundown."

He grinned at her sharp tone and resumed shaving. "No need to be jealous, Harry."

He didn't even try to deny her accusation, which only added fuel to Harriett's pique.

"I'm surprised the clerk didn't mistake you for a lady of the evening. Most of the women in this town are."

"He did," Harriett told him icily. "I set him straight."

"I'll just bet you did."

"I came to pay your wages." Harriett watched Jake draw the straight razor slowly up his neck and along the line of his jaw. A quiver started in the pit of her stomach. Why had her heart been so heavy when he left her at Edwin's? Why couldn't she let him go and be done with it? He was trouble on two legs, without morals, without decency, always sinking to the lowest level whenever the opportunity presented itself. He'd already resumed gambling and drinking. An empty whiskey bottle sat on the table beside his bed.

And whoring. Of course whoring. Cavorting with women on that rumpled bed. He bought cheap, musk-scented floozies and took them to the place he'd claimed only Harriett could take him to.

She ought to take that razor and put an end to one of his vices for good.

"You look like the Devil bit you," Jake told her with a grin.

"Maybe he did," she said darkly. She'd ask someone else to look for John MacBride. Jake Carradine could go to Oregon or to hell for all that Harriett cared. "When are you leaving for Oregon?"

Jake washed his razor in the basin of water and put it away. "Don't get your hopes up," he said, pulling a shirt over his head. "I've decided to stay here awhile."

His eyes met hers, and she saw a glimmer of amusement. What the spit was so funny? "I thought you were very anxious to get your land back and kill Mr. Kane."

"That can wait. I figured I'd prowl around town for a week or two. There's a lot of opportunity here for a man like me, you know."

"Yes," she agreed dryly. "I can imagine."

"Maybe I'll get better acquainted with Edwin," he continued. "He seems a right interesting fellow."

Now Harriett knew he was up to something. Edwin was intelligent, cultured, considerate, and generous—but to a man like Jake Carradine, Edwin Garrett certainly wouldn't be interesting.

"As long as you're staying, perhaps you'd accept employment." If the Devil was going to be here, she might as well get some use from him. With him out looking for MacBride, she at least wouldn't have to think about how many whores were entertaining him. Not that she gave a fig, of course.

But she did. Why lie to herself? Fool that she was, she did care.

"Edwin has pointed out to me that John MacBride has the right to know about his wife's death—and his children," she told him coldly. "I need someone to find him, and you seem to have the requisite talents to prowl through mining camps."

At the mention of Chad and Indy the mocking light in Jake's eyes died. Whatever else he was, Harriett reminded herself, Jake had been good to Sadie and her children.

"You're going to let Edwin send off the children?" The question was dark, Jake's face still darker.

"Of course not. But Edwin is right. Their father has a right to know they're alive. He won't want to take them."

"And if he does?"

"He won't. And if he does, I . . . I'll do whatever's best for the children."

Harriett could see her own concern reflected in Jake's eyes. He took a step toward her, and she almost thought he was going to reach out a hand in comfort. But then he blinked and halted.

"I'll try to find him," he said.

Harriett reached into her reticule and counted out a handful of silver coins. "Here's your last month's wages. I'll pay you for this job when you return."

"Yes," he answered obliquely. "I figure that you just might."

The tone of his voice made Harriett's stomach turn in a full somersault—or so it seemed. The feel of his eyes bored into her back as she turned to go out the door, the bore holes still burning even after she'd closed the door firmly behind her.

When Harriett and Lucille returned to the house on Stockton Street, Martha Loggins told them the master was out seeing to some business matters, but would join them for the noon meal. Harriett asked to be told when he returned.

"I have to speak to him today," she told Lucille as they mounted the staircase to their rooms. "I can't marry him, and I don't want to accept his hospitality under false pretenses."

Lucille tagged along into Harriett's room. "Surely you don't mean to go back to Boston!"

"Oh, no! Of course not, Aunt. I was thinking that perhaps you and I could start a nice, respectable boardinghouse here in San Francisco. From the looks of that hotel we were in this morning, this town could certainly use one."

"A boardinghouse!" Lucille cried. "Do you know how much work it takes to run a boardinghouse?"

Harriett removed her bonnet, smoothed the satin ribbons that decorated the side, and ignored her aunt's shocked tone. "Of course it would take work. But in this town a good boardinghouse would thrive. And think of all the interesting people we would meet."

"Harriett, dear. Your parents left you a large fortune. Enough that you never need to worry about money."

Harriett shrugged. "I'm not worried about money. I just find the prospect of spending the rest of my life stitching samplers and receiving callers a bit dull."

"You could write for Mrs. Bloomer's publication. She's printing your journal, isn't she?"

"Yes. And I'd like to write something about the West —the interesting people, the gold mines, you know. But as for women's equality and social reform, I . . . I feel like I'm too far away from the heart of the revolution. And I'm not quite as sure of the solutions as I was."

"Hallelujah for that!" Lucille commented, a twinkle in her eye.

"I wasn't that bad!" Harriett declared.

Just then Chad burst in through the open door. "Aunt Harriett! Mr. Loggins is gonna take me to see the Seal Rocks! If you say I can go! Can I go?"

"Did you pester Mr. Loggins to take you?"

"No! Honest! He just up and said let's go! Can I go?"

"Yes. If you promise to do everything Mr. Loggins tells you to do."

"Yeah! Sure!"

The boy sprinted for the door. Harriett and Lucille both smiled as they heard him thunder down the stairs.

"This house probably hasn't heard noises like that since it was built," Harriett said.

"You didn't tell him that Jake was going searching for his father."

Harriett looked away. "I'll tell him when Jake comes back."

"Heavens above. I never thought to see the day

when you would be fighting to keep two children under your roof. The old Harriett Foster would turn over
in her grave."

"What is that supposed to mean?" Harriett asked
sharply.

"I think you buried yourself somewhere between
here and Independence, and some other woman took
your place. Same hair, same eyes, same face. Same
temper," Lucille added impishly at Harriett's scowl.
"But a different Harriett Foster, nevertheless."

Harriett sometimes suspected the same. She knew
exactly where the grave was. City of Rocks. And she
herself had done the digging, with a fair amount of
help from Jake.

"Do you know he's already had floozies up to his
room?" Harriett asked, her face gone sad.

"How interesting." Lucille seemed no more shocked
than if Harriett had told her that the sun had come up
that morning. "Was one there when you visited?"

"Of course not! But her perfume was."

Lucille turned a not quite sympathetic look on her
niece. "My love, what did you expect? Jake Carradine
is a rather . . . elemental man, after all. And you and
he are a thing of the past. Aren't you?"

"Oh, most definitely!"

"Then why begrudge him a floozy or two? I'm sure
the man has earned them, after all, with so many
weeks on the trail with only you and Caroline MacKenzie to flirt with him."

"Aunt Lucille!"

"I think I hear Indy crying," Lucille said, ignoring
her niece's crimson face. "It's feeding time, and
Martha isn't very good at giving him his nipple."

"I have never flirted with Jake Carradine! He's the
one . . . !"

"Temper, dear." Lucille smiled sweetly. "I think
we'd better go downstairs. Motherhood calls."

Edwin came back while Harriett was feeding Indy. He gave Harriett a warm smile, and the infant a stiffer one.

"He certainly is an enthusiastic little fellow, isn't he?"

Indy's little face was spreckled with milk from the nipple, some of which had run down into the folds of baby fat at his neck. He slurped as he ate, waving pudgy little fists in the air as if demanding more milk, faster. Indy was not a dainty baby.

"He loves the goat's milk," Harriett said. "I'm grateful Jasmine in still producing after enduring that steamer ride crowded among the cargo and other livestock."

"Jasmine?"

"The goat," Harriett explained.

"Ah, yes. I didn't know the beast had a name."

Jake had told her once that all creatures had names, Harriett remembered. In the middle of crossing a swollen river, with Harriett clinging white-knuckled and fearful to the wagon box, he'd laughingly dubbed all four of their faithful oxen. And by the time they'd driven out onto the opposite bank, Harriett had almost been laughing with him, fear forgotten. Although now that she thought of it, she had been distracted as much by Jake's looks as by his clowning.

"I suppose we'll have to build a shed out back for your . . . uh . . . Jasmine."

"What?"

"A shed," Edwin repeated, frowning in reproof of her lack of attention. "For the goat."

Now was as good a time as any, Harriett thought. Her stomach started to roil.

"Edwin. I need to talk to you."

He raised a curious brow at her tone. "Of course you can talk to me, Harriett."

Indy squirmed. Harriett shifted him closer to her

chest and he continued to slurp. "I don't . . . quite know how to say this."

"Then just say it, dear." Edwin sat down opposite her, his face somber and attentive.

If the man weren't so doggone sweet, Harriett thought with a sigh, this task would be a good deal easier. Why hadn't he defied all her memories and turned out to be a lech, a cad, a money-grubbing tightwad. Then she wouldn't find hurting his feelings so painful.

"Edwin, dear. As fond as I am of you, I can't be your wife."

For a moment Edwin was silent, as if her words took time to sink in. Then he shook his head. "Harriett. You came all this way. I thought you came to marry me."

"I did. But . . . along the way, circumstances . . . changed."

Again he was silent. He stood, paced a few strides, then turned. "Do you want to tell me about it?"

No anger darkened his voice. Only concern. If she had to fall in love, Harriett wondered, why couldn't she have loved Edwin?

"On the journey here, I . . . uh . . . formed an inappropriate alliance with another man, Edwin. I didn't intend for it to happen. But it was of my own free will. I betrayed you, and I apologize for that."

Edwin took a deep breath and looked away. "Jake Carradine," he guessed.

Harriett's silence was enough of an answer.

"Are you going to marry him?"

Harriett sighed. "No, Edwin. I'm not. Mr. Carradine and I make a most unharmonious match."

"But you fancy yourself in love with him."

Harriett was silent again. She had admitted that failing to herself, and to Jake. She wasn't ready to admit it to anyone else.

Edwin turned back toward her. "You must love him.

Otherwise you never would have given yourself to him."

Harriett's eyes flashed. "I didn't give myself to any-one, Edwin." All men thought alike! Jake, the cad, had used the very same phrase to imply that once a woman was bedded by a man, she gave up all rights to herself —as if she were some piece of merchandise. And here was Edwin spouting the very same nonsense. "I sup-pose I did love him, and it seemed very natural to ex-press my feelings in a way that was . . . not very wise. But that does not make me a parcel that has been deeded over and delivered!"

"Then there is no reason at all why you can't marry me, is there?" His face was somber, his eyes fixed in-tently on her face.

"Edwin, did you understand what I just told you?"

"Yes indeed, Harriett. I'm not yet a deaf old man." For the first time he revealed a bit of annoyance. "You yielded yourself to Jake Carradine. You thought you loved him and allowed him to seduce you."

"I didn't say . . ."

"You didn't have to, dear. I know men of Carradine's stamp."

Harriett clamped her jaw on her anger. She'd never met another man of Jake Carradine's "stamp" and doubted if Edwin had either. But Edwin was entitled to be put out, after all.

"I can understand, Harriett. It was a long, difficult journey. You were probably frightened much of the time. Carradine offered strength, support, protection. Like any young, inexperienced girl would have, you developed an infatuation. I don't really blame you."

Edwin's understanding attitude was beginning to se-riously annoy. "Edwin, I was not frightened." Not all of the time at least. "And I am neither that young nor inexperienced."

"God, how I wished you'd come by boat!"

"You know I get seasick."

"I'd rather have you seasick than pregnant."

"I am not pregnant!" She stood abruptly, making Indy hiccup. The baby looked at her with wide blue eyes before she boosted him up to her shoulder. "I can assure you that I am not pregnant. But that is no concern of yours, Edwin. I can't presume on your friendship any longer by accepting your hospitality. By tomorrow I and my entourage, as you call it, will be gone."

Edwin waved at her to sit back down, and when she ignored his invitation, sat down himself. "I'm sorry, Harriett. I shouldn't have made that remark. It was asinine. Please forgive me."

"There's nothing to forgive," she said stiffly. "You have every right to be vexed."

"Don't leave, Harriett. I do understand your feelings for this fellow."

Which was more than Harriett could say.

"But as you said yourself, it's a most unsuitable match. And all this doesn't change my feelings for you, dear. If anything, your forthrightness and honesty make me admire you all the more. And if I can be honest with you, Harriett—I am not a young man with a young man's passions. I would not give you up simply because I'm not to be the first in your bed."

"Edwin, I'm not sure I want to marry anyone at all."

"Don't make a hasty decision, dear. Give yourself time to recover from your . . . journey . . . before you reject my suit. We have similar backgrounds, similar tastes, common goals. I think you owe me . . . and yourself . . . some time to consider."

Indy belched—every bit as daintily as he ate. Harriett swung him down from her now wet shoulder into her arms. His blue eyes blinked up at her, and Harriett imagined that the grimace on his face was one that urged her to show sweet Edwin the door, even if the door did belong to him.

"You must at least stay here until Mr. Carradine returns with news of the children's father. There is absolutely no place in town suitable for a respectable woman with children."

Harriett sighed. "All right, Edwin. I will stay, and consider. But it isn't really fair to you."

"You let me decide what's fair," Edwin said.

Let the men decide what's fair, and everything else in a woman's life. Even Edwin.

Carefully avoiding Indy's grasping, milky hands, Edwin kissed her—a gentle, dry, very civilized kiss.

"I'm sure you'll see things my way once you've recovered your objectivity, my dear. We could be very content together."

As Edwin left the room, Harriett bounced a spitting, gurgling Indy in her arms. She felt like doing a bit of spitting herself. Was her whole future to be as dry and dull as Edwin's kiss?

The roaming life wasn't what it used to be, Jake concluded as he rested his arm on his saddle horn and leveled his pistol at two wide-eyed prospectors. The rifles they'd grabbed as he'd ridden into their camp lay in the dirt—where they'd dropped them when Jake's two slugs had plowed the ground between their feet.

"Now, you yahoos. Obviously I don't want your damned gold, or I could've shot you both and taken it. All I want is to know if you've seen a friend of mine."

"Yeah?" one of the men growled. "What friend?"

"Fellow by the name of John MacBride."

"What's he look like?"

"Got me," Jake said.

"Some friend." The man spat.

"Know him?"

"Hell no," the other partner chimed in.

Jake slanted one brow. "If you did know him, would you tell me?"

"Mister, you keep that gun pointed this way and I'll tell you anything you want."

"Well, if you happen to cross his path, tell him to look up Harriett Foster in San Francisco. She's got a couple of his kids."

"Sure thing," the man agreed.

Jake reined his horse backward, pistol still in hand.

"I figure there's a couple a whores in San Fran that could have a kid a' mine, too," the partner snickered. "Ain't no call to go huntin' a man down."

In at least fifty little claims Jake had played out the same scene over the last seven days. He'd learned early that a man didn't just ride onto a working claim. Prospectors were jumpy about their gold, whether it was on top of or still in the ground, and they were more likely to greet a stranger with hot lead than a friendly cup of coffee. Good thing for these damned jackasses that Jake had tamed his temper. Elsewise more than one prospector would have ended up being buried in his claim rather than getting rich from it.

As it was, they'd all been eager to answer his questions while staring down the business end of his pistol. Having the gun between him and them made the conversations less belligerent, Jake discovered.

But no one had seen hide nor hair of John Mac-Bride. Jake wasn't really surprised. The prospectors swarming over the hills had eyes only for gold. Even partners sometimes didn't get past first names. And how many Johns were there in California?

In earlier days his task might have been fun—riding from camp to camp, money in his pocket, no one to look out for but himself. His gun hand was as fast as ever, his fists as hard. In a couple of the larger camps he'd had to prove it.

When he was sixteen Jake had left his father and

Elijah and set off to have fun doing just what he was doing now—playing tough guy with guns and fists. He'd been tough then, almost as tough as he was now —but not very smart. In those years he'd enjoyed the game. Bored with swinging an ax, angry with his father's dictatorial demands, and foolish with youth, Jake had reveled in the feel of a pistol in his hand and the crack of bone under his flying fist.

The second time Jake had taken his gun on the road, he'd left his family in their graves. Numb with grief and angry at the world, he hadn't cared who got in his way or who got hurt. His gun had been all he had left, a thing to cling to as the only anchor in life that he could depend upon.

And now? Now his gun and his fists kept him alive, but he was bored with the game of who was tougher and faster than whom. Being a badman just didn't have the charm that it used to have. Besides, Jake had two children and a woman waiting for him in San Francisco. And if the woman wasn't waiting for him, by God she was going to get him—if he had to turn her up by her heels and shake until some sense landed in that red head. He'd stopped chasing to make her realize she wanted to be caught, but he hadn't figured on her prickly pride. He should have realized that such simple tactics wouldn't work on a woman like Harry. He needed something more direct, like a rope and a branding iron.

If Jake was fated to reform, he figured Harriett was his prize for good behavior. And damned if she wasn't going to be happy about it even if he had to convince her at gunpoint.

Two days later Jake came to a sizable mining operation on the American River not too far from the town of Coloma. Thirty or so men were digging the gravel and operating the sluices—employees of a rich easterner who'd built himself a grand house in Sacramento. The gold didn't belong to the men who were grubbing for it, so here Jake didn't have to use his gun as passport into the camp. The grubbers didn't mind at all stopping work to answer his questions, and even offered him a cot for the night. No one seemed to know anything about John MacBride, but Jake decided to stay awhile anyway. Sleeping on the hard ground was getting almost as boring as gunplay.

The mining camp was big enough to have a saloon, which was merely a large tent with plank tables and stools inside. The whiskey was watered, the beer so light-colored it looked like mule piss—and tasted much the same. But sitting in a saloon with a whiskey at his elbow and a good poker hand in front of him was better than a sitting at a lonely campfire with only himself for company.

The poker game was a raucous one. Jake bet Harriett's silver coins against tiny piles of gold dust, playing with little interest but consistent luck. By the time an hour passed he had more in gold than Harriett had paid him in wages from Independence to California. The other players began to rumble their displeasure, and because he wasn't in the mood to shoot his way out of camp, Jake bet half his winnings on the next hand.

The tent flap pushed aside and an oldster walked in, gray hair down to his shoulders and mouth puckered into gaps of missing teeth. From the lay of the man's face Jake guessed the old-timer was missing more teeth than he kept. He headed straight for Jake's table.

"Hey there! Fella outside said a tall, gunhung stranger's offering good money for news about a Mac-Bride. You him?"

"I'm him." Jake discarded, then drew two cards.

"I knowed a MacBride."

Jake's eyes narrowed as he looked at the oldster. "Which MacBride?"

"Johnny MacBride. Only we called him Babyface. Made him cuss somethin' awful."

"You know where he is now?"

"Sure do. He's up Lost Man Creek, ten miles upstream and about six feet under. Died o' pneumony last winter, and we planted 'im."

Jake smiled and silently apologized to John MacBride for being relieved at such grim news. I'll take good care of your kids—he promised the man's ghost —and a hell of a lot better care of my wife than you did yours.

He looked at his hand—two aces and three jacks— folded the cards, and set them on the table. There was still enough light left to ride. "I'm out gents. Got business in San Francisco."

19

Jake arrived at the Garrett residence just as the sun was setting on September 17. Matt Loggins greeted him at the door with a hearty grin, and when Chad heard Jake's voice the boy bounced down the staircase three steps at a time and ran across the entrance hall, Dodger bounding at his heels. From a full body's length away he launched himself at Jake, fully trusting that he would be caught. And he was. Jake lifted him high into the air and swung him around before setting him back on his feet.

After enduring Chad's assault, Jake knelt and presented his face for Dodger's tongue. The dog's tail wagged furiously and his tongue slopped in wild abandon.

"Chad, why don't you take Thunder around to the stable and give him a little grain. He's had a hard ride."

"Sure thing!" The boy jumped up. The dog jumped with him, dancing on hind legs and pawing at Chad's shoulders with muddy feet. "Let's go!"

Matt shook his head at the muddy trail boy and dog left in their wake.

"What's he still doing here?" Jake asked. He'd come only to find out where Harriett was staying, not ex-

pecting to find her here after she'd said that she
wouldn't marry Garrett. His face darkened. "I suppose
Harriett's here too."

Matt shrugged. "Last time I noticed Miss Foster was
in 'er room primpin'. She an' Master Garrett are goin'
to some singin' program tonight at the Italian Theatre
—once the master gets home that is. I can git 'er fer
ye."

"You do that," Jake said.

Jake wandered through a wide archway and into the
parlor while Matt scurried up the stairway. He imagined the fancy carpet cringing from his muddy boots.
In an oil painting above the mantel ladies with elaborate curls and even more elaborate gowns cavorted in
a flowery meadow. They seemed to peer down at him
in disapproval. Jake scowled back at them.

"Jake!"

He turned to find Harriett in the parlor doorway.
His scowl didn't fade. She paled a shade, then quietly
closed the double doors behind her.

"Did you find the children's father?" Her face was
rigid, her hands clasped tightly in front of her.

"John MacBride's dead," Jake said. "Died of pneumonia last winter."

Harriett closed her eyes. Jake watched her try to be
sorry for the man's death. Always thinking of how she
ought to react rather than accepting her feelings as a
natural part of who she was.

"Sadie once mentioned that she'd gotten a letter
from her husband. Said he was working the area
around the American River. So I rode around that
country for a while. Found a man in a camp near
Coloma who dug with Johnny MacBride. John's buried at their claim, up a little trickle called Lost Man
Creek."

Harriett opened her eyes. They were green as ever,
now dark emerald with emotion and brilliant with

gathering tears. "Jake, thank you. If you don't mind, I'll tell Chad. I . . . I didn't tell him that you were looking for his father. I didn't know how he would react."

Jake didn't answer. His mind wasn't on John Mac-Bride, or Chad MacBride. His mind was full of Harri-ett; his eyes also. She was dressed fancier than he'd ever seen, in a green silk dress that echoed the color of her eyes. The stiffly boned bodice and V-waistband emphasized her narrow waist. Three full layers of lace fell from fitted, elbow-length sleeves, and a chain of gold circled her slender neck. She looked like a woman who would be found on the arm of a rich man like Edwin Garrett.

"What are you still doing here, Harry?" His voice was soft, but the tone demanded an answer.

She looked up. He noted how dark her lashes were against her skin. She was losing the bronze glow she'd acquired on the trail. The parlor lamps, dim as they were, flashed fire off her hair.

"What do you mean?"

"You said you weren't going to marry Edwin Garrett. Yet here you are living in his house, dressed in fancy clothes and jewelry like a . . . "

"Like a what?" she demanded.

"Like a woman who's set on getting married."

"That's not what you were going to say, you jackass. For your information, Edwin did not buy me this dress, or jewelry either. I am quite capable of providing for myself, and I am not some rich man's trollop!"

"I didn't say you were."

"You were thinking it! Men assume that a woman is beholden to some man for everything she has, and the law makes it fact once she's married." From under thick lashes came a suspicious glare of glittering green ice. "You mean that all the time we were together this summer you had no idea that I was a wealthy woman?''

"I don't care how rich you are, Harry. What are you still doing in Garrett's house?"

Harriett lifted her chin in a stubborn gesture that Jake knew only too well. "Where I stay or what I do is none of your affair, Jake Carradine."

"When I ask questions," he told her in a voice dark as a building thunderstorm, "I generally get an answer. One way or another."

Her eyes grew round, then narrowed. "You think you have some say over what I do?"

He smiled and folded his arms across his chest, waiting.

Harriett lifted her chin another notch. "I am not a woman to be bullied!"

"Am I bullying you?" He smiled innocently.

A sheen of perspiration appeared on her upper lip. "You're trying."

"Maybe you need a lesson in what bullying really is." He unfolded his arms and took a step toward her.

Harriett hastily backed away, directly into Edwin's magenta velveteen settee, and sat down with with a notable lack of dignity. "All right!" she surrendered before he could come any closer. "I explained everything to Edwin."

"Everything?"

"Well, I didn't go into minute detail!" she snapped. "Edwin was very understanding. He still wants to marry me, and he asked me to stay awhile and consider his proposal."

"And you're considering." He folded his arms again, his face black.

"It's only fair that I give the matter some thought. He's been very nice about this whole thing and—"

"And certainly wouldn't let a little thing like his

woman being in love with another man interfere with his getting to your money."

Harriett surged to her feet. "Edwin does not need one cent of my money! Not one cent! And I suppose your motives were all so pure!"

"Lady! You can take your money and burn it! What I wanted was you! And I got you, didn't I?" His very soul winced at the hurt that flooded her eyes. But dammit! She wasn't the only one who hurt. "Harry, I knew you had some growing up to do, but I always figured you were honest. How could you consider marrying Garrett with what is between us?"

Harriett gasped in outrage. How dare he stand there and say there was something between them when he had treated her like a sack of flour all the way from the Humboldt River to San Francisco? How could he condemn her perfectly proper behavior when he had been amusing himself with trollops within hours of leaving her at Edwin's!

She pushed herself from the settee and stalked forward, ignoring the warning glitter in Jake's eyes. "What is between us?" she demanded, jabbing lethally with an index finger. "Just what do you think is between us? You were the man who said I didn't know how to love and was too cowardly to learn. You were the man who said I didn't need to worry about you any longer because the chase was over! You were the man —you . . . you fresh buffalo pie!—whose room reeked of whores not a day after we parted!"

"An attempt to make you jealous." The words were a statement rather than an apology. "There was a whore, but she left without earning her pay, Harry." His mouth slanted in wry amusement. "Too late I discover I'm a one-woman man, and the woman is you."

Harriett snorted her contempt.

"And I stopped chasing to let you discover that you wanted to be caught. One word, Harry. That's all it would've taken to bring me back. One lousy word. But you were just too stubborn to say it."

Or too scared, Harriett admitted to herself. Scared that he would say yes, scared that he would say no. And scared of herself.

"But I'm not too stubborn to say it. I thought I'd have some time to persuade you, but I don't, not with Edwin fixing to throw a rope and hog-tie you. You don't belong with him, Harry. You belong with me. I'm done with roaming, with fighting—even with gambling and drinking, if you want to get testy about it. But I'm not done with you, Harriett Foster."

There was a fire inside him. Harriett could almost feel the flames licking at her as he slowly came forward, could see the heat in his eyes. Worse yet, she could feel the kindling start to burn in herself.

"No, Jake." She held out an arm to fend him off. "This is useless. Really. Stay away from me!"

Harriett stayed rooted where she stood. These last days she had missed Jake so. At night he walked into her dreams, leaving her breathless, sweating, heart pounding, and achingly empty when she woke to find herself alone in her bed, entwined only with her rumpled sheets, enfolded only by a goose down mattress. By day she had tried to lose herself in Edwin's collection of books and plays, in beginning a new correspondence with Amelia Bloomer, in Edwin's affection—which seemed so calm and serene (*boring* was also a word that came to mind) compared to Jake's passion. Soon, she had told herself, very soon the things of her life that had been so important before Jake would seem important again.

But not if Jake kept bounding back into her life to light her fires.

And yet she had been the one who couldn't let go, a resurgent orneriness reminded her. Or had it been both of them who couldn't quite give up?

"Stay away!" Whether she pleaded with Jake or herself Harriett didn't know. But the entreaty didn't work for either, it seemed. Because as Jake drew closer, stalking her like a hungry predator, Harriett felt the fire inside her spread to every nerve. All he had to do was look at her and she lost all claim to common sense.

"You wanted to know what is between us, Harry." He reached out and took her shoulders. Harriett stood frozen. Terrified. Delighted. "I'll show you what's between us."

He kissed her—no dry, civilized, gentle peck as Edwin was wont to give, but a searing, penetrating demand for her very soul. He bent her back, pushed her down until she found herself on the settee with his weight pinning her to the velveteen cushion. His mouth burned a path down her throat, over her exposed shoulders, until his lips tasted the soft flesh of her cleavage. Efficiently he dipped his hand into the boned bodice and freed one tingling breast. His lips fastened gently on the nipple, tongue teasing and torturing, while he lifted her skirts with his hand and traced a path over her stockings to her garter, and thence onto the soft, bare flesh of her thigh.

Harriett moaned. She was burning, aching, just as in her dreams, only worse. Much, much worse. She was shameless, reason gone—like hot candle wax, flowing, bending, opening to every demand, unable to harden around reason and determination as long as Jake fed the fire.

He pulled away, his mouth inches from hers. One callused hand rested on the inside of her thigh, the other warmly enfolded her breast.

"I could take you right now, Harry. You wouldn't fight me. You can't fight me." His voice was soft, confident. It slid into the deepest part of her soul and made her shiver, because he was telling the truth. "I'm in

your blood, just as you're in mine. You'll never be able
to give yourself to another man—Edwin or anyone
else.''

He slid his hand from under her dress; she felt cold
without its warmth. As if she were a senseless doll he
sat her up and gently straightened her bodice.

"I'm in the same hotel," he told her. "I'll be there
when you want to bring me my wages—and anything
else you might want to give me."

Harriett closed her eyes. Jake's footsteps didn't
sound on the plush carpet, but she sensed him leave
the room. And once again her heart was empty.

Two hours later Harriett sat in the second row of the
Italian Theatre, an establishment occupying the upper
stories of the Occidental Restaurant. The first three
rows of seats were reserved for ladies and gentlemen
who attended the performances; the rest were occupied by what Lucille's escort called riffraff.

Edwin sat beside Harriett, and Lucille and her escort—a gentleman merchant friend of Edwin's—on
Edwin's other side. Lucille's escort had very little to
say, and Harriett was silent. Edwin and Lucille were
the only ones in the foursome who laughed and talked,
and they seemed to have a grand time. If Edwin noticed Harriett's broody manner, he didn't comment.

The "celebrated artiste" Fanny Marten was to sing,
as were a Signor Rossi, Signorina Canova, and Signor
Suar. The theatre was full to bursting with a colorful
conglomeration of enthusiasts—bearded, flannel-and-
denim-clad miners rubbed shoulders with dandies and
gamblers and the golden newly rich. Laundresses and
blacksmiths laughed along with storekeepers and physicians; plain workmen and despised "Sydney ducks"
sat next to sea captains and warehousemen—all sitting
within sight and smell of San Francisco's "elite," of
which Edwin Garrett was definitely one. Only the Chi-

nese, or "Celestials" as they were called, were missing representation; and they kept much to their own society in the narrow alleyways and shabby buildings of Chinatown.

Any other evening Harriett would have found the audience itself entertaining, for she was fascinated by the relaxed and almost egalitarian nature of San Francisco's society. The performance onstage was hardly what one would find in Boston, but Harriett did admit, in one of her few moments of attention, that the "celebrated artiste" had a fine soprano voice.

But for the most part Harriett neither heard the musical program nor noticed the audience's antics. Her mind wasn't sitting straight in her head; most of it was still back on the parlor couch with Jake, reeling from the things he'd done and said.

All the time Harriett had smarted from Jake's rejection he had merely been biding his time—waiting with devilish patience until she came crawling back. The fiend! When she thought of the painful attempts to swallow her pride and seek reconciliation—and Jake probably seeing clear through her stumbling efforts, laughing at her! Or if he hadn't laughed, he at least had let her suffer. How dare he manipulate her in such a manner! She hated him, despised him. He could jump off a cliff and she would merely wave and wish him good journey.

Yet when he touched her, she melted. He held out those strong arms of his and some force pulled her inside their embrace. Her own childish passions were enslaving her more surely than Jake Carradine ever could. When Jake was near, reason didn't stand a chance. He brought a new Harriett to life—Ornery Harry, as Harriett had come to think of her alter ego. Harry had almost buried the old, comfortable Harriett on their odyssey across the continent—almost, but not quite. And now, just as sensible Harriett was beginning to flourish again, Jake had to come along with his declarations and demands, waking Ornery Harry from restless slumber.

If Jake stuck around long enough, Ornery Harry was going to win. Harriett could feel defeat in her bones. Then what would she do once Jake's passion wore thin, once reasonable Harriett woke again and found herself in the thrall of a man who, in spite of all his wonderful qualities, thought love was more important than freedom, thought women's rights stopped where his passion began, and already had proven himself ruthless in going after what he wanted? Not to mention that his greatest talent—other than melting women at a touch—lay in violence. A fast gun and hard fists. He'd said he was ready to change, but in the same breath promised to fight, to kill, if necessary, to regain his land. Could any man truly change?

Harriett wanting Jake Carradine was like a child craving candy with no thought for the tummyache that would follow. But what she was asking for was far worse than a tummyache.

"Harriett?"

Harriett blinked as Edwin's voice broke into her brooding. The Signor Rossi and Mrs. Marten had stopped singing. Lucille and her escort were rising to go to the lobby for intermission.

"Would you like to adjourn to the lobby, my dear?" No reproof for her moodiness, no prying into her personal feelings and thoughts. Sweet Edwin.

"I'll stay here if you don't mind," she replied.

"Then I'll stay with you."

Always accommodating. That was Edwin.

"Are you enjoying the performance, dear?"

"Oh, yes," she lied. "They're quite talented, aren't they."

"Indeed. Though a bit common. We have the legitimate opera as well, you know, and it won't be long before the best companies from Europe and the East Coast are making San Francisco a regular stop. Some day soon this is going to be a center of culture and commerce.''

"No doubt you're right, Edwin.''

"I'm going to be a part of it. You know, Harriett, this is what I've always wanted to do—open the roads of commerce to a thriving new world. I used to envy the Spaniards for finding Mexico and the English for landing on our own shores—lands untouched by anyone other than savages. And here I have my own opportunity. People just don't realize that the true wealth of this land is not the gold, but the chances for trade and business.''

"Yes, Edwin.''

He reached over and patted her hand. "But you understand, don't you, Harriett, because you're an intelligent woman who isn't easily dazzled by glitter, despite your relative youth. That's what I value the most about you, my dear.''

For the first time Harriett wondered how Edwin would behave in lovemaking. Cool, she decided. Cool, dry, intellectual, if that was possible. She shivered.

"You could be a great help to me here, Harriett. And think of the opportunities for advancing your own causes. True, statehood has been achieved, the state constitution already written, but many fresh-thinking people are emigrating to this land. Soon it might be possible to achieve some needed reforms for the ladies.''

"Yes, I'm sure that's true.''

"Then you've given my proposal some favorable thought?''

Had Edwin been formally proposing again? Was marriage to him such a dry thing?

Of course it was. Why else had she once consented to wed him—to have companionship without those "childish passions," as her mother had called them; to have friendship without the risk and pain of emotional commitment. That was the kind of marriage she had wanted, still wanted. Wasn't it?

"You've had time to consider, Harriett—time to recover from your . . . journey. I do have great respect and affection for you, my dear. I would count myself a lucky man if you would consent to be my wife."

Harriett closed her eyes. Her time was up. Edwin was a good man, sweet and considerate, and would never demand more than respect and mild affection. He would never be able to hurt her with a glance, lift her to the stars with a smile, send her plummeting with a single word. Edwin would protect her from Jake Carradine, protect her from her own passions. He would give her the life she had always wanted, and banish Ornery Harry forever.

Edwin offered her escape from her own foolishness.

"Yes, Edwin." She opened her eyes and squared her jaw. "I would be honored to be your wife."

Edwin's announcement of their formal betrothal was received by Lucille and Edwin's friend Mr. Carsden with very little ado. It was only appropriate, Harriett thought, that such a sedate prospect of marriage should receive such sober felicitations. Indeed, Lucille looked less than happy. Though her aunt hid her feelings well, Harriett knew Lucille well enough to read through the smile. Knowing Harriett's uncertainties, her dear aunt was fearful for Harriett's happiness. Bless her sweet heart.

But Harriett wasn't uncertain any longer. She was sure, terribly sure, that she was doing the right thing. Terribly sure.

The curtain rose; the audience thundered applause to welcome back Mrs. Marten. Harriett tried to clear her mind and listen to the performance. After all, she had made her decision. The turmoil was over. She had nothing more to worry about. Had she?

Thirty minutes into the performance a faint cry sounded from the lobby. Someone in the back of the auditorium took it up, and soon it rippled through the audience like wind through the prairie grass.

"Fire!"

"Fire down the block, coming this way! Fast!"

The "celebrated artiste" stopped singing. The audience, first one by one, then as a mass, surged to their feet.

"Fire!" Edwin cried. He grasped Harriett's arm. "Don't panic! Don't panic! We must be calm above all!"

If anyone was on the verge of panic, it was Edwin. His eyes were wide, his hands shaking. Harriett felt a brush of terror herself. She'd heard how fire had ravaged the town twice already that very year, and in December of the year before. Harriett could imagine too well what would happen if even a small fire got started in this crowded conglomeration of scrap timber and canvas.

"Edwin!" Harriett pulled at his arm. "I think we should get out of this building."

"Quite right, my dear. Stay calm, ladies. Here now, that's right. Take hold of me, Mrs. Stanwick. We must stay together at all costs."

Getting out of the building was easier said than done. The house was packed full, and the aisles weren't nearly wide enough to accommodate a mass exodus. The "ladies and gentlemen" in the first three rows had a herd of pushing, shoving humanity between them and the doors that led out.

Finally they threaded their way through the aisle and into the lobby. San Francisco's elite, Harriett noted, was not behaving with any more dignity than the horde of "riffraff" that surrounded them. The

lobby was chaos. Smoke was everywhere. Breathing
was agony, and though no actual flames were visible,
Harriett suspected that the building itself might be already afire. And they still had to get downstairs. Mr.
Carsden pushed through the logjam of bodies that
crowded the lobby. Behind him, Edwin held firmly to
both Harriett and Lucille, the three of them plus Carsden forming a wedge. Pushing, shoving, cursing, the
crowd of theatre-goers slowly made its way down the
one stairway. Just as Harriett set foot on the ground
floor, the stairway railing halfway up gave way to the
pressure of humanity. Those crowded behind it fell
shrieking to the first floor, some immediately trampled
under the crowd still trying to escape.

Harriett gasped.

"Don't look back!" Edwin warned. "Come on! Come
on! No time!"

Coughing, stumbling, eyes streaming, they finally
broke through to the street—literally jumped from the
frying pan into the fire. Harriett could scarcely see, the
smoke was so thick and her eyes streaming so, but
what she could see was a facsimile of Hell itself. The
entire street was a wall of orange-white fire, and a
fireborne gale of wind whipped the flames into an incandescent fury. The air around them whirled in a
hurricane of smoke and glowing cinders. Every breath
was searing torture. A few steps away an "iron house"
—fireproof, Harriett had heard—glowed white. A man
lay facedown halfway across its door, hair singed and
skin blistered and charred. Harriett grew sick at the
sight. Down the avenue a hook-and-ladder company
with its little hand-drawn fire engine worked furiously,
a gnat spitting at a giant.

"This way!" Carsden shouted above the roar.

He pulled them toward the only avenue that was not
yet completely engulfed. They swam through the heat,
incandescent cinders blowing around them in an evil,

searing rain. Harriett stumbled along blindly, Edwin's fingers biting into her arm. Through the tears she could see smoking pinpricks on her gown where red-hot ash had burned through the silk.

Edwin jerked to a halt. "Lucille!" he croaked. "God! She got plucked right out of my hand!"

A crowd of fleeing people was surging around them. "Lucille!"

Edwin's voice was hoarse, but if he'd had a speaking trumpet, his voice would not have carried above the roar of wind and flames.

"I've got to find her!" he said.

He pushed Harriett toward Carsden and swam back into the crowd, this time fighting the current instead of going with it.

"Oh, God!" Harriett cried. Lucille swept away by the crowd to heaven knew what fate, and now Edwin gone as well.

Carsden shouted at her to follow and grabbed her arm. Harriett shook her head frantically and jerked away. She couldn't leave Lucille and Edwin behind.

Then Elias Carsden was gone. The crowd eddied around her, and the heat came in waves that battered and scorched. Resolutely she pushed forward in the direction that Edwin had disappeared, knowing with a grim resignation that none of them were going to come out of this alive.

20

The Singapore Saloon was as good a place as any for a man to forget his woes. The proprietor, One-Legged Dickie, was an amiable sort who let his customers drink or brawl as they pleased, as long as they didn't break up the property too much or had the where-withal to pay for damages. His wife, a lady with flam-boyant magenta hair and breasts that were the talk of San Francisco's waterfront, ran the brothel next door. She did her best to snag Jake as a customer when he walked in the saloon door, but he wasn't interested. He wished that he was. A whore would prove a wel-come relief to the gnawing ache in his groin, but he'd tried that before. His body had a mind of its own, and it wasn't going to stand up and perform for any but the right woman.

He sat down and ordered whiskey. When Dickie brought the drink, Jake took a swig and spit it out. "How do you expect a man to get drunk on this horse piss?" he growled. "Bring me some real goddamned whiskey!"

Dickie shrugged. Jake's size and the comfortable way he wore his gun—as though it were part of his thigh—didn't encourage argument. The proprietor fetched another bottle.

Jake was determined to get drunk if the task took him the whole night. Harriett Foster was a goddamned expert at driving men to drink. For all her prim admonitions about "spiritous liquors," she had to be one of the distilling industry's biggest assets—Harriett and women like her. Jake would be striking a great blow for American temperance if he married her and kept her under lock and key.

Jake poured another glass and downed half of it in a single swallow. It burned all the way down, competing with the fire of his frustration. For the first time he allowed himself to wonder if he might be wrong. He was so sure that Harry loved him, that she couldn't give herself to another man even if she tried. But then, how much experience did he really have with women —especially with respectable women who had intellect, education, and an independent streak worthy of a mule? Not much, he admitted. His mother had died almost before he knew the difference between women and men; Elijah's wife had died within a few months of Jake's settling in Oregon. Decent women were rare in the lumber camps where he'd grown up, and they were nonexistent in the places he'd frequented in his years as a hired gun. Whores were more Jake's style.

But that was in the past. Harriett Foster was his future—unless she did something stupid just to prove how damned independent she was. He might have made a mistake in pressing her so hard. Harry had a lot in common with a mule, temperamentally speaking. Jake had once seen a mule back right over a cliff in pure spite of something it didn't want to do. Just like the mule, Harry might back away from him so fast she would step right off that cliff—and into Edwin Garrett's arms.

Not if Jake had anything to say about it!

Jake slammed his glass down on the table. "Dickie! Another bottle."

"Comin' up, sir!"

But before the proprietor could reach into his store of rotgut, a sooty messenger appeared at the doorway. He brought with him the smell of smoke.

"Fire!" he rasped. "There's at least four blocks afire uptown, maybe more. The whole city could go. We need men for bucket lines."

Jake snapped to attention. "Is the fire near the Italian Theatre?"

"Hell yes, man. The Italian's gone."

Jake stood so abruptly, his chair toppled backward. He pushed through the crowd, and before his mind could even formulate a plan of action, he was out the door and running. The image of Harry's face swelled in his mind. After all she'd survived—storms, rivers, Indians, cholera, and a jackass gunman named Carradine—she couldn't die in a lousy fire! Harry was too smart to die in a goddamned stinking fire, too smart, too stubborn, too ornery. And if God was worth His salt at all, He wouldn't do this to Jake twice.

Ten minutes later Jake stopped, doubled over, and gasped for breath. At first he had followed the stench of smoke, but he no longer needed a guide. The smoke was so thick, he could hardly breathe, and just ahead flames lit the night like a message from Hell. Confused human turbulence swirled around him as the crowd escaping the fire collided with the few going toward it —grimly determined volunteers with buckets in their hands, frantic merchants desperate to save what they could of their inventory.

Jake stumbled on, fighting the crowd. Surely Garrett had gotten Harriett to safety. After all, the man wasn't a total incompetent. Jake hadn't seen them in the fleeing crowd, but they might have gotten out earlier, or taken another avenue of escape. Or he might have missed them. Harriett was probably safe in the house on Stockton Street, washing soot off in a steaming bath and thinking of more ways to bedevil Jake Carradine.

But he couldn't convince himself. Matt had said Edwin and Harriett were going to a singing performance at the Italian Theatre, and the Italian Theatre was in the middle of an inferno. Harriett was somewhere in the frantic crowd. Jake could feel her in his very gut.

Five minutes later he saw her, swaying, staggering, heading away from escape, not toward it, the little fool. The fire was all around now, and the crowd had thinned. A few people still fled, and the one bucket-line remaining in the area was pulling out. One bucket-toting volunteer took Harriett's arm. She shook him off.

"I'll take her," Jake told the volunteer.

Harriett turned at the sound of his hoarse voice. "Jake!" She willingly melted into his embrace and clung to him, sobbing. "Lucille got lost!" she wailed. "Edwin went to find her. And I can't find either of them!"

Her dress was smoking, her face blistered, her hair a singed disaster. But she was the most beautiful sight Jake had ever seen. "Is there another way they could have gotten out?"

"No! This is the only way open." She raised a tear-streaked, sooty face to his. "Oh, Jake! Where could they be?"

Jake was tempted to throw her over his shoulder and carry her out, but the desperation in her eyes reminded him of what he'd felt when Elijah and Joshua had burned to death in their cabin. "We'll find them," he said.

He grabbed a bucket that a volunteer had left behind and doused them both with water, then soaked his kerchief and tied it about Harriett's nose and mouth. Then, with Harriett stumbling beside him, they searched.

A few minutes later, in a side alley that threatened to become an inferno at any moment, they found Lucille, weeping into blistered hands, hair charred, dress blackened and partly burned away. She knelt beside the scorched remnant of a wooden beam that pinned Edwin to the ground. From the look of her hands, Lucille had been trying to push the beam away.

Jake gently moved Lucille aside and lifted the beam. "Pull him out," he grunted.

Edwin cried out in pain as the two women tugged him to safety. Lucille descended upon him in another flurry of weeping while Harriett took his hand with a tenderness that made Jake's heart feel suddenly hollow.

"We can't move him!" Lucille cried as Jake started to pick Edwin up.

"It's either move him or leave him to be fried," Jake growled.

"At least bind his chest," Harriett said. "He could have broken ribs." She ripped a large square from her skirt and tied it tightly around Edwin's chest.

Jake shucked his shirt and used it for the same purpose. Then he lifted Edwin as carefully as possible, though why he was helping this man to live he didn't know. The expression on Harriett's face when she'd seen Edwin lying under the beam frightened Jake more than the fire. Far more.

"Let's go," he ordered gruffly. "That avenue's not going to stay open much longer."

When the ashes from the fire settled, the entire area bounded by Montgomery, Washington, Grant, and Pacific streets had been gutted, burned nearly to the ground. Many of the buildings destroyed were mere shanties of timber and canvas, but the fire had also leveled several restaurants, the offices and equipment of the *Pacific News*, the Italian Theatre, and many other businesses, as well as almost destroying the courthouse.

Lucille's blisters and burns healed rapidly, as did Harriett's. Edwin lay abed with cracked ribs, a concussion, and badly burned hands. He healed—more slowly than the women, but just as surely. Elias Carsden called the morning after the fire, frantic with worry for their safety. He suffered minor burns and a burden of guilt for losing track of them all during the conflagration, but his wounds also healed.

The only one permanently injured was Jake. His injury was visible only in the depths of his eyes—and then only when his guard slipped to reveal the darkness of defeat. Harriett had finally convinced him that she belonged with Edwin Garrett, not with Jake Carradine—and she'd done it without a show of red-headed temper, without even a word of reproof, denial, or objection.

When they'd made it back to Edwin's house that grim night, Harriett had been profuse in her thanks for getting them all to safety. She'd had Martha feed him while they were waiting for the doctor to tend Edwin's injuries. Ignoring her own hurts, she washed and salved Jake's burns and tended to Lucille, who was still nearly hysterical. All the while she told Jake how much they owed him, how much she owed him.

But her heart had been upstairs with Edwin. Jake could see the distraction on her face. And all the next week she spent constantly at Edwin's side, whether or not the man needed her. Jake went back to the St. Francis and had a long talk with himself. He remembered the luxury of Garrett's home. Two maids, one for each floor, did all the cleaning. A cook imported from Europe prepared the meals. Martha Loggins, the housekeeper, supervised the domestics, and her husband, Matt, was both butler and valet. Books lined every shelf, fine paintings graced every wall. Luxury, art, the gentle life—things Harry had valued all her life. He thought about her expression when she'd seen Edwin lying beneath the beam, her frantic concern for his recovery. And he reluctantly concluded that Harriett did love the man. Perhaps not with the passion she reserved for Jake. But would passion—one that she didn't want, at that—make up for the loss of everything Edwin Garrett could give her? Especially since she did love Edwin in her own prim and proper way.

Jake finally faced the fact that he had lost. Harry had been right all along. They were mismatched. Jake wasn't of her world, she wasn't of his. Harriett would do very well with her rich cold-fish merchant, and Jake would go back to Oregon, settle a few debts, and take back the land that was rightfully his. If Homer Kane blew him to kingdom come, so much the better.

He packed his things and checked out of the St. Francis. The *Mary Connor*, advertised in the *Alta California* daily newspaper to be a "fast and commodious" sailer, was leaving early the next day for Portland. Jake planned to spend the night getting drunk at the Singapore Saloon and stagger aboard the ship before she sailed. Or maybe he would get so drunk that someone would have to carry him aboard. That might be even better.

But first he would go to the house on Stockton Street and tell Edwin he had won. The man had a right to know that the battle was over.

Arriving at the Garrett house, Jake was glad to learn that Harriett and Lucille had taken Chad and Indy on a picnic, it being a fine day. He didn't need to see Harry; she would only mess up his noble resolve. Edwin, recovered enough to be up and about, greeted him with an unreserved welcome that got even more enthusiastic when Jake stated the purpose of his visit.

"You're a good man," Edwin told Jake. "Hell, Carradine. You're a better man than I thought."

"I figure you'll treat Harry the way she wants to be treated." Jake's words were amiable, but his tone held a threat that neither man mistook.

"Don't you worry about Harriett," Edwin assured him. "She'll be a leader in San Francisco society; she'll have clothes, servants, books—everything her heart has ever desired. And plenty of vice and social prejudice to combat. Believe me, she'll be as happy as a kitten in a basket of yarn."

Jake wondered what Harry would say to Edwin's comparing her to a kitten. He figured Edwin might be in for some surprises.

Woe be to the man if he didn't live up to Harry's ideal of perfection. She would read to him from Margaret Fuller and Mary Wollstonecraft, lecture him about his piddling little vices, prod him to reach his full potential as a human being, and harass him about women's property laws and women's rights conventions.

Good luck to the poor man. He would never have a moment's peace.

But Jake would trade places with him in the blink of an eye.

"I'd better be going," Jake said. "I have some loose ends to tie up before the ship sails tomorrow." Loose ends—like three or four bottles of booze. "Will you tell Harriett good-bye for me?"

"I certainly will."

Probably with great glee, Jake thought.

Edwin shook his hand in a firm good-bye. "I want to thank you again for all you've done for us, Jake."

"A pleasure." In spite of his mood, Jake couldn't resist a wicked grin as his words brought to mind several things he'd done for Harry that could not be to Edwin's liking. Not at all. The slight flush on Edwin's face bore witness that the older man followed a similar line of thought.

As he left the house, however, Jake was not grinning. Finally, it was over.

Harriett gazed out the window of her bedroom at the fine October afternoon. On the next day she would become a married woman, and when night fell she would climb into bed with the man who was her husband. That bedding would be accompanied by none of the overwhelming helplessness she had felt with Jake —none of the flood of passion that washed away reason and control and dignity. Why did that prospect not make her glad?

"I can't imagine why he hasn't answered any of my notes!" Harriett complained to Lucille.

Lucille took a pin from her mouth and made a final tuck in the bodice of her niece's wedding gown. "Hold still!" she warned. "I'll prick you for sure. Who hasn't replied to what notes?" she added as an afterthought.

"Jacob. I've sent at least four notes to his hotel. One of them was an invitation to the wedding. And he's not sent back a single word!"

"Maybe he moved to another hotel. That St. Francis is a bit expensive."

"He would've told me."

"Turn around," Lucille ordered. "Stand straight; don't slouch. Hmmm." She made a minute adjustment in the waist seam. "All right. The hem seems to hang straight now. Take it off and we'll stitch the final seams."

Harriett perused her wedding gown in the bedroom mirror. "You don't suppose something might have happened to him, do you?"

"Who?"

"To Jacob! Haven't you been listening to me?"

"Oh, I'm sure Jake can take care of himself." Lucille slanted a wise look at her niece. "You seem awfully anxious for him to attend the wedding. Don't you suppose it might be a bit painful for him?''

"Well, he doesn't seem to care at all!" Harriett huffed. "You'd think we could remain friends, at least, with all we've been through together." All that bluster and steam right before the fire—not to mention the way he'd pushed her down onto the settee and demonstrated quite graphically just how much power he had over her—and Jake hadn't made a move toward her since. Had his efforts stopped because her engagement had become official? Her commitment to Edwin had certainly never stopped him before. Perhaps he'd decided she wasn't worth the effort after all. Was she disappointed, or simply relieved?

"Um," Lucille replied. "It is difficult to turn a lover into a friend. And vice versa."

Harriett sensed a cutting edge in her aunt's tone. But then, silly Lucille had always favored Jake's suit, for some reason.

A knock sounded on the door just as Harriett slipped carefully out of the half-sewn gown. "It's Edwin, my dear. May I come in?"

"Half a moment, Edwin."

Lucille helped her niece climb back into her day gown and then patted Harriett's cheek. "I'll leave you two alone."

"Come in," Harriett called to Edwin.

Lucille glanced up as the door opened, then hastily dropped her gaze. Edwin and she did not meet each other's eyes as they passed.

"Ah! You look absolutely lovely today, Harriett. You're going to make a splendid bride."

"Thank you, Edwin." She obediently presented a cheek for his dry kiss. "You're looking quite fine yourself."

As usual, Edwin was impeccably dressed in a single-breasted frock coat, embroidered brocade waistcoat, and faultlessly tailored trousers. The points of a snow-white collar were starched and turned down over a red cravat. Gloves hid his hands, which were scarring quite unpleasantly from the September fire. Harriett had told him several times that she'd seen much worse on the journey out, that the scars didn't bother her in the least, but still he insisted on the gloves, saying that Harriett had experienced quite enough unpleasantness in her life and should have sweetness meet her eyes from this time forward.

Harriett hadn't bothered to voice her opinion of that soppy sentiment, fearing to hurt Edwin's feelings. And she hadn't said another word about the gloves.

"Fine day for October, isn't it?"

"Yes, it is," Harriett agreed. "Perhaps the winter will not be as rainy as you say."

"Tsk, yes! We'll be swimming in the streets before the new year."

"Well, I daresay one gets used to it."

"Soon we'll have the streets planked. Then the mud won't be such a bother."

Edwin sighed, massaged an aching spot on his brow, and motioned Harriett to a chair. "Sit down, my dear. Pleasant as our conversation always is, I didn't really come for small talk."

Harriett sat.

"Tomorrow we're going to be joined as man and wife," Edwin reminded her.

"Yes." If her response was not quite as eager as Edwin hoped, he didn't betray his disappointment.

"I believe that husbands and wives must be very honest with each other, Harriett. Otherwise their relationship sinks into a sham of what a marriage should be."

Harriett's brow furrowed. "I have been honest with you, Edwin."

"I know you have, dear. I'm afraid it is I who have not been quite as forthright as I might have been."

"You?" Her brow inched up.

"Indeed. I have pondered over the past two weeks if a little deception was not in your best interests, my love. For a while I convinced myself that it was. But if I am strictly honest with myself, I must admit that this untruthfulness—actually more of an omission than a lie—was more for my good than yours."

Harriett began to think she would be sprouting gray hairs before Edwin got to his point.

"Therefore, Harriett, I feel that I must set this matter straight before we are legally joined on the morrow."

"Yes?"

He clasped his gloved hands behind his back and began to pace. "Martha tells me that you are concerned that your missives to Mr. Carradine have not been answered."

Harriett frowned.

"I'm sure she heard it from her husband, whom you entrusted with the messages," he explained. "Really, my dear. You must learn that servants are not good at keeping a confidence. Learn to be more careful around these people."

"Edwin! What is this about my notes to Jacob?"

"I'm afraid I intercepted them."

Harriett's heart jumped with sudden joy. Jake was not ignoring her. Then anger took over. "You what?"

"You see," Edwin explained, eyes fixed on the floor as he continued to pace. "I knew Mr. Carradine was no longer at the St. Francis."

"He moved?"

"He went to Oregon, my dear, and quite truthfully, I didn't want you to know. If your messages had reached the St. Francis, some overefficient clerk might have sent a note back saying that he had checked out."

He paused and wiped at his brow as Harriett's face grew flushed. "Mr. Carradine told me of his decision the day you and Lucille took the children on an outing. I must admit that I was surprised at his wisdom—seeing the sort of man he is. In spite of his obvious affection for you he recognized that you would be happier with me."

"That's what he said?" Harriett asked incredulously.

"Yes, my love. He bade me say good-bye for him."

Harriett's breath rushed out in a gale. Gone. Jake was gone. "Where in Oregon did he go?"

"The Willamette Valley. Seems he has some unfinished business there."

"Yes. He does." Gone. How could he have gone without saying good-bye?

"You're taking this very well, my dear. I know you were fond of the man. He was a good sort, in spite of being a bit rough around the edges. Well—more than the edges, actually. I can see that I needn't have worried myself about your reaction, but I debated and debated over the right thing to do . . ."

Edwin droned on while Harriett's mind grew numb. She shouldn't care. Hadn't she wanted Jake out of her life? Now she didn't need to worry that he would appear and sweep her away with some nonsense about love and passion. Now she could get on with her sensible, safe, reasonable life—the life she had always wanted in the world to which she was born.

She shouldn't care. But she did.

"Harriett, dear? Have you been listening?"

"Oh, yes, Edwin. To every word." There was a lie to start out their splendid marriage. How would she bear Edwin's pompousness for the next thirty or so years? How had she failed to notice that as well as being sweet, handsome, considerate, educated, and liberal-minded, Edwin was also pompous. And condescend-

ing. Minor faults, surely, when one considered his
other fine qualities. Minor, but irritating.

"Edwin? Could I be alone for a few minutes?"

He gave her a surprised look. "Of course, my dear. I
will see you at dinner. Remember, eight sharp."

"Yes, Edwin."

The door closed softly behind him. Harriett was
alone. Very alone. Somehow, with Jake still in town,
she hadn't felt alone. Now she felt lonelier than she
had in years. How could he go to Oregon without telling her? Telling Edwin instead, damn him. Damn Edwin! Damn Jake! Damn every man who thought he
knew what was best for a woman and did it without
her consent!

The door latch clicked. Lucille came in, hesitantly.
"Edwin just told me that Jake left."

"He just told me, also," Harriett said sourly. She got
up and paced across the carpet, much as the agitated
Edwin had paced earlier. "Jake didn't even say good-
bye."

Lucille was silent.

"How could he not say good-bye?"

"Maybe he couldn't."

"Spit!" Harriett's skirts swirled around her as she
walked, echoing the agitation in her mind. "He told
me I could never give myself to another man," she
grumbled more to herself than to her aunt. "Then he
up and leaves without so much as a fare-thee-well."
She took a final turn, then plunked herself down into
the chair. "Not a good sport at all! Poor loser."

She frowned at the floor. If they'd been alive, the
flowers on the carpet would have withered under her
glare.

Lucille sat on the bed and regarded her niece with
canny eyes. "Harriett, why are you so upset? You're
marrying Edwin. You wanted Jake to leave you be.
Haven't you gotten everything you wanted?"

Harriett rose, unable to stay still. She crossed to the window and looked out. The day had been fine, but now the fog was rolling in, gray and chill. The chill seemed to melt through the walls of the house and sink into her very bones.

She had gotten everything she wanted, or at least everything she had asked for. Her future stretched away in a barren plain of colorless, featureless years. No battles, no triumphs, no passion. Security, respect, even affection—but no love. And she had brought it upon herself.

Harriett's eyes took on a tinge of gray to match the pallor of her skin. "What have I done?" she asked, a sad whisper. Then louder: "What have I done!" She turned to Lucille as if her aunt held the answer.

"I don't know, dear. What have you done?"

Harriett started to pace again, hands clenched at her sides. "I've botched everything! That's what I've done! Oh, Aunt!" She threw up her hands in despair. "I've been so incredibly stupid!"

"My dear, I've told you that often enough."

"And I should have listened. I think there's a hole where my brain ought to be. And now . . . now my heart, also." Her anger dissolved into despair, and like a puppet whose strings have suddenly been cut, she collapsed onto the bed with tears dribbling down her cheeks. "I won't ever see him again."

"I don't imagine that you will." Lucille scooted closer and took Harriett's hand.

Never to see the sun strike gold off his burnished hair, or to see his eyes crinkle in a smile. Never to see the dimples that appeared in his cheeks with his audacious grin, or hear the soft rumble—sometimes thunder—of his voice when he spoke her name. Never again to see those clear gray eyes darken with desire and feel an answering passion in herself. How could she bear it?

"I see you didn't really want him to go," Lucille guessed.

"I didn't know what I wanted," Harriett wailed. As her aunt's arms went around her she let go a flood of tears onto Lucille's shoulder. "I fell in love with him so long ago," she sobbed, "but I just couldn't give in. I was afraid to lose the part of myself that would belong to him." She sniffed loudly.

"Not to mention all the property and stocks you inherited from your father," Lucille added.

"That too," Harriett admitted in a choked voice. "How was I supposed to know if I could trust him?"

"You could have listened to your heart for a change," Lucille suggested.

Harriett looked up, eyes red, nose running. Lucille handed her a handkerchief. "My heart wasn't talking to me," she said, wiping her face.

"Yes, it was," Lucille told her. "You just didn't listen."

"Lord! I've been such a ninnybrain!" She wiped at her streaming eyes.

Lucille shook her head and rose. Now she took a turn at pacing. "Harriett, I know you're very fond of Edwin, but why on earth did you consent to wed him?"

Harriett sniffed and wiped at her nose. "I told myself that I could make him happy—and that he would protect me from my own foolishness over Jacob." She flushed at the memory of how Jake had frightened her that night of the concert. Or had she been more frightened of herself? She pleated the coverlet of the bed with nervous fingers. "I suppose part of me thought that Jacob would dash in at the last moment like a wild Pawnee and carry me off. Then, you see, I could blame him and not myself if we turned out to be a disaster." Her voice sharpened into self-derision. "Not a very pretty picture of Harriett Foster, is it?"

"Oh, my dear!" Lucille sat down on the bed and took Harriett's cold hands into hers. "Always so serious, with the weight of the world on your shoulders—and now the weight of your own weaknesses as well? Harriett, love, don't berate yourself so. We all make foolish mistakes."

Harriett snorted.

Lucille smiled gently, ruefully. "Some of us make foolish mistakes and get saved from them—like me."

"You?"

"You think yourself foolish? I was hoping to marry Lawrence Steede, even though I knew very well he was nothing but a well-spoken drifter. Good fortune saved me from such foolishness when he flaunted his colors so that even I had to see. But I was certainly saved through no wisdom of my own."

Harriett sniffed back tears that once again threatened. "You're right, I suppose. Everyone makes mistakes. Some people are lucky." Her voice cracked. "Others are caught out by their own damned stupidity."

"Yes, my love." Lucille took Harriett's tear-streaked face by the chin and firmly turned it toward her own. "Some are saved from their foolishness, some are caught out, and some—some very lucky ones—are given a second chance."

"A second chance," Harriett whispered, the idea slowly taking hold.

"You aren't married to Edwin quite yet, dear. It's very safe to say that you love Jake and rail against your own foolishness when he's out of reach. But is he truly out of reach?"

Harriett's mouth twitched in a tentative smile.

"Just how much do you love Jake Carradine?" Lucille asked, one brow arched in challenge.

A gleam appeared in Harriett's eye.

21

Homer Kane looked up and saw a ghost leaning casually against the door frame to his office. His mouth fell open, and his hand reached instinctively to the top drawer of his desk for the pistol he always kept there.

"Don't go for your gun, Homer." Jake Carradine sent Kane a smile that was anything but friendly. "I'd hate to kill you before we get a chance to talk."

"I thought you was—"

"Dead," Jake supplied. "So did I for a while, but I wasn't, as you can see."

"Shit!"

Jake twitched a brow. "Glad to see you're so happy about my fine health." He pushed himself off the door frame and sauntered into the room. "You've changed it a bit." Cold gray eyes wandered over the oak paneling, fine carpet, and etched-glass lamps. "When this was the Carradine mill, we didn't have all these fancy fixings in the office. Just plank floors and log walls. Must have done right well for yourself, Homer. I hear lumber hit three hundred dollars in San Francisco during the peak—a hundred and fifty at the mill. That's a mite better than the forty we were getting before the gold."

A muscle in Kane's jaw twitched; his hand still lingered close to the gun drawer. He cursed himself for carelessness; someone should have put some extra lead into Jake Carradine on that night, just to be sure. Leaving a man like him alive was like leaving a stick of dynamite with the fuse lit—and then sticking it down your pants. Sooner or later you were going to be sorry.

"So you're back," Kane said quietly. "Figger to kill yourself some Kanes?"

Jake shook his head and smiled again—a smile that made shivers run down Kane's spine. "Now, Homer, if I'd wanted to kill you, I could've just walked in here and blown you to hell. No one would stop me. There's still not enough law around here to matter, and I don't figure that many of your neighbors would've gotten too upset about it. But I made a bargain with someone a while ago. Part of the deal was leaving you alive."

"You maybe oughta worry about keepin' yourself alive, Carradine. I gotta whole crew . . ."

"That's out in the timber. And one man in the mill yard." Jake grinned. "I checked."

Homer's jaw tightened; his hand, concealed behind the desk, inched ever closer to the gun drawer.

"Want to take me on yourself, Homer?" Jake held his arms out from his sides. "I welcome you to try it. God, I wish you would."

The overconfident son of a bitch was asking for it, Homer thought, and Homer Kane was just the man to give it to him. "You think I'm a fool?" he asked in a conciliatory voice. His fingers urged the drawer out a little at a time. "You don't make trouble and I got no fight with you, Carradine. You got no proof that me or my boys had anything to do with your family gettin' burned. 'Ceptin' maybe the word of a damned half-breed, an' nobody's gonna listen to him."

Jake's eyes were fixed on Homer's face. Seemingly at ease, he stood not five feet from the desk, a perfect target for the slug that Homer was going to send his way. Killing Jake Carradine was going to be easy, almost too easy to be satisfying. Homer's hand curled around the butt of the pistol, sliding it forward. His thumb touched the hammer.

Then suddenly he was staring down the business end of Jake's Navy .44. Homer froze, his pistol still half in the drawer. One instant Carradine had just been standing there, and the next his gun was in hand, cocked, ready to blow a hole in Kane's forehead. Homer hadn't even seen it happen.

"It would feel good to blow you through the back wall," Jake said.

Jake's trigger finger grew white with strain. Homer's breathing almost stopped. All he could see was the unwavering muzzle of the gun pointed at his head. It looked hungry. The gray eyes behind it looked equally hungry, and were just as unwavering.

"But"—Jake pointed the pistol toward the ceiling— "a promise is a promise."

Homer drew his first real breath in several minutes. With the next breath he vowed that Jake Carradine was going to regret the day he'd returned.

"However," Jake said, "I didn't promise that you would live happily ever after." He gave Homer a speculative look that was full of menace. "You're not going to make another dollar from the lumber business. That's another promise I intend to keep. And you're going to be sorry that you ever messed with the Carradine family."

Plans were already whirling in Homer's fertile mind. Carradine was a fool for not finishing this when he had the chance. And fools were easy targets.

Jake chuckled at the look on Kane's face. "I'm not as easy to kill as Elijah and Josh, Homer. They didn't have a mean bone between the two of them, and I've got nothing but. You can't take me, old man, not you, nor your sons, nor all your goddamned crew. You're welcome to try." He settled his pistol back into its holster, as if Homer were no threat at all.

Homer was tempted to raise his gun, but the chilling look in Jake's eyes froze his hand.

"Just wanted you to know who's going to be behind your fall, Homer. Have a nice day thinking about it."

Jake left as casually as he had appeared, no ghost at all. But the flesh-and-blood man frightened Kane more than any apparition. Though what could Carradine do against the Kane power? He was one man. Just one man—a man whose days were numbered.

Homer started breathing again and bellowed for the yardman to find Rufus and Nathaniel. Kanes had killed Carradines before. One more shouldn't be a problem.

The hills were still black with Oregon pine. A stream still splashed between rocky banks on its way to the Willamette River. Yet to Jake, who had lived and worked there for two years, the little valley seemed naked without the log cabin that had stood on the hillside above the creek. Charred remnants marked the spot, a blackened skeleton of what had once been a home. Ferns and tiny sapling trees had sprouted where Elijah had once slept with his wife, grass and weeds covered the spot where Jake and his brother and nephew had eaten their meals. A rusting wood stove was now a home for squirrels.

Jake urged Thunder down the hillside, following the overgrown path that once led to the house. Amos came behind on his stocky Appaloosa mare. They reined to a halt a hundred feet from the cabin site, at the little spring that once had supplied the Carradines with drinking and washing water.

"Ain't nothing more to see down here, Jake." Amos's hand rested uneasily on the butt of his holstered pistol, as if Homer Kane and his sons still milled in the clearing, torches held high.

Jake shook his head, his face dark. "Not even a proper grave."

The place repelled him, made his stomach rise into his throat. But something had made him swing by the old cabin site. Penance, he supposed grimly. Penance for Elijah and Joshua, who were now one with the ashes and soil, perhaps a part of the saplings that had sprung to life where death had taken such a toll. Only parts of the bodies had been found, and those charred and twisted past recognition. A plain wooden cross had marked the grave where Amos had laid what few remains he and the mill crew had found, but now even the cross was gone—destroyed by Kanes, no doubt. Those vultures didn't want any mark of the Carradines to remain on this land.

"They're not here, Jake. They're somewhere else, somewhere good. You won't be helpin' 'em by openin' old wounds."

"I plan to open some new ones as well," Jake said stonily.

Harry suddenly walked uninvited into Jake's mind. She wouldn't approve of what he was doing, would no doubt give him a lecture on leaving revenge to the Almighty and concentrating on nobler pursuits. Harry didn't understand hatred. Her soul was too gentle for such things. She had never been haunted by ghosts who wouldn't rest until an old wrong was righted.

But Harry wasn't there to fume and fluster. Harry was another man's wife, finally safe from Jake Carradine.

"You look like you're itchin' to kill somebody, Jake."

"I'm not aiming to kill anybody," Jake snapped. "I just want the Kanes so miserable they'll wish they never heard the name Carradine."

Amos scowled. "Well, I figger you know what miserable is. You been doing nuthin' but growlin' and gritchin' since you got back. Just the same, I ain't never seen matters like this get settled without somebody's blood gettin' spilled."

"Somebody's blood has already been spilled," Jake reminded his friend. "Several somebodies. All Carradines."

"They still got the men and the money. You got nuthin'."

"I've got something. Like you said once before, Amos—I've got a devil riding my shoulders." Jake slid his pistol from its holster and sighted down the barrel. "The Kanes started this game," he said. "A Carradine is going to finish it."

That thought should have given Jake satisfaction, but it didn't. Somehow his heart still felt hollow.

Astoria had been wet with fog and drizzle when Harriett's ship made landfall there. Several hours up the Columbia River, Milton had looked much the same. Farther inland yet, Portland huddled under clouds that seemed to brush the treetops. But at least the drizzle had stopped.

When Harriett stepped ashore from the sailing brig *Wakula*, a ship of the Crosby & Smith's Regular Packet Line to Oregon, the air smelled of mist and evergreens —fresher somehow than San Francisco. The waterfront was busy, but not frantic, and what she could see of Portland beyond the wharves seemed better ordered than the frenetic shantytown metropolis she had left a few days ago.

Captain Sherwood appeared at Harriett's side. "Here you are, Miss Foster. I've written down the name of the boardinghouse and the widow woman who runs the place. Anyone can tell you how to find it —up Washington Street a ways. It's a very respectable

place, and much cleaner than any of the hotels. Tell
Mrs. Kerry that Asa Sherwood sent you around."

Harriett took the proffered slip of paper. "You've
been so kind, Captain Sherwood. Thank you again."

"It's been a pleasure, miss." He eyed her pantaloons
in mild amusement, his salt-and-pepper beard twitching with a smile. "Always glad to see decent young
women with spunk come into the territory. Keeps us
men in line, you know. Hope that young man of yours
appreciates such a fine lady as yourself."

She gave him a startled look.

"Didn't have to tell me, Miss Foster. Seen the look in
your eye, I did. You make sure that man of yours takes
care of you, you hear?"

While Captain Sherwood whistled a hackney over,
Harriett mused on her lack of offense at the notion
that "her man" should take care of her. All this time
she hadn't realized that she did need taking care of.
She needed Jacob. And Jacob needed her in equal
measure—if he hadn't already gotten his fool head
blown off. Perhaps they could take care of each other.

Captain Sherwood handed her into the carriage.
"We'll be here in Portland for two days. Any time you
want to send someone round for the rest of your baggage will be fine." He gave her a fatherly smile. "You
take care now, miss."

Widow Kerry's boardinghouse was as spotless and
warm as the captain had promised. The flowered
chintz coverlet on Harriett's bed matched the curtains
at the window, and a faded but clean rag rug added
warmth to the plank floor. A damp breeze blew the
scent of evergreens into the room, along with the rattle
of wagons, jingle of harnesses, and voices of passersby
from the busy street.

Harriett looked out the open window. Under gray
clouds she could see the Columbia River flowing past
mast-studded wharves on its way to the sea. On either

side of the river were hills carpeted with a forest of fir, oak, and maple, rising gradually until they disappeared into clouds and mist.

Closer at hand, Portland stretched back from the river. Wagons, buggies, horses, and pedestrians all slogged through muddy streets, winding their way around unremoved stumps of trees that had been cut down to make room for the burgeoning town.

She liked Oregon, Harriett decided suddenly. These people were more solid than the California gold-rushers. They weren't down-and-outers desperate to find gold and rich merchants trying to live like aristocrats in a city that was all mud and cholera and fire. The people in the street below were lumbermen, farmers, merchants—many of them were here to stay, to build a new land. One could feel the energy and enthusiasm rising up from the street below like heat rising from a stove.

Harriett drew the curtains closed and stretched out on the bed. Afternoon had just begun, but she was exhausted. How quickly her life had swung about! She could still not quite comprehend the change. Only days ago she had been in San Francisco feeling the lead weight of marriage to Edwin slowly sink down upon her shoulders. And now hardly a week later she was in Oregon, feeling light and careless as a skylark. The *Wakula* had covered in a few days a distance it had taken her weeks to travel with oxen and wagon.

Edwin had been his usual understanding self when Harriett had explained her decision. He had merely nodded his head sagely, making her feel like a child seeking her father's blessing.

"I thought the wind might blow Mr. Carradine's way," he had said with a rueful shake of his head. "He seems a good man, all in all. Rough, but good nevertheless." He'd given her a canny look. "Are you sure that you want to do this, dear? You don't have to run to

Carradine to escape me, you know. With your wealth there's no need for you to marry at all if it's not your wish."

She squeezed his hand. "For once I have truly made up my mind, Edwin. I love Jacob Carradine, and I'm going to find him."

Lucille had volunteered to take good care of Chad, Indy, and Dodger until Harriett returned, though Chad stubbornly insisted he was plenty old enough to take care of himself. As aunt and niece kissed good-bye at the dock, Lucille promised also to take excellent care of Edwin. Excellent care, Lucille repeated to Harriett, eyes atwinkle. Harriett guessed that Edwin's just-restored hopes of continued bachelorhood were about to be snatched away before he could enjoy them.

A knock sounded on the door. "It's Mrs. Kerry," a voice said. "Are you quite settled yet, Miss Foster?"

Harriett swung herself off the bed and smoothed the wrinkles from her skirt. "Come in, Mrs. Kerry."

The widow bustled in. Her eyes swept the room as if looking for anything out of order. With her tightly bound light brown hair, round face, flour-smudged apron, and buxom figure, Widow Kerry looked like Harriett's image of the frontier mother. Of course, her own mother had been redheaded like Harriett, with a slender figure and snapping blue eyes. And baking flour had never come near a garment Catherine Penn Foster wore. For the first time in her life Harriett wondered how it might have been to have a mother who cared more for home life and children than the burning social issues of the nation.

"Unpacked already?" Widow Kerry noted approvingly. "My, Miss Foster, you are a tidy one, aren't you." The woman's face grew even rounder as she smiled.

Harriett couldn't resist a smile in return.

"Well, my dear. I wouldn't have disturbed you—I

know you must be simply exhausted after spending days on Mr. Sherwood's ship. Myself, I get seasick just thinking of such travel, but I imagine a young thing like you has a sturdier constitution."

The widow looked no less sturdy than an ox, Harriett thought in silent amusement. "I confess I spent a few undignified hours at the railing, Mrs. Kerry. We seem to share an affliction."

"Oh, my goodness! You poor child. Has your stomach quite righted itself yet?"

"I'm very grateful to be on dry land," Harriett admitted.

"I must bring up some of my special tea. That will settle you right up, my dear. Oh, tea! That reminds me. You were asking after the Kanes earlier?"

What tea had to do with Kanes, Harriett couldn't guess. But she had asked the widow about both Jake Carradine and Homer Kane when she had first come in. The woman had known nothing about Jake, but the Kanes, Mrs. Kerry had told Harriett, were a very prosperous lumber family with a mill downstream of the Falls of the Willamette, between Portland and Oregon City. Homer Kane's two sons were no-accounts, the widow had confided, seeming delighted to voice her opinion. The old man wasn't much better. They were an untidy, wild lot, and in spite of all the money they threw at merchants in both Oregon City and Portland, they weren't much admired.

The widow had stopped her chatter with a bright-eyed inquiry. "You aren't a friend of the Kanes, are you, dear?"

Harriett had the feeling that if she'd answered yes, she would have had to look for a room elsewhere, in spite of Asa Sherwood's recommendation.

Widow Kerry crossed to the window and brushed aside the curtain. "Since you were asking about the Kanes, dear, I thought you would be interested that

the boys just rode into town." She peered down the
street as Harriett came to look out. "I don't see them
now. They must have passed on by. Me and my chatter. My husband used to say that I'll be gossiping away
when the Good Lord returns and miss the Judgment
Day itself."

Harriett was eager. The characters of Jake's drama
were finally coming alive, bringing her closer to Jake
himself. "Do the Kanes often come to Portland? I
thought you said they lived close to Oregon City."

"Oh, that's not so far away. They do most of their
business here in Portland. The two boys especially
come here a lot. I'd say they're headed for the bank,
then the mercantile, and they'll wind up in one of the
saloons." Her voice was dark with disapproval. "Like I
said earlier, they're wild ones. Isn't a decent woman in
town that won't cross the street to stay out of their
way."

"Where is the bank?" Harriett reached for her bonnet and wool shawl. She met the widow's frown with a
determined thrust of her jaw. "I'm looking for a man
who has business with the Kanes. They might be able
to tell me where to find him."

Widow Kerry relented reluctantly. She pointed
down the muddy street to an imposing two-story frame
building. "You stay on the right side of the street, now,
you hear. The other side's got all the gambling parlors
and saloons, and other places a young lady like yourself shouldn't even know about. This is a good town,
but that stretch down there isn't a place for a lady to
be walking alone."

Harriett wondered what Mrs. Kerry would say if she
could have seen Mrs. Hornsby's wagonload of "entertainers" in the Indiana Company, or if she could have
listened in on the evenings when the salty madam herself had attended Harriett's combination reading lessons and ladies' discussions.

"I'll be very careful," she promised. "But I can't think of any other way to locate Mr. Carradine."

As Harriett left the boardinghouse, the object of her search was enjoying a whiskey in the Half Moon Saloon. Back to the wall, feet comfortably propped up on the table in front of him, Jake indulged himself in a bit of grim satisfaction for the progress of the last two weeks.

The Kane timber operation had hit a few snags—all named Carradine. Their upper holding dam had blown up, the waterwheel at the sawmill had collapsed (almost as if its supports had been axed), their remuda of mules had spooked and knocked down the main corral, and a wagon hitch had snapped—sending a load of logs careening down the wagon track to the mill. Word was that a third of the Kane crew had walked off the job, saying the operation was jinxed—a jinx by the name of Jake Carradine, with the help of Amos Walking Horse.

All that was only the beginning. Jake and Amos had ridden into Portland to do a little damage to the business end of the operation. Already merchants who had heard of the Kane troubles were scrutinizing the Kane accounts. In spite of their wealth, the Kanes weren't well liked. Only a little push was needed to get most of Portland to deny them credit. Jake and Amos had provided that push, with the help of a few prominent bankers who remembered the Carradine family. The jinx had struck again. Soon, in addition to all their other problems, the Kanes were going to bog down in a swamp of poor cash flow.

The sight of Kanes floundering was sweet indeed, but Jake wondered if being a jinx was enough. Almost every day he returned to the cabin site and stared at the blackened remnants. He itched to fight, to see his family's murder repaid in Kane blood. But he'd made a promise to an empty-seeming sky when Harry had almost died, and he was a man who kept his promises. Usually.

This promise he had to keep. As if the Almighty watching him weren't enough, every time Jake's hand drifted close to his pistol, Harry marched into his mind, arms crossed disapprovingly, brow lifted in rebuke, and one foot tapping out a disparaging tattoo. Early in his life Jake had become an expert at ignoring his conscience, but now it had grown red hair and green eyes, soft lips and a sprinkling of freckles. He could ignore it no more than he could ignore Harry herself.

He downed another swallow of whiskey. Somehow this attack of redheaded conscience seemed unfair. He'd done the noble thing and set Harry free. Why wouldn't she set him free as well?

The doors to the saloon creaked and swung open. Jake looked up, expecting to see Amos walk in. Instead, he saw Nate and Rufus Kane shouldering their way toward his table, an ugly gleam in their eyes. Jake's heart leapt. He grinned with pure joy. Finally he was going to get his fight. Even that damned redheaded conscience couldn't object to him defending himself.

"We got business with you, Carradine." Rufus strutted up to the table belly-first, which, given his mountainous build, was how Rufus did everything.

Jake's grin grew broader. "I take it you boys have been to the bank."

"Think you're smart, don'tcha?" Nate sneered. "You think we don't know who's behind everything that's been goin' on?"

Jake cocked a jaunty brow. "Glad to take the credit, boys. As I remember, I even gave your pa fair warning."

One of the numerous flies that patronized the Half

Moon Saloon chose that moment to come buzzing around the table. Rufus grinned and made a lightning swipe that defied his ponderous size. The buzzing abruptly stopped.

"You think you got us runnin'?" he chortled. "You're nothing more than a pesky fly." He squeezed his hand mightily, then opened it to show the spot of goo on his palm. "You see what Kanes do to pesky flies."

Jake obligingly looked at the mess. "You've gone down in the world, Rufus. Used to be your pa let you murder peace-loving men and five-year-old kids. Now you've been relegated to flyswatter."

Rufus's face grew red; a muscle in his jaw twitched.

"You gonna come out and fight like a man, or do we swat you like a fly?" Nate offered.

"Swat away, if you think you can."

"Damned smartass!"

Rufus drew. With a push of his foot, Jake sent the table crashing against both Kanes. Before they could recover their balance, Jake kicked the pistol from Rufus's hand, then whirled and grabbed Nate's wrist as Nate clutched at his gun.

"Shame on you for wanting to shoot up this respectable place of business!" Jake admonished with a crooked smile. He recovered both pistols and threw them, along with his own, to the bartender. "Keep these for a few minutes, will you, Charlie?"

"Whatever you say, Jake." Charlie grinned in anticipation of entertainment. His customers left their card games, set down their drinks, and pushed aside their bought women to watch the action.

"We don't need guns for the likes of you," Nate boasted.

Rufus crouched, his posture reminiscent of an overweight gorilla's. Jake's grin had disappeared, but his eyes gleamed in grim delight. "Come on, Kanes. Let's shed a little blood for the good ol' days."

Both Kanes sprang at once. Jake brought up both fists and drove into two bellies at the same time. His victims doubled over. He came to their aid and straightened them both with an undercut to their chins.

Nate staggered back, groaned, then recovered and charged forward just as Rufus managed to grasp Jake in a bear hug that all but broke his ribs. Jake met Nate's advance with a bruising kick and at the same time drove his elbow into Rufus's gut. Rufus let go abruptly, and Jake landed in a heap on the floor, his ribs still creaking. Nate kicked out viciously, but Jake caught his ankle and twisted. Nate crashed to the floor.

"Two on one!" someone cried from the audience. "That ain't exactly fair!"

"Five bucks says the tall one wins!"

"You're on."

"I'll give three-to-one odds on the Kanes!" another cried.

"You ain't got the money to buy your own drinks! Shaddup!"

"Shut up yourself!"

The clamor increased as the Half Moon customers watched Jake, Nate, and Rufus kick, punch, gouge, jab, and otherwise maim each other. Inevitably someone decided the three brawlers were having all the fun. Someone threw a glass at someone else, another took a wild swing, and within moments the whole saloon erupted in an uproar, scrapping just for the sheer hellish fun of it.

Jake didn't even notice what went on around him. All his fury was focused on the Kanes. The pain of their blows didn't register, only the satisfaction of feeling his fists crash into muscle and bone and seeing the scarlet of his enemies' blood. That he was equally covered in blood didn't matter. He gave vent to the hatred that had driven him for the last year. The fire that had burned within him, almost destroying him, now flared out to sear the Kanes, and they gave way before its fury.

Rufus went down under Jake's hammerlike blows. He didn't rise. Nate was about to suffer the same fate when Jake froze. He jerked erect, eyes wide and unbelieving. There in the door stood his conscience come to life—red hair, green eyes, freckles, and all. His gaze met hers in wide-eyed astonishment just as Nate's fist connected solidly with his jaw.

"Jacob!"

Jake heard the cry even as he bounced off the plank floor. He opened his eyes to see a redheaded angel of vengeance grab a chair, lift it high in both hands, and clobber Nate from behind. Nate dropped like a felled tree.

Jake groaned and eased his head back to the floor. His conscience walked over to where he lay, peered down at him, straightened, and shook her head. Arms crossed disapprovingly, brow lifted in rebuke, foot tapping out a disparaging tattoo, she spoke.

"Jake Carradine. It seems every time I'm out looking for a man, you get tossed at my feet."

22

"The first time I saw you, you were brawling," Harriett said with a smile. Jake leaned on her arm as they emerged onto the street outside. "Can't you find a better way to entertain yourself?"

Jake didn't ask what she was doing in Oregon. Somehow, in the depths of his heart, he knew. He straightened, lifting her left hand. The absence of a wedding ring made him grin. The smile she gave him in return answered every question.

"Come on." He pulled her along with him as he headed toward his hotel, suddenly charged with energy in spite of bruises, a cut eyebrow, and raw knuckles.

"Jacob! Wait! Where are we going? Who were those men in the saloon? Shouldn't we find the sheriff?"

"There's no sheriff here, Harry."

"But . . . !"

"And for once"—he swung her around to face him in the middle of the street—"stop talking. You've delivered yourself into my hands, lady. And now you're going to suffer the consequences. One noble sacrifice is about all I have in me. You're not about to get a second chance."

Harriett's eyes widened as he bent down to kiss her

in full view of every passerby. "Jacob!" she whispered furiously when he gave her back her mouth.

Jake arched a brow in appreciation of the sudden surge of color to her face. "Unless you want to be tumbled in full view of Portland, we'd better hurry along."

Her eyes widened even further, but an impish gleam in their green depths gave him all the encouragement he needed.

The clerk at the Oregonian Hotel sputtered when Jake headed for the stairs with Harriett in tow. "Mr. Carradine! No women are allowed . . . !"

"It's all right, Joe. She's my wife!"

"What a bald-faced lie!" Harriett looked as though she didn't know whether to laugh or cry. Jake didn't give her time to decide. He closed the door to his hotel room and, with a slam of finality, fastened the bolt.

"It'll be true in an hour or so. Like I said, you're not getting a second chance."

"Jake, I—"

"Quiet." He moved behind her and worked loose the buttons of her bodice. "Time for that later. I've been wanting you so long I ache inside and out."

"I only wanted to say that I love you."

Jake hesitated. He turned her around so that he could look into her eyes. "I always knew you loved me, Harry. But sometimes I thought you'd never admit it."

She reached out to touch his face, to run a finger down the groove that sculpted his cheek and chin. "I confess that I do love you past anything."

Jake scarcely dared to breathe for fear he would wake and find he was dreaming. "Do you know how much I love you?" he asked softly.

Harriett smiled, a smile of a girl become a woman. "Enough to marry me. To give me children in the joy of our souls and bodies. Enough to put up with my fears and foibles—and my lectures."

"And more," Jake whispered. His hands moved to

her waistband, and Harriett's skirt and petticoat fell in
a pool around her hips. He pulled her against him and
slipped his fingers into the top of her pantaloons,
slowly, ever so slowly, peeling them down from her
hips.

"I'm beginning to like these things," he confessed
against her ear. "Just like eating an orange, with a
treat underneath that stubborn peel."

He felt her face grow hot where it rested against his
chest. Laughing softly, he smoothed his hands around
her buttocks. Her skin was like silk. He would never
get enough of the feel of her under his hands. Slowly
he caressed, until he felt her stiff form relax against
him. His fingers ventured fleetingly into the cleft between her legs and met with moist, warm invitation.

She moaned, her face buried in his chest. The sound
sent a knife-sharp stab of desire into his groin, which
was already swollen with need.

"God, woman! What you do to me!"

With almost frantic haste Jake picked her up and
deposited her on the bed. He ripped at his own clothes
and hurriedly rid Harriett of the remainder of hers.
Rock-hard and huge, he ached to bury himself inside
her waiting softness. She lay before him, all his at last,
thighs slightly parted in acquiescence, nipples erect
with passion, eyes dark with love. Suddenly, hot as he
was, Jake wanted her to understand that this act was
more than bodies joining, flesh pleasuring flesh. This
was not just a woman on his bed; she was his Harry—
special, beloved. She'd come to him at last, and he
wanted to show her just how loved she was.

Jake covered her with his body, supporting himself
on knees and elbows. With one knee he nudged her
thighs farther apart.

She closed her eyes. "Jake," she sighed.

"Harry."

"I love you."

He bent to take a nipple in his mouth, teased and tortured until she surged against his hard thigh. "I adore you," he said, "lectures and all. And I'm going to teach you what love means. This is just a start."

He rolled off her. Harriett tried to roll with him, but he gently pushed her onto her back and pinned her there with one strong arm. He leaned to possess her lips while his fingers slipped inside her, first one, then two. She moaned into his mouth as he thrust and withdrew, thrust and withdrew, echoing the rhythm with his tongue.

"Oh, Jake! Please."

"You want something?" he chuckled. He kissed her nose, her chin, her throat, and then moved to her breast, where his tongue gently teased as his fingers worked their implacable torture of ecstasy between her legs. She bucked against his hand and then climaxed in frenzied spasms. Her cry of joy he swallowed with a fierce kiss.

Harriett lay in limp aftermath while Jake painted a *J* on her belly with the moisture clinging to his fingers. "You belong to me, Harry. I offered to let you go, but now you've given yourself up to me."

She reached out to touch his chest, ran her finger down his ribs to his taut belly, and smiled beatifically. "So I have."

He caught her hand and pinned it to the bed. Much more of that and he was going to bust.

"Does that still frighten you?" he asked softly.

"Yes." She turned dark emerald eyes up to his. "Wouldn't it frighten you?"

"But you're here."

"I'm here. You're stuck with me, God help you."

"He already did."

She reached up and pulled him to her for a kiss.

"I swear I'll never hurt you," he murmured against her throat. "I'll never use you, or what's yours."

She put a finger to his lips. "All I have is yours. Everything I am is yours. I belong to you, just as you, Jacob Carradine, belong to me." She smiled slowly and rubbed her thigh suggestively against his. "And I could use some of you right now, I think." A glint of mischief twinkled in her eyes. Her hand closed around him, ending the possibility of all the vows he wanted to make to her. He could feel himself grow even harder at her touch. "We're not finished, are we?" she asked with a throaty chuckle.

"Not nearly," he groaned.

She welcomed him with parted thighs, wrapping her slim legs around his hips as he thrust. He tried to be gentle; he couldn't. He tried for her sake to go slowly, but desire ripped his good intentions to shreds, and Harriett finished the job by meeting him thrust for thrust with an eagerness that matched his own. Jake gripped her buttocks and sealed her to him as he swelled with power, with animal satisfaction, and finally exploded inside her with brutal force, sensing at the same time the joyful pulses of her own climax.

Rigid with ecstasy, Harriett let herself be swallowed into the maelstrom of Jake's power. Joy allowed no fear. Sweet fulfillment banished doubt. Harriett was finally complete, whole as she'd never been in her life. Seducing her with desire, surrounding her with passion, and teaching her, finally, the truth of love, Jake had chained her and set her free at the same time.

Two hours later Jake and Harriett stood before the local part-time preacher, whom they'd rousted from his job as carpenter and towed to the one-room frame schoolhouse that doubled as a church.

"I don't see what the dag-blamed hurry is," the preacher complained. He glanced at Harriett, prim and proper in a green wool gabardine dress she'd bought in San Francisco. Head properly bonneted, hands folded meekly at her waist, pantaloons conspicuously absent, she looked a picture of maidenly modesty. "Doesn't look like an emergency to me. Couldn't this wait until Sunday?"

"Preacher Hobbs, you don't know how fast this lady can change her mind." Jake squeezed Harriett's hand, his eyes crinkled in silent laughter.

"All right. Let's get this done, then. I've another cabinet to finish today."

"Oh! This is so romantic!" Widow Kerry had been hastily commandeered as a witness. She'd been gushing sloppy romance ever since Harriett pulled her from the boardinghouse.

Amos was in attendance also, though his status as a legal witness was in question because of his race. Unsmiling in the best Indian tradition, his eyes gave him away. His ugly face almost broke into a grin when Harriett gave him a spontaneous hug.

A few moments later Preacher Hobbs pronounced Jake Carradine and Harriett Foster man and wife. He closed his service book with an emphatic snap. "Now may I go finish my cabinets?" he asked with exaggerated civility.

"Be my guest." Jake had eyes only for Harriett.

"In that case, you may kiss the bride." He gave the couple a tolerant smile, nodded to the widow and Amos, and took his leave.

Jake took the preacher's suggestion. His lips lowered almost reverently to Harriett's mouth. The widow, watching with a plump-cheeked smile, sighed and clasped her hands.

Harriett allowed her head to fall back into Jake's supporting hand. His mouth moved over hers in gentle affection, not passion, but she could feel a hot spark ignite in the core of her. The same spark was dancing in Jake's gray eyes as he drew back and looked down at her. He kissed her again—a quick brush of his lips.

"Tonight," he promised for her ears alone.

She touched the groove in his cheek, smiling. Tonight she would sleep with her husband, a wife, under
the law little better than a slave. But she didn't feel like
a slave. She felt like queen of all the world.

Amos cleared his throat. Widow Kerry's sigh was
soupier than ever.

"I think this calls for a celebration," Jake suggested.

Arm around Harriett's waist, he led the foursome
out of the schoolhouse and into the fading afternoon,
where the long shadows concealed a bruised Rufus
and Nate Kane standing in an alley across the street.

"I tol' ya Carradine went in there!" Rufus growled.
"Preacher Hobbs was with 'em. That asshole up an'
got himself hitched! Whaddya bet?"

"Too bad, pretty little girl." Nate smiled toward the
lady in green. "You're gonna be a widow woman
soon."

Rufus's meaty brow wrinkled in thought. "I've got a
better idea," he finally said.

What did men do when they prepared for their wedding night? Harriett wondered. She sat on the bed in
Jake's hotel room, brushing her hair with slow, soothing strokes. Mrs. Kerry's establishment did not allow
couples, so they had fetched Harriett's one satchel
from the boardinghouse, then Jake had kissed her and
left with Amos to collect the rest of her baggage from
the *Wakula*—while she prepared for her first night as a
wife.

Harriett climbed down from the bed, padded barefoot to the window, and looked out to the dark street.
She let the curtain fall back into place and returned to
stand by the bed. But her nerves would not be still. The
hotel room suddenly seemed a cage. Five paces in one
direction and six in the other. Restlessly she paced,
then stopped before the cracked mirror on the dresser.
The image staring back at her was pale. Freckles stood

out like beacons on her nose and cheeks, and her hair, released from its severe bun, curled around her face in a red halo before falling in fiery waves to her waist. A plain cotton robe fell open at the neck to reveal the lacy trim on her nightgown—a fanciful thing she'd bought for her honeymoon with Edwin. Would Jacob like it? Would he continue to like her, or discover some disappointing little detail he hadn't noticed before? She couldn't recall if he'd ever seen her hair loose and brushed before—the color didn't look quite so unfashionably red when it was confined. And they had never been together in a real bed—on a bed only this afternoon, but never in one as true lovers and companions. Would it make a difference?

Harriett sighed, sat back down on the bed, and resumed her brushing. Why was she so nervous? She wasn't a virgin bride who feared her husband's touch. The torrent of Jake's passion was familiar territory, and her own response a thing of joy instead of fear. The moment she had seen Jake again—even brawling, sporting a bloody nose and bruised face, looking like a mad bull—even then she had known she couldn't do without him. And Jake himself—he'd taken her back without a word of rebuke, as if he'd known all along she would come to him. All those hours of worry over how he would greet her! And here she was, only hours after finding him again, sitting in his hotel room waiting for her wedding night. A wife, in spirit and truth as well as law. A wife.

She put down her brush and hugged her knees to her chest, hoping that Jake would come back soon. For the first time in her life she felt sorry for her parents. The respect and lukewarm affection that had been the measure of their relationship seemed pitiful beside what she had with Jacob.

The door latch rattled. Her husband had returned! Harriett sprang up from the bed to launch herself into his arms. Only to jerk back when the door swung open and a pair of ruffians stood framed in the doorway. Black eyes, split lips, and swollen jaws testified that they were the men who had fought Jake in the saloon.

"Evenin', missus." The bigger one tipped his hat while his smaller companion leered. "I be Rufus Kane, and this here's my brother Nate."

Dawn was only a promise in the east as Jake reined his horse to a halt atop the hill. Below him, a darker splotch in the dark valley, the Kane cargo mill—formerly the Carradine mill—squatted on the bank of Tanner Creek. The waterwheel was still, locked on its axle. The whole valley was quiet except for the splash of the creek as it danced its way down to the Willamette. Even the birds were not yet awake.

Jake reached into his jacket pocket and pulled out a slip of paper. The scrawled contents were burned into his memory—*Carradine. Come to the mill to fetch your wife. First light. You for her. No tricks. Come alone.* No need to read it again. No need even to have it in his pocket. But crushing the note in his hand gave him some satisfaction—the feel of the paper crumpling down to a twisted little ball. He'd like to do the same to the Kanes.

Glancing up, Jake grimaced. The sky was still bright with stars. "All promises are off," he growled to Whomever up there might be listening. Inside him was a killing rage, red-eyed, crouched, teeth bared, ready to spring the moment Jake released the iron vise of will that was holding the monster back. No matter what the cost, the Kanes were not going to harm another of his loved ones. They might find a way to kill Jake Carradine. But they were not going to hurt Harry.

His mount shifted and whuffed, its breath puffing out steam in the cold air. The eastern sky was finally growing light. Jake wondered if Amos was in place.

They had spent the better part of the night planting dynamite in strategic locations around the mill and yard. Jake was no stranger to private wars. As a hired gun, war was how he had earned his pay. His own private war had been delayed long enough. Now was the time to see some Kane blood. And perhaps pay for it with some of his own—but not with Harry's.

Time dragged slowly. The night faded to gray and then to the pale rose of dawn. A first hint of sunlight filtered through the trees to touch the mill. The valley woke; the trees came alive with birdsong. Tendrils of fog snaked through the brush, slowly retreating before morning's advance, and little Tanner Creek began to wink and sparkle in the sun. Soon the mill crew would appear to man the saws. By then, Jake knew, it would all be over.

Finally the door swung open—slowly, cautiously. Homer's pistol appeared first, then Homer himself. His eyes scanned the yard, the valley, then came to rest on Jake sitting atop his horse on the hillside. Homer grinned and gestured with his gun for Jake to ride down.

Jake urged his horse forward. The Kanes were going to kill him, or at least try to kill him. And he wasn't fool enough to think they would release Harry. They thought they held all the cards in this game. But Jake was going to cheat.

"Nice of you to drop by, Carradine," Homer spat as Jake dismounted. "We were about to feed your little lady to the saws."

Kane held out his hand, a nasty smile twisting his face. Jake unbuckled his gun belt and handed it over. "Little spitfire she is," Homer smirked. "My boys had to knock her around a bit before she turned sensible."

Jake kept his face stony. He looked down the barrel of his own gun as Homer took it from its holster and thumbed back the hammer.

"They wanted to do a mite more—you young fellas are always thinkin' with your peckers. But I says to 'em that we got bigger prey in the woods. Can't be messin' with the bait until the trap springs shut." Kane's face darkened. "You ain't givin' us no more trouble, boy. No more trouble at all."

Jake preceded Homer into the building. Kane nudged him past the office and into the mill itself, where the saws sat in strange silence, no lumber to chew on, and Rufus and Nate stood holding Harry between them. She looked battered, defiant, and achingly beautiful, but at the sight of him her head dropped in despair.

"Well, now, boys," Homer crowed. "For once you had a good idea run through your empty heads. Here's Mr. Jake Carradine himself, come to fetch his bride."

The sons snickered. Harriett looked up. Her eyes flashed green, begging Jake to run. The only comfort he could offer her was a smile.

"That's just dandy," Rufus rumbled. "Can we have 'er now?"

"I don't see why not, boys." Homer shoved the snout of the pistol against Jake's temple. "For all the trouble Carradine has caused us, I think he should watch you both humpin' on his wife before we send 'im to Hell."

Jake's fists clenched at his sides. Where the devil was Amos?

As if in answer, an explosion shook the mill. The saws whined as they vibrated, then settled back into silence.

"What the shit was that?" Homer cried.

Two more explosions shook the mill and rattled the saws.

"God damn!"

For a split second Homer let the pistol waver. Jake moved like lightning, knocked the gun from Kane's hand, let go a punch that would have felled an ox, and then launched himself at Harry. Rufus stiff-armed him, knocking the wind from his lungs, but as Jake went down he dragged Rufus with him. One blow of Jake's fist laid the man out. Jake sprang to a crouch, Rufus's pistol in his hand, to find Nate clutching Harry as a shield.

"I'll kill her," Nate snarled. "Move one muscle and I'll blow her brains all over this mill."

Jake didn't think twice. He prayed to whichever saint was the patron of gunmen and fired. His slug whizzed close enough to Harry's head to singe her hair, and it drilled Nate between his eyes. Harriett dropped to her knees, wide-eyed, then got up and ran. She screamed when Jake reached out to grab her, but her struggles ceased when she realized whose arms were around her. Jake pushed her behind a frame that held a conveyor track leading to one of the saws. He forced her down, and when she started to speak he pulled her head back against his chest and covered her mouth with his hand.

"Stay down," he whispered. "And be quiet. The old man isn't where he fell. He's slinking around here someplace, and you can be sure he'll have lead flying our way any minute."

He should have finished Homer off when he had the chance. Old man Kane was big as an ox and just as tough. Jake should have known that one blow wouldn't be enough to put him out of action.

Harry nodded. Jake released her, turned her face up to his, and placed a quick, fierce kiss on her mouth. "We'll have our wedding night yet, Harry. Just hang on."

Killing Kanes was no longer important, Jake realized. The only thing he wanted was to get Harriett safely out. "Homer!" Jake shouted. His voice echoed in the cavernous mill. "Let's call it a draw. Enough blood has been shed in this war." Silence answered him, and Jake surveyed the building with wary eyes.

Harriett crouched beside Jake and tried to look brave. With his kiss still burning her mouth, she reminded herself how deadly her husband could be when he set his mind to it. She wasn't afraid, Harriett told herself, just tired—tired of being knocked around, tired of seeing Rufus and Nate lick their chops over her, tired of listening to Homer Kane chortle over the death he would give Jake Carradine. Suddenly Jake's appalling talent for violence was the only thing between Harriett and a most unpleasant demise. The situation made her see her husband in a new light—defender, not predator. If they got out of this mill alive, Harriett vowed, she would apologize to Jake for ever thinking him a savage. Before she met the Kanes, she hadn't known what a savage was.

Abruptly the stillness ended. A whine started slowly, then continued to build until the mill itself seemed to vibrate. Someone had started the saws.

Jake grimaced and pushed Harriett farther back under the framework that hid them. "The bastard doesn't want us to hear him coming."

A shot exploded, and a slug plowed into the planking on the other side of their flimsy shield. "You want to call it a draw, Carradine?" Homer's laughter sent chills down Harriett's spine. "Why should I call it a draw? I'm not the one who's pinned down."

Jake popped up for a quick look over the framework, then ducked. "The man's got a point," he muttered. "He's out there just out of the line of my fire, and he's going to sit out there until we decide to do something stupid, like make a run for it." He glanced around the mill, and his eyes finally came to rest on the spinning headsaw. "Maybe not . . . This ought to give the bastard second thoughts."

Jake took careful aim and fired. His shot bounced off

the headsaw and whined back into the mill. Homer's cry of surprise bore witness to how close Jake had come to his mark.

"Get down, Harry," Jake warned. "With that blade spinning, these slugs are going to fly all over the place. Maybe we'll get lucky and one will head right for Kane."

Jake was right. The spinning blade sent his shots flying in every direction. There were no more taunts from Homer.

"Stay here," Jake ordered Harriett. "And keep your head down. I'm going to go take care of that son of a bitch."

"Jacob!" She clutched his hand, a terrible fear rising in her throat. The savage light in his eyes made the words stick. Telling him to be careful would be useless. "I love you," she whispered.

For a moment his eyes softened. "I'll be back, Harry." He leaned forward and gently kissed her lips. "I'll be back."

The moment Jake sprang from cover the air was full of Kane lead. Harriett saw Homer's head appear for just an instant from behind a huge barrel. Jake fired, and the head ducked down like a turtle zipping into its shell. Then Jake disappeared also. Harriett's hands balled in fists so tight that her nails dug into her palms.

Lead ricocheted around the mill like bees buzzing in a hive. Both men were firing. Harriett buried her head in her arms and crouched into as small a ball as she possibly could. Someone cursed. She couldn't tell if the sound came from Jake or Homer, but the shooting had stopped.

Harriett peered from behind the framework. Both men crouched in the open space in front of the headsaw, circling like wolves. Both pistols had been tossed aside on the floor, presumably empty.

Harriett whispered a small prayer. "Deliver him back to me! Please!"

The men lunged at each other. They grappled. If any man on earth stood a chance against Jake's strength, it would be Homer Kane, Harriett guessed, for the older man was every bit as big as his adversary, and age seemed to have taken no toll at all.

But apparently the old devil didn't trust a fair fight. He pulled out a long-bladed, wickedly curved knife.

A movement at the door distracted Harriett's attention. Her heart leapt when she saw Amos stumble in. Without a second thought she dashed from her hiding place to the half-breed's side, dodging around the two Kane bodies stretched out in her path.

"Amos!" She grabbed his arm in desperation. "Do something!"

Amos circled her with one long arm. He watched with seeming unconcern while Jake dodged the knife thrusts that Homer aimed toward his belly. "Jake can take care of himself."

"But Mr. Kane has a knife!"

Amos looked down at her. "This is something Jake has to do himself. Best thing for you and me to do is stay out of it." He shook his head at the terror in her eyes. "Ain't no meaner fighter in these parts than Jake Carradine. He's beat me a few times, and there ain't no other man that can brag about that."

The fight went round in a stalemate until a kick from Jake sent Homer's knife flying. Harriett gasped as Homer raged forward, red-faced and cursing, toppling Jake dangerously close to the spinning headsaw. Amos's arm tightened around her as she instinctively started forward. Then Jake was on his feet again, grinning. Blood ran from one corner of his mouth, and a cut over his eye streamed scarlet down the side of his face. Kane looked no better.

"I can take you, you bastard," Homer boasted.

"When I was your age I used to wrestle three men at a time."

"Come show me," Jake invited, eyes narrowed. "The only ones I've seen you take were my little brother and a five-year-old kid. And my brother could've fought a fly and lost."

Homer swung, connecting with his fist to Jake's jaw. Jake didn't even stagger, but came back with an uppercut that sent Homer stumbling back. Homer kicked out, missed, and scrambled to his feet while Jake crouched, eyes hard as steel. He seemed to wait for Homer's next blow, welcoming it. They exchanged blow for blow, Homer flailing desperately, Jake with an aura of cold fury that made a shiver run down Harriett's spine. For a moment she almost felt sorry for Homer Kane.

The fight ended abruptly when Homer spotted his knife out of the corner of his eye. One eye on Jake, he dove for the weapon, not seeing that his momentum would take him in the direction of the whirling saw. Jake grabbed for him—too late. Homer Kane's blood sprayed in a vertical fan that painted a crimson stripe from floor to rafters.

Harriett shrieked and buried her face in Amos's stocky shoulder. Jake stood frozen, eyes cold steel, and stared at the mess that used to be a man. The fight was over. Two Kanes were dead, the other helpless. Somehow he found that he didn't feel any better for his grisly victory.

Amos's hand clutched Jake's shoulder, waking him from his trance. "Come away, friend. You've a bride to attend to."

Jake turned. Harriett stood still and pale, horror in her eyes. Forgetting himself, forgetting the Kanes, Jake walked over to her and gathered her against him. He could feel her weeping into his shirt, her sobs all the more painful for being silent. Lifting her into his arms, he took them both out the door into the morning sun, where fresh air could wash away the smell of blood, where they could both start to forget.

Amos followed. While Jake set Harriett down on the grassy bank of Tanner Creek, the half-breed stood with spread legs and fists on his hips, looking down at the couple. "Is it over, Jake?"

"It's over," Jake said. The steel had gone out of his eyes. The rage inside him had died a violent death.

"Rufus? Shall I kill him?"

"Let him go."

Amos nodded, looking satisfied.

"You took a hell of a long time getting here," Jake observed wryly.

"Got a little too close to one of the dynamite charges."

Jake grunted. Amos colored under his already dark skin and almost looked sheepish. His expression brought a tentative smile to Harriett's face.

"Speaking of dynamite"—Jake's eyes began to dance—"that reminds me, woman. We have a wedding to celebrate."

Harriett's smile was still shaky, but the hand she slipped into his was warm.

"And a wedding night," he said for her ears alone.

Harriett blushed. "Whatever you say, husband."

"I'd be willing to wager this'll be the last time I hear that sweet phrase." Jake rose and pulled Harriett to her feet, then slipped his arm around his wife's slim waist and grinned down at her. Harriett gave him a dimpled smile that was all the answer he needed.

The three of them walked together down the bank of the stream toward the peacefully grazing horses. Behind them, the mill wheel turned and creaked, the saws continued to hum, and the mill awaited the Kane crew to arrive for the day's work. And a half-mile away, in the blackened remains that had once been the Carradine home, at the spot where Eli and Josh Carradine had died, a newly sprouted blossom spread its petals to welcome the morning sun.

Epilogue

Journal entry—January 10, 1851—San Francisco:
The start of a new adventure, and a new journal—
one in which, thank heaven, I will not have to mince
words, for the only reader will be myself.

Today will be a day of sad good-byes. I fear I will
make quite a blubbering fool of myself at the gangplank, for though my heart is eager for the adventure ahead, it weeps for those dear friends we leave
behind. But Edwin and Lucille have assured me that
they will visit us at Puget Sound once we are settled.

I wonder if one can ever be truly settled in a place
so wild. We will be living in a land which is not yet
even a territory, though Jacob assures me that it
soon will be. I can see his eyes light when he speaks
of the wealth of timber there—timber that marches
right down to the sea, he says.

My dear husband! He struggled so with himself
before asking me to give up our relatively civilized
Oregon and travel to this new country. But I managed to convince him (sometimes, I have discovered,
there are more effective persuasions than words!)
that wherever he was I would be content. I don't
blame him for wanting no part of the Carradine operation on the Willamette. As he says, too much

blood has soaked into that soil. Amos, now a full partner, will do an admirable job of managing both the Carradine workings and the adjacent Kane forests. (Rufus was only too happy to sell and be gone. I believe he is here in California looking for gold.)

Chad is anxious to be off, every bit as eager as Jacob to help in opening this new land. Seeing the two of them together, anyone might think they were really father and son. I hope Sadie can see them from whatever part of Heaven she graces.

Indy has grown like a weed and has gotten to be quite a handful. As much as she loves the little sprite, Lucille was more than happy to hand him over to me, I think. Now that the children are gone, she and Edwin will travel to Europe for a delayed wedding.

Edwin has promised to see to the selling of my properties in Boston and transfer the funds to a bank here in San Francisco. Jacob hesitates to use my wealth to set up our new operation in the north. He says our income from the Carradine mill is sufficient. But I will persuade him. (Persuasion can be so delightful—though I suspect that in my eagerness with this new diversion I have gotten myself with child. Or more appropriately, have seduced my ever eager husband to get me with child.)

I surprise myself by having no apprehensions about the coming venture. I trust Jacob with my life, and more. How could I ever have feared him and the lovely longings he inspires in me? I give thanks to God that I found a man so gentle, and yet, when needed, so strong. With Jacob beside me, loving me, I fear nothing—not this wild new land, not childbirth, not life itself. No woman on earth is as fortunate as I.

* * *

Lucille held back tears as she watched her niece wave a final good-bye and turn to walk toward the gangplank of the *Nisqually*. Chad ran on ahead with Dodger bounding by his side, and Indy squirmed inpatiently in Harriett's arms. Jake smiled and took him from her.

Edwin circled Lucille's waist with one arm. "Good man, Carradine. Looks rather curious, though—a pistol on one hip and a baby on the other." He sighed. "But I don't suppose this country is ready yet for a man to go without a gun."

"Is this country ready yet for Harriett?" Lucille wondered aloud.

"In what way?" Edwin asked.

"Last night I overheard her telling Jake that these new territories in the northwest are the logical place for women to first be granted the vote."

Edwin chuckled. "Carradine is certainly going to have his hands full." He squeezed Lucille's hand as they turned to walk back to the carriage, a silent affirmation of his affection.

Lucille smiled up at her husband, then stole a final look at the ship, which was bustling now in preparation for sailing. Harriett stood at the rail, Jake and Chad on either side of her. She waved, a sad gesture that was at the same time eager. Lucille almost laughed. The predominantly male population of Puget Sound was due a surprise in the person of one Harriett Foster Carradine.

The gruesome death of Ned White as pictured in Chapter 8 is a fictionalized account of an actual incident that occurred along the California Trail.

Quotes from Margaret Fuller were taken from *Woman in the Nineteenth Century*, S. Margaret Fuller (a facsimile of the 1845 edition, University of South Carolina Press, 1980).

The September 18, 1850, edition of the *Alta California*, a San Francisco daily newspaper, reported that the September 17 fire started around four o'clock in the morning. For the sake of the story, I took the liberty of changing the time of the fire to late evening.

Bloomers were not worn as a symbol of feminist independence until 1851. I took the liberty of pushing that style back a year because of other time elements of the story.